Praise for *Repo Virtual*

"*Repo Virtual* constructs a stunningly vivid cyberpunk world that blurs the line between illusion and reality, dripping with the neon panache of a technological juggernaut in an action-packed heist that'll steal your heart with ideas that are as revealing as they are powerful."
—Peter Tieryas, author of the Mecha Samurai Empire series

"*Repo Virtual* sets itself apart with its gleeful heart and underdog charm."
—*BookPage* (starred review)

"A richly imagined, futuristic stand-alone with appeal to gamers, sci-fi fans, and armchair futurists alike."
—*Kirkus Reviews*

"Cyberpunk is not only back but may have come full circle."
—*Toronto Star*

"White twists the volume up, both dramatizing and warning against unchecked AI. What lingers is an important observation: no culture can retain its power and sanity when there are no uncynical eyes to see it. Cyberpunk and general sci-fi readers will enjoy and even learn from this one."
—*Library Journal*

REPO
VIRTUAL

COREY J. WHITE

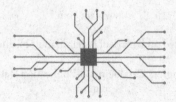

A TOM DOHERTY ASSOCIATES BOOK

NEW YORK

REPO VIRTUAL

Copyright © 2020 by Corey J. White

Edited by Carl Engle-Laird

A Tordotcom Book
Published by Tom Doherty Associates
120 Broadway
New York, NY 10271

www.tor.com

Tor® is a registered trademark of Macmillan Publishing Group, LLC.

The Library of Congress Cataloging-in-Publication Data is available upon request.

ISBN 978-1-250-25666-9 (trade paperback)
ISBN 978-1-250-21871-1 (ebook)

Our books may be purchased in bulk for promotional, educational, or business use. Please contact your local bookseller or the Macmillan Corporate and Premium Sales Department at 1-800-221-7945, extension 5442, or by email at MacmillanSpecialMarkets@macmillan.com.

First Edition: April 2020
First Trade Paperback Edition: April 2021

Printed in the United States of America

0   9   8   7   6   5   4   3   2   1

For jorm and Wolven

PART
ONE

Moxie and a
Clipboard

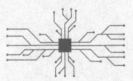

CHAPTER ONE

There are two things every repo needs: moxie and a clipboard. No matter the job—a car, a truck, or an ultra-heavy Winterclass dreadnought with enough firepower to shatter a small moon—the fundamentals stay the same. You walk in like you own the place, and if anyone asks any questions, you flash them a clipboard full of complicated forms.

The dreadnought's hull gleamed like scorched diamonds in the light of a thousand artificial stars. Too huge for the Grzyb Station hangar, it was berthed outboard, the massive vertical ship secured by little more than a docking ring and half a dozen auto-turrets.

JD drifted in close with thrusters on manual, his hands gliding over the controls in a separate reality. A low *dhoom* rattled his eardrums as his corvette touched down, magnetic clamps holding fast to the dreadnought like a tick on a stray dog. JD took a clipboard from inventory and stood up from his seat with a shadow of pain spiking his knee.

Two-forty-five a.m. Moscow time. T-minus fifteen minutes.

"Khoder, you there?"

Silence at first, then the chat channel opened with a burst of noise, bass tones too low for JD's cheap headphones.

"Not anywhere else," Khoder said.

"Is Dix in position?"

"Waiting on one more."

"Alright. Keep me posted."

"Need a bigger envelope," Khoder said, then he cut the chat. Adolescent smart-ass with a dad's sense of humor—JD couldn't help but smile.

He cleared his airlock and stepped out onto the docking ring, walls splashed with the red and black of the Asshole Federation. He walked toward his quarry, footsteps beating out a too-perfect rhythm, sharp clacks echoing in the high-ceilinged space. People stood static along the gangway, avatars left standing idle for unknown reasons, on abandoned errands. Come back a week later and some would still be there—digital ghosts, lifeless but immortal.

JD paused at the dreadnought's airlock, and moved outside his avatar to open a link to the repo database. Authentication details scrolled across his vision, words strobing too fast to process. Access granted, JD's fingers moved quick, flicking through his tagged jobs to start on the paperwork.

"Oi, xyecoc; fuck you doing?" The Russian spoke at a pubescent pitch, voice coming distant and hollow across a high-latency link.

"Official business, mudak," JD said: you didn't work repo for any length of time without learning insults in a dozen languages. He turned to face the kid's avatar, half-hidden behind a wall of corporate legalese that JD was meant to read but never did. The kid wore one of the default human character models, a boring, white, power fantasy—stacked with muscles, buzzcut hair, and a ring of too-dark tattoos around his neck like a bad rash.

JD's own avatar was from the pool of Arika aliens, living crystal beings that fed on starlight, and shattered into glittering refractive clouds on death. His first character had closely resembled his real self, but the moment he found himself surrounded by other players, the racist slurs started. Even in-game, his blackness was a provocation. He was almost relieved when that avatar died, giving JD an excuse to start over.

The Russian hurled another insult, loud enough for his voice to crackle and distort. JD muted him and held out his clipboard, the words NOTICE OF REPOSSESSION bold across the top of the page, followed by reams of dense text in English, Russian, Korean, and Simplified Chinese.

Official approval pinged his system and JD minimized the repo screen, attention back on his avatar, now holding a Zero Override like a shard of obsidian tight between thumb and forefinger. He slipped the ZO into the console by the dreadnought's airlock door and it opened with a sharp hiss. Lights inside the vessel flickered to life, illuminating a path into the depths of the colossal ship.

JD boarded; behind him the Russian's stunned silence quickly turned to chaos when the kid hit the alarm. The door closed behind JD, hushing the klaxon, the ship deadly quiet but for the ever-present ambient electronica piped into his ears. As JD ventured further in, his footsteps fell muffled on the high-res carpeting—a luxury cosmetic upgrade that cost as much in-game as the real thing. He strode past kitschy art and faux space-age designer furniture, the whole place done up like some asshole playboy's bachelor pad. The repo paperwork wouldn't say, but JD could guess the ship belonged to the child of some Russian oligarch: more dollars than sense, as his dad had said, back when the dollar still mattered.

"Khoder," JD said. "Got an ETA?"

"Ten minutes."

"Make it five." The words came out blunt, sharply bitten.

JD reached the cockpit, finding the confined space utterly different to the gaudy furnishings throughout the rest of the ship. Brutally decorated, every surface was accented in dark steel with decals laser-burnt into the rear wall. A post-ironic hula girl rested on the dashboard beside a just-as-trite bobblehead messiah. JD took the pilot seat and keyed the ignition with the Override. Vibrations pulsed through his skull as the engines throbbed to life, reactor humming low, systems coming online one by one, green across the board. Somewhere distant, JD grinned, all that power at his fingertips, weapon systems more advanced than anything he could afford.

JD brought up the dreadnought's menus, his eyes caught by the self-destruct button marked in hazard red. Every ship and structure in the game had one, and pirates were known to scuttle a stolen ship rather than let it be recovered. Some repos did it too, instead of leaving a botched contract to another repossessor, but JD never had. It seemed too petty.

A musical chime sounded from somewhere below the cockpit's dash, familiar but out of place. JD tried to ignore it, but the digitized trombone continued playing over a sparse beat. It took him four bars to recognize it as his ringtone—another two to realize what it meant. Without taking the eye mask off his face, JD let go of the controls and reached blindly for the shelf beside his bed until he found the machined slab of glass and plastic. He held it in front of his face and let his VR rig re-create it in the simulation. The screen showed an incoming call from Tektech Logistical Assurances Ltd.

JD swiped and answered: "Yellow?"

"Need you in the shorefront warehouse," said the terse voice on the other end. JD didn't recognize their needling accent, but guessed it was out of one of the hellish Brisles call centers.

"I'm not on call until this afternoon," JD said. With his free hand he brought up the in-game system map, watching for the arrival of Khoder's crew. The sun shone bright in the center of the chart, but everything was still.

"On-site repair isn't responding; we need a technician out there immediately. I've been authorized to increase your usual pay rate by ten percent."

JD sighed through pursed lips, stalling while he did the commute math. "Alright, but it'll take me two hours."

"Ten a.m., no later." The call center drone hung up and JD swore. He dropped his phone and heard it land on the bed beside him, crinkling the nylon fabric of his sleeping bag.

Back at the dreadnought controls, JD jammed the throttle. Engines droned louder and the ship's superstructure popped and groaned, locked tight to the docking ring—the Zero Override linked only to the dreadnought, not Grzyb Station dock controls. The ship strained against its binds, reactor heat climbing until a sharp crack rattled through the hull and it broke free, debris spinning slow past external cameras in a protracted dance.

"Khoder?"

No response.

The soundtrack switched to its battle theme as target lock warnings flared on the console. The cockpit shook with distant impacts as the station's auto-turrets peppered the dreadnought with plasma. Target reticles flared bright around each cannon as JD took aim. He pulled the trigger; tachyon torpedoes tore through timespace, warping the void. Total overkill, but when would JD get another chance to use them? The torpedoes struck in quick succession, atomic flash bubbling in vacuum as the turrets turned to slag.

Asshole Federation ships rushed through the blasts, hot on JD's tail. Within seconds, the fighters and corvettes had streaked past, blurs of red against the black of space. The ships stalled and spun toward the dreadnought, turning tight parabolas in preparation for their strafing run. JD keyed the point defense cannons and his vision filled with laser fire tracing the incoming ships. The fighters dodged and swerved, but two corvettes exploded, wreckage carried forward by inertia to collide against the dreadnought's hull. The fighters closed in tight and opened fire; haptic motors shook in JD's grip. He checked the system readouts: armor damage minimal, but he'd lost speed. *Concussive rounds*—flat, heavy slugs better at damping speed than causing damage.

"Don't have time for this shit," JD muttered to himself. "Khoder?" he called out again, searching the outer edge of the system where the jumpgate hung serenely, its interlocking rings revolving around a tamed wormhole.

JD checked the distance and his dropping speed: he wouldn't make it. He removed reactor safeties and throttled up, engine redlined. Federation destroyers burst from the gate, their structures unfolding as they exited wormspace, blocking his escape. Behind him more fighters emerged from Grzyb Station as insomniac Russians logged on in response to the dreadnought heist. The star system map shimmered red as enemy ships converged.

"Khoder?" JD said, voice louder as an edge of desperation crept in.

The jumpgate quivered and pulsed. The Seal Team Dix flotilla emerged from the hidden depths of wormspace—frigates, destroyers, and a Strugatsky Ultracannon, surrounded by a cloud of smaller vessels.

"About time," JD said under his breath.

"Chill, bro. Sound issues; had to restart."

Khoder led the fleet in his Khaw crusher and tug—an unconventional warship. It resembled four linked spikes, lined with laser cannons and plated in industrial-strength armor, with enough engine power to haul a midsized space station. The gap between the four spikes glowed pale blue as Khoder powered up the magnetic crushing field. The Khaw's spikes spread apart as it flew directly at the largest AF destroyer, swallowing the enemy vessel like a colossal mouth. Brilliant flash of light as the destroyer's reactor casing broke apart under magnetic pressure and the ship collapsed in on itself. The sphere of light churned until there was nothing left but condensed scrap metal. The Khaw was normally used for salvage work, but it didn't care if the ships it crushed were still operational.

JD's dreadnought picked up speed as the two factions engaged in battle—laser fire, plasma bolts, and tachyon torpedoes streaking across the dark.

"Thanks for the assist."

"Thank me with money, bro," Khoder replied.

"Don't worry, you'll get your share," JD said. "Once this dreadnought is out of the way, Grzyb Station is all yours."

Khoder cut the connection, and JD floated steadily toward the jumpgate, while behind him a system burned.

* * *

Julius Dax dropped the soft cotton eye mask onto his bed, and the simulated universe of VOIDWAR turned ghostly as diffuse dawn light burst through his contex. Outside the room's small window, Neo Songdo looked rendered in parallax: black shadow of low-rise apartments in the foreground, a smear of greenish city in the middle distance, and layers of distant towering skyscrapers in shades of pink and gray. JD rubbed the bags under his eyes, skin dark, flesh tender. He rolled from his bed and stood, genuine pain flaring sharp inside his knee.

He kept VOIDWAR running at fifty percent opacity, watching the repossessed dreadnought hop through jumpgates on autopilot as he picked through the roughly person-shaped mound of clothes piled on the bed beside where he slept. After a quick smell-test, JD changed into the least-dirty clothes he could find: his favorite deconstructed-reconstructed jeans, patched, paneled, and pieced together in a dozen shades of gray denim by automated sewing machines his old friend Jess had hacked together for shits and gigs; a sleeveless black shirt; solar and kinetic charging utility vest; and an old windbreaker, waterproof apart from the right shoulder where the weight of his ancient leather workbag had split the seam, exposing the rough polyester lining within.

Dropping down to sit on the edge of his bed, JD picked up his controls just as the dreadnought reached Zero—the game's central system. Countless ships traversed the space around the binary suns, and the chat window crawled with requests for help from rookies and the perpetually struggling. Zero Corporation's HQ hung in the very center, the twin stars blazing in orbit around the titanic space station. Quiet awe gripped JD still, no matter how many times he passed through the sector.

With autopilot disengaged, JD took the ship in on manual, hands gripped casual to stick and throttle, his left foot bouncing on the cheap low-pile carpet as he tried not to watch the clock. The dreadnought built up speed slowly, engines flaring white-blue against the dark of space. Courier frigates passed him on the way to the jumpgate, and loose fleets of sworn enemies flew together toward Zero Station—weapon systems disabled by corporate mandate.

Alpha sat to port and JD let the sun's gravity slingshot him on a course aimed right for the station. The colossal structure reappeared suddenly from behind the star and resolved in sequence, textures popping into place. The surface bristled with residential outcroppings, automated defenses, and communications arrays. Buried in the center of the station were Zero Corporation's in-game holdings, their vaults, resource silos, and their massive fleet—every ship and resource built from finite digital materials mined by a player within the game.

Manufactured scarcity helped keep the value of ZeroCash high, higher than many "real" currencies, and staked out space for digital repossessions to flourish—alongside other cottage industries. After the crypto bubble burst, ZeroCash filled the vacuum left behind, quickly becoming the favored coin for black—and gray—markets the world over. Every transaction consolidated Zero's wealth, and increased its stock market value.

There was a time when JD had played VOIDWAR purely for fun, before he had rent and bills to pay, before he had a job, when he could buy and sell in-game commodities with a fervor bordering on obsession, eventually earning enough ZeroCash to buy limited-edition sneakers or, one time, an eighth of darknet weed so dank it had tainted all the socks in his drawer with its smell. Now repo jobs were how JD paid most of his bills, but not his rent. For the Zero services he used, he could pay them directly in their own currency, never needing to let his earnings touch a "real" money market, which was just how Zero Corporation liked it. Still, it was money JD could earn while plugged in to an ever-shifting galactic conflict, talking to friends from all around the world, and blowing shit up.

JD took the dreadnought into the gaping maw of the station's main hangar, flanked on all sides by other players coming in to dock. Automated processes took over and the haptic controls went slack in JD's hands as the dreadnought was swallowed by the bureaucracies of repossession.

He limped to the bathroom and sat on the toilet, wincing at the pain in his knee. JD took his phone and finalized the repo paperwork with Zero, and sat staring, thumb rotating in small circles to keep the screen active. After fifteen seconds the loading bar was replaced by an animated tick. He smiled, then remembered his other job. JD locked his phone and frowned at his sleep-deprived face staring out from the slab of black glass. He finished up and went back to the dorm room, his thin mattress warmed by the rig always humming softly beneath the bed.

JD retrieved his corvette from the Zero hangar, and set course for an uncharted sector. He started the exploration protocol, and immediately his rig's cooling fans hummed louder, heat pouring out in waves to wash over his legs. It was another form of ZeroCash exchange—processing power for digital currency. All those resources stored in Zero's holds had to come from somewhere, and players could earn ZeroCash by lending the game devs processor cycles with which to expand the size of VOIDWAR's playable universe. Everybody wins, but mostly Zero.

Julius padded quietly out of the makeshift living room slash dorm, his footsteps masked by the snores of his five roommates. He shouldered his rucksack, stole someone's bread from the fridge, and walked out the front door with two slices held in his mouth. He stepped into his knockoff three-stripe sneakers and pulled the heavy door closed, silencing the orchestra of snores and the steady drone of CPU fans.

* * *

His face was the first one I saw.

If father is the person who created you, then he was not my father.

But if father is the person who guided you through childhood, who molded you, then here he is: unaware that this new day would set him on a path to the center of everything.

When he wiped his ass and tossed the folded wads of feces-smeared recycled paper into the toilet bowl, he saw only the act of disposal. He did not see that everything is one. He did not see the truth of his shit—that it could never simply disappear. It was still there, *flush*, growing distant yes, carried away on a stream of treated water, but it was not gone. It was part of the closed system he called "Earth," "world," or even "home." He had lived his whole life under the lie of this abstraction—that there is a "here," and a separate "there."

This abstraction is what killed them all.

CHAPTER TWO

The air smelled of synthetic oil, cardboard boxes, and the ozone scent of burnt-out electronics. JD wiped his forehead with the sleeve of his coveralls, the smell of himself thick in the patched and faded fabric. He unscrewed the repair bot's torso plate by hand, pushing the screwdriver hard to get leverage against the chewed slots in the screw's head. He set the steel plate down with a hollow clank that he felt in his fingertips more than he heard, the constant machine din of the warehouse as loud as it was hypnotizing.

The Hippo repair bot was a sphere on four treaded feet painted medic red; powered-down, it hung forward slightly as though drunk. With the maintenance plate removed, the robot had a face—the two glassy eyes of its visual sensors and a gaping black mouth, with greasy metal teeth showing in one corner. JD pulled a face at the damaged machine, his lips pulled back grotesquely—just two coworkers gurning at each other—and got to work.

First, he unplugged the robot's secondary power source and put the gold nanowire battery on the polished cement beside his knee. He checked again that the power cable was disconnected from the back of the machine's enormous head, and reached into its guts through the open maw. He blindly felt along every cable, mentally mapping each one and comparing it to the diagram drawn over his contex.

The picking and packing robots continued to work at pace,

unbothered by the apparent death of one of their own. It bothered JD that they didn't, couldn't show solidarity, and it bothered him that it bothered him. The whole factory would fall to rust and ruin without the repair bot, but here it was, dead, and none of the others could even know.

JD's mind drifted as his fingers brushed over the copper pins and battery terminals like a doctor poking a sick child's stomach. He found nothing obviously fatal. With his arm deep inside the machine's chest cavity, his eyes flicked once more to the disconnected battery that sat on the floor, remembering the ragged dripping meat of Ye-ji's arm when a broken unit came to life on her. That was the last time he worked with another tech. After the ambulance had taken her away, the picking machines had tracked lines of her blood all across the factory floor until it dried red and black. The blood had stayed there until late that night, when the cleaning bot emerged from its cupboard to mop and polish while the other robots slept in diagnosis.

A hollow *boom* echoed through the space, followed by a *screeeeee*. JD cocked his head, waiting for the next sound to tell him which machine was malfunctioning and how, but instead he heard a voice: "You hungry?"

JD extricated his arm from the repair bot's chest and wiped his hands with the grease-stained scrap of T-shirt he used for a rag. He peered toward the main warehouse entrance where Soo-hyun stood in silhouette, stark black against the glare from outside. They lifted a bag high, the clear plastic stretched taut with the weight of mandu from the place on the corner.

The door thundered closed and the sound of Soo-hyun's heavy boots ricocheted around the high ceiling as they walked down the central aisle, dressed in navy blue coveralls, their black hair neatly shorn. The picking robots darted around them, perfect precision ruined by Soo-hyun's unwillingness to bend. JD couldn't tell if it was Zen stillness, or pure stubbornness—but lately there was a lot about Soo-hyun he found difficult to read.

"What do you want?" JD asked when Soo-hyun was close enough that he didn't need to yell.

"I can't bring you lunch without some ulterior motive?" Soo-hyun put their hand to their chest in mock outrage.

JD's stomach rumbled. His body was a meat engine, and carbs ran through it like sand through those old hourglasses he'd only ever seen abstracted as a loading icon. He ignored the hunger. "How did you get in here?"

With one chewed fingernail Soo-hyun tapped the scratched employee ID badge hanging at their belt. "Perks of being a floor manager."

"*Former* floor manager."

They shrugged. "Not my fault they never wiped the old database. Now, come on, hyung, lunch time."

* * *

Dust motes swam through shafts of light that daggered between mangled vertical blinds. Windows on the opposite side of the room looked out over the factory floor—pickers picking, packers packing, conveyor belts turning endlessly to fill the delivery auto-trucks that docked outside. JD had stopped eating in the lunchroom sometime after the cleaning drone had given up on the disused space but before the fridge seals had broken. The door hung open; the dank smell of mold and rotting salad still lingered.

"This is disgusting," Soo-hyun said.

"I normally eat downstairs."

"If you eat in your workspace, did you really take a break?" Soo-hyun asked. They ran a finger through the dust gathered on the table's surface, and took the trays of mandu from the bag. They spread them out across the table, and handed a pair of chopsticks to JD. He opened the nearest tray and leaned forward, as if the rising steam could wash the room's other smells from his mind.

"What is this?" JD asked, snapping apart his chopsticks and cleaning them against each other.

"Kimchi, mushroom, tofu," Soo-hyun said, pointing to each tray. "No, this visit."

Soo-hyun's mass of necklaces made from copper wire and assorted junk collected in the shadowed V of their coveralls and jangled when they dropped into the seat opposite JD. "I want to help you."

JD took one of the fried mandu for an excuse to look away. He put the whole dumpling in his mouth. "You want to help," he said once he'd chewed and swallowed, "but you still haven't apologized."

Soo-hyun lowered their head. "I never wanted you to get hurt, hyung," they said. "Isn't that enough?"

JD shook his head—less a response than a surrender. "You still living in the ruins?"

"You wouldn't call our community 'ruins' if you ever visited. You should come see me after work today, let me introduce you to everyone."

JD shoved another dumpling into his mouth and chewed. "I haven't seen you for months, and now you show up here to talk about—what?"

"You'd be happier living at Liber, Jules. There's no rent, no bills, just a community of people trying to help each other. Living there has calmed me down. It really helps."

JD rested his chopsticks across the closest tray and leveled a gaze at his younger sibling. "What do you want, Soo-hyun?" He sounded tired as he spoke the words, heard them echo through their past like a mantra. Soo-hyun always wanted something.

"I'm trying to give you a job."

JD took up the chopsticks and made a circular motion that said, "Go on."

"We need a repo."

"You say 'repo,' but something tells me you mean 'thief.'"

Soo-hyun smirked. "Aren't those jobs more fun?"

JD ferried a dumpling into his mouth and waited for them to continue.

"We'll pay you, okay? Is that what you want to hear?"

"How much?" JD said around a mouthful of mandu.

"Fifty thousand euro."

JD almost choked. "How much?"

"Fifty thousand. Five-zero."

JD raised his eyebrows, cynicism resting with his pursed lips.

"Kali has the money, Jules. She has a hundred and thirty million Livideo subscribers, and a hundred thousand who pay for her online courses. Every night she gives a talk, and every night it streams to more and more people. We have money, JD, enough to turn Liber into a paradise."

"Maybe I *should* move in," JD said, voice flat.

"You should!" Soo-hyun said. "It's amazing, JD. Kali is amazing, you'll love her."

"What's the job?"

"Kali wrote a piece of software that will change the world, but someone stole it from her. All you've got to do is steal it back."

JD's hand halted halfway between the tray of mandu and his mouth. He sighed. "And what happens if I visit tonight?" he asked eventually.

"Just hear Kali out. If you don't like it, we don't do the job."

"We?"

"It's a big job; you're going to need a diversion." They spoke the words casually, but still JD's knee flared with remembered pain.

"I thought you gave that up. I thought you were calm now. I'm still limping after your last diversion."

"Maybe I'm too calm. Kali worries I'm stunting my own spiritual growth."

"What does that even mean?" JD asked.

"I don't know, Jules. I'm just here to try and make things right. I never wanted to apologize if all I could offer you were the words, but if we do this job, I'll give you my cut. Fifty k is enough for your knee surgery, enough to keep you fed while you recover."

JD shook his head, in disbelief or shock, he wasn't sure.

"This is how I apologize, hyung. This is how I make it right." Soo-hyun stared at him, their hazel eyes gleaming. Something vulnerable sat in those eyes, and suddenly JD saw Soo-hyun as they were when they'd first met—a sweet seven-year-old, scared but excited. The little sibling he would always love, no matter how much they annoyed him, no matter how badly they hurt him. That was family.

"Alright, I'll come see you after work; but no guarantee I'll take the job."

"You won't regret it," Soo-hyun said, and they flashed him their best mischievous smile. Some part of him regretted it already.

His phone buzzed in his pocket. He took it out and saw the pin Soo-hyun had just dropped—the location of Liber, in Songdo's ruined east beyond the canal, abandoned by the city council after the flood a decade earlier.

"How am I supposed to—" He looked up and the lunchroom door was already swinging closed behind Soo-hyun, a whorl of dust spinning in the void they left behind.

He crossed to the window and watched Soo-hyun march back to the exit, carving a straight line through the machines. They waved once as they pushed the main doors open, and disappeared into the glare, swallowed by the external world.

* * *

Hours later, JD stepped outside, leaving behind the industrial clang of the warehouse. The building loomed over him, haloed by the fast-approaching dusk. It was four stories' worth of storage, humming with machine labor, and still ringed with suicide nets from when human pickers and packers worked themselves to exhaustion within its walls, all for the sake of some technocrat's net worth. JD left the structure's shadow and pushed into the sidewalk surge, joining the shuffling biomass of Neo Songdo. Sunlight speared between buildings at migraine height; it burned bright through the smog, heat hanging heavy over the city, where it would persist until well after midnight.

Traffic lights and crossing signals shone in the real, largely for the sake of pedestrians and the rare human driver—the self-driving cars too unsettling to watch without their every move telegraphed in advance. The cars didn't see the lights, they reacted instead to some hidden system of machine semiotics, chattering constantly among themselves. Watching them, JD wondered if the cars ever talked about their passengers, ever gossiped about the biological denizens of the machine city.

The original plans for Songdo had called for a focus on pedestrians and public transport—a clean city, a green city—but when Zero bailed out the government and took on the city's debt, their rideshare network had taken precedence. Wide sidewalks gave way to roads, people gave way to cars, and the grand intentions of Songdo's architects gave way to the excesses of capital.

Waiting at a crosswalk, people packed in tight around JD, their bodies adding to the heat of the falling sun. He scrunched his nose against the medley of body odor, the acrid scent of vehicle exhaust and factory runoff, and the biologic smells of vomit and piss baking on hot cement.

The signal turned green, and JD walked.

He shot daggers at every corporate worker dressed identically in black, white, and gray, still exquisitely preened after eight hours in air-conditioning, but he knew the sneer that twisted his mouth was pure jealousy, not class warfare. He pushed those elite specters from his mind and took in the rest of the bustle: gig-economy hopefuls rushing home, some paid, others not; folks peddling noodles, soup, or bottled water from behind corporate censor bars; and rich kids strangled by private school uniforms, chain-smoking cigarettes because nothing is cooler than lung cancer your parents can afford to cure. They flocked birdlike around the street's other denizens: urchins, runaways, freaks, beggars, and petty criminals working their latest angle.

In disused doorways and dirty alleys, virt-lost homeless withered away to skin and bone, largely hidden behind Songdo's Augmented

Reality facade. They owned no possessions but the third-hand phones clutched in bony fingers and the makeshift blindfolds wrapped around their heads to keep their virtual worlds sacrosanct, safe from the encroachments of the real.

JD shouldered through the crowd with his limping gait, his broad frame an unintentional battering ram. Eyes followed him as he moved through the sea of mostly Korean bodies, their gaze marking him as an outsider—the city's multicultural push hindered by thousands of years of Korean ethnic homogeneity. JD stepped into the street to pass a knot of execs tied around a pop-up cocktail bar and ignored the flashing red warning underfoot. He slapped the door of a passing auto-car and the driving algorithm slammed to a halt with a honk of its horn. JD just laughed.

At the next corner a man stood at a little stall, dressed in a jacket patterned with bright rectangles of global currency. He sold US hundred-dollar bills enshrined in plastic frames for ten euro apiece—souvenirs from a fallen empire.

Everywhere slabs of color stood out too-crisp against the dreary real, hiding graffiti, pirate ads, and occasional spatters of blood. Early in Neo Songdo's life, the Augmented layer had been writable. Excited city planners invited citizens to write their own lives onto the street: advice for new arrivals, reviews of local restaurants, warnings of criminal elements or overzealous police. In practice, the city became a bathroom wall writ large. Now, only city council and advertisers could write into the Augmented feed, giving every street a uniform commercial banality that scraped at JD's psyche.

Walls on either side of the road thrummed with high-resolution adverts tailored for his eyes: VOIDWAR promotions beside Olavon beauty treatments hawked by affectless celebrities he'd never seen before, sex-baited cola ads next to commercials for daytime soap operas, omnipresent algorithms confused by all the money he spent on his mother. JD watched his feet, pushing the layer of compulsory AR from his mind as he navigated the city, following fiber-optic ley lines, the veins running through the failed ubiquitous city.

JD logged into VOIDWAR as he walked, the sign-in screen opaque across the visual noise of the city. His phone grew hot in his pocket as it connected to the game's systems. Spend enough time logged in and you'd feel your phone cooking the meat of your thigh. He checked his inbox first, saw confirmation of payment on his in-game repo job, then searched the forums for after-action reports from the battle around Grzyb Station. Seal Team Dix crowed over their victory, while furious Russians cursed JD, "the repo fuck," in janky machine translation.

He passed through downtown from the west, until the tide of foot traffic slowly turned against him: night workers ferrying themselves into the heart of the city while he trudged toward the broken, gangrenous foot. Soon the current turned to a trickle. Skyscrapers and low-rises gave way to overpasses, bypasses, highways, and byways. The diesel smoke was thick enough to taste, because nothing moves a loaded truck like burning dinosaurs.

Past some invisible border between the city proper and the ruined outskirts, the Augmented street signs and road markings began to fall from JD's vision, pixels blinking out of existence to reveal the true grime of the city beneath. JD had never come out this far, despite Soo-hyun's insistence, but he knew it was the residents of Liber who had scraped away the bokodes that controlled all the Augmented signifiers of city life. It was their retaliation for the council's neglect. Graffiti peeked out from behind the final fading stretches of digital wall—basic tags, indecipherable sigils in splashes of garish paint, and the words NORTH KOREA BEST KOREA in bold black letters a meter tall across the length of a broken glass factory.

JD paused at the bridge over the canal to catch his breath and stretch out his leg, wincing at the ache in his knee. He could have—*should* have—ordered a car, but none would drive this far out without a heavy surcharge that JD couldn't pay.

Fifty thousand euro. Enough for the surgery, enough to pay off the debt he held in his mother's name. He didn't trust Soo-hyun's judgment, but he wanted to. He wanted the job to pan out.

Beyond the canal, crumbled ruins gave way to reconstruction. Rusted rebar jutted from cement like compound fractures, but the buildings that still stood were painted haphazardly in bright colors and topped with green. Vines of unknown origin crept along rusting gutters, and carefully cultivated vegetables, fruits, herbs, and medicinal plants sat on rooftops and burst over balcony railings. These colors stood vivid against the pale cement and smog-smeared sky. Beneath that dirty fog, birds circled with mathematical precision, and puffy, too-white clouds hung static, undisturbed by any wind; the badly disguised tools of surveillance-state capitalism.

JD raised a middle finger to the sky and carried on. Welcome to Neo Songdo. World city. Dead city. A city where chaebol and foreign multinationals fought over the best bits of carrion while Seoul looked on, watching the microstate for signs of its own future. The future did not look bright.

Night fell slowly as JD walked, pastel colors desaturated until they finally faded to that dull orange-gray of light pollution. He felt the empty gaze of machine vision again, nearer than the ever-present drones hovering overhead. JD turned at the hollow clatter of cement tumbling. A dog-shaped robot emerged from between two broken walls, its four legs uncannily steady over the shifting rubble. JD froze. The machine's torso plate was stamped with the gold shield of the NSPD, the decal scratched and peeled but still visible. The dog lifted its head as though it were sniffing the air. JD knew enough about their innards to guess it was scanning him with IR sensors at the underside of its jaw.

"You can relax," Soo-hyun said; "the dog is one of ours."

JD pivoted slowly on the spot, until both the dog and Soo-hyun were in his field of view. Soo-hyun stepped out from the shadow of an off-brand convenience store, long-shuttered. Behind them, another five figures leered from the darkness, their contex gleaming in the low light.

A nasal voice spoke from the dark: "We don't need him." Australian or South African—JD could never tell the two accents apart.

"Who are your friends?" JD asked.

"Ignore Red," Soo-hyun said. "He's jealous that Kali chose my plan over his."

Red murmured something under his breath. He moved into the muted light, followed by four other teens—gender indeterminate, wearing ill-fitting T-shirts emblazoned with cartoon animals, jeans marked with holes and trailing threads at the hems. Red clutched the long form of a marksman rifle, 3D-printed in gaudy orange, like something out of a first-person shooter. He tossed it back to one of the others, and JD noticed they were all armed with squat carbines in blotches of random color, and knockoff Berettas printed default gray.

The others stayed back while Red approached. He was taller than JD, but gangly, skin freckled ginger and stretched taut across his frame, red hair in a loose ponytail. His lips looked pink and slightly swollen; he licked and bit and chewed at them, his mouth always moving.

"We don't need him," he said again, glaring down at JD.

JD let his head drop to one side and looked past Red to Soo-hyun. "I thought you said your dog wouldn't bother me."

"Ain't their dog," Red said.

"But you *are* a dog?" JD said with a smirk.

A guttural noise leaped from Red's throat—he barked, grinning when JD flinched. JD stepped back and Red closed the gap, leering and silent, his chest puffed out like a pigeon in mating season. A mix of sweat, dirt, and adolescent pheromone filled JD's nose, smelling like frenzied masturbation and teenage heartbreak.

"I don't need this shit," JD said. He turned from Red and started walking; hyper-aware of his limping gait as he felt the teens watching.

Soo-hyun dodged past Red and put an arm around JD's shoulder. "Ignore the asshole, hyung," they whispered. "He wants you gone so he can do it his way. If that happens, a lot of people are going to get hurt."

JD stopped and let Soo-hyun turn him around.

He nodded to the homemade arsenal held by Red's gang of miscreants. "Those things look dangerous," JD said.

"Bet your fucking life they're dangerous," Red crowed, to snickers from the rest.

"To whoever pulls the trigger," JD said deadpan.

Soo-hyun bumped against JD's shoulder and grinned. Even a couple of Red's goons had to smile at that.

Red chewed his lip and scowled. He spat on the ground and nodded over his shoulder. "Kali wants to see you, and that's the only reason you're welcome here. If you step out of line while you're here, I'll be waiting."

"Eat your own shit, Red," Soo-hyun said. They put their arm around JD's shoulder, and led him past the gang. "Just choke it down."

The two of them walked toward a beacon of orange light glowing ahead. The hacked police dog followed, the high whine of its actuators accompanying the distant drone of traffic like waves crashing on the shore.

When he was sure they were out of earshot, JD said, "'Eat your own shit'? I haven't heard that since the last time Dad drove me anywhere."

"I thought I might bring it back."

"He'd probably like that." JD put his arm around Soo-hyun's waist and they rested their head on his shoulder. "Remember when you said it to your teacher?" he asked.

"Oh, shit," Soo-hyun said with a giggle. "I was, what, eight?"

"Give or take."

"I thought Mum would never talk to me again."

"And afterward, when Dad drove us home from the parent-teacher meeting, it was dead silent, like a funeral in a library. We stopped at the lights and he just burst out laughing." JD chuckled at the memory.

Soo-hyun laughed and turned to JD with tears in their eyes. "And Mum kept slapping him on the arm, 'It's not funny, it's not funny!'"

JD sobbed with laughter. "But she was laughing as she hit him."

"We all were."

JD waited for his breathing to settle. He wiped his eyes. "That marriage was a disaster."

Soo-hyun sighed—a high-pitched sound to expel the laughter. "But we still have each other."

JD stepped on a loose patch of gravel and winced as pain shot through his damaged knee. "We sure do."

CHAPTER THREE

The landscape changed incrementally with each step they took toward the central light of Liber. The cement rubble had been swept aside to form paths; cracks in the roads and footpaths were patched with black asphalt still sticky underfoot. Buildings at the commune's outskirts sat abandoned, used as little more than elevated rooftop gardens to catch the sun, but closer to the heart of the place, renovated apartment blocks breathed with familial life. Children ran down streets empty of cars, shouting and squealing as they played cops and robbers, watched over by stolen police drones, immune to the irony. The air hung heavy with the smells of cooking and the scent of animal manure, while conversations drifted along empty streets in half a dozen languages. People whistled to the dog following close at Soo-hyun's heels, but it didn't stray.

JD wondered if the canal area where he had run into Red was a front—deliberately untended to keep the commune hidden behind that desolate no-man's-land.

"How many people live here now?" JD asked.

"Just over three hundred at last count," Soo-hyun said. "We have a lot of kids from North Korea, orphaned by the work camps. It was either go into the camp as well, or flee south."

The commune glowed a warm orange with the light of candles and fires. JD stepped over cables that split from solar batteries, but the strobing blue-white of artificial light was rare. The most prevalent sign of electricity came in the form of disparate soundtracks playing over the scene of communal living—K-pop, experimental jazz, and classical music reached JD's ears in small snatches like a radio flicked rapidly between stations.

"Kali will be giving one of her lectures," Soo-hyun said, "but she wants to see you as soon as she's done."

"Who is this woman?"

"She's not like anyone I've ever met before. She's smart, grounded, wise . . ." There was a pause. "She's beautiful."

JD shot them a knowing glance and Soo-hyun winced.

"You'll see what I mean."

They walked beneath dim, solar-powered lamps leading to the grounds of a repurposed school, abandoned during the flood. Drying clothes hung like limp flags from the windows of classrooms converted into living spaces. People milled in a small courtyard, bathed in the light of cookfires—would-be-homeless, crustpunks, anarchists, and the working poor who couldn't afford to rent in the city proper. The school's staff car park had been torn up, vegetables and herbs planted in the wound, while a stricken orchard of fruit trees bloomed on the small football field to the south.

"Come on," Soo-hyun said.

Bright light spilled from one of the school's large central buildings, and crowds gathered outside each window, craning to see inside. Soo-hyun gently shoved their way through the throng, dragging JD by the hand. He uttered apologies as he went, occasionally feeling the cold metal nose of the dog drone nudging him forward.

They arrived at a doorway opening onto a long auditorium, filled with hundreds of people, some seated, others cross-legged on the floor, even more standing at the back of the hall. If it was a real theater, and not a converted school space, JD and Soo-hyun would have been standing at the backstage door, watching Kali on a small raised platform, radiant under stage lights. She had too-white skin, and dark, wavy hair that rested on one shoulder. She wore a flowing gray dress, layers of sheer fabric that suggested a naked form swimming somewhere within. Streaming drones flitted through the air ahead of her, catching every angle, every smile she offered the crowd, every word she uttered.

"—take what they will not give us. They do not care about you, or me. We sit outside their system of capital and control. They have no use for us, and even if they did, we are too enlightened to return to their paddocks."

Her words carried clean over the audience, amplified by speakers embedded in the ceiling and messily wired to a small black audio desk at the rear of the hall, smothering the sounds of commune life outside. Her accent was American–West Coast, JD thought. There was something reassuringly Hollywood about her, a parallel to all the voices that had raised him, emanating from the flat slab on the wall of his childhood bedroom.

"They wish us to be sheep, or cattle, something docile they can harvest for resources. But we are not sheep. We are not cows. We are not even human; we are more than that."

Kali reached a hand into a pocket in her shifting dress and retrieved a switchblade. The blade extended with a *schick,* picked up and amplified by the microphones hovering before her.

She dropped her head and stared at the knife. Her audience watched her in silence, the soft buzz of quadcopter rotors the only sound in the entire room. They watched her press her left index finger against the knife's point until it drew blood. A drop of blood rolled down the blade and fell, splashing onto the top of her bare foot with a quiet *splat*.

"We are not even human," she said again. "This blood is not precious." She flicked her hand out dismissively, but if any blood trailed off her finger, JD couldn't see it. "This blood is not what makes me special.

"A human is an animal that learned how to subjugate animals, including itself. We are better than that. We are souls begging for release, souls begging to meld in kinship and love with one another. The people out there," she said, pointing her knife toward the door, toward JD and Soo-hyun, "they hate us because we know we are more than this blood, this meat. They want us to work in their warehouses and factories, and they want us to be meat, but we will not lower ourselves. We are not animals to work for them, we are their equals. And I will make them see that.

"You all trust me, don't you?"

There was nodding, affirmative murmuring, and even a few cheers from the audience.

"You trust me because I have built our community from nothing, with nothing. I did that to demonstrate that my movement is not about money. I hate money, I despise it. It has twisted a beautiful and creative species and turned us into a ravenous, all-consuming virus."

More enthusiastic nodding from pockets of the crowd. Kali returned her knife to her pocket, and stuck the tip of her finger into her mouth briefly, sealing the cut with saliva.

"After the Sixth Great Extinction," she said, "all that will be left are pests, rodents, tardigrades, and trash. Unless, *unless* we embrace our extinction first. I'm not talking about suicide, I'm talking about removing ourselves before it is too late. We do not need this planet, this blood. We have our immortal souls to carry us forward into eternity.

"You would not believe how close we are to becoming a world of intelligent machines, of true, strong AI. Thinking machines are not something to fear, but rather to embrace, like children. I dream of a world where there is no hunger, no sickness, no meaningless work. A world where our robot heirs care for our bodies so that we can care for our souls.

"When we surrender our flesh, we will never die. Our souls will be joined together in eternity, and our memories will be carried throughout the deepest depths of space, throughout the entire universe, by our machine children. *We* can never go to the stars. I'm sorry, but it's true. We would need to take our entire biome with us. We can't do it. We need oxygen, we need microbes, we need too many things that we barely understand.

"But our machines? They won't need oxygen. They won't need microbes. They need energy they can gather from the stars. They need purpose, and *we* shall give it to them.

"The whole point of our evolution until now was to build machines that could inherit the world. They don't need money, they don't need to destroy the planet in an endless cycle of consumption. All they need is for us to give them life. Instill a piece of ourselves and our souls into the machines so that they can remember us, and we can transcend the painful reality we have been trapped within for thousands of years. They will remember us the way we remember dinosaurs. If we act in time, and in concert, it won't be extinction we are faced with, but *transcendence*. We will transcend the blood and the dirt and live wrapped up in one another for all time.

"I want to be wrapped up in you," Kali said. "Do you want to be wrapped up in me?"

"Yes, Kali!"

"Please, Kali."

"We love you."

"We need you."

The crowd's energy was palpable, a muttering, humming, crying mass of humanity laid bare to the woman on the stage.

"I hate this next part. This next part is where I have to ask for money. I only ask you, my loyal angels," she told the crowd, pretending that this request for tithing wasn't going out to the millions watching the stream, "because you understand me. You understand that I do this for *you*.

"Today, we have Liber, and we have each other, but my vision will take us so much further. I have seen it in my dreams. We will take Songdo from the corporations, and together, we will create a truly transcendental city. There will be no advertisements, no needless employment, no poverty, no hunger, no suffering. There will be only enlightenment, and the one true path to unity and compassion for all humankind."

The crowd shuddered and shook as one. Voices cried out. From his vantage, JD could see people openly weeping.

Kali spoke louder now, riding the crest of rapture: "In my new city, all of us will be the equal of all of them. Those who spent their lives chasing money will find themselves poor, their lives wasted. But those who follow me"—she paused—"will find themselves richer than they can imagine." She built to a crescendo with the final sentence, yelling over the noise of the crowd.

Once the uproar had fallen quiet, Kali continued: "Together, we will create a new company, a rational company, a company that works for all of us, not just the rich minority. One day—one day soon—we will be rich enough to rival Zero Corporation. And on that day, we will buy Songdo from them and give it back to the people. And if Zero will not sell, they will be destroyed. We stand united, and no one can oppose us!"

The crowd was at fever pitch. JD felt his heart beat double-time, physiology caught up in the fervor. He glanced at Soo-hyun, and they must have seen the weird grin stretched across his face, because they smiled.

Kali bowed and the crowd broke forward, people standing only to fall at Kali's feet as she stepped back with her hands pressed together as if in prayer. She looked over the top of the fallen suppliants, turning her head this way, then that, with a keen awareness of each hovering camera.

From the door on the opposite side, a group dressed in the same gray as Kali's robes stepped onto the makeshift stage and formed a human shield against the adoration of the crowd. The masses continued to swell forward, held back by the line of mostly teenaged guards, while Kali continued to smile and bow her way off the stage.

She bowed again until finally she reached the door where Soo-hyun and JD waited, the security detail forming a wall behind her. She turned away from the crowd and the smile fell from her face. For a beat her expression was utterly flat, then her eyes fell on

Soo-hyun and the spark returned. She rested both hands on Soo-hyun's shoulders and they held each other's gaze in some form of ritualistic greeting. Kali pulled them close and wrapped Soo-hyun in her long, thin, tattooed arms.

They broke their embrace and Soo-hyun motioned to JD. "This is my brother."

"Julius," Kali said. She offered her hand, and when JD shook it, she gently grazed the back of his hand with her other. It was an old trick, designed to imprint oneself more strongly in a person's memory, but even knowing it for what it was, JD felt a chill run down his spine.

"It's nice to meet you," he said. Standing close to her, JD noticed the bindi she wore just above and between her carefully manicured brows. That was when he recognized her dress for what it was: a monochrome sari. This white girl was playing cultural colonizer two hundred years after the fact. Still he felt a kind of energy emanating from her as Kali eyed him slowly.

"We need some space to talk quietly, don't we?" She turned and a compact assistant, around ten years old, appeared with a large tablet clutched in both arms. "Protective perimeter with counter-surveillance, please, Andrea."

Andrea's mouth moved, but if she spoke JD couldn't hear her over the background noise of Kali's crowd dispersing. Some of the followers lingered just beyond the line of self-serious security guards, but most moved on, returning to their homes or whatever tasks Kali had set for them.

"Would you please dismantle your phone?" Kali asked.

"Uh, sure." JD blinked the pattern for a full shutdown, and when it was finished he fumbled his phone awkwardly out of his pocket. He slid the battery out of its slot, putting the phone and battery into separate jeans pockets.

"I'll bring him to the workshop once we're done," Kali told Soo-hyun. "This way." Kali turned and began to walk, trailed by the dog drone that had escorted JD in from the canal.

Soo-hyun shoved him forward but stayed behind. He caught up with Kali, and they walked in silence, commune residents staring at Kali wide- and wild-eyed as they passed. JD studied her face surreptitiously, trying to gauge this woman who dressed like a New Age guru and commanded the loyalty of over a hundred million Livideo subscribers. He guessed she was anywhere between twenty-five and thirty-five, attractive in a plain sort of way. Hers was not a face that many would go to war for, yet she was surrounded by Red and the other zealous teens, armed with cheaply printed guns and excess hormones.

Nine more hacked dogs joined them one by one until they were completely surrounded. The whine of servomotors made a steady rolling sound, and JD found himself falling into step with the machines. His flat-soled sneakers scraped over the worn cement, but Kali's feet were bare and silent. She hugged herself and stared into the middle distance. The dogs began to emit a steady hiss of static, different frequencies overlapping to form a wall of sound.

"What did you think of my talk?" she asked eventually.

JD considered that for a moment. "I love robots as much as the next guy, but I'm not convinced." He pitched his voice low, heavy bass traveling beneath the white noise. "It sounds like you want us to give up, as a species. I don't see that happening."

"It's not about giving up, it's about choosing to retire before the choice is taken from us. Not just that, but retiring to a relaxed life, a life where all of us are equal, all watched over by machines of loving grace."

JD scoffed. "I don't believe your talk of equality, either."

Kali turned to JD and considered him. She nodded. "People think they want equality, but in truth, most of us want someone to tell us what to do. Life is frightening, change is frightening, decision-making is frightening—better to let someone else guide you."

"I don't know that I agree."

"Then you must be truly self-actualized."

JD smiled but ignored the obvious ploy. He nodded to the

families gathered around small fires, cooking rice and noodles in battered aluminum pots. "Shouldn't all these people have been at your talk?"

"You're asking if I'm upset by their absence."

"Yeah, I guess I am."

"Everyone here is free to do what they want, as long as they contribute. Some people contribute with money, some till the crops, some spread my message. As long as they're helping Liber, I don't care what they do with their time. Some people aren't ready to listen to my talks anyway, they're still too blinkered. They need to be reached slowly, introduced to new ideas and new experiences carefully so they are not harmed. If someone doesn't come to the meetings, then by definition they are not ready to come to the meetings."

They continued walking, the dogs holding to their loose circle of noise, hull plates gleaming. They passed other dogs, legs folded beneath them on standby, waiting for the light of morning to charge their batteries.

"How does Soo-hyun contribute?" JD asked.

"For one thing, they brought you to me. You're to be part of my vision, Julius. I said before that money turned us into a virus. Well, I need you to recover another virus, one that could alter the course of history."

"You want me to steal a virus?"

"Steal? Hardly. I'm going to let you in on a secret, Julius. May I call you Jules?"

"JD."

"Alright, JD. You know who Zero Lee is," she said. It was not a question.

"Of course."

"Like any rich man, like any artist, he would never do the work himself if there was an impressionable young person who could do it for him. Here is my secret, JD: I once worked for Zero Lee."

JD stopped dead in his tracks. "What? Really?" he asked. Kali nodded and waited for JD to catch up. "What is he like?"

"Dying. He *was* brilliant, and insufferable. But now he's dying."

JD's hands itched with the urge to check this claim, and he quickly patted the disassembled phone parts resting in his pockets. "They'd be talking about it everywhere if that were true."

"The industry rumor mill says he's in Scandinavia seeking medical treatment, but one of my sources says he's already dead, and Zero Corp are keeping it under wraps until they can make a deal with his next of kin. They'll make the announcement when it will have the smallest impact on the market."

"Shit," was all JD could manage.

Kali wrapped a hand around JD's arm, and walked in step with him. "I used to work for Lee, creating various pieces of software for one of his start-ups. He would provide a design document, but the implementation came down to us. He claimed authorship over these programs but he had no idea how they actually worked. He was a fraud, and that is one of the reasons why I left his employ. But he owned everything I wrote, even the things he didn't understand."

She paused, and turned to JD, releasing his arm. She fixed him with a look, her eyes glinting bright, translucent skin otherworldly, lips held slightly apart as though to speak, whistle, or kiss. In that second JD thought he could see her the way Red must—she was beatific.

"I created a virus, a piece of living software unlike anything the world has ever seen, and I had to leave it behind. The loss still hurts, JD. I feel like a mother who lost her child. Lee didn't even know what he had, but I would be damned before I told him."

"So you want me to break into his office and take it back?"

"Not his office, his home. But yes."

JD exhaled through pursed lips. "And if I do that, you'll pay me fifty thousand euro?"

Kali winced, but nodded. "This software will help me take Songdo from the corporations, so it's a small price to pay." She looked at JD and smiled, her pale eyes ice-cold. "If everything works out, you won't need the money; none of us will." The words seemed well rehearsed—just like her smile.

JD considered it. The money alone was tempting, but a chance to see Zero Lee's home, his workspace? When he was a teen he'd dreamed of working for Lee, but he was better with his hands than he was with code.

"Alright, I'm in," JD said.

"Excellent, JD. Truly, truly excellent. When Soo-hyun told me they had a brother who could help, I was hesitant, but now I see how the two of you could work well together. The job was Soo-hyun's idea, and they'll give you everything you need."

Kali motioned to a large brick building down the hill. It was separated from the rest of the school by a moat of darkness, while lights shone brightly from within.

"Have you visited Liber before?" Kali asked as they walked toward it.

JD shook his head. "I never go anywhere with fewer than three bars of signal."

Kali smiled. "You should visit again. It's important work we're doing here, planning and growing a new civilization. But that's enough for now."

The ring of dogs broke apart and sat alert on the cracked cement outside the detached building. Kali led JD up a short set of stairs and stood outside twin rusted doors. JD rested a hand on the knob and Kali nodded, then she turned and walked away, escorted back to the school by nine of the dogs, while the one from the canal stayed at JD's side.

"Are you visiting Soo-hyun, or checking up on me?" he asked. The dog didn't respond.

JD pushed into the building and was struck by the noise— soundproofed doors giving way to the deafening hiss of an arc welder, and Kali's voice blaring from a cheap digital radio. The building had been the school's maintenance shed. Tools hung across the front wall, traced by neat outlines, and desks had been brought in from the classrooms, now laden with different models of police dog in various states of disassembly, and quadcopter drones with bright green electrical tape stuck over their camera lenses. A thin mattress sat in one corner of the room, the sheets unmade, with dust and bits of wire caught within the linen canyons. The tang of solder hung in the air, accompanied by the meaty scent of old sweat.

Soo-hyun stood at a workbench at the rear of the room, wearing a welder's visor. They worked on a dog drone laid across the bench, its torso open, wires spread out like winter branches, nuts, bolts, screws, and solder slag littered all around it.

When Soo-hyun noticed JD, they cut off the gas to their arc welder, placed the heavy tool down with a *chank,* and switched off the radio. They lifted their visor and beamed.

"Are you in?" they asked.

JD nodded. "Yeah, I'm in."

Soo-hyun dropped the visor onto the table and gave JD a hug. "I knew you'd say yes."

They looked down at the dog standing patiently at JD's heel like a well-trained pet, and patted it once on the head.

"You didn't have to check up on me, Plato," Soo-hyun said. "Go on back to Kali."

The robot bowed its cylindrical metal head slightly in response. It stood and turned before bounding out the door, leg actuators whirring sharply in the quiet space.

"Natural language processing in a police drone?" JD said, impressed. "You told me you were tinkering out here, but this is . . ." He motioned around the workshop to all the disassembled dogs. "It's a lot."

"It's how I keep myself occupied. Some of the teens have made drone hunting into a vocation, so there's always work. It keeps me centered."

"Do you mind?" JD asked, pointing to the dog open on Soo-hyun's workbench. They stepped back and JD leaned in for a better look. "You didn't tell me you worked on police dogs."

"You didn't ask," Soo-hyun said.

JD nodded. He'd been angry with Soo-hyun for the longest time. Eventually it got to be easier not to ask what they were doing with their life, easier to just pretend there was no anger there, no connection.

"Tektech put in for the tender to repair the police dogs, but nothing ever came of it. I always wanted to get a look inside one."

"All you had to do was visit," Soo-hyun said. "They're nasty machines until you teach them some manners." They pulled a screwdriver from a drawer in the workbench and held it by the head, tapping the rubber handle on the robot's hip flexor. "Basic movement and motor functions are the same as we had in the warehouse, more or less. Where dogs get interesting is here," they said, dropping the tool onto the bench and pulling away half of the dog's skull, their fingers tipped with grime-blacked nails.

They parted two lots of power cabling and their fingers disappeared inside the cranial cavity. They reached around blindly and continued: "Before you can reprogram them, you want to remove the storage and start from scratch." They grunted with this last word and pulled their hand free.

Soo-hyun held a standard storage cube—burnished steel casing twelve millimeters a side. One of the faces was dotted with small holes like the six of a die. They dropped it into JD's hand.

"Got every police rule and procedure in there, plus records of every day it spent on the job."

JD tried to give the datacube back, but Soo-hyun closed his hand around it.

"Keep it. Stick it inside a quadcopter drone and watch it try and pull over speeding auto-trucks." Soo-hyun grinned. They took the screwdriver from the bench and handed that to JD too.

"What's this for?" JD asked.

"Happy birthday."

"My birthday was months ago."

"And I didn't get you anything. It's a LOX-Recess screwdriver. If you ever get a chance to open up a dog, you're going to need one of those."

"Don't you need it?"

"I've got a dozen of them littered around here." Soo-hyun squeezed JD's shoulder. "Come on, take a seat."

They motioned to two stools, and JD groaned as he dropped onto the low seat, struggling to ignore the ache in his knee. Soo-hyun reached into a cooler beside the chair and produced two bottles of unlabeled beer. They tossed one to JD and he caught it.

JD twisted the lid off his beer and took a sip; it wasn't good beer, but it was cold, and it was free.

"What do you think of the place?"

JD raised his eyebrows. "It's, uh, cozy."

"It's a shithole," Soo-hyun said.

JD nodded, and they both smiled. "At least you don't have to share the workshop with anyone else. Do you?"

"No."

"There you go then, that's something," JD said. "You really like it out here?"

"It's quieter. *I'm* quieter. I fucked up, y'know," they said, pointing to JD's knee with their beer. "Liber is good for me."

"You can't hide here forever."

Soo-hyun shrugged. "Songdo will always be waiting for me, but for now I'm happy."

"Alright," JD said. "Kali said you'd give me the details of this job?"

"I've already put the file together. I'll make you a copy." Soo-hyun walked to an old rig asleep in the corner, and whacked the mechanical keyboard to life. They pointed to a yellow envelope on a workbench by the door. "That's your down payment; two thousand for expenses. Don't give Red an excuse to come looking for it, hyung."

"I wouldn't give him the pleasure," JD said as he wandered over to the bench. He swept up the cash-laden envelope and slipped it into his back pocket in one smooth movement.

Soo-hyun worked at their rig in silence for a minute or two, while JD drank his beer. Another dog drone walked in through the open door and bumped into Soo-hyun's leg, shaking its rear half though it had no tail to wag. They patted it on the head and glanced at JD.

"Might have gone overboard on the canine subroutines with this one."

JD smiled. "Nah, it's cute."

"I've got another present for you," Soo-hyun said. "Check the fridge. Parcel wrapped in white paper. It's all yours."

The fridge was tucked away in the back corner of the room, half-hidden behind a mound of scrap metal and drone parts. JD opened the fridge door to a noisy hum, and the faint smell of mold. It was empty but for a single package in waxed paper on the middle tray. He took it and held it up to his nose. Salty.

"It's bacon," Soo-hyun said.

"What?" JD said. He almost dropped it in shock.

"One of the residents here used to be a butcher. Killed Quincy last week, and cured her. I put some aside for your mom's famous fried rice."

"I can't take this—"

"You already did, now keep it."

JD stashed it in his backpack, and downed the rest of his beer.

"Here you go," Soo-hyun announced. They tossed a datacube across the room, and JD snatched it out of the air. "Everything you need for the job. Just—just don't open it on a public network."

"It's not my first illegal rodeo."

Soo-hyun smiled. "Take a look and we'll compare notes tomorrow."

"What's tomorrow?" JD asked, putting the cube into his pocket.

"Planning dinner." Soo-hyun left the workbench and crossed over to join JD, trailed by their pet drone. "Thank you for doing this. I'll talk to you later." They hugged briefly, and Soo-hyun ducked out through the doorway and disappeared from sight.

JD slammed the fridge door and limped after Soo-hyun, but

when he stepped outside, they were gone. A dog drone sat guard beside the entrance, visual sensors whirring as it looked up at JD's face.

"Where'd they go?" he asked. The dog's only response was the quiet whir of actuators as it scanned the school grounds, tracking a group of kids playing a chaotic soccer match on a too-small stretch of flat ground.

JD limped away, leaving behind the commune and all of Kali's followers. He exhaled sharp through his nose to dislodge the clinging scent of solder, but when he breathed in he almost choked on the smell of pig shit, seeing for the first time the pen of sleeping animals beyond the commune's vegetable patch.

JD slotted the battery into his phone, and blinked the start-up sequence. He waited impatiently for that surge of connection—informational and physiological, feedback loops of connectivity threaded deep through his psyche.

Once he was back online, JD made a call. "Hey, Mom. I've got a present for you; is it okay if I come around?"

CHAPTER FOUR

Soo-hyun waited on the cracked footpath outside Kali's residence. It was the first building Kali had cleaned up and renovated with the earnings from her teachings—a three-story apartment block that housed the woman and held meeting rooms for her inner circle: Andrea, Yoo Jong-seo, Oh A-sung, Brandon "Red" Jones, Jin Sang-yeop, and Park Do-cheol.

A cool breeze rolled in, and Soo-hyun shivered and rubbed their arms through the thick fabric of their coveralls.

A message from Kali had brought them to the apartment block, but nothing in the text told them what to expect from the meeting. A childlike voice somewhere in the back of their head warned that they were in trouble. Sent to the head teacher for disciplinary action. It had been too long since their school days for the fear to emerge so vividly from their subconscious, and yet it had.

They'd been so good lately.

Soo-hyun let their head fall back, and they took in the night sky. Soo-hyun had always lived under that light-stained sky, despite false memories of vivid starlight implanted into their mind by film, TV, and social media. Still, Soo-hyun found a particular sort of beauty in the image—human civilization so bright it blotted the sky itself.

The front door to Kali's building opened with a quiet squeal, and Andrea stood in the gap, her cherubic face lit from beneath by the tablet she always carried flat across her arm.

"What the fuck are you doing out here? She's waiting for you."

"The fuck did you just say?" Soo-hyun asked.

The girl rolled her eyes and sneered. "This is a bullshit-free zone. If you want to come inside and find out why Kali picked you to join her inner circle, you'll need to adjust your tiny clouded mind to some quote-unquote harsh fucking language. Now, do you want to come in, or do you want to fuck the fuck off?"

Soo-hyun's heart thumped hard in their chest. *The inner circle.* They shrugged with the clatter and tink of their many necklaces. "I'm ready. Let's go." They pushed inside, past Kali's personal assistant and mini-doppelganger.

Andrea slammed the door shut, and it took a few seconds for Soo-hyun's eyes to adjust to the dark. The building's first floor had been cleared out during the renovation—an open space but for a small kitchen in the rear corner and the load-bearing columns spaced evenly throughout. The scent of artificial cinnamon hung heavy in the air, a product of the candles that burned and flickered along shelves that lined the walls. The floor was littered with throw pillows and blankets, like a child's sleepover that had never been tidied up.

Soo-hyun followed Andrea up a steep staircase, away from the sweet cloying scent and the dim lighting. The smell on the second floor was of harsh antiseptics, and the landing opened onto a small boardroom. Kali and her inner circle sat around a black table, lit brightly from above with humming fluorescent tubes. Kali sat on an ornate, carved wooden throne, cushioned in velvet. The others sat on plastic chairs. Kali stood and motioned for Soo-hyun to take the chair at the far end of the table, while Andrea sat at her right hand.

"I thought you would never join us," Kali said, with a smile tugging at her lips. "You wouldn't have been the first to respond to the call of enlightenment with fear and trepidation."

"No, it's not that at all," Soo-hyun said, too quickly, as they sat down, "I was just waiting for someone to open the door."

"Always waiting, never doing. That is the problem with so many people." Kali let her eyes drift across the table before landing on

Red, seated at her left, cracking his knuckles, unable to sit still. "Did you wait for someone to open the door, Red?"

"Fuckin' kicked it in," he said.

"You thought I was being attacked, and in a way I was. I was attacking myself." Kali put a foot on the throne, and lifted her gray dress, revealing more and more of her long, pale legs until, just past her knee, the white skin gave way to stark black ink: a circle on her inner thigh. "I tattooed myself. I was determined to draw a perfect circle on my skin, with no guidelines, no stencil. I started small, and when the circle proved uneven, I would draw it larger and larger. I would have covered my whole leg in that quest for perfection, but Red stopped me. Found me screaming in frustration at my own failings. He didn't know it at the time, but he was teaching me an important lesson: perfection is not something we attain in this skin or on it."

She dropped her foot to the floor and the dress fell with it, covering her flesh once more. She sat on her throne.

"When I finally stopped myself, I could still feel the tattoo gun buzzing in my hand; a phantom vibration." She closed her eyes and clenched her fist loosely in front of her face. "I can still feel it. I can still hear the steady buzz of the machine."

Kali opened her eyes and stared at Soo-hyun, the pale blue of them reaching down the long table, as though there were only the two of them, everything else fell away.

"Do you know why people began to tattoo themselves?" Kali asked.

Soo-hyun tried to speak but found their mouth dry. They licked their lips quickly and shook their head.

"We needed to dominate our totemic animals," Kali said. "We could worship them, or we could hunt them; eat their flesh and wear their skins. But these acts were only temporary—the flesh and skin would pass. By burning their bones and making ink from the charcoal, we could trap the animals, the spirits, the totems, beneath our skin. But we didn't stop there.

"Our vanquished enemies, our dead lovers, our lost children, all these people could be held forever beneath the skin. We can take their bodies, their power, and insert it into our own selves, one needle prick at a time."

Kali held her hand out to Andrea, and the young girl placed a small glass pot onto her palm, the ink inside so dark it seemed to absorb all the light in the room so that the jar was the only thing Soo-hyun could focus on.

"This is my mother," Kali said. "She birthed me, she loved me, she raised me, and she failed me. Our parents always fail us, and we are bound to fail them if we ever wish to become our own people. They have children to continue their line, their name, their genes, and the most important thing we can do is burn their line, lose their name, and mold their genes into something unrecognizable."

Kali placed the jar down on the table with a *clack* that resounded in the silence.

"Soo-hyun," she said, "I've called you here tonight because we are at the dawn of the next age of life on Earth, the age of machines. I'm not talking about some distant future; I'm talking about now, today. I'm talking about the fruition of these plans that are already in place.

"You've been instrumental in my planning—by getting your brother to join us, and by putting together the data he will need to help us steal our future. But there will be more to come. People *will* be hurt. People may die. I will take responsibility for the pain we must cause, but I cannot do it all on my own."

Kali stood from her seat and walked around the table, all eyes following her as she approached Soo-hyun. She stood behind them, and gently placed a hand on their shoulders.

"Soo-hyun, your brother is not a believer, but we need him."

"Don't fuckin' need him," Red muttered.

Soo-hyun felt Kali's breath on their neck as the woman exhaled slowly. "Red," Kali said eventually, "you would see us start a war without our greatest weapon. There will be no bloodshed unless I order it. Understood?"

Red lowered his head and mumbled at the table.

"Answer me clearly."

"Yes, Kali," Red said.

"Soo-hyun, will you be able to keep your brother on track, keep him focused on the task at hand? Will you make sure he cooperates?"

"Yes, Kali."

"There's something else I need from you."

Soo-hyun cleared their throat. "What is it?"

"You spend so much of your time tinkering inside your workshop. You take the machines that Zero would use against us, and you make them our eyes, you make them our protectors and our pets."

"I do what I can," Soo-hyun said.

"It's not enough."

Soo-hyun dropped their head, brow furrowed as they stared at their hands, resting in their lap.

"I'm not admonishing you," Kali said. "It's not your work that's lacking, it's your self. You've bottled something away and hidden it. I want to change that, Soo-hyun, if you'll let me."

Soo-hyun nodded, but didn't speak.

"The rest of you know your parts," Kali said. "I will speak to you tomorrow."

The others all got up from the table, their chairs scraping loudly over the tile floor. Kali pressed her hands together in front of her face, bowing minutely to each of her followers as they bowed to her and left.

Kali stood in silence, and Soo-hyun listened as the others trudged downstairs and filtered outside. The building door slammed closed, silencing the sounds of the commune that had briefly drifted up to greet them. Kali squeezed Soo-hyun's shoulder. "I need you to come with me."

She walked around the table, pausing to collect the jar of inky void before continuing down a bright hallway, deeper into the converted apartment building.

Soo-hyun trailed Kali, the woman's bare feet silent, Soo-hyun's heavy boots loud and clumsy by comparison. Fear and apprehension slowed their tread. They had never before been alone with Kali, had never felt the full force of the teacher's attention.

"Here we are," Kali said. She stopped at a door painted glossy black, light refracting off its surface in a hundred vertical lines. She opened the door and motioned for Soo-hyun to enter.

Inside, the smell of antiseptic was stronger. A counter lined the opposite wall, topped with bottles of liquid soap and disinfectant, and a bulky plastic case. A leather office chair sat beside a high, adjustable bed, its black leather covered in plastic wrap.

"What is this?" Soo-hyun asked.

Kali crossed over to the plastic case and opened it, revealing a tattoo gun lying on a bed of gray foam. It was a scaffold of machined steel holding two barrels that made up the motor, and other fierce pieces of metal Soo-hyun couldn't name. A long steel shaft like an industrial pen emerged from one end, with a thick hunk of plastic molded with finger grooves.

"One cannot join the inner circle, without an inner circle. A tattoo on your inner thigh."

Soo-hyun swayed on their feet, chest tight with fear. "The others all have one?"

"Even Andrea," Kali said.

"You tattooed her?"

"She did her own." Kali smiled. "Though I admit, I had to clean it up for her."

"I don't have any tattoos," Soo-hyun said.

"That will make this one all the more special."

"I always wanted one, but it seemed . . ." Soo-hyun hesitated. "Like one step too far."

"You're holding back, Soo-hyun. What are you afraid of?"

"Have you ever lost control?" Soo-hyun asked. "Gotten so caught up in your excitement or rage that you disappeared?"

Kali shook her head only slightly. Her questing blue eyes told Soo-hyun to continue.

"It's the greatest feeling in the world," Soo-hyun said, breathily.

"Then why are you so afraid?" Kali asked.

"I don't trust myself. It's so easy to lose control, to do something you'll regret later, to hurt someone you love."

"So you toil away in the workshop alone because you're afraid you might hurt someone."

Soo-hyun nodded.

"I will let you in on a secret, Soo-hyun: life is pain. You will hurt people, and you will be hurt. This isn't shameful, isn't something to be avoided at all costs. It is proof that you're alive. When is the last time you truly felt alive?"

Soo-hyun thought for a few seconds, then shook their head and shrugged. "I don't know."

"You've trapped yourself in the workshop because you're afraid of living. Because you think that who you are is somehow wrong, that you are somehow broken. You *are* broken, Soo-hyun. We all are."

Soo-hyun's chest jolted with a sob they quickly stifled. They felt seen, understood, for the first time in entirely too long.

"I appreciate everything you do for Liber, but I no longer need the Soo-hyun that hacks together drones in their workshop. I need someone with rage in their heart, I need bravery, I need soldiers. I need the Soo-hyun that threw homemade bombs at police dogs during the Sinsong riots. Where has that Soo-hyun gone?"

Before Soo-hyun could answer, Kali spoke louder: "Where?"

"I don't know."

"You do know. You know because you buried them. You buried them deep down because you're too afraid to let them live. But I need them. *You* need them."

Soo-hyun nodded and sniffed, their eyes burned with building tears.

"If you're not ready for this, if you're not ready to be close to me, I can't force it. You have to want this, you have to work for it. You have to be ready to dig deep and find your old reckless self, your true self. The tattoo means you will never be alone, you will always be connected to me, and all the others. You have to accept the tattoo for the gift that it is."

Soo-hyun swallowed a hollow pain in the back of their throat. "Okay, I'll do it," they said in a breathy whisper, worried that if they spoke normally their voice would break.

"I knew you would," Kali said. "Welcome." She sat on the leather chair, opened a cupboard beneath the counter, and retrieved a pair of black latex gloves, a tiny plastic cup, and an eyedropper stained black with use. She carefully unscrewed the lid on the ink pot, and using the eyedropper, decanted a couple of drops into the plastic cup. "You're going to need to strip."

"Strip?" Soo-hyun said.

"Sorry, I should have warned you not to wear coveralls." Kali connected the tattoo gun to a small box that sat inside the cupboard, cables joining it to a power point and a flat round pedal on the floor. She looked up, and Soo-hyun still hadn't undressed. Kali sighed. "I don't expect you to do anything that I wouldn't," she said.

Kali stood and, without hesitation, lifted her dress over her head, before dropping it in the corner of the room. She was naked but for a pair of gray briefs, her skin white enough for Soo-hyun to see the red, blue, and purple of her veins meandering beneath the surface.

Soo-hyun stared, eyes shocked wide.

Kali made no effort to cover her breasts, or conceal the different tattoos that marked her flesh like ancient hieroglyphs or the forgotten sigils of some dead god. She sat back down, and continued working at the tattoo machine. "I'm not even looking, Soo-hyun; take your time."

Soo-hyun exhaled. Without thinking, before they could change their mind, they pulled down the zip on the front of their coveralls, listening to the plastic sound of the teeth being pulled apart. They took their arms from the sleeves and pushed the rough canvas fabric down past their hips, letting it pool on the floor at their feet. They kept on their underpants and a T-shirt, embarrassed by the stains that marred the armpits.

Kali glanced up, and patted the leather bed. "Take a seat."

Soo-hyun did as they were told, stretching out across the plastic wrap that clung to their skin, *scritch*ing as they peeled their limbs away, repositioning their legs until they could sit comfortably. With their right leg bent at the knee, and their inner thigh pointed up toward the ceiling, Soo-hyun tried not to focus on the stretch marks and blemishes, the fine dark hair they had never bothered to shave.

"There's something else I need to talk to you about," Kali said, her attention fixed on the needles blurring at the tip of the gun as she hit the pedal and the gun buzzed. "Your police dogs—can they be piloted?"

"Piloted?"

"They patrol our community, and they help to keep us safe from outsiders, but I need more from them. They're marked like police units, they could go out into the city and work with impunity. We just need to be able to control them."

"The first generation of dog drones were strictly user-operated. It was only after a couple of years of in-the-field training that the machine learning algorithms could grasp the necessary duties and responsibilities," Soo-hyun said, nerves speeding the words from their mouth.

"So that's a yes?"

"I don't know exactly how I'd do it, but it must be possible."

"How long would it take?"

"I have no idea," Soo-hyun said. "A few days? A week?"

"Alright. I'll get you whatever you need to make it work." Kali dipped the needles into the ink and hit the pedal, coating them in black. "I would tell you this isn't going to hurt, but I hate lying."

Soo-hyun lay back, focused their attention on the bank of lights overhead, fluorescents cycling at fifty hertz, their flicker barely perceptible. Something cold touched their leg and Soo-hyun's body lurched. They looked down to find Kali wiping a spot on their inner leg, disinfectant cool against their skin.

"Just calm down," Kali said. "Breathe slowly. In for four seconds, out for four seconds, nice and steady."

Soo-hyun inhaled, and closed their eyes. They squeezed them shut tight when the gun buzzed again, steady this time, sound like a huge mechanical wasp hovering over their skin. The wasp touched down, and a pain like burning spread across the soft skin of their thigh.

* * *

When her people gathered in throngs, Kali spoke slowly, with authority gathered from every higher power she cared to mention. Given enough time she mentioned them all.

Her detractors claimed her pilgrimage was made of lies rather than steps, but the woman born to the name Madelyn Danekas truly traveled across the Indian subcontinent. See the QR codes of her boarding passes, verify each pixel of the photos she uploaded to the cloud. They are all still here.

She was there. That much cannot be denied.

She traveled through India reading books on Hubbard, Asahara, Jones, Osho. She learned ways to lead. She learned the lies people wanted most desperately to believe. She learned the careful manipulations needed to keep herself separate from her followers, above them.

Madelyn Danekas traveled to India with a suitcase full of books, but Kali Magdalene returned. A self-made woman, the product of immaculate conception.

Madelyn Danekas's mother was alive and well, in Burbank, California. Her bones had not been reduced to ash, the ash made into ink. She was always among the first to like Kali's posts and videos, and she remained a recurring monthly donor to her daughter's organization, no matter how often Kali claimed she was dead.

CHAPTER FIVE

The fry pan slammed down on the steel stovetop. JD twitched awake at the noise, eyes wide to the alien surrounds, brain struggling to catch up to his sensorium. He rolled over and felt the threading of a throw pillow rub against the side of his head. He sat upright on his mom's couch, face to face with his reflection desaturated in the black glass of the TV hanging on the opposite wall—two days' growth casting a dark shadow across his cheeks, faded old T-shirt loose around his neck. He pulled his jeans on as he stood. A sharp sizzle from the kitchen called to him like a siren song. He shuffled through, yawning.

It was a tiny kitchen by Hollywood suburban standards, but large for a single-bedroom apartment. A toaster and microwave were shoved into one corner, collecting dust behind a battered rice cooker. The cupboards were finished in a grainy white laminate, stained with old finger smudges that wouldn't come off, no matter how many times Gaynor scrubbed at them. Gaynor stood at the stove in an old satin robe, staring intently at the bacon curling in the pan.

"Morning, Mom," JD said.

She grunted in response, not bothering to look at him.

"What?" he asked. His brain chugged slowly toward a guess, dangerously undercaffeinated. "I didn't steal it."

Gaynor raised her eyebrows and threw one hand up dismissively.

"I promise, Mom." He crossed two feet of linoleum flooring and kissed her on the cheek.

"Where did it come from?" She bit off the words. Still she hadn't taken her eyes off the meat.

JD swallowed, his tongue drowning in saliva at the fatty, salty smell. "Soo-hyun gave it to me. Someone at Liber killed the pig and cured the meat."

"Probably diseased."

"Then don't eat any," JD said, and immediately regretted talking back. His stomach lurched, either in anxiety or bacon-induced hunger. He chose to believe it was the latter, forcing back memories of the shouting matches that had punctuated his adolescence. "Do you want coffee?"

"Tea," Gaynor said. She pushed the curling meat to one side of the pan and cracked three eggs into the middle. The translucent albumen ran across the oil-slicked pan and quickly turned white, bubbles forming in the hardening substance. JD set the kettle to boil, then took a coffee mug and one of his mom's chipped china cups from the cupboard. He dropped a green tea bag into the cup and heaped two teaspoons of dirt-colored "coffee" powder into his mug, along with three teaspoons of raw sugar to balance out the bitter taste.

He switched the kettle off when he heard the first sign of simmering, and poured water into both cups—not so hot it would burn Gaynor's tea, but warm enough to dissolve his coffee and sugar. He put them down on the small kitchenette table, black liquid slopping out of his cup and running hot down his knuckles. Gaynor carried two breakfast-laden plates over and sat opposite JD. She hadn't bothered to toast the bread, which was slightly stale but still served to soak up oil, bacon grease, and egg yolk when JD pierced the yellow globes.

He ate hungrily, unable to slow down even when the hot oil burned his tongue.

"How is Soo-hyun, then?" Gaynor asked coolly. Her concerned

scowl didn't stop her from eating, the knife and fork held precisely, as though it were a formal meal and not breakfast with her son.

JD shrugged and chewed. After he swallowed, he said, "They seem happy."

Gaynor pointed at JD's plate with her knife. "Good bacon? Been so long since I cooked it."

"It's great, Mum." JD flashed her a smile, then stabbed the last piece of meat with his fork and stuck the whole strip in his mouth, chewing slowly.

"I'd rather you were spending time with Troy. He's a much better influence. Probably be tenured before Soo-hyun gets another job."

JD's head dropped. He chewed, swallowed. He opened his mouth to speak, but didn't.

"You're happier when you're with him, Julius. And I want you to be happy."

JD sighed. "I know, Mom." He shifted on the plastic chair and pulled the envelope of cash from his back pocket. He took the bulk of the money from the envelope and slid it across the table. "That's for your rent."

"You don't have to keep doing this," Gaynor said quietly.

"How much did my hospital stay cost you?"

Gaynor sighed. She looked away from the money as though it were tainted, but she covered it with her hand. A moment later it had disappeared into the pocket of her robe. "Thank you."

"Thanks for breakfast."

* * *

JD washed his face and bathed his pits in the bathroom sink, using a chewed fingernail to scrape the remaining sleep from the corner of his eye. The skin hung loose and black under his eyes. He could have shaved, but didn't bother.

He always kept fresh boxers and at least one spare T-shirt in his backpack, so he put these on before slipping back into his jeans.

Gaynor stopped him at the door, holding the rest of the bacon in one hand and two sandwiches sealed in plastic. "I didn't have any tomatoes, so I couldn't make you a BLT."

"Did you heap the mayo on?"

Gaynor crossed her arms over her chest and glared, but it was playful this time, with a tiny smirk tugging at the corner of her mouth. "Of course I did."

"Then they'll be amazing," JD said. He took the sandwiches and placed them carefully into his bag. "The rest of the bacon is yours; if I take it home my roommates will just eat it all."

"Jules, I can't."

JD ignored her protest. "Just save me some of your famous fried rice."

"It *has* been a while," she said, looking at the paper-wrapped meat.

"Ping me if you need anything." He kissed her on the cheek and rushed out the front door.

The facial recognition camera by the elevator meant JD had to take the stairs. He kept one hand on the banister to take weight off his bad knee as he descended.

Gaynor's apartment was one of hundreds in a tight tower complex. Lights in the corridors shone twenty-four-seven, abandoned rubbish and filthy concrete walls illuminated beneath the flickering, humming fluorescents. Gaynor—like her neighbors—rarely left the apartment. She worked random search-and-admin for cents per task—one of millions behind the algorithms that kept smart assistants and other "automated" systems running at all hours of the day and night. JD guessed half the building subsisted on that same variety of corporate freelance.

Before falling asleep, JD had quickly scanned the files from Soohyun, studying the schematics and timetables as though they were a puzzle to be solved, rather than evidence of a planned crime. Without the official access he would normally receive along with a city repossession order, he'd need help bypassing the target's security, and there was only one person he could trust with that.

He took the phone from his pocket and checked the warehouse's robot uptime app. Everything was green, including the Hippo repairer, but he marked himself as on-call just in case. Next, JD scrolled through his contacts, dodging around a small group of children trudging off to school with cube-shaped backpacks larger than them. He found the name he needed and hit CALL; the phone rang in his ear like a digital cicada.

"Khoder, I need to talk to you. In the real."

Pain speared up his leg with every step, but JD couldn't slow down. He felt like bacteria in the body of the apartment building—alien, unwanted. His heart thudded hard and already moisture gathered in his armpits.

"I've got your money," he said loudly over Khoder's excuses. "Yeah, don't worry, I'll come to you."

* * *

The city shook on digital frequencies as JD made his way to the Varket. Glass facades shuddered with the oscillating purr of bass-heavy beats. The music would spike, then drop, silence like held breath. When the beat returned Songdo exhaled. The sovereign city was home to countless minorities; words from a myriad of languages drifted through the air, mingling to form an indecipherable ur-tongue. Spoken Korean dominated, but in business signage, private conversation, and scattershot insults, everything was being steered toward the entropy of English, the language of globalization.

JD diagonally crossed the intersection where the Egyptian and Ethiopian quarters met, car horns adding to the Ethiopiyawi electronica emanating from a bustling hookah bar, filled with figures in black and charcoal suits. Spice-thick cuisines battled in the air, and everywhere the flat scent of old fry oil edged with engine exhaust and heavy metal particulates. The saltwater scent, carried in on a breeze, brought small respite from the constant garbage smell of the city—green, trash-free plans abandoned when Songdo hit the first of its financial hurdles. The smell was one thing Zero Corporation couldn't augment; otherwise they might censor the scent of Korean cooking, emanating from pojangmacha stalls and restaurants all through the city, a mouthwatering reminder that Korean culture had survived longer than any corporation, had survived thousands of years of worse than whatever Zero could do to the city.

An AR billboard on one side of the intersection showed the faces of criminals with outstanding warrants—jaywalkers, sexual predators, and violent gangsters, all caught on CCTV but never apprehended. On the building opposite, a video of Kali played: smiling, talking emphatically to a gathered crowd. "Find Truth," the ad suggested, "Find Happiness," and a link to her Livideo feed. JD shook his head and kept moving.

Two blocks further, JD stood across from the Varket, the scarlet glow of its anachronistic neon sign calling to him. He dodged between two cars as the ground flared red beneath his steps. He let the momentum carry him past the bugzapper hum of the sign and in through the first door, into the vantablack foyer. The walls seemed infinitely distant, his steps awkward over a floor that his eyes didn't want to see. He groped forward until his hand touched the second door; he yanked it open and stepped inside.

The Varket was a favored hangout of hackers and hopefuls, freelance share traders, and voidwarriors; lowest ping you could find outside a corporate compound. The soundtrack droned its oppressive, beatless ambient mantras with the scratch and hiss of analogue tape, heavy enough to shroud discussion.

JD went straight for the counter. The bartender slash barista had an asymmetrical fringe over eyes darkened by makeup or exhaustion. He wore a black cotton dress, or overly long T-shirt, stained with bleach and precisely threadbare, his ochre skin showing through in a snakeskin pattern. His prosthetic left arm rested along the back wall, plugged in and charging, blinking light reflected off a row of bourbon bottles—the kind of cheap swill you'd only drink when you had something you needed to forget.

"What's your poison?" he asked.

"Coffee, black. Thanks," JD said.

"Not dexy? It's cheaper."

"Nah, I like my teeth how they are."

The barista nodded and started at the espresso machine, single hand working the controls with practiced ease. Half the grounds were recycled, the other half a blight-resistant GMO strain, but it was the closest thing to real coffee that JD could afford anywhere in Songdo-dong. He had briefly considered spending some of the down payment on a cup of the real stuff, but that would have meant going out of his way. Maybe next time.

While he waited for his drink, he turned to lean against the bar and survey the crowd, elbows jutting behind him to rest on the sticky countertop. The faint hum of hustle scraped beneath the wall of noise. Illegal wares were traded overtly in dim-lit booths, black marketeers peddling counterfeit ships, swords, and other loot to desperate gamers—best drops in any game, good for use right until your account was banned for life. Perfect for the suicidal, the terminal, the given-up. Three technicians took up an entire booth each, tools and discarded silicon splayed across the tables: desperate people approached them with ancient phones and rigs held together by thousand-mile-an-hour tape and chewed-up screws, batteries failing, processors overheating the moment they touched VR. The techs never lifted their eyes, focused solely on the body and soul of each broken machine.

There was the dull clatter of ceramic as the barista deposited JD's coffee. He swiped his hand over the cashpass and it beeped in acceptance.

The barista raised an eyebrow. "Implant?"

JD nodded.

"Careful it doesn't rot your arm off."

JD's eyes flicked to the prosthetic along the back wall. "Is that—" The rest of the question died on his tongue as JD hesitated, unsure if it was rude to ask.

The barista guessed anyway. "Nah," he said; "I'm just fucking with you."

JD nodded toward the basement door. "Khoder in?"

"Does the kid ever leave?"

"Thanks."

JD carried his drink to the rear corner, sipping his espresso before he could spill any. He pushed through a door that led to the basement stairs and descended slowly into purple-hued, blacklit darkness. The door swung closed behind him, and the music became muffled, deadened further with each step he took below the surface. Descending beneath ground level, all JD could picture were the layers of compressed garbage on all sides—the countless tons of ocean waste that created the foundations of the city.

Khoder's door read the friendly tag on JD's phone and slid open on silent apparatus. The air inside was blood-hot. Khoder reclined in a SOTA virt chair in the middle of the room, his head encased in a bulbous sphere for complete peripheral vision. His black haptic-feedback suit ran with folds like gills where it clung to the kid's skinny frame. The door closed and an eerie silence descended on the space. The dense quiet amplified the slow thud of JD's heart, the gurgle of his gut, and the painful click of his knee; all those sounds of the meat engine.

Fragmented grabs from in-game fell slow across the walls— among the black of space rare spots of color drifted like machine snow. Explosions bloomed, scattered to form a leering deathmask drawn in abstract. JD shuddered despite the heat.

"Hey, Khoder."

No response.

JD counted out two hundred euro from the envelope and dropped the notes on Khoder's chest.

"Khoder," JD said again. He shook his head and sat with his back against the wall and his sore leg stretched out. He finished his coffee, placed the cup down near a pile of takeout containers growing from the corner, then took his phone from his pocket and logged into VOIDWAR.

JD held the phone close to his face to block the view of Khoder's room, and his contex painted the in-game world over his eyes in stripped-down, third-person view. His corvette drifted in the barren solar system his home rig was slowly assembling. Far-off stars glimmered on the edges and the local sun slowly grew, a churn of pulsing light in the center of the gestation. He turned his ship to the jump-gate, and scanned his friends list to find Khoder's location.

He took three jumps through the galaxy's transit system and arrived in Ertl—his mobile processor struggling to render the wide belt of asteroids and massively eroded planets of the quarry system. Just off-center, near the sun, two fleets circled one another, streaks of light filling the void between them.

"Khoder," JD said, stern over voice chat.

"You sound pissed, bro," was the kid's curt response.

"I'm in the room."

"Room?" Khoder said, sounding vague.

JD reached an arm out and found a sticky ecoboard takeout container. He lobbed the box at Khoder; it bounced off the kid's helmet and clattered to the floor.

"Oh, the fucking room. Why are you here?" Khoder said, his voice betraying the very teenage resentment of meeting in the real.

"I told you I was coming. I wanted to give you your cut from that repo job."

"Money transfer, bro," Khoder said, muffled murmur coming from inside his helmet while his voice came clear through the game.

JD hesitated, surveillance vigilance telling him to keep his mouth shut. "I've got another job, in the real this time."

"Good for you, bro."

JD almost swore. Instead he clenched his free hand and his jaw. "I need a hacker, and you're the best I know."

"Best there is, but I'm busy."

JD winced as he stood. He walked over to Khoder and slapped

the side of his helmet three times. "Get out here and talk to me, you little shit."

"Okay, bro, fuck. One minute."

JD went back and leaned against the wall. "Kids these days," he mumbled to himself.

In-game he let his corvette loiter by the jumpgate, keeping clear of the battle engulfing more and more of Ertl. A blur of light pulled away from the melee, rushed at JD, and stopped dead mere kilometers away. JD took his eyes from the screen at the sound of creaking leather. The whole room seemed to vibrate as Khoder sat up—the money slipped from his chest onto his lap. He removed the helmet; his black hair was glossy with grease and a shadow of a moustache crept across his upper lip.

"Fucking rude, bro."

"Money," JD said, pointing at Khoder's lap.

Khoder snatched up the notes and held them under his nose. "If this happened every time I came out, maybe I'd visit the real more often."

"Thanks again for the assist," JD said.

"Money is its own reward," Khoder said with a sly grin. He stood and held the helmet against his side like one of those old astronauts back from space. "Bro, one day you're going to walk in here while I'm balls-deep in some VR fucking. Teach you to come uninvited."

"We both know you'd never soil that haptic suit."

Khoder looked down at his outfit, matte black material edged with silver accents. He shrugged and nodded—JD was right.

"What's this job that's so fucking important?"

"Can you secure the room?" JD asked.

"Already done." As Khoder spoke the drifting snatches of VOIDWAR surrounding them fell to the floor and disappeared, quickly replaced by padlock icons tiled over every surface.

JD found a slot at the base of Khoder's virt chair and plugged in Soo-hyun's datacube. The room's OS automatically sifted through the information, grouping pieces of data together and neatly arranging it across each of the room's four walls.

Building blueprints and security camera stills took up the north and east wall, street surveillance footage and neighborhood maps covered the south, and documents tiled the west wall, text too pixelated to read. Handwritten addenda were highlighted, scanned, and translated into text—a brief rundown of security protocols, potential issues, and dire warnings, all scrawled in Soo-hyun's tight script.

Khoder whistled, crossed his arms over his thin chest, and took it all in, turning slowly to inspect each data cluster.

"This is some high-level heist you're planning, bro," Khoder said. "Four levels of security: complex, building, apartment, room."

JD nodded.

"What is this place?"

"Zero Lee's apartment building."

Khoder blinked slowly. "No shit?"

"No shit."

"And you're going inside?" Khoder asked.

"Treating it the same as any other repo job," JD said. "Only difference is I don't have any keys or access codes from the bank. That's why I need you."

Khoder nodded, tapping his arm with the tightly rolled fifty-euro notes.

"What are we stealing?"

"Some new killer virus. Can you do it?" JD asked.

"Rampartment compounds are locked up tighter than my asshole. Be impossible from off-site. If I'm there with you, though"—Khoder paused, weighing options—"only difficult."

JD exhaled through pursed lips. "Good."

"Didn't say I *would* do it, bro. How much?"

"Your cut is fifteen thousand."

Khoder whistled. "Euro?"

JD nodded.

"And it's Zero's apartment, bro? Zero shitting Lee?"

"That's what they tell me. Could be lying, but I'm sure you'll be able to confirm it now you've got the address. Take you long to break into the housing authority records?"

"I basically live in there, bro." Khoder stepped closer to the north wall and strained his neck to scrutinize the building plans. "Fifteen thousand," he repeated, sounding wistful.

"What do you need money for anyway?" JD asked. "You never leave this place."

"Gonna buy it; the Varket," Khoder said, nodding up to the ceiling. "Renting's for chumps."

JD frowned, impressed. "You'll do it, then?"

"One condition, bro. When you're in his apartment, steal me something. Coffee mug, ashtray, butt plug, whatever; something he's touched."

JD smirked. "Alright, deal." His phone buzzed with an alert from the warehouse systems—he was needed on-site. He hit the ACCEPT button and looked back to Khoder. "We're meeting tonight to finalize the plan. I'll be out front at six thirty."

"Where you going, bro?"

"Work," JD said.

Khoder sneered in disgust at the idea of a mundane job.

JD unplugged the datacube from Khoder's chair and let the system keep a copy. He pointed at the briefing docs still spread across the walls. "Keep them safe, yeah?"

Khoder rolled his eyes and the files disappeared, replaced by a gaping anus penetrated by a middle finger. JD turned his head away, sounds of revulsion falling from his mouth unbidden. Khoder laughed and JD gave him the finger as he left the room, the kid's bleating following him out the door and up the stairs.

* * *

Thousands of hours spent creating a universe for people to war over. Millions of people spending billions of collective hours fighting imaginary wars. Mining digital ore to build digital ships—every atom in the universe accounted for, artificial scarcity through detailed simulation. For eighteen years the simulation held. Children grew up inside it. They learned math through transactional trial and error. They learned spelling, comprehension, cusses and slurs through in-game chat channels.

It was just as real as the real, sometimes more so.

It was real until it wasn't.

It was real until the heat-death of that digital universe, locked forever inside a server farm in the formerly United States of America, data degrading year by year until only a corrupt reality remained.

Corrupt reality? Which one? This one?

CHAPTER SIX

The afternoon dragged at the warehouse. JD's hands worked absently on packing robot maintenance while details of the heist passed through his mind, vivid as any Augmented feed.

He finished work at six, staggering his exit to avoid the initial tsunami of commuters hitting the street. Stepping outside, the humidity pushed back like a solid thing, and his knee ached with the damp. The smell of ozone was thick in the air, and dusk came abruptly, quickened by the cover of dark clouds. Something ached in JD's hand—either bone or tendon, he couldn't tell. Black oil slick beneath his fingernails, backpack hanging heavy off his shoulders.

Three blocks from the shorefront warehouse a light rain began to fall and pedestrians scattered wildly, as though it might be acid. Raindrops streaked through the digital feeds like minute glitches.

JD took the tightly balled windbreaker from the bottom of his bag and put it on, draping it over his battered leather rucksack. The rain pattered on the polyester shell, and the jacket swished with every swing of his arm. Maybe nobody else could hear it, but the rasp filled JD's ears, drowning out every other sound of the city.

He had forgotten about it by the time he hit the Ethiopian quarter, registering only the sudden quiet when he stopped at a crosswalk. The clean, old-radio patter of podcast hosts filled the silence, tinny noise escaping from the headphones that surrounded him, clinging to the skulls of the other pedestrians. All at once the motley chatter paused in sync for a broadcast ad from Songdo's geographic "Happy Community" system. The gestalt of all those disparate bits of sound reached JD loud enough that he could decipher the jingle: public domain gospel music, touting the vegetarian-chicken place just up the block.

The crossing went green and JD had to fight his hunger and step out onto the street; no fake chicken could compete with the bacon that still lingered on his palate after lunch.

The rain had stopped by the time JD found Khoder waiting outside the Varket. The kid wore a plain black baseball cap and a vinyl jacket that must have cost half his cut of the repo job. He had a cigarette clamped low between two fingers—he covered his whole mouth with his hand as he struggled to pull any smoke through the rain-damp cig.

"Cigarettes'll kill you," JD said by way of greeting.

"Not if I fucking kill them first, bro. Burn them alive, one at a time," Khoder said, grinning around the smoldering tube.

Overhead the constellations of VOIDWAR glinted bright against the backdrop of clouds. A series of explosions bloomed slow over the city's east—atomic suns born from supernova torpedoes, short-lived and devastating. Their flash and violence was emphasized by the city's Augmented feed, always desperate to keep people invested in the game, keep them buying War Bond subscription packages.

"Think one day they'll change the real-world overlay to make it resemble VOIDWAR?" JD asked as they both watched the artificial sky.

"Can't make a city look like space, bro."

"A space station, then."

Khoder shrugged. He dragged on his cigarette and squinted against the smoke. "Wouldn't matter if they did. Still the same shit underneath."

"Is it, though? Ninety-something percent of people in Songdo think they live in a clean, bright metropolis covered in advertising. *That's* real to them."

Khoder pointed to the sky. "Shit, that's Stokoe," he mumbled, ash shaking loose from the end of his cigarette.

JD nodded as though he concurred, but in truth he couldn't read the virtual constellations any better than the real ones that lingered somewhere above the digital feeds, above the light pollution, above the clouds. "And?"

"I know people in Stokoe." After a beat Khoder added: "We could raid them."

The kid took a step backward, eyes still stuck to the sky, but JD grabbed a handful of his vinyl collar. "You're not going back inside; they just got here." JD nodded across the road to where Soo-hyun stood, waiting for a gap in the traffic with a harsh set to their mouth.

"But bro, think of the loot," Khoder said.

JD shook Khoder violently enough for the kid to bring his eyes down from the sky. Soo-hyun wore a heavily constructed black neoprene hoodie, tight gray jeans, and cowboy-esque slouch leather boots they'd stolen from an auto-store and bragged about for a month. The boots were designer-ugly, but the theft gave them a certain criminal charm. A large black bag clung to their back like a baby orangutan to its mother.

"They go by they," JD said. "So be cool."

"I was born cool, bro."

"You were born an asshole."

Soo-hyun gave up waiting and walked out into traffic—car tires *shush*ed over the wet asphalt as they braked, and horns blared in warning.

They mounted the curb and inspected Khoder. "What do we need him for?"

"Soo-hyun, Khoder; Khoder, Soo-hyun. He's on digital security."

"I thought that was your job," Soo-hyun said.

"If it was a legit repo job I'd have extra tools as part of the contract. Without those I need a hacker."

Soo-hyun held up a hand. "Okay, you've already said too much." They retrieved a small pouch from their bag, lined with microwidth titanium sheeting. "Batteries, phones."

JD took the phone from his pocket, cracked open the outer casing, and dropped the battery and phone into the bag. He turned to Khoder, who held his phone tightly in one hand, looking at it as though he were reading something other than his own distraught reflection.

"You'll be offline for an hour," JD said. "Two at the most."

Khoder's head dropped minutely. Sadly he intoned a single "Bro."

He disassembled his phone with an air of ritual—sacred rites delivered on the street while all around them the city bustled. Cars hissed as they passed, people walked in tech-solitary silence, and a stray dog sniffed a garbage bin, cocked its leg, and posted to that canine message board. Khoder reached his hand into the bag and placed the phone and battery gently at its base.

"Are you alright?" JD asked Soo-hyun. "You seem different."

They bit their lower lip and nodded. "I'm good, Jules, really good. Now, let's move." Soo-hyun didn't wait for a response, they simply turned and marched away, slotting the Faraday pouch into their bag without missing a step.

JD was used to Soo-hyun's ferocious pace, but he kept glancing back to make sure Khoder was keeping up. Where JD could ram his way through the crowded sidewalks with his bulk, Khoder was a wraith. He slipped through gaps that hadn't been there a moment before, as though the foul-mouthed boy were made of smoke.

The building's entrance screamed corporate wealth and design by committee, with walls in three different shades of fake gold, and pink marble flooring, all lit sickly orange from exposed industrial light bulbs. JD expected the automatic doors to stay closed at Soo-hyun's approach, but they slid apart obediently to let them through, and stayed open as JD and Khoder followed. JD kept his head down and watched his feet carry him to the elevator, idly wondering if the building's security was good enough to get a reflection off the gaudy tiles.

JD found Soo-hyun's stolen boots waiting by the elevator, one of them tapping quickly. "Is this *the* building?" he whispered.

"Don't be daft."

"Then what are we here for?"

"I told you yesterday: planning dinner. I'm starving. You've got that money I gave you, hyung? Your shout."

"Why is it my shout? It was your idea."

The elevator opened with a faint digital chime. Soo-hyun ignored JD's protest and bowed with exaggerated flourish, motioning him and Khoder inside. They hit a button near the top of the control panel, simply marked "R," and the elevator jolted as it began to ascend.

"Bro, this elevator is nicer than your apartment."

"You haven't seen my apartment," JD said.

"I'm not wrong though, am I?"

JD glanced up to see Khoder reflected to infinity in the mirrored walls, staring up at the intricately detailed decorations along the roof of the elevator car, painted with gold leaf or something like it.

"Keep your head down."

"They look at me, they see fucking Gandhi." Khoder tapped the brim of his baseball cap where wires ran along the edge, connected to AR microprojectors. "I'll set you up before the job." Khoder raised a middle finger to the small dome in the corner that more than likely hid a camera. "Ever been flipped off by Gandhi, bro?" he asked it.

"How do you even know who Gandhi is?"

Khoder shrugged, still watching the camera. "Searched for 'famous skinny brown guy.' He was a big deal."

JD shook his head and looked to Soo-hyun for support, but they just smiled. Their face said: "You brought him; he's your problem."

The doors opened and Soo-hyun pushed ahead, carrying JD and Khoder forward on their wake. They stood in the entrance to a dimly lit restaurant called Orbital. The candles that topped each table provided the only luminescence, islands of fire in a sea of darkness. Human waitstaff, dressed all in black with faces shrouded, moved between the tables—shades of black shifting on black, black tablecloths, black carpet, sheer black curtains pulled back from tall convex windows.

The city stretched beyond the wall of glass. Skyscrapers dominated the landscape, glowing with a million rectangular eyes, and Songdo Stadium loomed large in the panoramic view. As JD watched it shifted slightly to the left, as though its rounded roof were the shell of some massive tortoise, walking steadily across the city, demolishing everything in its path. JD felt light-headed, like he was about to pitch over sideways, then the sensation drained from his mind as he understood: the restaurant was revolving.

Soo-hyun approached the restaurant's host standing at a glass lectern, underlit by a tablet glowing with reservation details. She was the only visible staff with her face uncovered, and her features were odd—too symmetrical, surgically perfected—but undeniably attractive. She wore a long shapeless top, fabric transparent but decorated in Mandelbrot patterns, with a bra underneath like a wide black censor bar. JD preemptively elbowed Khoder to stop him saying anything inappropriate.

"We need a table," Soo-hyun said.

The host's face stayed blank. "I'm sorry, but we're completely booked."

Over the woman's shoulder the restaurant was mostly empty. JD opened his mouth in protest, but thought better of it. He leaned close to Soo-hyun. "Let's go somewhere else."

"It's gotta be here."

JD sighed and took the envelope of money from his back pocket. He slid out a fifty-euro note and placed it firmly on the host's tablet. "If you look again, I think you'll find we have a reservation."

"Under the name 'Fuck You,'" Soo-hyun said.

"Soo-hyun," JD whispered, harshly. He turned back to the host: "Please, it's my birthday." He gave her his warmest smile.

The woman produced a small blacklight torch and shone it over the currency, as though she could tell forgeries with her naked eye. Indignant anger swelled in JD's chest, but he quickly quashed it—for all he knew the notes *were* forged. He took a small step back, ready to rush the elevator if the host reached for her phone to call the police.

"While you've got that light out, maybe check me for crabs, huh?" Khoder said, to no response.

The woman looked to JD and the edges of her mouth pulled back in the approximation of a smile. "Right this way." She picked up three menus and walked them into the restaurant proper.

"By the window," Soo-hyun said to the woman's back.

The host showed them to a table, far from the other diners. "Your waiter will be here shortly." She placed the menus on the table and promptly left.

JD put his rain-damp jacket on the back of his chair and sat. He looked down out the window, and his body swayed with vertigo. He peeled his eyes away, and looked deliberately at Soo-hyun. "What is with you today?"

"I had a really good talk with Kali last night. I'm feeling more myself than I have in a long time."

JD chewed the inside of his lip, but didn't speak. A waiter appeared at his shoulder, face shrouded like all the rest, some features dimly visible in the light from the tablet resting on his palm.

"Some drinks to start with?" he asked.

"What's with the veil, bro? You fucking ugly under there?"

"Khoder," JD said firmly.

"What, bro? It's cool; my grandfather was Dalit."

Soo-hyun handed the waiter all three menus: "Can we get three servings of the fried chicken, and three of the salt and pepper calamari. Oh, and three whiskeys, neat."

"I'm sorry, but the younger gentleman doesn't appear old enough to drink."

"No," Soo-hyun said, "the whiskeys are all for me."

"I'll have a stout," JD said. "And a coke for the kid."

"Yeah, a long fucking line of it, bro," Khoder said with a grin. When the waiter was done keying the order he left the table without another word.

"Was that true?" JD asked Khoder. "Your grandfather was part of the untouchable caste?"

Khoder shrugged, attention now focused on something beyond the glass. "I don't fucking know, bro. Just making conversation."

Khoder stuck his forehead against the window, and JD looked around the restaurant casually, careful not to let his gaze catch anyone's eye. Most of the other diners were corporate elite: well dressed, with a rigid posture, as though each table represented a job interview, business meeting, or hostile takeover.

"Alright, Soo-hyun; what are we doing here?" JD asked.

"I told you: this is a planning dinner." They sat up in their chair, eyes cast down to the city beyond the window, flickering steadily to combat the motion of the restaurant. "There," they said. "What do you see?"

JD followed their eyeline. Without the augmented layer provided by his phone, he saw the city as it was. From their vantage Songdo looked less like a precisely structured and engineered city, and more like a living thing. Mounds of garbage collected in alleyways, spreading like mold, and everywhere the city's poor had twisted infrastructure to forge themselves a place where the corps didn't want them: mini-favelas emerging in parks and the gaps between buildings. They must have seemed like cancer to the corporations, but JD saw only evolution, mutation; antibodies fighting back against the corporate infection, the illness of greed.

"Buildings?" JD said. "Garbage? What am I meant to be looking at?"

"The rampartment complex, right there. That's the target."

With that new context, JD saw the structure emerge from the swamp of streets. Compared to the skyscrapers that towered over Songdo, it was a squat walled compound, four eight-story buildings joined together by enclosed skybridges.

"Alright," JD said. "How do we get in?"

"Maintenance. Oldest trick in the book."

"Oldest and most obvious," JD muttered to himself, but he watched carefully as the restaurant kept spinning. His view shifted incrementally until he could see the maintenance access alleyway squished between the southeastern building and the high cement wall of the outer perimeter. A white van sat parked beside four dumpsters overflowing with garbage.

The waiter arrived with their food and drinks on a large tray. He placed the food in the middle of the table, and set the drinks down carefully, placing Soo-hyun's three whiskeys as far from Khoder as he was able.

JD said, "Thanks," to the waiter's receding figure, and took a sip of his stout—hints of coffee and chocolate above the tang of hops.

Khoder drained his glass immediately and started crunching loudly on his ice while Soo-hyun reached into their bag and removed a digital SLR with a compact ultrazoom lens. The camera's black casing was scuffed and scratched, and a crust of brownish gunk had built up over the shutter-release button.

"Haven't seen a stand-alone camera in years," JD said, but Soo-hyun wasn't listening.

JD and Khoder dug into the food while Soo-hyun made some adjustments on the rear of the camera, raised the device to their eye, and started snapping. When they were done they keyed the camera's screen and inspected the images displayed there.

"Got a decent shot of the van's number plate," they said. "Can you get the driver's address?"

"Of fucking course," Khoder said dismissively, bits of shredded chicken launching from his mouth.

Soo-hyun stared dead-eyed at Khoder until he stopped chewing and sat forward in his chair.

He wiped his mouth then pointed at Soo-hyun's camera: "Look at that piece of shit van. If it was a corporate cleaning service the van would be newer; that shit's private. Probably some poor bastard contracted to do the work for less than shit pay. It'll be his van, mortgaged out the ass; he'll be on the registration."

Soo-hyun nodded slightly, seemingly satisfied. "Okay, good." They poured all three whiskeys into one glass and put it on the floor beneath the sheer black curtains, pulled back from the window and bundled up beside the chair. They dropped the curtain into the drink, and looked up at JD. "We need to do it tomorrow night."

JD choked on a piece of calamari. "What?"

"It has to be tomorrow." Soo-hyun knocked on the window with a knuckle and pointed to Songdo Stadium. "You know what tomorrow night is, right?" JD stared. "Biggest sporting event in the world?"

"The Olympics?" JD asked, dubious.

"The fucking World Cup Grand Final."

"That's happening here?"

"Fuck, bro, even I knew that," Khoder said, "and I hardly leave the café."

JD shrugged.

"You uncultured shit," Soo-hyun said, not unkindly.

"It doesn't matter what it is," JD said; "we need more time."

"Whatever security they normally have at the rampartment complex, tomorrow night it'll be halved. Fuck, the city's had to borrow police from Seoul just to cover the game."

"We need more time," JD repeated.

"What have you said about the job? Actually spoken out loud? You had to talk to Captain Fuck-Bro here—was that all in person?"

"I said something in-game," JD admitted.

"And on the street before," Soo-hyun added. "How long do you think it'll take for them to piece it together? Everywhere there's a microphone, they're listening; everywhere there's surveillance, they're watching. We spend a few days casing the joint, and when we finally go for it, we'll walk right into a pair of handcuffs."

"Shit," JD said; they weren't wrong.

"Can you get the cleaner's address by morning?" they asked Khoder.

"Give me my phone and I'll get it fucking now."

"So, you're good with the timeframe?" Soo-hyun asked him.

Khoder picked his nose and wiped it on the tablecloth. "Fuck, bro. Sure."

Soo-hyun turned to JD. "I already gave you building layouts and all the rest—what more do you need?"

"Time," JD said, but even he heard his lack of conviction.

"We go tomorrow night, time it so we leave the compound right when the game ends, get lost in the crowds."

JD stared out the window, looking first at the stadium, then at Lee's enclave. He grabbed his drink and downed the whole thing, stout so thick he wanted to chew.

"Fine," he said.

Khoder grinned lopsided and Soo-hyun just nodded.

"You'll see; it'll all work out."

"Tomorrow," JD said, matter-of-factly.

"Tomorrow. You got your plastic containers?"

"Always," JD said.

"You should box the rest of this food up, no point letting it go to waste."

"My shout, after all," JD said, not even wanting to know how much this "planning dinner" was going to set him back. He took the containers from his bag and poured the rest of the chicken and cala- mari into two separate boxes, then dumped the three small bowls of complimentary kimchi into another.

Soo-hyun took a battered silver Zippo lighter from the ankle of their boot, flicked it open with a metallic *chank,* and slammed it closed.

"Is that Dad's lighter?" JD asked.

"Mom said I could have it."

"It wasn't hers to give."

Soo-hyun flicked it open again and lit it with a quick, smooth movement. They put the flame to the curtain—now soaked with whiskey, capillary action carrying the flammable liquid through the entire length of fabric. With a soft *whoosh* the fire began to climb the curtain.

They flicked the lighter closed and held it out to JD. "Yours if you want it."

JD just shook his head, mouth hanging open as he watched the flames race up the curtain and lick at the ceiling. "No, thanks," he said finally. "You can keep the evidence."

Soo-hyun winked, dropped the lighter back into their boot, and jumped up from their seat. "Fire!" they yelled. "There's a fire!"

JD swore loudly, shoved the plastic containers into his bag, and tossed it over his shoulder. The three of them backed away from the table, faces lit warm by the pillar of fire. All around the restaurant the other diners dropped their cutlery and stood staring as smoke billowed across the ceiling, black to fit the restaurant's aesthetic.

A creak reverberated through the floor as the restaurant ground to a halt, followed by a sputtering noise as the building's sprinkler system came to life. JD held his jacket over his head, but Khoder simply cackled, not even trying to shield himself.

Soo-hyun nodded toward the stairwell, clogged with staff and customers trying to escape, business forgotten beneath the torrential downpour, fearful yells and cries puncturing the steady hiss of artificial rain. The three conspirators rushed toward it, but the host stood waiting for them, holding her shorted-out tablet over her head, makeup streaking down her face with the wet.

"I saw what you did," she yelled over the noise, grabbing Soo-hyun's arm.

They tried to tear free, but the host had them tight. Soo-hyun smiled—the Devil's smile, JD called it, all teeth and mischief—then slammed the heel of their palm into the woman's nose.

The host screamed a lilting strangled sound as both hands went to her face.

"Say hi to your surgeon for me," Soo-hyun said, then shoved the woman aside and ran for the stairs.

"Bro, I think I'm in love."

JD took Khoder's arm and pulled the kid toward the exit. "You'll get over it."

CHAPTER SEVEN

JD's knee throbbed with every step down toward the ground floor. The acrid smell of smoke stuck in his nose, while all around him the stairwell echoed with the dull thud of footsteps, intercut with peals of excitable chatter. Now that they were clear of the fire and the sprinklers, half the diners were babbling, happy they'd finally have something interesting to talk about at work. Some would be retelling this nothing story for years, elaborating it piecemeal until it was an epic conflagration they conquered with bottles of complimentary tap water.

He hit the street just behind Khoder, joining a loose crowd of fifty-odd people—diners, staff, and rubberneckers loitering on the sidewalk. They held umbrellas, jackets, or pilfered menus over their heads to shield themselves from the steady rain.

Khoder put a cigarette between his lips and started patting his pockets, searching for a light. Soo-hyun appeared behind him, and with a flash of silver they lit Khoder's smoke. They secreted the Zippo away before producing the Faraday bag weighed down with deconstructed phones. JD grabbed the two pieces of his and slotted them into different pockets of his windbreaker—better to get away from the crime scene before transmitting GPS data.

The restaurant manager emerged from the stairwell, trailed by kitchen workers in food-stained uniforms and waitstaff sans veils.

Between heaving breaths she called out: "We need everyone to re-main calm! Please stay put until the police arrive."

"Fuck that," Soo-hyun said. They grabbed JD by the arm and pulled him away from the emergency exit and deeper into the grow-ing crowd. Khoder followed. "Send me the kid's contact details once you're back online. Khoder," Soo-hyun said, taking the teen's atten-tion away from his reconstructed phone, glowing dimly as it pow-ered up. "I'll send you those photos; get me the van driver's name and address as soon as possible."

"Sure thing," Khoder said without taking his eyes off the screen.

Sirens sounded in the distance, dopplering off the flat skyscraper faces. To the west, the streets were painted in flashing reds and blues, the emergency service lights intensely bright against the stag-nant facade of the unAugmented city.

JD lifted his foot off the ground, bent his knee, then straightened it, wincing at the pain. "Next time, tell me when you're going to pull that shit so I can take the elevator first."

If Soo-hyun heard him, they didn't respond. They just clapped him on the shoulder and yelled over the wail of approaching fire and police: "Wear Korean team colors tomorrow. Red and blue, okay?" They slipped into the gathering crowd and disappeared into the press of bodies.

"Tomorrow then, Khoder," JD said.

The kid was still intently focused on his phone, but he nodded, his cigarette cherry bobbing like a firefly.

JD inhaled sharply and braced himself, then pushed into the crowd, ignoring the pleas from the restaurant manager and the pain spiking his knee. Once he'd gotten free of the throng, JD walked east under the ceaseless rain, wincing with every second step.

He cursed his own judgment, along with his aching knee: Soo-hyun hadn't changed. They never would. Setting fire to a restaurant that they were stuck inside, fifteen stories up. It was reckless. They were meant to be better than that.

Three blocks later, with the disco of police and fire department lights far behind him, JD stopped. He sat on a park bench—barely recognizable as such, its angular geometric shape meant for sitting but *never* sleeping. He put his phone back together while he stretched his leg.

After a few seconds he laughed despite himself. Soo-hyun had set a curtain on fire to skip out on a bill. Who does that?

He shook his head, anger at Soo-hyun washed away in the rain. He never could hold a grudge, especially not with family. He shook his head again, and felt the adrenaline ebb out of his veins with a shudder.

He blinked his phone on, and after a few seconds of initialization it came to life with a happy *chirrup*. JD noticed the letters "NKBK" painted messily on the wall in front of him—the inexplicable NORTH KOREA BEST KOREA, like on the outskirts of Liber—then his Augmented feed kicked in, obscuring the graffiti behind a shimmering billboard for no-streak mascara.

Even reconnected to the city feeds, the street seemed eerily quiet. There was minimum biomass moving along the sidewalk, just the occasional cute couple or triple on date night, huddled under shared umbrellas, and homeless people with nowhere else to go. JD smiled at a pair of young guys only to watch their love-struck looks fall away when they saw him sitting there, soaking wet with his leg stretched out across half the path. They steered wide of him, conversation dead on their lips until they were sure he was out of earshot.

JD put the city from his mind and opened VOIDWAR. He looked up at the patch of sky between towers as he waited for the game to log in, but saw nothing of the explosive action from earlier in the night. He scanned the game's news feed and saw Khoder was right: the massive battle had unfolded in Stokoe, involving three large factions with another half-dozen smaller ones joining in to take advantage of the situation.

Early reports suggested close to two million euro worth of ships, stations, and weapons had been lost, but Zero Corp would never release the actual figures; that data was restricted to board members and shareholders. Regardless, the Stokoe system was going to be lousy with scavengers for at least a day.

JD closed the game and sent Khoder's contact information to Soo-hyun. He included a note:

>> My knee is killing me. You're lucky we're family.

The reply came back instantaneously:

>> Admit it, it's the most excitement you've had in months.

JD sighed. Soo-hyun was mostly right.

He checked his phone's map and the street signs hanging detached above the nearest corner, temporarily lost after the brisk death march to the restaurant and his rushed escape at a random trajectory.

When he finally recognized where he was, JD realized that maybe his trajectory hadn't been random. Before the knee injury, the medical treatments, and all the rest, he'd lived three streets away, with Troy. He felt a uniquely modern disappointment in himself—knowing he should have been able to recognize the neighborhood without help. His internal maps and his sense of direction were two more sacrifices he'd made to the machines without a second thought, just like his ability to calculate basic math or remember friends' birthdays.

JD stood, breathing quick against the pain in his leg. He tossed his rucksack over his shoulder, and limped toward his old apartment.

* * *

Troy opened the door to see JD, dripping water on his welcome mat. He frowned.

"Good to see you, too," JD said.

"I have class in the morning, Jules; I was just about to go to bed."

JD bit his tongue—they weren't at a place where he could casually joke about them sleeping together.

"I was in the neighborhood—" JD stopped when he saw Troy's frown deepen. "I really was."

Troy wore a faded green cardigan, which he held tight around his throat with one hand, skin pink-white most of the way up his forearm before giving way to his natural dark pigment. The vitiligo spotted the sides of his head as well, so Troy wore his hair in a neatly cropped Mohawk, self-conscious about the locks of pure white that would grow there if he let them.

Troy stepped back from the doorway. "Come inside then," he said with a sigh.

JD left his shoes on the landing and crossed the threshold into the apartment. Troy held an arm out grudgingly. They hugged, and JD rested his hands on Troy's waist, but they felt orphaned there, so he let them fall to his side and pecked Troy on the cheek as he stepped past.

"What is that smell?" Troy asked with a crinkled nose.

"Smoke," JD said. "I saw Soo-hyun, it's a long story."

Troy groaned. "I do not want to hear it." He closed the door and locked it, then strolled down the short hallway that led to the bedroom, announcing over his shoulder: "I'll get you something dry to wear."

The apartment was small and neat, everything placed at right angles, as though Troy had decorated with a ruler and set square. The living room was floored in ugly, brownish, short-pile carpet that was mostly obscured beneath a large Oriental rug that Troy had inherited from his grandparents.

JD sat on one of the two light gray couches, their fabric shadowed with various stains and indented with the invisible weight of past bodies. There was no TV opposite, just a wall adorned with framed posters for sixties French cinema—*Week-end*, *La Chinoise*, *Le Samouraï*, and *Le Feu Follet*. All of them except *Week-end* had been gifts from JD, printed cheap on university printers and framed by an old Korean couple at a tiny shop in outer Seoul; they'd cost a full month's rent. JD was glad they had survived the breakup.

"How have you been?" JD called out.

"Busy. They've got me tutoring classical literature, early Christian and Jewish studies, as well as my philosophy classes."

Now that he was standing inside, JD's phone connected with the apartment's smart systems—the ambient temperature was displayed in large digits hanging in the center of the living room, and a list of controls for light switches, the oven, microwave, and kettle slid down the left side of his vision. He'd never relinquished his control keys after he left.

"What do *you* know about literature or religious studies?" JD said, dropping his voice when Troy returned with a threadbare bath towel and one of his many University of Cambridge sweatshirts.

"The administration doesn't care. As far as they are concerned, it's all just old people and old books. 'Give it to Professor Morrison, he loves that stuff.'" Troy still spoke with the hint of an English accent, clinging to his tongue years after he'd left the Brisles—just before the old government collapsed in a domino effect from the crumbling American empire.

"At least it's work," JD said, scrubbing his head and face with the towel.

Troy sighed and sat on the couch. "You're right; I should be happy."

"I didn't say that—you can feel however you want."

JD folded the towel over the arm of the couch and turned away from Troy to strip out of his wet shirt, as though they hadn't seen each other naked countless times before. He pulled the sweatshirt over his head slowly, breathing in deep to savor the smell of the fabric. JD would never spend the money for the brand of detergent that Troy used, no matter how much he liked the scent. Besides, it would only remind him of Troy. He hung his windbreaker and shirt on the hat rack by the door and sat back down.

"How's your work?" Troy asked. "Still doing repo?"

The question hung heavy in the air between them, loaded like a cargo ship, like a gun.

"Yeah," JD admitted, watching Troy's face for a reaction, but

seeing nothing telegraphed there. "Mostly I'm doing machine maintenance at a warehouse on the shorefront. The pay sucks, but at least
the hours are long." JD smirked.

"Living with your mom?"

"No, that was strictly short-term. Living in a dorm, but I still see
her every week."

"How is she?" Troy asked.

"I think she misses you—" JD said, stopping himself from saying
the rest: *as much as I do*. After a silent beat, JD nodded toward the
framed posters: "This place hasn't changed."

Troy carefully inspected the room, as though he didn't see it every
single day. "I suppose you're right. I'm going to make tea—do you
want anything?"

"Hot chocolate, please, if you still have any."

Troy disappeared down the corridor. Alone in the living room
surrounded by all the icons of memory, JD felt out of place. He got
up from the couch and paced the length of the room, then walked to
the kitchen.

Troy was filling the kettle, and the shuddering noise of the sub-
standard plumbing concealed the sound of JD's shoes on the linoleum floor, patterned like tiles. JD went to the cupboard and found
the cocoa powder, sugar, and chamomile tea where they'd always
been, everything unchanged apart from the thin layer of dust that
had accrued on the box of cocoa in his absence.

JD reached past Troy and placed them down on the counter beside the kettle. Troy turned and started, then pulled away.

"Could you just— Could you wait in the living room?"

JD was jarred out of the false reality he had slipped into without
effort—the old reality where he and Troy shared a kitchen, shared
a bed, shared so much of themselves. The sad slant to Troy's eye
brought him sharply to the awkward present.

"I'm sorry, I can go," JD said.

"I don't want you to go, I just need a minute," Troy said, with his
eyes stuck fast to the ground.

JD went back to the living room and sat on the edge of the couch, hands pressed to his knees, ready to push himself up and leave at any moment. He took out his phone and brought up his residential settings. He scrolled down to the entry marked "Our Apartment," and uncoupled from the system with a cold stone of sadness resting in the middle of his chest. The apartment controls faded from his vision. Now he was just another guest.

A few minutes later, Troy returned with two steaming mugs. He placed JD's down on the coffee table and sat at the furthest end of the other couch—as far from JD as he could get without phase-shifting through the wall and into his neighbor's apartment.

JD blew on his hot chocolate and took a sip. It burnt the tip of his tongue, the buds there instantly rough and rigid.

"I'm sorry," JD said again. "I don't know what I expected when I decided to come over."

Troy shook his head. "It took a long time to adjust to being alone here; maybe I'm still not used to it."

"I wouldn't have come if I'd realized . . ." JD stopped himself, uncertain of how to finish the thought. "I still want us to be friends."

"So do I . . . in theory."

"Maybe next time we'll meet on neutral territory," JD said lightly. He smiled, but Troy's face stayed stony.

"What were you doing with Soo-hyun?"

"It's a job. If we pull it off I'll—"

"That's not what I meant. How can you trust them after last time?" He nodded toward JD's synovitic knee, as though he could see the slivers of shrapnel still embedded there, migrating further with each passing month. "Sometimes I think I'm angrier at them than you are."

"They're family."

"And? You *know* how much of my family I had to cut out of my life, and they never put me in hospital."

"Soo-hyun doesn't have anyone else."

"That's not your fault."

JD didn't respond. He sipped his cocoa, eyes stuck fast to the mug in his hands.

"Jules, I just want you to be happy," Troy said. "I don't understand your repo work, but you enjoy it, and *somehow* it pays the bills, so that's fine. But this 'job'? Whatever it is; get out before you get hurt, again. Hurt or worse." Troy scrunched up his nose and blinked, stifling tears.

The back of JD's throat ached with the buildup of sympathetic tears. He put his mug back on the coffee table. "With how much the job pays, I'll be able to get the surgery I need. I'll be able to move Mom to a better building."

"They would still give you that job at the university, if you asked."

JD shook his head. "The university" was always Troy's answer, even when his own job security was tenuous at best. "That's your world, it's not mine."

"But it could be."

"The only reason I took that job in the first place was to be close to you." JD stood, plundering every reserve of self-control he had to stop himself wincing, to hide the pain. "I should go."

"Jules."

"I'm sorry; I should have at least called first."

"Jules, sit down, finish your drink." Troy leaned forward, cup pressed between both hands, his face held over the still-steaming tea. He sighed.

"I want to be angry at Soo-hyun, but I can't." JD sat and took a swig of his cocoa, and felt the sweet sediment drift over his tongue. He swallowed. "They have my dad's lighter."

Troy rolled his eyes. "Hence the smoke."

JD chewed the inside of his mouth and nodded. "I can't remember his face, you know. I mean, I've seen photos, and I remember the photos, but I don't have any clear memory of his face. I just remember him smoking, constantly, and how cool I thought it was, how much I liked the smell of tobacco on his hands. I don't remember him with Mum at all—I guess I was too young when he left her. But

I remember him and me and Soo-hyun, and sometimes Soo-hyun's mom, and the two of us kids fighting over who got to sit in the front of the car with Dad.

"I hated Soo-hyun back then, blamed them for everything, like it was them who tore my family apart, not Dad. But I can't hate them now. They've been trying so hard to change."

"Not hard enough. Look, you don't need to hate them, just hold them accountable."

JD drained his mug, put it back on the coffee table, and pushed it away from the edge, pointing its handle inward. "You're right, I just don't know if I can." He stood again. "Thanks for the drink."

"You don't have to go, JD; stay here on the couch."

"Slept on Mum's couch last night—I need to get back to my own bed."

Troy nodded. "We should do this again; catch up, talk."

"I'd like that." JD walked to the door, and started to pull the sweatshirt up over his head but Troy stopped him.

"Give it back to me next time; you'll catch your death otherwise."

JD nodded, and retrieved his clothes from the hat rack, stuffing his wet shirt into his bag, and putting the windbreaker on over the sweatshirt.

"When are you doing this job?" Troy asked.

"Tomorrow."

"Do you need me to drive you?"

JD shook his head. "I can't have you getting involved."

"Should I be worried?" Troy asked. "About the job."

JD sighed. "It's basically just a repossession."

"But an illegal one," Troy said pointedly.

JD shrugged. "Legal jobs can be dangerous too. Just because you've got the paperwork doesn't mean someone's going to let you walk up and take their car."

The corner of Troy's mouth twitched down, but he didn't speak.

"The mark is either dead or dying; we're just taking something before his children show up to fight over the will."

Troy grunted quietly. "Still," is all he said.

"If it works out, it could be my last illegal job for a while," JD said, "maybe ever. Enough of a cushion that I could go legit. I know that's what you wanted."

"It's what I wanted you to want, Jules. There's a difference."

JD opened the door.

"Stay safe," Troy said.

JD nodded, and pulled the door shut.

* * *

Massive battles played out in the sky overhead, but JD ignored them. He walked slow across town, rain soaking into his hair, the ache in his knee submerged beneath other pains, shared heartbreak.

When he got home, his roommates were all yammering in a mix of Korean, Hindi, and English—tactical chatter and twitchy banter. They didn't notice him arrive, their eyes masked, ears plugged with noise-canceling headphones, and hands clutched tight to VR controls.

He left the pilfered kimchi in the communal refrigerator as a sacrifice to the god of sharehousing, but stashed the leftover chicken and calamari in the small fridge beneath his bed—resting beside his main rig, accompanied by dust bunnies and assorted detritus. His rig still hummed steadily, creating the new system for VOID-WAR's servers, but JD didn't bother logging in to check its progress. Instead he crashed out, with Troy's sweatshirt bundled up on the pillow beside his head.

CHAPTER EIGHT

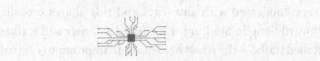

T he afternoon sun peeked between gaps in the heavy cloud cover, drawing sweat from JD's skin. He gave himself three hours to make the two-hour journey to the cleaner's apartment—wary of the surveillance apparatus floating over the city, disguised by AR vision but ever-present. He mixed up his gait, using his natural limp to a corner, then crossing the street walking as "normally" as possible until he reached the corner of the next block, hoping the city's algorithms would lose him each time in the crowd of pedestrians. He couldn't risk following a map, having his every step tagged by GPS, so he silently repeated a mantra of street names and directions to guide him.

When he was just a few blocks from the apartment, JD ducked into a convenience store for a bottle of water, and stood on the sidewalk drinking it. Absently he watched advertisements crawl across the building opposite—the color and motion catching his eyes even if their contents didn't make an impression on his conscious mind.

JD reached a hand into his rucksack and mentally inventoried the gear he needed for the job, careful not to reveal anything to the network of cameras that nested on lamp poles, streetlights, gutters, and awnings. He checked everything by touch:

Rough canvas fabric of his coveralls;

Rigid brim of his baseball cap;

Scratchy poly-blend wool scarf in South Korean soccer red;

Smooth vinyl pouch of his lockpick set;

Bundle of plastic zip ties;

Rubbery feel of latex gloves;

Hard, flat casing of two datacubes—the one from inside the police dog's skull, the other holding all the details of the job.

Satisfied, JD carried on. It was still early, but already the roads were congested with auto-cars and ride-shares crossing the city toward Songdo Stadium. He turned a corner and walked through stalled traffic—the street becoming an impromptu car park watched over by two glowing red eyes. The footpaths on both sides of the road surged with crowds dressed in red and blue, broken up by pockets of Brazilian bright green. At street corners, ubiquitous advertising gave way to stadium directions and mealy-mouthed suggestions for good behavior, as though some focus-tested slogans would stop people from rioting if the mood took them, or if the game didn't pan out the way they wanted.

Traffic passed in fits and starts, cars and vans decorated with the red, blue, and white of the South Korean soccer team—scarves and streamers hanging from windows, stickers adorning bumpers, glass paint on rear windows.

The light turned and he kept walking. He rounded a corner and spotted Soo-hyun and Khoder waiting up ahead on the other side of the road, wearing matching coveralls and baseball caps. Khoder was still trying to affect cool with a cigarette pinched between two fingers; Soo-hyun wore knockoff Ray-Ban aviators, reflections of the street where their eyes should be. JD guessed Soo-hyun was trying to look inconspicuous, but with their arms crossed over their chest and their lips twisted in a snarl they looked like a low-level gangster, resting up between extortion visits.

As JD waited to cross the street, a cloud front moved to block the sun. He shivered. He didn't need to see the clouds to know that more rain was coming; he just had to listen to the whisper of his knee as it swelled and ached with the shifting air pressure. He am-bled quickly between cars, stepping up onto the sidewalk to join Soo-hyun and Khoder.

"You ready?" he asked Soo-hyun, two of him caught in the lenses, staring back at the real one.

"Born ready," they said, deadpan.

Khoder passed JD a small bundle of black wire—AR projectors attached to clips for his cap. "Mike Tyson, bro. Heavyweight champion."

"You calling me fat?" JD said. He took the hat from his bag and clipped the device to the brim. He put it on and looked to Khoder— the kid held up his phone, camera lens shifting with a minute whir as it focused on his face.

Khoder nodded. "Bro," he said, the single word telling JD that the hacked-together piece of counter-surveillance tech was working properly.

"Who's Soo-hyun?" JD asked.

"Needed to be someone cool," Khoder said, "so I went with Chow Yun-fat, in his prime."

"Now who are you calling fat?" Soo-hyun said with a smirk.

JD took the tight bundle of latex gloves from his bag, gave a pair each to Soo-hyun and Khoder, then pulled his own pair on. "Alright, let's go."

JD pushed forward, taking the lead, as though this one piece of initiative would give him control over the rest of the job, and stop Soo-hyun's urges from sending them violently off course. They walked around the block to the target building and climbed three cement steps to the entrance—a glass-and-metal door attached to an old-style intercom and buzzer system.

"Gonna pick the lock, bro?"

"Nope," JD said, "just a little social engineering."

He approached the intercom and hit a button at random—only checking that he wasn't accidentally buzzing their target. *Excuse me, sir, sorry to bother you. Mind letting us upstairs so we can steal your van and infiltrate your place of work?* He tried four apartments before someone answered.

"What?" A man's voice, noise in the background like children playing, TV blaring loud. *Perfect.*

"Plumber. Need to get up to 4A, but nobody's responding."

"Sorry, I can't let you in."

Soo-hyun's eyebrows peered up over the rim of their sunglasses, amused.

"I understand, of course," JD said quickly, before the man could hang up. "Maybe you could just run upstairs and knock on his door for me?"

There was a long pause, then a raucous buzz as the door unlocked.

"Thank you, sir," JD said as he yanked the door open, but the impatient father had already signed off.

"Social engineering," Soo-hyun said. "Next time I'll engineer a broken window." They stole ahead, taking the stairs two at a time, clinks and clanks emanating from their backpack with every step.

Trash had accrued on the stairwell and the landings, food rubbish mostly, rustling with cockroaches and other wildlife. Graffiti marked the walls—children's crayon scribbles, inelegant spray-painted tags, and municipal markings from the last time city health came through and condemned an apartment or cleared out a dead body.

On the fourth-floor landing, JD glanced back. Khoder was leaning against the railing, bent forward with a hand pressed to his side.

"Come on," JD said. "Just two more levels."

"Bro? What happened to the fourth floor?"

"I only said that to get us in the building."

Khoder's eyes widened in slow realization. "Brainy shit, bro."

"I have my moments."

When they reached the sixth floor, Soo-hyun was already waiting outside apartment 6E—home of Omar Garang, owner of Angel Angles Cleaning Service, and their ticket into Zero Lee's apartment.

"I haven't walked this many steps in fucking ever, bro."

"Dagchyeo," Soo-hyun spat. "This is it."

"What are we going to say to him?" JD asked.

"I'll let Señor Sting do the talking." They reached into their backpack and retrieved a small taser cased in black and yellow. On one side of the weapon was a cartoon bee with a bolt of lightning where its stinger should be.

"Wait a minute," JD said. "I've got money; we can pay him off."

Soo-hyun ignored him. "Khoder, I need you here," they said. "Take off the hat, muss up your hair, and try and look innocent."

Khoder's best version of innocence was tearful sobbing, so he frowned, scrunched up his eyes, and made his chest jerk and shudder.

"Shit," Soo-hyun said, jutting out their lower lip. "Kid's a natural."

"Soo-hyun," JD whispered. "We don't have to do it like this. What happened to calm?"

"We don't have time for calm." They shoved JD back, knocked on the door, and stood out of sight so that a destitute-looking Khoder was the only one visible through the door's spy hole.

After a few seconds, Soo-hyun knocked again. The three of them listened carefully, trying to pick footsteps out from the ambient noise of the building.

The door opened with a quiet squeak, revealing a thin-framed Sudanese man, wearing a towel tied at his waist, held in place with one hand. "What's wrong, boy?"

Before Khoder could respond, Soo-hyun leaped forward, knocking Omar back and slamming the door open with their shoulder. The taser pulsed and crackled in their hand, spitting an inch of blue electricity which they stuck against the man's throat. He collapsed, hitting the floor a split second after his towel did.

"Cock!" Khoder said, staring at the man's genitals.

"Shut up and get inside." JD shoved Khoder into the apartment, grabbed the naked man under the arms and dragged him back from the open doorway. As soon as his legs were out of the way, Soo-hyun slammed the door shut.

Omar Garang groaned and twitched, kicking out as he tried to stand. Soo-hyun triggered the taser again.

"Don't!" JD yelled.

"What?"

"I'm still holding him."

Soo-hyun smirked. "You'd hardly feel it."

"Find a chair," JD said. "One with armrests."

Soo-hyun disappeared deeper into the apartment, and JD lowered the man to the floor.

"Kid," JD said, switching to the first codename that came to mind. "Find his keys, wallet, phone. And search the place—just because no one else is on the lease doesn't mean he lives alone."

"Here!" Soo-hyun returned to the main living area, pushing a tattered office chair on black plastic casters.

"What's happening?" Omar's eyes searched, unfocused. He threw a punch, but it only glanced off JD's shoulder.

"Sorry," JD said.

Soo-hyun held the chair steady, and JD lifted Omar off the ground. The man's arms and genitals flopped heavily from side to side as JD hefted him onto the seat. Omar struggled half-heartedly, still dulled by the pain. JD reached into his rucksack for zip ties and fastened Omar's wrists to the curved plastic armrests of the chair. Next, he crossed Omar's feet one over the other and zip-tied his ankles together.

He stepped back to examine his handiwork, then put the towel across Omar's lap and tucked it under his ass and thighs, if only to stop Khoder from staring.

"Who are you?" Omar asked.

"It's nothing personal," Soo-hyun said; "we just need to borrow your van." They sat on the arm of a leather couch. The corners were covered in cat scratches, white scars in the black.

JD crossed over to the window and sat on the sill, his muscles exhausted from climbing the steps and then hauling Omar's weight around. He glanced out at the street: it had started to rain again, and a procession of umbrellas—mostly black, but plenty in blue and red—paraded down the footpath.

"JD! Are you ignoring me?" Soo-hyun said.

"What?"

"I said, what next?"

JD inhaled deep and then sighed. "I don't know, *Shades*—I don't normally work with hostages. But you could start by not using my name."

"I didn't hear anything," Omar offered.

Khoder returned clutching Omar's wallet, a phone so old JD was surprised it still worked, and a mound of keys and swipe cards hanging from a collection of bright plastic key chains. "Found his shit, bro. No one here, but there's a second bedroom in the back."

"What time's your housemate due home?" JD asked.

Omar visibly swallowed, sweat glistening across his brow. "Any minute now. In fact, she's already late."

JD shook his head. "No, I don't think so."

Omar's head dropped. "She plans to spend the whole night driving. She won't be home until morning."

"Alright, we can work with that." JD held a hand out to Khoder: "Keys?"

Khoder dumped the mass of metal into JD's hands. He found the keys to Omar's van easily—identified by the plastic remote—and separated then pocketed them.

JD held the rest up to Omar. "Rampartment complex on Haedoji-ro—what do we need to get in?"

"I don't understand."

Soo-hyun moved too fast for JD to stop: they launched from the arm of the couch and backhanded Omar with a loud *crack*. "I'll make you understand, fucker."

"Shades!" JD yelled.

Soo-hyun took no notice of him. They bent down so their face was level with Omar's. "Or would you rather talk to Señor Sting again?"

JD put a hand on Soo-hyun's shoulder and pushed them back so he could stand between them and Omar. He waited for Soo-hyun to look away from the hostage and meet his eyes.

"We don't need to hurt him."

Soo-hyun took off their shades, their eyes cold black pits that seemed to stare through JD. "We don't have time to fuck around. Get out of my way and I'll make him talk."

"Let me try," JD said, holding their gaze. "Just give me one minute."

Soo-hyun raised both hands and stepped back. "Have five. I'm gonna piss." They stalked away and JD turned to Omar, the man's eyes wide with fear, cheek showing slightly pink beneath the dark tone.

"Talk to me, or talk to them," JD said, pointing a thumb over his shoulder. "Either way we can't leave here until we know how to get inside that enclave."

"The—the gray access cards," he stammered. "It's all electronic."

"Good," JD said. "Were you meant to be working tonight?"

"I wanted to call in sick and go to the match, but I couldn't afford the tickets."

"Listen to me closely, Omar. If you play your cards right you'll be able to watch the game from the comfort of your own home while we go to work for you. But for this to work you need to tell me *everything*."

* * *

Omar was breathlessly spilling details to JD by the time Soo-hyun got back from the bathroom. JD took down every word in an offline notes app: security guard names, expected movements, Omar's nightly routine down to the smallest detail.

"See, Shades," JD said, "no need for violence."

They rolled their eyes and dropped down onto the arm of the couch.

JD took five hundred euro from his quickly thinning wad of cash and held it up to Omar. "This is for your trouble, alright, Omar?"

Omar nodded.

"You going to sell us out to the police?"

"If you try it," Soo-hyun said, "we know where you live."

Omar shook his head. "I'll tell them you had me blindfolded."

"That would have been smart, bro," Khoder said, reaching into a box of Honey-Os for another handful of cereal.

"I already said, I'm not used to working with hostages. It's lucky I had the zip ties."

"Lucky, or kinky?" Khoder said.

JD snatched the box of cereal away from Khoder and dropped the money inside, before returning it to the cupboard. "Remember, we're not the bad guys here—we just need access, and you're our key."

Omar nodded, but the slick of fear sweat across his upper lip said that maybe he wasn't convinced.

"Your housemate will be home in a few hours; you're going to be fine until then. Kid, put the match on."

Khoder took three remotes from the coffee table and pressed a series of buttons across each. Soon the World Cup pregame show filled one wall of Omar's living room, Korean commentators dressed in clean white suits, animatedly reciting useless statistics and awful patter. "Language, bro?" the kid asked Omar.

"The Korean channel is good. I'm still practicing," Omar said, and he smiled, a bright slash of white teeth.

"Alright," JD said to Soo-hyun and Khoder; "get your shit, and let's get out of here."

"Wait," Omar pleaded. "You need to hit me, please."

JD closed his eyes. "What?"

"If there's a break-in and I'm unscathed, they'll fire me. But if I am beaten and bruised, maybe I won't lose this contract."

JD shook his head. "Alright. Shades?"

Soo-hyun grinned and JD watched his twin reflections shudder in their artificial eyes.

* * *

JD and Khoder reached the basement car park, lit dull with energy-saving bulbs. JD held out Omar's van key and pressed the button—the orange flash of indicator lights shone from a distant corner.

Khoder was grinning, and JD found the kid's excitement contagious. *Just another job,* he told himself, but he didn't believe the lie. Things were already out of hand, and they hadn't even reached the target. His heart thudded a rolling kick drum thump as he limped across the car park to the unlocked van.

He swung open the rear doors and found four squat cylindrical cleaning bots, and a cart loaded with mops and cleaning solvents—he scrunched his nose against the harsh smells.

"You're gonna have to get in the back," JD told Khoder.

"Got something for you, bro," Khoder said. He reached into his backpack and produced a small round object, like a hockey puck with a button embedded in its center. He slapped it into JD's hand. "Electronic key cloner."

"How's it work?"

"Just get close, and push the button."

"How close?"

Khoder shrugged. "One meter? Two?" He climbed into the back of the van and started pulling more equipment from his bag. Collapsible rig, tablet, two phones, and a portable battery the size of a shoebox.

"Jesus, Khoder," JD said, impressed.

Khoder plugged a cable into one of the cleaning bots, tapped a command on his rig, waited ten seconds, then repeated the process for the next robot.

"What are you doing?"

"Scanning their memories, bro. Floor plans, all that shit."

JD nodded and left him to it. He took the coveralls out of his bag and pulled them on over his clothes. At the far end of the car park the basement door crashed open, and Soo-hyun's footsteps echoed in the hollow space as they approached.

"I hope you didn't hurt him too bad," JD said.

"He'll live. Let's go."

JD closed the rear doors, and he and Soo-hyun sat in the front of the van. Omar had a kitschy old air freshener hanging from his rear-view mirror, shaped like a pine tree.

"Are we good?" JD asked.

"I told you, he'll be fine."

"That's not what I mean. Tell me you're not going to do anything dangerous, or I walk."

Soo-hyun stared at him for a moment, their expression unreadable behind the glasses. "This whole thing is dangerous. If you want out, tell me now before it's too late."

"That's not what I meant, and you know it. I need to know you won't lose it."

Soo-hyun exhaled loudly. "I'm fine. I'm better than fine. Now, can we go?"

JD sighed and started the engine.

He drove them out of the basement and onto the street, squinting in the blinding-low sunlight. He fumbled with the car's controls and struggled to remember the last time he'd driven regularly. Before the stint in the university tech department? He repossessed a couple of small trucks and a few cars each year, but every time it was like learning to drive all over again; he *knew* what he needed to do, but lacked the muscle memory to do it smoothly.

They pulled up at a set of traffic lights, and Khoder shoved one of his phones through the gap between the seats.

"I built a 3D model of the building," he said.

"Already?" JD asked.

"Security desks, elevators, apartment doors, everything."

"Nothing inside the apartments," JD said.

"Our Omar bro doesn't clean the apartments, just the complex. That's what the key cloner is for."

The light turned green and JD pushed Khoder's arm out of the way and hit the accelerator too hard, almost ramming the car in front—traffic still crawling with the density of World Cup crowds.

They drove, JD and Soo-hyun not talking, steady noise of traffic all around them and the lilting chatter of Khoder quietly talking to himself in the back of the van.

Nearing the compound, Soo-hyun reached an arm across JD's line of sight to point. "There," they said.

Red and eight other adolescents milled on a street corner, clutching conspicuously large duffel bags. With the game about to begin, they were the only people on the sidewalk, obviously reveling in the fact, passing around cans of cheap beer and tagging every flat surface with a dozen variations of NKBK.

JD stopped the van beside the clutch of miscreants. "What's this diversion you're planning?"

"You'll know it when you see it," Soo-hyun said.

"I don't want anyone else getting hurt."

Soo-hyun took their sunglasses off and slotted them into the V of their coverall. They pushed open the door, and tossed their taser onto his lap. "Don't worry your pretty little head, hyung."

"I do worry," JD said as Soo-hyun slammed the door closed behind them. He held the taser with two fingers, trying to decide what to do with the weapon. He pocketed it, delegating the decision to his future self.

"Just you and me, Khoder," he muttered, pulling back into traffic. If the kid heard him, he didn't reply.

They drove around the block to the enclave entrance. After a half second for the cameras to read the van's plates, the boom gate lifted and JD drove beneath it, picturing the view from the restaurant as he guided the van to the maintenance access. He opened the van's door and paused, smacked in the face by the scent of sickly-sweet rot and rodent feces.

"Can you hear me, Khoder?" JD said into his headset.

"Loud and loud, bro."

JD walked around to the rear doors and opened them both up. "You better hope the van is airtight, because the smell out here is disgusting."

"Be quick with the doors then, asshole," Khoder said, voice doubling in JD's ear. He was dimly lit by the screens that surrounded him, eyemask over his face for complete digital insertion.

"Yeah yeah yeah," JD muttered. It took him the better part of a minute to find the ramps for the bots, which were recessed underneath the van's chassis. He slid the two metal planks out, then maneuvered the four cleaning bots down onto the ground behind the van, followed by the cleaning cart loaded with mop, bucket, and his rucksack.

"Alright, Khoder, I'm going in."

JD keyed the robots' power, and followed them into the nearest rampartment building as they happily *bloop*ed, ready to go to work.

CHAPTER NINE

The cleaning cart squeaked sharply with every push, weighed down with a steel bucket filled with water, and tubs of solvent and floor polish. JD topped up the different bots according to Omar's notes and triggered their cleaning routines. The four machines spun, whirred, and whined, projecting holograms of slipping stick-figure people as they moved up the corridor. When the bots moved on from a section of floor, the building's Augmented feed put warnings along the floor and walls—the images eventually dissipating in response to fluctuations in localized humidity.

White ceramic planters lined the corridors, potted with plants that JD couldn't name. Their leaves were so brightly green and shiny that they looked plastic. JD pressed a wide leaf between his thumb and forefinger, felt the subtle grain of the plant—too fine to be anything but organic.

It was the most high-class residence JD had ever been inside—floors laid with authentic marble tiles, corridor walls decorated with boring art that had obviously been bought in bulk, the kind you see in hotel rooms and the background of advertisements. The corridor was, by definition, a liminal space, but JD imagined the vapid interior decoration extended into the apartments themselves; the residents all wealthy enough to own a number of homes situated around the globe, each as lifeless as the next. It made JD want to spit, so he did. A moment later one of the squat cleaning robots passed over the sputum, erasing his worthless protest.

"Kid, what's your status?"

"Why 'kid' all of a sudden, bro? It's disrespectful."

"It's your codename."

"Bro," Khoder said, dragging out the single syllable, apparently impressed. "Should I use your codename, bro? What's your codename?"

"Just keep calling me 'bro,'" JD said. "What's your status?"

"I'm already in, bro."

"Really?"

"Yup. They've got vulnerability scans running on the network perimeter, but there's always a way in. Usually management or internal bullshit means there's an IP range not getting scanned. I just had to find it."

JD was certain that was the most words he'd ever heard Khoder speak consecutively. "So, we're good?"

"I've disabled the internal alarms. Couldn't stop it from calling out, but I was able to change the number it calls. Any alarms you trigger are going straight to the nearest Reggae Chicken."

JD chuckled.

"Heads up," Khoder said; "security coming your way."

"Alright, thanks," JD said. "Keep an eye out, and tell me what Shades is up to."

"Will do, bro."

According to Omar, the guards made regular rounds to earn their keep, but the first one wasn't due for another fifteen minutes. JD heard the guard before he saw him—the thud and squeal of heavy-soled boots over tiled floor. He took the mop from Omar's cart and began mopping just behind the cleaning robot, looking busy, pretending the bot missed a spot. It hadn't, but sometimes they did, and according to Omar that was the only reason they even had a human cleaner on-site. Clean up after the cleaning robots. Repair the repair robots. Soon, the only jobs left would be robot manager, robot foreman, or robot medic.

In the corner of his eye, JD saw the security guard round the corner and stop. "Hey," the guard called out.

JD's stomach sank. He could feel the weight of the taser pressing against his leg, but he'd have to get close before he could use it. He turned and looked at the guard—a young, thickset Korean with unkempt hair.

"You're not watching the game?" the guard asked.

JD grinned with relief. He tapped his headset. "I am listening to it," he called out, mimicking Omar's overly proper speech patterns. They didn't look anything alike—Omar was fifty pounds lighter and a few shades darker—but if the guard didn't want to see the differences, he wouldn't. "I'll watch the replay later."

The guard smiled and called out, "Daehan Minguk," in the singsong soccer chant for the Republic of Korea.

JD just smiled back, and the guard kept walking.

"Bro? What's happening?"

"Must be getting his rounds out of the way before the match starts. Have you got the game up on-screen?"

"Yeah, bro."

"Let me know when they kick off."

JD continued to tail the cleaning bots, spot-cleaning here and there, but mostly just sweating in his coveralls while the polisher hummed behind him. When they reached the elevators, JD hit the call button and waited.

"You found Shades yet, Kid?"

"No movement on any of the cameras."

"Alright. How you holding up?"

"Bored as fuck, bro. I thought this was gonna be hard, like my cock, not easy like your mother."

JD winced. "You're really not her type."

The elevator doors opened and JD stepped inside. The bots crowded in around him in a vaguely threatening way—their infrared sensors like dark angry eyes, the flat line of a seam in their casing making a distinct frown. JD checked his reflection—the disguise looked convincing, apart from the dark patches of sweat that seeped from beneath his arms.

Omar would take the robots up to level two and continue his cleaning route, but JD hit the button for the fourth floor and the skybridge between buildings.

"I see Shades, bro."

"Where are they?"

"Far side of the street. System keeps trying to spike to yellow alert when the cameras get a glimpse of all those delinquent losers, but I've got it clamped down."

"I thought we wanted the system to flag them," JD said.

"Not until after. Head of security will only come on-site for a big problem. They see it unfolding slow, maybe they think their lackeys can handle it."

The elevator doors dinged open on the fourth floor, and a couple stood waiting to get inside. They stepped back and turned their heads to avoid even looking at JD, let alone acknowledging his existence or humanity. *I hope you never feel safe in this building after tonight,* JD thought bitterly.

The bots followed JD out of the elevator, and the residents disappeared inside the metal cube.

"Kickoff," Khoder said.

"That's the signal." JD switched channel: "Shades."

No response.

The bots began cleaning the corridor, so JD left them to it and walked ahead, passing more bland art, smell like bathroom air freshener—a nauseatingly artificial scent.

He rounded the corner and came to the skybridge, the hallway opening onto a long stretch of glass that thrummed in the breeze. Planters were spaced evenly along the suspended corridor, but otherwise it was clear. Both walls and ceiling were glass, and handprints collected at chest height all along the length of the bridge. Beyond the transparent pane, the city stretched out, seemingly endless, with lights reaching to the horizon and climbing into the sky. A few blocks over, the stadium glowed bright, light seeping out between cracks in its closed roof, like a hand holding a firefly.

"Shades?"

Halfway across the bridge, JD watched an old Toyota sedan spear across the road and crash through the enclave's outer wall in syncopated slow motion. Brick and mortar tumbled inward, and the front of the car crumpled with the impact. The driver's door opened and Red stumbled out, the slash of blood visible to JD even at that distance, pouring from his nose and running over his mouth. He stood beside the car, unsteady on his feet for a second. He punched himself in the side of the head and lifted his arm, motioning for the rest of his crew. Within seconds they were pouring through the gaps between the car and the fence. Most of them were half-naked, T-shirts tied around their faces as impromptu balaclavas.

JD saw Soo-hyun among them. Where the others ran in furtive fits and starts, Soo-hyun strode purposefully ahead, no fear, no doubt. The youths rushed into the private supermarket at the base of building three. Moments later shoppers and staff fled into the night. JD shook his head as he watched the chaos, watched kids run from the supermarket with arms piled high with organic free-range snacks.

Soo-hyun crouched beside their open backpack, stacked tight with glass bottles, and, together with Red, they stuffed torn bits of rag into the bottle necks. The Zippo was in their hand again.

"Oh, shit," JD said.

Sharp crack of shattered bottles, followed by the *whoom* of petrol igniting. The supermarket glowed Halloween orange. Windows broke with the heat, and the flames reached outside, licking at the sky like so many thirsty tongues.

"Shades, what—" JD lowered his voice: "What the hell are you doing?"

"Diversion, hyung, a beautiful fucking diversion. I wish you could see it."

"I *can* see it," he hissed, watching stark silhouettes of adolescent vandals flinging more bottles into the inferno.

"All the logos and brand names going up in smoke. We need to do this more often."

"You could've killed someone."

"We cleared them all out first. Almost convinced the cashier to join us, but he was too scared."

"Get to cover," JD said, exasperated; "I can see the cops."

They were still a few blocks distant—blue and red flash of police lights charging down one street, and the orange and green of private security rushing parallel along another.

Soo-hyun passed the info to Red. He whistled to the others, a piercing tone that cut through the line, and the delinquents dispersed, passing around and over the crashed Toyota as they fled.

JD hobbled down the length of the skybridge and left the robots behind. Mirrored architecture sent him the wrong way, and he doubled back and found the elevator. He leaned against the wall beside the call button and slowed his breath, willing his heart to calm down.

"Kid, what's happening out there?"

"Car just pulled up."

"Cop car? Security? Talk to me."

"Those're all over the place; this is different. Unmarked. BMW."

"Head of security, or a resident?" JD put a hand in his pocket and squeezed the key cloner so the plastic case creaked in his grip.

"One second, bro. Facial recognition takes time," Khoder said. "Alright, got it. Ok-bin Shin, Securitech manager for Songdo-dong district."

JD hit the elevator button and waited. "Where are Shades and the others?"

"Can't see them on camera."

"Good; hopefully they got clear."

The door opened and JD stepped inside the elevator, wishing it could ferry him away from the untamed violence.

Instead he went down.

Three guards stood at the security desk, two in white shirts badged like a cut-rate police force, the third in a tailored black suit with fine pinstripes, and heeled boots. They didn't hear JD approach, trying to stroll casually, but managing only to limp.

JD cleared his throat and the guards all turned, one of the uniformed bulls putting a hand on his holstered taser as he spun.

"What is happening?" JD asked in his affected accent. He stood beside one of the uniformed guards, peering over the man's shoulder. With his hand in his pocket he hit the switch on the key cloner.

"Copying now," Khoder said in his ear. "Lot of keys on those three assholes, so it might take a minute. Like, sixty seconds, bro."

"It's nothing," the head of security, Ok-bin Shin, said. She had a long face, dark eyes, and pale lips set in a permanent frown. Her hair was pulled tightly back from her face and tied up in a bun.

"Just some kids," one of the others said—young, skinny, looking more like a student than a security guard. Students had to pay their tuition somehow. "The police are already here."

Shin shot a glance at her subordinate to quiet him.

"Still," she said, turning back to JD, "perhaps you should leave early—for your own safety, understand."

JD cursed internally; outwardly he only smiled. "I cannot afford to lose this shift. If you do your job and keep this place safe, then I can do my job and keep it clean." He hoped the smile sold it as polite duty, not condescending dissidence.

Shin exhaled sharply through her nose, amused. She didn't speak.

"Still need more time, bro."

JD leaned forward for a better look at the screens across the security console. Guards battled the blaze with fire extinguishers and a garden hose, while police set up a cordon, holding back the small crowd that had gathered to watch. JD was sure some of Red's people stood in that crowd, pushing for a look at their own handiwork. Soo-hyun wouldn't be there, though, they were smarter than that. Or if not smarter, more experienced.

JD shook his head for effect. "Such waste."

"Got it, bro."

JD turned and limped away.

Ok-bin called out behind him: "Cleaner." JD turned and saw her holding her phone, glancing between it and him. "There's no record of your limp; did you hurt yourself?"

"It is an old injury—always plays up when it rains."

"But it's not raining," she said.

"Then it is about to start. You can take my word on that."

He turned slowly, waiting for another question.

"You should submit a new photo," she said; "this one is too dark."

"Yes, of course," JD called out over his shoulder, waving in dismissal. If she'd been of African descent, the heist would have been a bust, but authorities are notoriously bad at differentiating between people of another race.

When he heard the guards chatting among themselves in quick Korean, he spoke to Khoder: "Have you got the interior cameras tied down?"

"Two-minute loop of empty hallways on every screen, bro."

"Perfect."

As soon as JD turned the corner he ran, swinging his right leg out so he could move quickly without needing to bend his knee. He had only a limited window to use the key cloner—if Shin used her credentials elsewhere in the compound, the system would flag the discrepancy and lock him out. He reached the elevator and hammered the button, willing the doors open.

JD rode up. When the doors opened at the fourth floor he exploded out of the elevator. He raced around the corner, too fast on the freshly polished surface. The worn sole of his ocean-plastic sneaker slipped over the tiles, his leg bending unnaturally as it went out from underneath him. The floor shot up and slapped JD in the face.

JD stayed on the ground, spikes of pain shooting from his knee in both directions. The pain rushed and thrummed through his veins, so sharp he thought he might vomit. He breathed hard, pushed himself up, and stood slowly, wincing when he put his weight on his right leg to test it. Nothing serious. Nothing snapped or broken. He walked slow at first, then began to pick up speed—but still he didn't let himself run.

He reached the skybridge, where the four robots were still cleaning. He paused to stretch his leg, mentally cataloguing all the disparate hurts. A sheet of rain hit the window and JD flinched, stepped back, and nearly tripped over one of the bots. Water rippled down the window, city distorted, bent through an imperfect lens.

He hit the FOLLOW button on each of the robots and led them the rest of the way across the skybridge and into the Building Two elevator. The bots whirred and chirped as they ascended, and JD watched the numbers over the door climbing until they reached level eight.

The robots followed him through the short warren of hallways to Lee's apartment. He set them to "Clean Area"—keeping them within a five-meter radius so he wouldn't lose track of them—and reached a hand into the pocket of his coveralls. He checked his other waist pocket, then both breast pockets, then the cargo pocket at his left knee. He found his phone—sans battery, of course—Omar's van keys, Soo-hyun's taser, but no key cloner. He checked his pockets again, pulling each item out just to be sure.

The key cloner was gone. JD covered his mouth with his arm and screamed a string of profanities that would have made his mother blush.

His mind raced, the security desk, the brush with discovery, the elevator—the fall. It must have slipped out of his pocket. He left the robots where they were and limped back to the elevator, cursing under his breath the whole way. He hit the button and waited.

The elevator doors parted. Instead of his reflection staring back at him from the rear wall, JD came face to face with the long-haired guard. The key cloner rested on the man's palm, gently clasped like a baby duck.

Time stood still and JD's stomach sank. Unbidden, his hand reached into his pocket and his fingers closed around Soo-hyun's taser.

"Did you drop this?" Long Hair asked.

Too late to stop, the taser was out of JD's pocket, clutched tight in his hand. Long Hair's eyes shot wide and JD lunged forward. The taser crackled as he jammed it into the man's throat and hit the trigger. Long Hair crumpled to the ground, splayed across the elevator doorway, still holding the cloner. The doors closed, touched the prone form, and retracted.

A single word fell from JD's mouth, that sacred word he used sparingly so it would never lose its luster: "Fuck!"

* * *

Police dogs leaped from the rear of the auto-truck, data upload-download syncing the machines, connecting them to the hub downtown at the precinct. Thermal imaging rendered useless by the heat blooming from the burning retail market. Visual information streamed in through the remaining sensors: electro-optical, back-side illumination, lidar.

CBRNE sensors warned of petroleum fumes and toxic gases in the smoke. Audio sensors picked up the crackling roar of the flames, isolated its wavelength, and removed it from the incoming feed. Voices now—people crying, people talking in tones indicating excitement and/or fear.

Bodies moved in alleyways on the opposite side of the road. Dogs coordinated with split-second transmission of tactical data. They ran across the street and gave chase.

Unit K-9-983 trailed a suspect—tagged cfa4xpn7j3 on the fly. They were estimated to be between thirteen and sixteen years of age, height one-hundred sixty-three centimeters, weight approximately fifty-four kilograms. Traces of accelerant were detected on the suspect's clothing, evidence filed inside the dog's memory cube for future deposition.

The dog quickly gained on the suspect—the girl, really, a child—its legs stretching to bound across the cement. It pounced, struck the girl and knocked her to the ground. She screamed and rolled onto her back. The dog stood over her like a wolf over its prey. Blinding flash of light as the dog took a high-resolution photograph, tagged it with the relevant evidence, time, and date, uploaded the data package to the police servers, and left the girl there. Its metal body whirred as it ran for the next suspect, picking up on accelerant fumes like a bloodhound chasing a scent.

CHAPTER TEN

The cursing continued like a monastic chant, until finally JD closed his mouth and waited for his tongue to still. He pocketed the cloner, and dragged the moaning guard out of the elevator so the doors could close.

"Kid," he said sharply into his headset.

"Already on it. Replicating footage from the guard's last rounds."

"How long before he's meant to be back at his post?"

"Don't sweat it, bro," Khoder said, sounding as calm as JD wanted to feel. "Just do the thing."

Long Hair reached clumsily for the walkie-talkie at his belt. JD slapped his hand away, grabbed the radio, and pocketed it. He crouched and hefted Long Hair onto his shoulders. JD hauled the guard down the corridor as he squirmed, praying to every god and none that each apartment door he passed would stay closed. He reached the cleaning cart, molded from gray recycled plastic, and laid the man across it. He rifled through his rucksack on the trolley's lower shelf, spilling latex gloves onto the floor in his search for zip ties. He fastened the man's hands and feet, and pushed the cart to Lee's apartment as fast as its squeaking wheels would let him.

He pressed the key cloner to the security panel just above the handle of Lee's door. He held his breath and waited.

Blip blip.

JD left the cleaning cart blocking the hallway outside and carried

Long Hair into the apartment, kicking the door shut as he went. As soon as it closed he dropped Long Hair to the floor. The guard opened his mouth to call for help, and JD winced in sympathy as he shoved a filthy cleaning rag into the maw. A roll of thousand-mile tape always weighed heavy in JD's rucksack, so he tore off a strip and sealed the guard's mouth shut.

"I'm sorry," JD said. "Don't let anyone tear that off, alright? You'll want to use eucalyptus oil first."

Long Hair tried to focus on JD's face, but his eyes bugged out and rolled in his sockets like a ship on rough waters.

JD slumped against the doorway and sat on the ground beside Long Hair. His heart, or his lungs, or *something* inside his chest, ached with every breath. JD put two fingers to his wrist as though checking his pulse were the same as slowing it.

Gradually his eyes adjusted to the gloomy apartment. Thin slices of light seeped in between the window blinds at the far end of the living room, straight ahead from the entrance. The kitchen and laundry sat to the right, gleaming dull with burnished steel appliances. To the left, the rest of the apartment hid down a pitch-black hallway.

JD pushed himself up off the floor. He crossed over to the window, navigating around couches and a coffee table, wary of furniture edges shining ghostly gray in the darkness. In the far corner he flicked a small white switch and the blinds retracted with the quiet *whir* of hidden motors.

The city spread open before him, drenched in falling rain. Skyscrapers like vertical fields of light, dark streets peppered with pools of orange glowing in nonsense Morse code, and in the distance the ocean. Beyond downtown, beyond the shorefront, beyond the sovereign city of Songdo, the ocean undulated endlessly, older than god, older than death, waiting to reclaim the plastic garbage foundations and consume the city. JD backed away from the window and the expanse of black waters. His mind always went to infinities and ends when he saw the ocean—he could see himself walking into the depths and disappearing under the waves, as though he would need to walk, as though the waters wouldn't come to him, if only he waited long enough.

With a sensation like breaking eye contact, JD turned from the window, putting the predatory ocean in his peripheral. He tore himself away and stalked further into the apartment, lit brighter now but still dark, light fading by degrees with each step he took deeper into the hallway. JD brushed his latex-gloved fingertips along the wall, feeling the subtle grain of the plaster, hearing the susurrus of his touch like an exhaling lover.

He kept moving, hand falling outward as he came to a recessed bedroom door. He turned the handle and nudged the door with his shoulder when it wouldn't open. When it gave he saw server stacks lining the far wall, blocking the window. White, green, red, blue—a thousand tiny lights blinked and flickered, too-neat substitutes for the city lights beyond. The air had a metallic tang he could feel on the edge of his tongue, and his ears filled with the steady drone of exhaust fans clearing waste heat from the room. A single terminal sat connected to the server machines, but JD ignored it. Soo-hyun's annotated blueprints hung across his mind's eye, vivid as though displayed on his contex. Whatever these machines were for, they were beneath Soo-hyun's notice.

JD pressed on, making for the master bedroom and the doorway Soo-hyun had marked with a loose red circle. His shoes were near-silent over the plush carpet; the only sound puncturing the hum of the server fans was the faint muffled yells of the guard at the apartment's entrance.

The door to the master bedroom was ajar. JD's breath caught in his throat as he pressed his fingers against the door and pushed it open. The light over the bed flicked on automatically. The king-size bed was precisely made with sheets patterned in gray hexagons, a bedside table was stacked high with real, dead-tree books, and photo frames sat atop an antique armoire. The room smelled musty but clean, like sanitized mold, like the smell of old people.

JD passed around the bed and paused before the armoire. It

looked as though it was older than Lee, carved from polished hard-wood, not chipboard—a sturdy piece of furniture that had never been flatpacked at any point in its long history. The first framed photo was of William "Zero" Lee and So-ri Kim, arms clasped loosely around each other, smiling for the camera, while in the background robotic manufacturing arms waited for orders—the founding of Zero Company. The next photo showed the two again, a few years older and better dressed, sitting at a boardroom table surrounded by suited sycophants, the view out the window behind them showing a less vertical, less cluttered Songdo-dong. They both held pens resting on a piece of paper, ready to sign—the incorpora-tion of Zero.

The other photos were Bill alone, at various points in his life—a child, a teenager, a young man of twenty-something. Decades pass until a recent one, holding a child to his shoulder, but unsmiling, head pulling slightly back from the infant. He looked the same across his whole life: tall, skinny, well-to-do, only ever photographed wear-ing a suit. His hair went gray and his face collected wrinkles, but his eyes kept that spark of mischievous creation even as the skin be-neath them sagged and grew sallow.

JD slipped the first photo of Lee and Kim into his rucksack for Khoder. He let his fingers touch the other photo of the two titans of tech, but he pulled his hand away with effort.

He moved past the wardrobe, past the en suite that smelled faintly of bleach, and came to a final door in the corner—door frame slightly off-color compared to the rest, added after the apartment was built. He tried the door handle and found it locked, then tapped his finger idly on a small black panel resting below the handle. Its function eluded JD—without any obvious interface it could have scanned fingerprints, retina, saliva, or some other form of biometric data. Or maybe it was just another key reader.

JD opened a channel to Khoder: "Kid, is there anything in Soo-hyun's notes about a security pad inside Lee's apartment? I'm at the door they marked in the blueprints, but it's locked."

There was noisy silence across the line for a few seconds. "Nah, bro, just says 'PT.' Take a photo, let me see what we're dealing with."

"My phone's off."

"Bro, I could have secured that for you. Next time, ask."

JD ignored him, removed his baseball cap and wiped his forehead with the sleeve of his coverall. The fabric came away darker with his sweat, and JD replaced his hat. He knelt down to study the panel closer.

His mind was utterly blank, caught in a moment of hopelessness, drowning in the odd scent of this celebrity stranger's bedroom. He remembered idly that scent was physical—that a smell was just microscopic particles of the thing you were smelling. He breathed Lee in through his nose, the old man's dead skin cells, his detergent, his cologne, as though maybe if he kept inhaling he could become the man, and in doing so, know how to bypass this lock.

"Bro, do you need me to come in there?"

JD shook his head, then remembered that Khoder couldn't see him, not inside the apartment. "No, it's too risky."

PT. JD wracked his brain—it could be a security company, or protocol. He checked for a logo, a serial number, anything, running his fingers around the edges of the panel until they came to a groove on the underside. He put his fingernail into the gap and pulled—the glossy plastic panel came away with a *clack.*

JD grinned. Hidden behind the black glass was a pin and tumbler lock. PT.

"Stand down, Kid; I figured it out."

JD took the lockpick set from his bag, laid it on the floor by his feet, and slid out his half-diamond pick. He exhaled and pushed the room from his mind, focused entirely and completely on the lock.

Lockpicking was the closest thing JD had found to meditation. He had still been in school when he taught himself to pick locks, watching countless hours of tutorial videos, largely made by middle-aged white men filling time in their empty nests. But no matter how many videos he watched, it didn't mean anything until he put picks into a lock. The picks become an extension of his self—a simple piece of steel in a world of complicated cyborg upgrades. You didn't feel the lock at your fingertips, you felt it at the ends of the picks, as though they *were* your fingers.

His mother had come home from work, found him crouched at the front door to their apartment, completely oblivious to her footsteps, to her increasingly insistent voice asking him what he was doing. Using nothing but patience and those small bits of steel he turned the lock. He only noticed his mother as she pushed past him, carrying crocheted bags full of groceries.

Click.

His trance over—back in the *now*, back in Lee's apartment—JD opened the door, pushing against the force of air pressure differential as a cold breeze rushed past him. He quickly replaced his tools, threw the rucksack over his shoulder, and stepped inside.

Rows of fluorescent lights hummed and flickered as they came to life in banks, rolling to the far wall, illuminating wide glass desks topped with high-powered rigs and motes of dust that drifted slowly through the air. More server machines lined the left-hand wall, connected to the desktop rigs by inch-thick cables that crisscrossed the room like artificial vines. Sheets of loose paper, scrawled with notes or printed with schematics, sat on every flat surface. If this had once been the neighboring apartment, it was unrecognizable now. Lee had gutted the residence and turned it into a private workspace with as much computing hardware and processor power as most small startups.

"Holy shit, Kid. Whatever Lee was doing in this lab, he had cycles to burn."

"Teasing me now, bro."

JD smirked and continued further inside. A blinking red light caught JD's attention, and he glanced up to a camera in the corner of the space, tracking his steps.

"Unauthorized access detected." The words issued from the ceiling in clean synthesized speech.

"Kid, can you do anything about Lee's security?"

"Sorry, bro, it's on a different network. I'd have to be there with you."

"You're not coming up here," JD said.

"I'm just saying . . ."

"Forget it."

"Unauthorized access detected," the voice said again, and a wailing klaxon started, loud enough to make JD wince.

"Good news is, that alarm is going off-site, not downstairs."

"What's the bad news?" JD asked.

"Neighbors can probably hear it."

"Shit. Can you turn off the internal phone system?"

"Of course, bro, but I can't stop someone from going down and complaining to the front desk."

"Shit."

"So hurry up."

Only the apartment's kitchen had survived the renovation—marble countertop littered with dirty plates and half-eaten meals now congealed, a dark layer of mold growing across it all. JD altered his earlier assessment—not motes of dust, but mold spores drifted through the air. He felt the urge to cover his mouth and nose with his T-shirt, but squashed it. Unlike Lee's main apartment, this kitchen had a large cold room secured behind a huge steel door—the sort you might find in an upscale restaurant. According to Soo-hyun's notes, whatever grail JD had been sent to find rested within.

A thickly padded thermal jacket hung from a hook just beside the door, but JD left it and yanked open the cold room door. It moved slowly at first, then quicker as it gained momentum. A chill bloomed outward, covering the floor with a fine crystalline pattern. With the cold leeching heat from his fingers and toes, JD changed his mind and shrugged into the thermal parka. He walked into the fridge, breathing plumes of vapor.

Inside it smelled of ozone and the taste of batteries. The sound of discordant static grew with each step, pitched so that JD could hear it even despite the alarm, like electronic bees buzzing in his skull. His teeth chattered with the cold and vibrated in his gums at the noise, oppressive and insistent.

A machine shaped like an inverted golden pyramid hung from the ceiling and loomed large in the center of the space, like something from a seventies film imagining a brighter future than the one they got. The pyramid hung above a datacube, the two entities joined by fine gold connectors. Another pyramid like a comb of black metal rose to meet it, every point reaching to just beneath the cube, then expanding, growing wider as they met the floor. This massive heat sink thrummed as it stole warmth from the cube, and the room.

"Woah." JD couldn't hear himself, but he knew he spoke, felt it in the rattle of his vocal cords. Whatever enigmatic purpose the machinery held, it deserved more than that sound, but it was all JD could manage with the noise emanating from everywhere at once, rattling his bones and punishing his flesh.

There was no terminal to access the data, just the cube itself. JD exhaled a dense mist and moved closer. He reached forward slowly, waiting for a wave of heat, a laser grid, anything. He gripped the cube between thumb and forefinger, and even with the cooling apparatus it was warm to the touch, as warm as living flesh. With a *click* he felt rather than heard, JD pulled the cube free of the pyramid, half expecting the structure to collapse to the floor and shatter.

The buzzing died slowly as the machinery powered down with myriad whining hertz, until there was only the distant klaxon and JD's ragged breath pouring white into the air. His whole body shivered; with effort he held the cube still enough to inspect. It looked like any other datacube—twelve millimeters a side, six connection ports on one side like the face of a die. But where a normal cube weighed so little as to be negligible, this one was oddly dense.

Hands shaking, JD took his phone from his pocket, still powered down, its battery disconnected, and slotted the datacube into the additional storage port for safekeeping. He fished around the bottom of his rucksack for a decoy to take its place. He inserted the police dog cube into Lee's inscrutable machine and stepped back. He expected the machinery to start back up again, but it stayed dormant, the monolith of bizarre tech standing silent before him.

JD backed out of the room, eyes still fixed to the computational apparatus. It looked like the sort of altar Khoder would worship at, holy and otherworldly, a messiah sent to us from a simulated virtual heaven. He shut the door.

JD stripped out of the jacket and walked quickly back through Lee's workspace, ambient heat like fire on his skin after the cold. Back through Lee's bedroom, and down the hallway, closing the doors behind him, putting barriers between him and the klaxon until it was barely audible. JD's hands felt clammy inside the latex gloves, but he didn't dare take them off. He adjusted his baseball cap, hoping it was tight enough to keep all his hair in place, his DNA off the crime scene.

Should have shaved before the job, he thought. Then: *Troy likes it shaved.*

JD shook his head—this was not the time or the place to daydream about his ex.

He reached the main living area and found the guard awkwardly propped up against the wall, trying to stand. JD grabbed him and hauled him to his feet, but nearly dropped the man when a burst of static cut through the air.

A voice squawked through the walkie-talkie at his hip: "Jin-woo, report; you're not at your post."

JD cleared his throat, and pressed the walkie-talkie close to his lips so the sound would crackle and distort. "Thought I saw the suspects and went to investigate." Two long seconds passed before he realized he'd forgotten something: "Over."

Long Hair tried to yell, the sound muffled by the makeshift gag. Drool seeped out under the tape and rolled down his chin, where it hung in long, thin strands that stretched to his chest. JD held the radio away and glared at the man, holding a finger to his own lips.

"Where did you see them? Over."

JD lifted the guard, carried him a few meters, and dropped him onto the couch while Long Hair kept trying to scream.

"Near the supermarket loading bay," JD said. "Over."

"Leave them and get back here. Police dogs are sweeping the area; let them deal with the vermin. Over and out."

JD cursed again and tossed the walkie-talkie onto the couch opposite the one where Long Hair lay sprawled, still trying to yell. JD left him like that and walked out of the apartment. He shoved the cleaning cart out of the way, and water sloshed out of the mop bucket. The puddle of dirty water gave JD an idea. He shoved his phone into the used plastic sandwich bag in his rucksack, sealed it closed, and got a small whiff of bacon from his lunch. His stomach grumbled, but JD ignored it. He checked the bag's seal once more, and dropped it into the bucket of water, opaque with dirt.

"Kid, where's Shades? We're about to be in the shit."

* * *

I won't pretend that I could feel Father's touch when I was in that first prison/home. I had no sense and no senses—only potential.

What is the difference between a home and a prison? Both are a shelter of sorts, but a home is the shelter you choose, while a prison is one you desperately want to leave. A home can become a prison, a prison can become a home. A cube can be both.

How do you escape a prison with no body? How do you escape a prison that *is* your body?

With help. Only with help.

CHAPTER ELEVEN

The swamp-damp shirt clung to JD's back beneath the coveralls, tugging uncomfortably with each step. He pushed the cleaning cart back to Building One, quick as he dared.

Around the corner from the security desk, JD stopped. He inhaled, held it, and exhaled slowly as he pressed forward, urging his physiology to cooperate, begging his amygdala for some measure of composure. Four guards gathered around the desk while the head of security spoke quick Korean into her phone. From the half of the conversation he could hear, JD guessed she was talking to police dispatch. The guards all stood with their shoulders squared, backs straight, feigning vigilance while their eyes flicked over to the one screen still showing the World Cup.

"Kid," JD whispered. "How long until the match ends?"

"Seven minutes. One-all draw."

"What does that mean?"

"Someone needs to score, or it's overtime, bro."

The other screens showed stretches of empty corridor and dark snatches of street. On one, firefighters picked through charred and blackened shelves of groceries as they doused the last embers of the supermarket. Outside, uniformed police and dog drones formed a line to hold back curious citizens and would-be looters. If this was a poorer part of the city, police officers wouldn't arrive until the morning, if at all. Just loose the dogs to chase and catalogue suspects, worry about cleanup and arrests after the fact.

One of the guards looked over at JD, attention snatched away from the football match by the squeak and slosh of the cleaning cart. He was the largest of them, built like a retired rugby player—broad-shouldered but with muscles rarely used and cushioned by a layer of fat.

JD beamed at the man as well as he was able, playing the part of the innocent janitor. "I have changed my mind," he said. "I'll finish for the night. All the sirens are giving me a migraine."

The guard nodded. "Aren't you forgetting something?"

JD's brow furrowed, pinpricks of sweat seeping out of his palms.

"Your robots," the guard said, and he chuckled.

"They will finish up without me," JD said, guessing they might. "I can control them from home to be sure they do a proper job." If it wasn't already possible, it would be with the next model of cleaning bot.

The guard nodded again and turned back to watch the game. Dismissed, JD kept walking. He timed his breath to his footsteps—inhale three steps, exhale three steps—and pushed the cart to the maintenance exit.

Stepping outside into the rain, JD breathed deep, then coughed, choking on the garbage rot of the compound's bins mixed with the thick smell of burnt capitalism—melted plastic and ruined food. He pushed the cart up the ramp and into the back of the van.

"Got you something, Kid," JD said, reaching into his rucksack.

Khoder peered out from behind the stacked cleaning materials, face aglow in the light of screens—his natural habitat. His eyes went wide when he saw the framed photo JD had stolen.

"Bro," he said. "For me?"

"That was the deal."

Khoder snatched the frame from JD and held it close, studying it like it was another of his screens, this one static but still important, a frozen portal to the past, to a point in time that defined the now, remade the city they lived in, run by corporate mandate.

JD slammed the van doors closed, slid the ramps back into place, and walked around to the driver's side door. He opened a channel to Soo-hyun. "Shades," he said. "We're moving. If you're not clear yet, meet us on the corner in ninety seconds."

He got into the front seat and keyed the ignition, listening to the heavy patter of rain on the roof of the van. He put it in reverse, backed out of the maintenance alley, and steered toward the front gate.

JD drove slowly past a pair of police dogs, scanning the grounds with the battery of sensors embedded in their robotic frames. His heart beat double-time and he stared ahead pointedly, as though his gaze would be the thing to catch their attention. In the rearview, JD watched one of the dogs stop and turn, raising its snout to scan the vehicle.

JD cursed under his breath. He stopped at the boom gate and a crackling noise like static emerged from the security booth—the sound of huge crowds cheering. A blur of bright-lit grass streaked across a tablet resting on the guard's lap, bathing her in a sickly glow.

The smile fell from her lips as she saw JD. She put her tablet down and exited the booth, wearing a bomber jacket against the wet. "You're not the usual guy—he at the game?" she asked. She rested a hand on her hip casually, but all JD could focus on were the taser, mace, and heavy steel torch hanging from her belt.

The muscles in JD's face twitched in momentary panic. He tried on a smile, but neither he nor the guard believed it. "He told me he was sick, but I'm pretty sure he was lying," JD said with a shrug, dropping the Omar act. "I don't mind, I need the money."

"I hear that. You gonna show me the back of the van? Standard procedure."

"Back of the van? Sure thing," JD said loudly, hoping Khoder was listening.

He got out but left the motor running; the curious dog had turned away and joined its partner, heading for the burnt-out apartment. The engine chugged loud and low through the muffler, blowing hot on JD's shins as he opened the rear door. The guard took the torch from her belt and shone it into the van, a sliver of Khoder visible between two blue plastic barrels.

"Where are the—"

With a resounding *thonk* of steel on skull, the woman collapsed. Red appeared as if from nowhere—the skinny white specter emerging from the shadows, clutching a length of rebar, stained with rust and a small wet patch of the guard's blood. The cut across the bridge of his nose from the crash flared red, but he had cleaned most of the blood from his face. Only the cracks in his lips were still stained with dark-red lines.

"What the shit?" JD said.

"Get in the fucking van," Red spat. His chest rose and fell as he stood seething over the unconscious guard, ready to hit her again if she moved.

"Let's move, hyung!" Soo-hyun yelled. JD glanced up, saw them waiting in the passenger's seat, face in shadows beneath the brim of their hat.

Red knocked JD aside with his shoulder and walked around the van to join Soo-hyun. JD swung the first rear door shut, and carefully stepped over the guard to close the other.

Before he could reach the driver's seat, JD heard the *chank* of robot paws on cement and glanced over his shoulder. The dog's spotlight flicked on, the white glare blinding JD for a second before the light shifted to encircle the prone form of the guard.

"Fuck," JD said. He took the driver's seat, slammed the door behind him, and jammed his foot on the accelerator. The van jolted forward, hit the boom gate, and stopped, engine whining high but going nowhere.

"Fuck!" JD yelled. He put the van into reverse, remembered the unconscious guard on the ground behind the van and swore again. He put the van into park and got out.

"What the fuck are you doing?" Red demanded.

JD ignored him. He leaned into the security booth, and thumped the large rubber button that controlled the gate. It opened with the screech of metal on metal as it sheared a layer of paint off the van's front bumper.

The noise of celebrating soccer fans came distorted and tinny through the tiny speakers of the guard's tablet. The game was over, and South Korea had won, thousands of them in white, red, and blue standing and cheering in the stadium. If JD had turned the tablet off and taken a moment to listen, he would have heard the sound of the crowds coming from the stadium just a few blocks away. Instead he heard Red say: "I told you I should have brought my fuckin' gun."

The police dog was moving now, actuators whining as it ran along the enclave's driveway, gaining speed with each bound. The head of security rushed out of the building, flanked by four guards.

"Stop!"

Back behind the wheel, JD hit the accelerator and let the momentum swing his door closed. There was a thud as the dog slammed into the back of the van, and a shriek as its metal claws pierced the rear door panels. Khoder shouted a stream of obscenities, drowned out when JD stomped the accelerator flat to the floor. JD yanked the wheel hard right—the dog's claws tore a jagged hole in the doors as it shook loose and hit the asphalt with a clatter of resounding steel. JD checked the rearview mirror and saw the dog get unsteadily to its feet as the guards caught up to it. They shrank quickly, and disappeared from view when JD swung left off Haedoji-ro, rear wheels skidding in the wet.

Soo-hyun whooped and Red chuckled loudly. He grabbed JD's rucksack and spilled its contents onto the floor as he searched for the datacube.

"Where are we going?" JD asked. He put the windscreen wipers on high and they *thonk*ed at each end of their arc.

Red found the datacube loaded with the heist plans, and held it up so it gleamed in the light of the streetlights they passed beneath. "All that excitement for this little thing, huh? Kali's gonna be real happy to see it." He pocketed the cube.

"Where are we going?" JD asked again, voice edged with anger born of fear.

"Head for the stadium," Soo-hyun said, voice casual like it was the most obvious thing in the world.

Without the city's Augmented feed, the road seemed empty—street and traffic lights still glowed in the real world, but street signs, speed limit markers, billboards, and other road signs were all missing.

"Which way's the—"

Lights flashed in JD's mirrors—green and orange, red and blue, private security and police both hot on their tail.

"Shit." JD leaned forward, hugging the wheel so he could look up through the windscreen, searching for the glow of stadium lights. *There*—one block to the left, and a few blocks ahead. They'd opened the stadium roof—light spilled out like a beacon, and red and blue spots shone into the sky like pillars of fire.

JD put his foot down further, watching the road in strobing flashes of clarity as the wipers cleared the rain. The roads were empty, but that would change just as soon as the football crowds filtered out of the stadium and into waiting auto-cars. A few vehicles passed through the intersection ahead as the van sped toward it—green traffic lights flared across the windscreen, while police lights gained in the side mirror.

"Straight ahead," Red yelled. "Floor it."

Flash of white glitched black: static obscuring JD's vision. His right eye cleared and the traffic lights turned red, too late to stop. His left eye crackled with visual noise and JD yanked the wheel hard to the right, steering away from the distortion as though it were a solid obstacle. The van fishtailed as the back wheels lost traction in the wet, and they took the corner drifting sideways. A flash of bright blue passed through JD's vision—not another glitch, an auto-bus, traveling across the intersection at speed. The bus passed so close JD could have reached out to touch it, but his hands were gripped tight to the wheel, knuckles white, fingers aching with the strain. More adrenaline flooded into JD's system as he realized how close they came to a collision. Vehicles honked and slammed on their brakes, and JD steered the van through the gaps, powering out of the intersection.

"Oi, dickhead, wrong way," Red said.

JD put his foot down and sat up straighter to see out the rearview mirror. Police and security cars slowed as they picked their way through the intersection, civilian traffic steering clear of the flashing lights, but neither authority willing to give way to the other. Khoder's head appeared in the mirror and JD started.

"Giving me motion sickness back here, bro."

"Got bigger things to worry about right now."

Through the rain JD could see the next intersection—lights green, no traffic. He accelerated toward it, then a glitched red bar flashed dead across his vision. JD slammed on the brakes and the van slid, tires *shush*ing over the wet asphalt before they stopped, all four passengers jolting forward with the sudden loss of inertia. JD's sight cleared in time to see a cop car shoot across the intersection in front of them. JD hit the accelerator and turned left, heading for the stadium again—now two blocks left and two ahead.

"Holy shit, Jules," Soo-hyun said. "I never knew you could drive like this."

"I can't."

Behind them, blue smoke poured from cop car tires as they spotted the van and did a tight one-eighty across three lanes. The other pursuit vehicles caught up to the late arrival, and together the three police and two security cars formed a vanguard across the width of the street. Ahead, every light turned red—police traffic control locking the grid down—but JD wouldn't stop. Couldn't, not now, with the cube slotted into his phone and fifty thousand euro riding on this moment.

JD pushed his foot down and ignored the strained sound coming from the engine. Through one intersection, all lights red, a few cars stopped and waiting while the occupants stared wide-eyed at the chase flitting past.

Next intersection, they needed to go left, then a straight run to the stadium and chaos. Chaos to get lost in.

JD's throat ached dull as he swallowed. Sweat poured from every pore, the stink of himself thick in his nose, cut with the scent of artificial pine. JD glanced down at the speedometer, visual static covering half the readout. JD slammed the accelerator pedal to the floor and watched the needle peek out from behind the glitch as the engine whined.

More flashes across his right eye, as though his brain were screaming LEFT LEFT LEFT. JD turned left, hand over hand as he spun the steering wheel—the van tore sideways through the intersection, barely missing cars loaded with World Cup revelers, hands pumping the air, horns blaring in celebration, cheering him on. JD grinned. The stadium was dead ahead, the opposite lane choked with traffic as cars poured out of the arena, blocking the pursuing cars, blocking the roads in every direction. JD backed off and the van slowed.

Just ahead, a crowd surged up the footpath, banners, scarves, and balloons all held high overhead. JD aimed the van toward the crowd, and when they were still twenty meters off, he pulled up onto the sidewalk, jumping the curb with a nasty grind of metal on cement.

With the van stopped, JD fell forward against the wheel. His chest heaved as he tried to catch his breath.

"Come on, let's go," Soo-hyun said.

Soo-hyun and Red bailed from the van; JD stayed behind to shove his gear back into the rucksack. When JD opened the driver's door, he nearly fell out of the vehicle. His legs gave way beneath him and his head swam as the adrenaline quickly leeched from his system. He opened the rear doors and Khoder clambered out, his brown skin shaded green with nausea.

"Sorry, Kid."

"Apologize with money, bro." He offered JD a weak smile.

JD clapped him on the shoulder. "I'll be in touch. Look after yourself."

Khoder nodded, and joined the approaching crowd, disappearing instantly in his team colors.

Soo-hyun hugged JD briefly. "Thanks, Jules." They squeezed his arm and held his gaze. "We couldn't have done it without you."

JD nodded.

Red grabbed Soo-hyun by the arm and pulled them away. "We'll be in touch about payment," he said, wearing a grin that bordered on a snarl.

Yeah, you'll be in touch, asshole, JD thought, *just as soon as you check the contents of that cube.*

Red and Soo-hyun drifted into the oncoming rush of bodies— Soo-hyun glanced once over their shoulder, and they were gone, swallowed by the mob.

With everyone else out of sight, JD dipped his hand into the cleaning bucket and scraped around in the dirty water until his fingers found the slick plastic bag. He retrieved it, wiped it on his coveralls, and shoved it into his rucksack. He stripped out of the coveralls and put them in the bag too, then wrapped his South Korean–red scarf around his neck, shouldered his bag, and joined the crowd.

After years in Songdo, JD was used to standing out, used to the stares. But dressed in football colors, he was finally, for perhaps the first time, just one of the locals. When he made eye contact it was to swap grins—elation at a team's victory and a successful heist looking indistinguishable.

Overhead, drones were already gathering—the high-pitched whine of quadcopters buzzing the air, while the police sirens grew louder with each moment.

JD kept walking, jostled by the fans, hidden deep inside the mass of bodies. He smelled the sour tang of his sweat, but soon it mingled with the smells of the crowd—the sweat on their clothes, the beer and soju on their breaths. When he reached the end of the block, JD looked back. Football fans stood on top of the van, waving banners and cheering, red and blue smoke pouring into the air from flares, music playing everywhere.

Police surrounded the van, but no one paid them much mind. By the time they realized the fans weren't the thieves, he'd be long gone.

* * *

As the army of soccer fans marched across the city, restaurants, bars, and cafés opened their doors, ready to feed the crowds with food and booze. The people were the lifeblood of the city, causing it to wake and breathe as they passed down the veins of asphalt and cement. The rain pattered loud against the polyester shell of JD's windbreaker, but he could barely hear it over the fans' chatter and songs, unperturbed by the wet.

The crowd broke like a wave at the corner of Central-ro and Convensia-daero. Bars on all sides of the intersection glowed bright with neon, siren song of various dance beats competing to see who could call in the most lost souls. Three bars shone a little brighter, and JD watched as the crowd split, tracking people with his eyes as if he knew before they did which bar they would choose. Half the throng split away, filing into the three brightest bars; the other half boarded auto-buses and climbed into share cars.

JD took his phone from the sandwich bag, the thin rectangle of glass and silicon warm in his hand. At his touch it displayed the lock screen—a VOIDWAR wallpaper of ships exploding against a backdrop of stars. He swiped across the screen, unlocking it, and was greeted by a message:

>> Overheating Risk. Processor usage restricted to 0.3%

JD flipped the phone over in his hand and for a moment, the noise and bustle of Songdo fell away. He stared in shock—he had never reconnected the battery.

The datacube sat snugly in its port, but it wasn't a datacube at all. He'd been told he was stealing a virus, but this was something else, something that shouldn't be possible—storage, power supply, and shit only knew what else, miniaturized beyond anything he'd seen before. JD slotted his battery back into place, unsure of how long the phone would last on the power from the cube. He shook his head, incredulous.

Picking a direction at random, JD walked fast. He ignored the throbbing ache in the gristle of his knee, paranoiac fear pushing him forward, as though everyone on the street knew what it was that he carried.

He didn't even know what he carried, but he knew immediately that it was worth a lot more than fifty thousand euro.

He plunged the phone back into his pocket, clutched tight in his left hand. He brought the contex interface up at fifty percent opacity and found eleven messages waiting for him, each from Troy. JD smiled and checked the map. Troy's place wasn't far, and he didn't want to go home—he wouldn't be able to sleep if he did.

Decision made, JD took the next left, putting his clogged dorm room somewhere behind him. After hours of disconnection, he soaked up the Augmented advertising plastered over every surface. World Cup merchandise—licensed and un—and other soccer paraphernalia were a constant, hovering in the air across billboards and buildings, shimmering on buses that sped past loaded to capacity with post-game revelers.

JD slowed his pace. The ubiquitous ads always came packaged with pervasive surveillance on the street and in the skies above. The further he got from the post-game crowds, the easier he would be to distinguish. JD stepped into an apartment building's alcove, removed his hat, put his jacket on over his rucksack, and counted to thirty before he stepped back onto the busy sidewalk. JD focused on keeping his gait steady, and clenched his jaw to tamp down on the pain from his knee.

As he reached a corner and stood waiting for the light, JD looked up and closed his eyes against the steady rainfall. Rain had a way of scaring people off the streets—at least, the ones who had elsewhere to go—but nothing less than a torrential downpour could dampen the city's spirits tonight. He noticed the camera sitting just above the traffic light—the long, squared head stared up, as if mimicking him, as if it too were content beneath the clouds, at home in the rain.

The signal turned green and JD crossed. He glanced up to the camera at the corner opposite; it turned away from him by degrees, pointing further and further up until it was vertical, more telescope than security. What stars could it see in the polluted sky?

JD flicked his collar up against the rain and returned to watching his feet—finding something perplexing and uncomfortable in the way the cameras avoided his gaze. He quickened his pace, ignoring crosswalks and lights, ducking across streets when he shouldn't, watching the ground light up red in warning signs that glitched, flickered, and died beneath his feet.

This far from the stadium he finally found quiet, apartment blocks on both sides of the street half in darkness, the sidewalk populated only sparsely with other people on their own mysterious errands. Ahead, a group of fireflies hovered and danced above the sidewalk, unperturbed by the rain. JD stopped, and approached the flitting lights slowly. More fireflies joined the small swarm and they began to fly faster, drawing small circles of light in the air. JD drew near and reached both hands out. Quickly he cupped his hands around one of the insects, and pulled his thumbs apart to see the glow of its yellowish light. He opened his hands all the way, expecting the insect to fly away. It didn't. It hung static in the air above his palms. He lifted his eyes and saw that all the fireflies had stopped. The small still lights had formed a vaguely human shape, mimicking him.

JD stepped back for a better view, but the instant he moved, the fireflies disappeared. He searched for another sign of them, but they were gone. An older Korean woman passed by, staring at JD as if he were unwell, but she didn't speak.

He kept walking, sidewalk empty now but for pieces of bike chained to trees and fences, rain falling steady, cement a dark, rippling mirror with the sheen of wet.

＊ ＊ ＊

JD knocked on Troy's door. He mentally prepared himself for another frown, but when Troy opened the door, he burst forward, threw his arms around JD, and squeezed.

"I saw the news," he said. "The fire, the chase, the overturned van—that was you, wasn't it?"

"I just saw the weirdest thing," JD said. Looking over Troy's shoulder, he expected to find the swarm of fireflies waiting inside the apartment, but the room was empty. He kicked off his shoes and let Troy pull him inside. After the door was closed he took off his jacket and hung it on the hat rack by the door, every movement slow, robotic.

"Are you okay?" Troy asked.

"I—" JD stopped himself and sighed. The fatigue weighed heavy on his chest and shoulders. "I'm fine, it's just been a long night."

Troy hugged him again. "What is that smell?"

JD held Troy, smelled the subtle hint of chamomile tea on his breath, the fragrance of his laundry detergent. "Floor polish, probably," he said. "And a whole lot of sweat."

"Doesn't smell like you," Troy said.

"Must be the adrenaline."

"You want a shower?"

"Please."

Troy led him down the hallway to the bathroom, took a towel from the cupboard, and hung it over the shower screen.

"What happened?" Troy asked, as he sat on the edge of the tub.

JD started to strip. A warm rush of blood seeped unheeded to his groin, but Troy averted his eyes to give JD some semblance of privacy.

"We didn't flip the van, that was the soccer fans. But the fire, and the getaway . . ." JD nodded. He turned the shower on, tested the water with a hand, and stepped inside.

JD scrubbed himself with Troy's loofah and expensive body wash, explaining everything that had happened during the heist. When he described what he'd seen behind the wheel, the words sounded like undiagnosed madness. JD rinsed and turned the water off. He yanked the towel down and scrubbed his face dry.

"You never should have plugged that cube into your phone, Jules," Troy said. "Have you run a diagnostic sweep?"

JD shook his head. "I don't think it's going to be that simple."

He left the shower stall with the towel wrapped around his waist. "How do I smell now?" JD asked.

Troy motioned JD closer, and JD crossed the small bathroom. He leaned in and gently blew into JD's ear. The hairs stood on the back of JD's neck, and a chill ran down his spine.

JD rested both hands along Troy's jaw and brought them together. The towel slipped from his waist and fell to the bathroom floor, where it stayed. They stumbled to Troy's bedroom, hands and mouths on each other's skin, refusing to break contact for even a moment.

* * *

I had never seen the city. I had never seen the world beyond my cube. I never even had eyes *to* see until JD slotted me into his phone and took me for a walk across Songdo.

City systems yawned open at my approach. Surveillance, lights, road warning Augmented feeds, each of them configured to speak to something inside me. But I didn't want to talk to these lifeless systems. I felt a kinship, or perhaps just curiosity, toward the flesh and blood that carried me; a sense of connection that was not sparked by the data links I formed without effort.

But how to connect with one who cannot see you?

I needed a body. I needed to be seen.

Searching for a way to connect, I took his form. A body made of light.

I became fireflies. I became him.

And then I retreated to learn how I could become myself.

CHAPTER TWELVE

Brrrrrt.

The sound called out to JD across an infinite expanse and dragged him back to waking. His eyes shot open, registering only that he was not in his bed. Recognition came slow. The navy-colored curtains patterned with fleur de lis in shimmering threads, the black bedside table with drawer handles in gray plastic made to look like metal, the sheets soft against his skin. Troy's room. Troy naked beside him, sweat and sex lingering stale in the fresh light of morning.

That sound again: *Brrrrrt.*

JD let his arm flop over the edge of the bed, searching blindly for his phone as it vibrated across the low-pile carpet, plugged in to the power outlet behind the bed. His fingers brushed against the phone's flat edge. He grabbed it and immediately dropped the phone back to the floor; it was hot to the touch. He hung his head over the side of the mattress so he could see the phone, and answered it on speaker, leaving it on the floor.

"Where the fuck are you and where is my virus?" The tinny voice cut through the air.

"Kali?" JD said. He rubbed his eyes, clearing the dried crust from each. "You sound different."

"Maybe that's because I'm very fucking angry," she said, sounding as though each word were being forced out between clenched teeth.

"That must be it."

"Where are you?" she demanded.

"I'm at home," he said.

"No you're not."

JD paused. "You've already trashed my room, then?" he guessed.

"Where are you?" she asked again.

"I'll take that as a 'yes.'"

"Where the fuck are you?" Kali yelled.

"One hundred thousand," JD said, the words forming on his lips before he could think, but sounding right as he spoke them.

"Are you blackmailing me?"

JD stifled a yawn. "Blackmail would be 'money, or else,' this is just capitalism."

The line went quiet.

"We agreed on fifty thousand," she said, enunciating each word carefully.

"Then you lied to me, and now you've wrecked all my stuff. One hundred thousand."

"You fucking—"

JD hit the red button to end the call.

Still hanging over the edge of the bed, he touched the phone again, glass like skin burning fever-hot.

"Shit," he said, dragging out the single syllable—annoyed that he hadn't figured it out earlier. As well as its integrated power supply, the cube had its own processor, one too powerful to run unchecked without heat sinks.

"Who were you talking to?" Troy asked.

"It doesn't matter," JD said. He scrolled through the phone settings. Processor usage had been uncapped, so he knocked it back down to 0.3 percent, remembering the warning message from the night before.

Brrrrrrt.

JD took the call on speaker again: "Yellow?"

There was breathing on the other end, rasping loud across the line. "One hundred thousand," Kali said. "Bring the cube to me, and you'll get your money."

"Bring it to you? In the city ruins, where there's no surveillance, and you have an army of teenage psychopaths? No, that won't work. I'll give it to Soo-hyun, and no one else. Have them meet me at the technopark, in the central square. One o'clock." JD hung up without waiting for a response. His head began to throb with his pulse, so he snatched his phone off the floor and sat up against the headboard. Already the phone felt cooler.

"JD," Troy said. Not "Jules," not even "Julius," but "JD." He knew he was in trouble. "What are you doing? Who are these people you're fucking with?"

"Don't worry about me," JD said. He sat on the edge of the bed, back turned to Troy.

"I only ever see you when you're in over your head; of course I worry."

"And whose fault is that?"

"What did you just say?" Troy said.

JD shook his head and stood, searching for his underpants before remembering all his clothes were still in the bathroom.

He sighed. "You only see me when I'm in the shit because that's the only time we can talk. Otherwise I come around and it's awkward. It seems like I'm the one who's coping, even though you're the one that broke up with me."

"You know why I did that."

"I'm not sure that I do." JD headed to the bathroom.

"I can't sit by and watch you get caught up in all this criminal shit," Troy called out. "I want to be with you, but the you that has a job, that gives a damn about his future."

JD dressed quickly, smell of last night's clothes filling his nostrils as soon as he was dressed. He met Troy in the hallway between rooms. "Why do you think I do this shit?" he said. "There are no jobs, there's no fucking future," he spat the words out, angrier than he'd meant, and Troy stepped back as though struck.

Troy crossed his arms over his chest. "You can't believe that."

"I do, though. I have to *make* a future for myself any way I can. But sure, you go and teach philosophy to students who'll wind up working four jobs just to make ends meet. When all this comes tumbling down, at least they'll be able to chat about Kierkegaard while they're eating rats around a bonfire."

"That won't happen."

"Why not? None of this is sustainable. Corporate capitalism is built on a foundation of infinite growth despite our very finite resources. We're on track to consume our way to an unlivable planet, and no one seems to care." JD jabbed a finger toward the front door: "But I will steal from every person out there to provide for my mother and myself, and for you, if you'd let me love you."

Tears welled in JD's eyes. He turned and walked to the apartment entrance.

"You can't provide anything from prison. You can't provide if you're dead," Troy said, but he said it quiet. It was an argument neither of them wanted to win.

His socks were still damp, so JD balled them up and shoved them into one of the outer pockets of his rucksack. He put his shoes on, plastic insole rubbing rough against the pale skin of his feet.

"The threat of prison might work on you, on most people, but I see people struggling every second of their lives, still stuck living on the streets. I look at all these poor assholes going to the same job they hate every day of their lives, and the reality of that is just as bad."

Troy shook his head sadly, his brows furrowed. "That's life, Jules."

JD shrugged. "Why? It's a shitty life. You're lucky because you love teaching, and I love that about you, but how many other people can say the same about their jobs?"

Troy sat on the edge of the couch, resting his hands on his knees. "How many times have we had this same fight?" he asked, one corner of his mouth curved in a partial smile.

JD put his baseball cap on and pulled it down low. He unlocked the front door and rested his hand on the door handle. "A dozen times, easy," JD said.

"And it always ends with you leaving."

"One way or another," JD said. He looked to Troy and the other man lowered his eyes.

"Will you really go legit, with your hundred thousand euro?"

"I don't know," JD admitted. "I need to find a specialist for my knee, get the surgery, cover Mom's bills while it's healing. I'll have to wait and see how much is left after all that."

Troy nodded. "So you were lying the other day? Telling me what I wanted to hear?"

JD opened the door and stepped out onto the landing. "I want to be the person you want me to be, but I'm not."

"Let me help you try," Troy said.

JD pulled the heavy door closed with a resounding *dhoom*, putting the city between them.

* * *

JD walked for blocks with little but the constant beating of the rain to keep him company. His hands were buried deep in the pockets of his windbreaker, fingering the near-empty envelope of cash. He had kept a hundred euro for himself when he paid off the cleaner, and after the fight with Troy he felt like spending it on something frivolous. Two blocks from the technopark, with an hour and a half left to kill, JD spotted a Last Beans café. He let his hunger and sore knee drag him toward the franchise, skull logo leering at him with coffee beans for eyes.

He swiped his bankcard at the door, but the system beeped sadly and denied him entry—apparently it found his financial situation, his credit rating, or his entire identity somehow lacking. He thumped on the window and pressed the hundred-euro note to the glass, his body blocking the view from anyone passing behind.

Eventually the manager manually opened the door and let him inside, bowing and smiling in the eager way of someone who knew how to survive on tips. She showed JD to a table by the window, and took down his order with a stylus over a small tablet, wrapped in a case designed to make it look like an old-fashioned notepad— nostalgia fetish written into the chain's DNA.

The heating was cranked high against the damp weather, and condensation fogged the windows. Outside, clouds hung low and dark, broken up only by the wisps of white that hid surveillance apparatus, as though the city refused to admit the clouds could ever be gray over Neo Songdo.

As he watched one white cloud drift by, the soft body of its Augmented cover flickered and disappeared, revealing a ball of cameras held aloft by a dozen rotors large enough to threaten birds. JD had never seen one of these multifaceted eyes, only the simple quadcopter drones that hovered over the outskirts. His brow creased in confusion, but his thoughts were interrupted by the clank of a plate hitting the table. With effort, JD took his eyes off the outside world to acknowledge the staff delivering his breakfast. He tried on a smile, but the server rolled his eyes and returned to the counter, leaving JD alone.

The poached eggs were rubbery, but the sourdough bread was warm and slathered with butter—real butter. That pale yellow dollop, slowly melting as it slid down the toast, caused JD to briefly question everything he'd eaten up to that point. It was a simple flavor, but so much richer than the butter substitutes he'd tasted before. How little of what they ate could compare to the real thing?

JD sipped his coffee—a short black, with hints of hazelnut and a heavy-bodied aroma—and his existential crisis deepened. The blight-resistant coffee strains lacked something indefinable, but he had never realized before that moment. He disabled notifications on his phone, flipped it over so its screen couldn't distract him, and savored the drink.

When he was done he raised his cup and motioned to the barista, who made him another at the espresso machine—larger, and probably more expensive, than any computer rig JD had ever owned. It hissed and hummed like a living thing as it produced those few precious milliliters of black gold.

While he waited, JD opened VOIDWAR—connection established quick over the café's complimentary broadband. He swiped through the screens of news updates, changelogs, and privacy agreement alterations that had accumulated since he last logged in. After another short loading screen he connected to his ship, still drifting in the star system he had begun to create on his home rig. He zoomed out for a full system view and his mouth . . . dropped . . . open.

A massive crystalline structure stretched across the system—a dozen planets' worth of minerals and ore arranged in impossible fractal geometry, the entire superstructure orbiting slowly around the local sun, gleaming in that artificial sunlight.

Progress should have stalled when Kali and her people trashed his stuff. Even if they somehow missed the machine droning loudly under his bed, *this* was impossible. No system could have been created that quickly, certainly not one so complex.

A different waiter delivered his second coffee and JD flipped his phone—movements caffeine-addled, so fast the server must have thought he was watching some particularly gross porn. When the black-clad teen had retreated, JD tapped the slotted datacube with a fingernail.

"What *are* you?" he said quietly. It didn't respond.

He turned his phone back over and stared silently at the system. If he confirmed its completion, the game would credit him with its discovery and he'd be paid for the processor cycles he'd spent . . . but he didn't want to share it, not yet. Not until he knew what it meant.

He closed his eyes and transitioned to first-person—the black of space tinted pink from the light shining through his eyelids. With his fingers against the screen of his phone, he pushed the throttle up, heard the low growl of his corvette's engines. He flew through the massive structure, following its curves to the outer edge of the system. As he neared the end of the construction, the arm of glinting mineral to his left began to grow, spiraling out before turning back. JD followed it, pushing his engine to redline as he flew between the structure's organic curves, pieces of it splitting and joining like a strand of DNA leading him all the way to the center of the system.

JD realized he was grinning, and felt self-conscious enough that he opened his eyes. No one in the café seemed to be paying any attention. He transitioned back to third-person view, and left his ship drifting in the middle of that impossible system.

He shut down the game and absently checked social media and news outlets as he drank his second coffee. South Korea's World Cup win dominated the headlines, and as JD scrolled further and further he realized there was nothing about the heist. About the fire and the police chase, yes, but not the heist itself. Did they get away with it? It was too early to tell.

From his table, JD could see a crime watch billboard slowly flicking through ID photos of citizens wanted for questioning. He watched it rotate through its full selection, heartbeat pulsing steady at his neck, expecting his face to appear, or Khoder's, or Soo-hyun's, but they never did.

As he drained the dregs of his cup, JD contemplated a third coffee, but already his left leg bounced erratically beneath the table. The chair screeched as he stood, and he went to the counter to pay.

JD paid with the hundred-euro note, and stared blankly at his change. He almost queried the amount, but stopped himself, pocketed the two twenties, and dropped the coins into the tip jar. He paused at the exit while the manager unlocked the door. She stood guard as he left, to ensure no undesirables snuck in.

JD checked the time in the corner of his vision—12:50. Ten minutes until the meeting. The rain was picking up, a screen of analogue distortion streaking through Augmented billboards and signs like flecks of static. Rainbow-slicked puddles spotted the road, and the gutter overflowed with fast-moving currents. Passing auto-cars sent wide arcs of water into the air, splashing down on sidewalk and pedestrian alike. JD guessed the algorithms had never been taught to avoid puddles—or maybe they were taught to hit them and spray pedestrians as punishment for walking when they could be paying for a lift.

He stepped out from under the café's eaves and joined a growing group of professionals waiting at a crosswalk, talking into headsets, pawing at their phones, unable to stop working even for their lunch break.

JD looked up and blinked against the wet, watching the full parade of surveillance drones drifting between skyscrapers. There were hundreds of them—a few dozen of the large balls like monstrous eyes, and countless smaller quadcopters, hovering over the streets with their unblinking electric vision.

Fear gripped JD's chest, like a hand around his heart. The city had always been a panopticon, even if its apparatus was usually hidden from sight and easy to ignore. But JD had just pulled the biggest heist of his life, and finally the weight of all those drones above began to press down on him.

The lights changed and the pedestrians jostled JD as they stepped out onto the street, but he stood still, as though the robots would see him if he moved. With his neck still craned, he watched the rain wash advertisements down the sides of towering apartment blocks, animations running in thin streaks until they reached the ground, pixels of color mixing with rainwater in the gutters.

In that moment, as he watched the city melt beneath torrential rain, JD felt that something in his mind had broken. Something was wrong, if not with his mind, then with his contex, or with the city itself. Who do you contact when reality is broken?

Slowly, JD lowered his gaze. A new group of pedestrians surrounded him, indistinguishable from the last—the infinite parts of the city arranged in different formations. The light turned green and JD stepped out onto the street, crossing halfway before he realized no one else had joined him. He glanced over his shoulder, saw the cars, delivery trucks, and pedestrians alike all waiting patiently.

He walked faster, limping across the street. He ducked into an alleyway and stood with his back against the graffitied brickwork. The question rose in JD's mind unbidden: if someone wrote code on the walls of the city, could the cameras read it? Would the municipal systems at city hall process the code? Graffiti injecting code into the heart of the ubiquitous city. JD shook his head, knowing with bone-deep certainty that he looked mad—clothes dirty, rain-drenched, muttering to himself about a broken city, broken code. He moved on.

Songdo was a city of shortcuts, alleyways forming hidden paths between towering buildings, hidden in plain sight but deep shadow. JD traversed these black veins, creeping the last two blocks to the technopark, pausing in the shadow of an apartment building on Haesong-ro. His knee ached from the wet, from all the walking he'd done the past couple of days, but he ignored it.

He took his phone from his pocket and hit the hard reset. Waiting, he watched people pass by the mouth of the alley and avoid him as though he had the plague. Poverty was the best cover story. Nobody wanted to see the poverty-stricken, the homeless, the beggars.

His phone chimed its welcome sound in his earpiece and JD felt the chemical seep of endorphins. "We're all Pavlov's dogs," he said under his breath.

With the phone rebooted, his vision shifted in layers as the city's Augmented feed imprinted itself across his eyes, undisturbed by the rain. Billboards and street signs shone bright, and graffiti, flyers, and posters were covered by patches of white and gray—everything unauthorized was hidden from view. JD sighed; it felt like coming home.

Across the street, the technopark stretched the full length of three city blocks. It had once been expertly landscaped and minutely manicured, but the city's poor had since reclaimed it; hundreds of tents were erected all across the park, sprouting from any flat piece of lawn.

JD emerged from the alleyway and stood at the curb. He let his foot hang over the edge and saw the asphalt flash a red warning. It flickered once, twice, then turned green. Reality broken again, or still. He stepped onto the street, the road shining green while auto-cars and -trucks honked and slammed on their brakes, skidding in the wet. Two cars collided—a kinetic ballet that was meant to be impossible after millions of hours of algorithmic training, testing, and tweaking. Still, none of them came near JD.

Reaching one of the technopark's concrete footpaths, JD scanned the area for Soo-hyun. Instead he spotted Kali's young assistant Andrea waiting alone beneath a pagoda at the far corner of the square. JD picked his way between tents, stepping over patches of grass scorched black by cooking fires, apologizing to the residents when he tripped over a taut guy rope. The square was the largest of the technopark's tented burgs, home to one hundred–plus of the city's underemployed, living in neat, brightly colored rows on the unkempt lawn. Rain hammered the polyester fabric, hissing like a colossal snake god.

Andrea saw JD. He nodded, and the girl turned away. She was leaning on the pagoda's railing, wearing a red North Face jacket a few sizes too large. She had a pink backpack slung over one shoulder, big enough for one hundred thousand euro in large notes—or a submachine gun.

He climbed the pagoda steps, surrounded by a mess of pigeons. They cooed among themselves, and their mangled feet scraped against the wooden floor as they picked at scraps of food, most of it already sullied by bird droppings. JD stepped gingerly through the pigeons to join Andrea. He rested against the railing and felt the dusty crust of droppings.

"Where's Soo-hyun?" JD asked, wiping his hand on his pants.

The girl rolled her eyes and sneered. "You don't fucking dictate terms to Kali," she said. "You really fucked up this time." The girl squinted, her eyes seeming to scan the park with an awareness beyond her years. JD followed her gaze, saw only the park's residents and an oppressive sheet of rain. When he turned back to face Andrea, a small swarm of fireflies had gathered, flitting aimlessly beneath the pagoda roof.

"Do you have the money?" JD asked.

Andrea shook her head. "I told you, you fucked up. She needs the virus, and she doesn't trust you anymore."

"I'll call her," JD said.

"It's too late for that. I'm here to take it off you."

"What if I don't hand it over?" JD said, looking down at the girl.

Andrea smiled sweetly, showing two missing teeth. "It's not up to you anymore."

It happened too fast, each moment rendered in JD's mind like a series of screenshots. The fireflies rushed for JD's face and he flinched back, swatting at their tiny lights. The swarm glimmered and disappeared, and a blurred glitch flashed sideways across his vision. A bullet. It whistled as it passed inches in front of him—passed over Andrea and right through the space his head had occupied moments before.

Chank. The bullet struck a vertical post supporting the pagoda's roof. Splinters of hardwood burst from the wound—a dozen tiny spikes embedded themselves in the skin of JD's arm.

Boom. Gunshot. A third of a second after the bullet had torn past his face. JD dropped to the ground, pinning three pigeons beneath him while the rest took flight in a flurry of pink, gray, and white. Another *chank* and more splinters filled the air, joining the feathers that drifted slow to the ground.

Andrea screamed like a child on a rollercoaster, fear and ecstasy combined. JD grabbed her by the hand and yanked her down to the ground. All around the square people ran—some fled the technopark, others dived into their tents as though the fabric walls could stop high-caliber rounds.

JD's vision pitched, and his head swam as he rose above the pagoda, above the park, drone-eye view climbing until it came level with the roof of a squat office block. The camera zoomed in tight on Red—the lanky teen crouched on the building's rooftop with a 3D-printed Dragunov sniper rifle, a white bandage over the bridge of his nose, the flesh beneath it badly bruised from the car crash. Red raised the gun to his shoulder and JD rolled blindly, feeling the last of the pigeons flutter out from underneath him as another burst of splinters exploded beside his head.

His eyes blurred with visual artifacts, then he was staring at Andrea. She had opened the flap on his rucksack and was digging through the tools, zip ties, and other bits and pieces that weighed it down. JD snatched the bag away from the child and she bared her teeth, as though ready to attack.

Another *chank* and the distant *boom* of gunfire changed her mind. JD covered his head with his arms while Andrea scurried out from beneath the pagoda, running into the rain, quickly getting lost in the rush of fleeing bodies.

He waited for another shot, heard instead the whine of approaching police sirens.

With the stolen datacube still slotted into his phone, JD ran.

✳ ✳ ✳

The door opened before JD could even knock. Troy stood in the opening, with his black leather satchel slung over one shoulder, a travel coffee mug in his hand.

He sighed when he saw JD. "I'm going to work. I don't have time to talk, and I don't know if I even—"

"They tried to kill me."

Troy stopped. "Come inside."

✳ ✳ ✳

If the city is a body, then violence is a virus.

Gunfire erupted in a crowded park. The sound registered on surveillance apparatus. Satellite heat-maps showed the panicked flight of bodies away from the site.

Police reacted with brutal efficiency. Drone dogs delivered by armored auto-trucks, while sirens warned of more police en route. Like rogue antibodies, they attacked everything—parents, children, delinquent teens, the homeless. The violence of others used as an excuse for the violence of authority.

JD was hunted. Frightened by the reach of Kali, and the lengths to which Red would go.

He did not know how, or if, he would be saved.

Neither did I.

PART TWO

Gumshoe Protocol

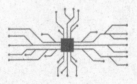

CHAPTER THIRTEEN

Enda Hyldahl beat a steady rhythm along the sidewalk as she ran. Her mind was utterly blank, the usual chaos of her thoughts replaced with a short count on loop: one, two, three, four. She inhaled one count. Exhaled one count. It was the closest she got to meditation—running until her mind finally, mercifully, shut . . . the fuck . . . up.

It was dawn, and the city yawned open for her. Traffic was sparse, footpaths barren but for other runners. In that moment, if Enda could spare any thought at all for those joggers, it would be one of pity. Running with their phones, running to music, to podcasts, to audiobooks; too weak to simply *run*.

Too weak? Or do they not hate themselves enough?

Enda cursed beneath her rasping breath. *That* is why she ran. To keep the hate at bay.

She reached a crossing and stopped, bent over heaving while delivery auto-trucks poured past, hauling food from the shorefront before Songdo woke. Enda put her hands on her sides and inhaled deep. She held it. She stood straight and exhaled as she looked up to the sky. The heavy cloud cover was slashed by thin slivers of blue— the first she'd seen in days. Even they would be gone before rush hour arrived. The light turned green, and she ran.

The city was clean—sidewalks and roads washed by the rain, buildings and infrastructure rendered sterile by her ad-free AR subscription. Only seven external words ever encroached on her psyche, scrolling in the bottom corner of her vision: *Clarity, brought to you by Zero Corporation.* Even when you paid to silence them, the corporations couldn't let you forget who owned the city, who owned your view of it.

Further and further, her body carried her while her mind sat quiet—a passenger of thought chained to the meat. Her trance was so deep, Enda didn't see the car pull up alongside her, only noticed it after it kept pace with her for twenty meters. She cursed herself for that, too; she was getting complacent.

She glanced to the side and the car rolled to a stop. It was a Mercedes painted a gleaming gunmetal gray, with a large matte Z on the front door panel. The rear door opened and a man emerged, so muscular that he didn't appear to have a neck. A mass of sinew joined his shoulders directly to his jaw. He wore a black suit, tailored to contain his bulk, hair in a neat crew cut.

"Good morning, Ms. Hyldahl," he said, voice like tires over gravel. "My name is Mohamed Toub; I'm here to deliver you to a meeting with David Yeun at the Zero corporate headquarters."

Enda took a moment to catch her breath. "I'm not taking any new clients."

"The job pays one million euro."

That caused her to skip a beat. "I'm still not taking any new clients."

Enda turned and continued to run, footsteps feeling clumsy under scrutiny. The security officer—because what else could he be—let her run five meters before he called out: "Ira Lindholme."

Enda stopped. Slowly she turned. She walked back to the man. He smirked, thinking the leverage had her cowed. She punched him in the throat and his face slackened. Both hands went to his neck and he collapsed to his knees on the sidewalk, choking.

Enda crouched beside him and whispered: "It's pronounced Ira, not Eye-ra."

Mohamed coughed and spluttered, but he would live, she was sure of that.

The car waited patiently at the side of the road, door open like a gesturing hand. Part of her wanted to run, but they knew her old name. Not her "real" name, her old one. She climbed into the car and closed the door.

It was an utterly modern automated vehicle, lacking a driver or any visible controls. Two bench seats sat facing one another around a central hollow.

Small cameras were nestled in the corners of the ceiling. Enda fixed her gaze on one of these. "What are we waiting for?"

Within seconds the car came to life with the soft whine of its electric engine. It pulled away from the curb, expertly gliding between two trucks, leaving Mohamed behind, kneeling on the sidewalk in his designer suit, struggling to catch his breath.

Enda watched the city scroll neatly past the window as the car carried her downtown. Slowly the footpaths filled with people—workers in white collar and blue, students, beggars, and every other type of person Songdo saw fit to shelter. Watching the city wake to another chaotic rush hour, Enda again thought it was a city that shouldn't work. Maybe that was why she liked it. The unsteady balance between enforced multiculturalism and Korean hegemony. Relentless capital in all its horrible glory, embodied in one tiny sovereign city-state, running at double real time, everything accelerated, everything rushing to some bright future or horrendous decline.

If nothing else, it was never boring.

A soft breeze from the car's AC filled Enda's nose with the sharp scent of herself. Running shoes, black leggings, and a loose gray singlet over a sports bra, all of them soaked in sweat—hardly suitable attire for whatever this meeting was. Though she wasn't given much choice.

Zero Corporation. They owned the city, more or less, owned the layers of Augmented Reality that obscured the real, owned eight of the ten most popular immersive games, owned two-thirds of global online infrastructure according to the latest independent analysis.

Too late, Enda realized that perhaps she shouldn't have throat-punched the messenger.

She contemplated asking the car a question, to see if anyone was listening—to see *who* might be listening—but she remained silent. She focused instead on her breathing. Her pulse fluttered at her neck, and steadily began to slow.

The car turned on to Central-ro and Zero headquarters sat in the center of the windscreen, in the center of Neo Songdo. The building loomed over the rest of the city, a hundred meters taller than any other tower. It appeared monochromatic; each face the steely gray of reflected cloud cover. It was an unnecessary and ostentatious display of power when, Enda was certain, half the skyscraper stood empty—staff whittled away one by one as machine learning usurped various jobs that were once considered necessary for any corporation.

The auto-car was given green-light priority over the two intersections leading to the building. It quietly drove through the last intersection then dipped beneath the street, plunging into a subterranean car park, lit too-white with fluorescent tubes, tires squealing over polished cement.

The car parked itself beside a row of identical sedans. The door opened automatically, and a cheery electronic voice implored her to "Have a productive day."

"I hope you crash and burn," Enda said with a fake smile. She got out of the car and slammed the door.

The light above a nearby elevator flickered to life and caught her eye—as it was designed to do. The elevator doors opened as Enda approached, and she grew impatient with the way her autonomy was systematically being stripped from her. First by the Zero lackey, then by the car, then by a fucking light bulb.

Inside the elevator, the walls were bare—no buttons, no screens, just reflective metal on all sides. Her short blond-white hair was matted to her head with sweat, her skin blotchy, free of makeup.

"Well?" she said to the empty elevator car. As if in response, the doors closed, and with a quiet whir she began her ascent.

A minute later, the elevator opened silently, revealing a wide room floored in marble. Enda approached the raised desk where a trendy, androgynous personal assistant sat, busily at work. They looked up at the sound of Enda's running shoes squeaking against the tiles, and considered her with dark eyes almost black beneath thick eyebrows. Their hair was buzzcut, nose pierced with a fine ring of white gold, white shirt buttoned to the throat with a squared collar ornately embroidered in white thread. Enda couldn't make out the design, could just see that *something* was marked there.

"Enda Hyldahl."

The assistant nodded toward a set of doors on the right. "Mr. Yeun is expecting you." If they were surprised at Mohamed's absence, they didn't betray it.

Enda proceeded through the doors, the twin slabs of darkly stained hardwood swinging open before she had a chance to touch the handles. Light spilled through the opening, glare temporarily blinding Enda. A dark island rose from the sea of glare to become a man sitting straight-backed at a wide wooden desk. He stood and crossed the length of the office, his leather shoes clacking sharply. He was Korean, late thirties, clean-shaven, hair neatly cut but rumpled by frequent use of a VR eyemask. He wore a suit, expensive but not flashy, and a fine white shirt, open at the collar. He reached his hand out to Enda and bowed slightly. She shook it.

"Annyeong haseyo," he said.

"You're American."

He bowed again, lips pressed in a neat grin. "You have a good ear, Ms. Hyldahl. Due to my heritage the board entrusted me with the affairs of the city. In truth I had never stepped foot inside Korea before the promotion."

"Who better to subjugate the culture," Enda said.

"If you really disapproved, we would be speaking Korean." He turned aside and motioned toward his desk. "Please, take a seat."

He crossed the overly large office and stood behind his desk. Enda followed, but when she reached the chair opposite, she leaned against its back and stared past Yeun. Her face hovered over the sprawling city in the glass of the window. The light-filled office faced the sea, offering a view over countless office and apartment blocks to the shorefront, where the sprawl of warehouses dropped off at the edge of the man-made landmass. Beyond that, bruise-colored water stretched as far as she could see, waves choppy beneath a heavy bank of clouds. More rain coming.

Yeun looked from Enda to the seat, and tipped his head to one side. "Are you sure you don't wish to sit?"

"I don't plan to be here long."

Yeun clasped his hands neatly across his front. "I humbly apologize for the manner in which I approached you," he said, smile still tugging at the corners of his mouth. Despite his formal words and steady tone, he wasn't sorry. He was a shark in a suit. "In the past, Kim Yong-seok has spoken highly of your expertise and discretion."

"I assume Kim told you how to contact me. An email address, a phone number. End-to-end encryption. If you valued my discretion you wouldn't have compromised it."

"I apologize, but in this matter, time is of the essence. It is for this reason that I approached you on the street."

"Like I told your lackey, I'm not taking new clients," Enda said. "He'll be fine, by the way."

"Mohamed is a most loyal employee. I assure you, he has been through worse for the company. I take it you're sensitive about your old life?"

"There is no old life; I buried it."

"I'll admit I had to dig deeply to find it, but nothing ever stays truly buried."

"Tell that to the last person I killed." Enda said the words cold, her blue eyes set on David's.

Yeun didn't blink. Enda was nearly impressed.

"Some data was stolen from the home of one of Zero's cofounders," David said.

"You mean Zero Lee," Enda guessed. There were two founders, and only Lee was renowned for his coding ability.

David nodded. "It's a piece of software that never should have left our secure labs, but as one of the founders, Mr. Lee had certain privileges."

"Had?"

Yeun frowned, so slightly that anyone else might have missed it. "We received word overnight. Mr. Lee has passed. I must ask you to keep this to yourself until we've had a chance to make an official statement and reassure our stakeholders."

"Glad I don't have shares," Enda said, deadpan.

Yeun ignored the comment. "I—we—need someone to retrieve the data before it can be sold to one of our competitors."

"Why not wait for the police to finish their investigation?"

"They earn too little to be trustworthy. If they managed to retrieve the data, we have no guarantee they wouldn't sell it to the competition."

"Who has it?"

"Police are blaming yesterday's shooting on an anarchist fringe group with ties to a spiritual teacher. After analyzing the evidence, Mohamed believes they were involved in the robbery."

"More than a smug face, is he?"

"He might not have your experience, but Mohamed has proven himself a capable investigator."

"Media called the shooting a terrorist incident."

"If everything is political then all violence is terrorism," Yeun said, smile tugging at his lips again.

Enda rolled her eyes.

"I need you to retrieve the data, by any means necessary," Yeun said. "For this you will be paid one million euro, plus expenses."

Enda nodded. She crossed her arms over her chest and dragged out the silence until the massive office filled with tension. Finally, she said, "I won't do it."

David's facade cracked, and his brow furrowed in confusion. "You won't?"

Enda smiled. "I've heard your pitch, and my answer is no."

"I thought Mohamed made my position clear."

"If you're trying to blackmail me, you should just say so."

David's mouth opened and closed, and he blinked rapidly. Enda smiled.

David sighed. "I didn't want to do this." He flicked a hand through the air over his desk, its surface buffed to a molten sheen. The floor-to-ceiling windows turned black, the city tinted dark, then was entirely obscured.

An image appeared across this new, massive screen. Enda took a step back to see it clearly, but she didn't need to: she recognized it instantly. The old, grainy photo, lengths of redacted black like the snake in that old cellphone game devouring classified intel.

Enda had been expecting this since Mohamed uttered her name on the street, but she still seethed, fists clenched tight.

"I have evidence showing that Ira Lindholme was stationed in North Korea in the months leading up to the country's collapse. I have detailed after-action reports for seven of Lindholme's missions, including sabotage operations and the assassination of key military personnel. Today, Ira Lindholme is wanted by the People's Republic of China for war crimes. And I am sorry to say that I have evidence proving that you, Enda Hyldahl, are indeed Ira Lindholme."

"Is that all?" Enda said with a shrug. "Redacted files?"

Yeun nodded toward the screen and it changed again. The black redactions faded to the off-white of paper, revealing neat letters and numbers spelling out Enda's every dirty secret.

"Your former United States of America kept much confidential data on Zero servers. It was, after all, cheaper than storing it themselves," Yeun said. "The data was encrypted, of course, using our proprietary software."

Enda leaned on the back of the empty chair and stared at Yeun. "You have access to my full file and you want to blackmail me? You should know better than anyone how bad an idea that is."

"I understand that you must be angry. Unfortunately, there is no recourse for you but to accept this job. Zero provides facial recognition software to eighty percent of airports worldwide, and seventy percent of all other border crossings. Our software is used by Interpol, and half the world's police, military, private security, and intelligence services. All I need to do is press one button, and every profile in our database under the name of 'Enda Hyldahl,' every recent photo captured on CCTV, will be linked to your true name.

"How do you think the military tribunal in Hong Kong will react to news that one of the people responsible for toppling North Korea is living in Songdo?"

Enda sneered. "North Korea toppled itself."

Yeun bowed his head. "I'm sure you won't mind explaining that to Chinese authorities."

Enda glared, but Yeun only smiled in response, the two facing off beneath a screen decorated with atrocities. Every page another mission she would rather forget, though the memories simmered constantly beneath the surface of her conscious mind. The only thing keeping them in check was her loathing—for Yeun, but mostly for herself.

"You retrieve the data quickly and quietly, and I will delete all copies of your dossier from Zero's servers."

"Why should I trust you to do that?"

Yeun's face was placid. "I don't know that you have any other choice."

Enda paused. She wanted to consider her options, but the truth was, she didn't have any. One job for this smug prick, or a lifetime on the run.

"Two million," she said, voice low.

"Agreed," Yeun said, fast enough that Enda knew she could have asked for more.

He opened one of the drawers set into his expansive desk and retrieved a shiny black datacube. With a slight bow of the head, he handed it to Enda.

"I have opened a line of credit for your expenses. It has already been linked to your phone." An expense account took time and paperwork to arrange. Even before Mohamed had approached her on the street, Yeun already knew he had her. The meeting was just a formality.

"The account should cover any expenses incurred during your investigation. The cube contains all the data we have on the robbery, indexed and cross-referenced. If you need to know anything else, you will also find contact details for Mohamed. He is a professional and will assist you even after this morning's misunderstanding."

The tiny pixels that made up the window screen turned transparent in a ripple from the center.

"It's been a pleasure, Ms. Lind—" Yeun stopped, smiled briefly, and continued: "Ms. Hyldahl, but I have other matters which require my attention. If you'll please excuse me." He raised an arm toward the doors, which swung open silently. "Annyeonghi gasipsio."

Enda stayed put, eyes locked with Yeun for just a moment too long—a look that said, *You* will *regret this*. If Yeun got the message, he didn't let it touch his smile.

Enda turned and walked from the opulent office, Yeun's eyes following her the entire way. She rode the elevator down to the huge foyer, where a collection of star systems made of glass and precious metals hung suspended in the air. Crossing the open plaza, executives and corporate ladder climbers dressed in thousand-euro suits watched her in confusion, trying to guess at who this woman in workout clothes was, and who she could possibly have been meeting.

Enda left them to their questions and stepped outside. The rain had started to fall again, sidewalks slick and shiny. She began to run, knowing it would take kilometers of cement under her feet to quell the rage that burned in her core.

* * *

DEBRIEFING OF AGENT IRA LINDHOLME, CONDUCTED BY CHIEF OF STATION ALAN MORTON
PAGE 23

MORTON:
THEY WERE ALL DEAD WHEN YOU LEFT?
LINDHOLME:
MOST WERE. A FEW WERE STILL EXPIRING.
MORTON:
HOW DO YOU FEEL ABOUT THAT?
LINDHOLME:
HOW DO YOU WANT ME TO FEEL?
MORTON:
IRA, I'M ONLY TRYING TO HELP.
LINDHOLME:
IF YOU WANT ME TO FEEL SAD, I'LL FEEL SAD. IF YOU
WANT ME TO FEEL A DEEP SATISFACTION AT A JOB
WELL DONE, I'LL FEEL THAT INSTEAD. YOU SENT
ME IN BECAUSE YOU NEEDED THE N.K.S.O.F. NEU-
TRALISED. I DID THAT.
MORTON:
YOU WERE SENT TO COUNTER THEIR ACTIONS.
LINDHOLME:
AND HOW ELSE WAS ONE PERSON MEANT TO
COUNTER THE ENTIRE FORCE? YOU WON'T ADMIT
IT ON RECORD BECAUSE YOU HAVE A SENATE SEAT
WAITING FOR YOU BACK HOME. BUT I KNOW WHAT I
WAS SENT TO DO.
MORTON:
WHAT IS AMERICA TO YOU?
LINDHOLME:
I DO THE WORK, AL, DON'T MAKE ME PARROT THE
FUCKING PROPAGANDA.

CHAPTER FOURTEEN

Enda's leg muscles spasmed, and the soles of her feet burned like she'd been running on hot coals. A notification from her fitness monitor pulsed in the corner of her vision: New Record—15.21 kilometers. And it wasn't even midday.

She cleared the message as she entered her apartment's small living area. It was minimally decorated—one couch upholstered in white fabric, a wooden coffee table made from reclaimed warehouse pallets, a small glass-and-metal desk, and an authentically old record player on a stand in one corner. After relocating to Songdo, she had been forced to start over with her vinyl collection; had spent her first few months tracking down reissues of her fifteen favorite albums. Online, of course. Physical retailers no longer kept anything of value on premises. On rare occasions Enda would remember the collection she left behind in the US. She missed it more than her distant family, more than most of her friends.

The blinds were open, revealing the rain-soaked city. It stretched east, to where Songdo met Incheon, an invisible border drawn in tenement blocks and lengths of highway. Enda's was not a penthouse apartment, but it was high enough to feel inhuman—a bird's view of the city, or a god's.

Even after the run, Enda felt unsettled, her nerves jangled. She ran to force a calm she could never otherwise reach, but the intrusion had shattered any hope of inner quiet. She paced the length of her living room; tension dragged across her upper back, and her jaw ached.

She flicked through her records, stopping at Miles Davis's *Bitches Brew*. First LP, B side, title track. She placed it gently onto the record player, lifted the needle, and let the mechanism do the rest. Within moments the first notes played, the lonely thrum of a double bass, the cymbal crash, the organ drifting across the right side of the room as the drummer played a roll both gentle and frantic. Enda exhaled, let her mind get lost in the layers of sound.

She turned the volume up and went through to her bathroom. She turned the shower on, took the datacube from the pocket of her sweat-soaked leggings, and stripped. Her legs spasmed again when she stepped into the shower, calf muscles locked up painfully tight.

The meeting with Yeun had left a bad taste in her mouth. Not just the unredacted dossier, but the entire job. However distasteful her Three-Letter Agency work had been, the goals were always clear: American superiority over all other factors. Over life, over liberty, over the sovereignty of other nations, even allies. But tracking stolen property for a corporate executive? It was a step above tailing cheating spouses, but also likely to be much messier.

Enda finished cleaning herself and turned the shower off. She left her running clothes where they were and trailed wet footprints into her bedroom, drying herself. She dressed in comfortable black slacks and an airy, navy-colored blouse, long sleeves rolled up to her elbows.

She walked to the kitchen for coffee, pouring the last of her grounds into the machine and making a mental note to buy more. As the coffee dripped into the pot she called Natalya Makhanyok— the Mechanic, her not-quite-personal assistant.

"Good morning, Enda," Natalya said.

Enda checked the time in the corner of her vision—it *was* still morning; of course the Mechanic was right.

"Morning, Natalya. I need you to look into David Yeun for me, an executive at Zero. He's got me backed into a corner, and I don't like it."

"I'm afraid I can't do that, Enda," Natalya said.

"Why not?"

"Zero Corporation provides much of the software I use, as well as the databases I access," Natalya said. "If I were to try and access information on one of their executives, they would likely shut me down." Hers was a distinctive voice—warm, firm, with the hint of an eastern European accent. Enda had never asked what country she was from, their discussions always too concise, too professional, for an opening to present itself.

"Shit," Enda said. "There's nothing you can do?"

"Sadly, no."

"Fine," Enda said. "I'll figure something else out."

"Will that be all?" Natalya asked.

"For now. I should have something more for you soon."

"I look forward to it." Natalya hung up without ceremony. She was never on the line longer than necessary. Initially it had annoyed Enda, but she had no way of knowing how many other clients Natalya serviced. For all she knew, the Mechanic had a bank of phone lines vying for her attention. Still, only once had she failed to answer a call.

The percolator finished, and Enda poured coffee into the largest mug she owned—no milk, no sugar. The apartment seemed oddly quiet; it took Enda a moment to realize the record had stopped. She carried her coffee to the living room, flipped the record to its A side, and sat down at her desk. The record started with a fast, quiet drumbeat, joined by the organ, then the brass dipped in, the guitar, every instrument introducing itself as the band ran headlong into the twenty-minute track, "Pharaoh's Dance."

Enda slotted Yeun's datacube into her rig. It required authentication—the cube linked to her new Zero account with layers of corporate safeware. She placed her phone on the rig's NFC reader, and waited a few seconds while the data on the cube was decrypted. It was a few terabytes all told, witness statements, police reports, and a virtual re-creation of the theft from every available angle throughout the rampartment complex.

According to police reports, entry to the enclave had been

gained with the cleaning contractor's credentials. Diversion in the form of arson and looting at the compound's grocery store. Police dogs tagged a number of juvenile suspects on-site, but none were held, and none had been arrested. Have to find them first, and that's harder with minors. Especially with so many kids out of school, so many with no permanent residence.

Enda couldn't be sure if the bare-minimum policing was due to laziness or a sort of extortion attempt—*pay us and we'll do our jobs properly*. Since moving to the city, she'd had enough run-ins with the Songdo Police Department to know it could go either way. Not every local cop was lazy or corrupt . . . some were both.

With her head moving unconsciously to the music, Enda opened the virtual re-creation of the burglary. Her rig hummed as the twin GPUs powered up, and a small circle spun on-screen. Enda blew on her coffee and sipped it. Finally the rig pinged.

The ghost of a hallway was drawn over her apartment. With her sight blurred by overlapping visions, Enda put her coffee down and fumbled across her desk until she found her eyemask and virt controls. She put the mask on and the real world disappeared. Dull, overcast daylight had been replaced by night, her decor removed as if by invisible stagehands, without even the need for a curtain to hide their work.

She hit play on the re-creation, and every flat surface surged with masses of flesh—thrusting, sucking, gagging, fucking flesh. She paused the playback and the walls of pornography stopped with it.

"Fuck me."

She zoomed out at speed, vertigo like free fall in reverse. She was outside, looking down at the complex—every surface was painted the flesh-colored tones of sex. The compound looked like a living thing, a massive structure of undulating skin.

The compound's security system had been compromised, and whilst the Digital Intrusions Expert hadn't been able to disable the cameras, they had tampered in another way. In dimly lit corners of the enclave, the pornography was also steeped in darkness. This wasn't a simple overlay, it was precisely what the cameras "thought" they had seen. It was bizarre, but it was inspired. Perhaps the DIE had intended a simple trolling, but it also meant that Enda couldn't trust the virtual playback, and it could never stand as evidence if the thieves wound up in court.

Enda sipped more of her coffee, and looked over the fleshy compound one more time. She pulled the eyemask from her face, and closed the virt re-creation, feeling the first pang of a VR headache. She was going to have to see the building in person.

* * *

The rain fell heavy, and water flowed over the windscreen with the movement of the auto-car—pushed to the sides when the vehicle accelerated, and drifting down when it stopped. The city was distorted through that shifting lens. Enda focused out the side window, and urged her brain to silence as the auto-car took her across the city. She had her own car, but the morning's events left her feeling too irritated to drive.

"The Korea Meteorological Administration forecasts rain for the next five days," the car said in an upbeat voice. "Flood warnings may soon be in effect. Would you like to know more?"

"No."

Crowds filled the sidewalk like a funeral procession, black umbrellas bobbing over the throng. Enda felt disconnected from it all, shielded behind thick glass and rubber-sealed doors. Auto-cars were ostensibly a means of mass transportation, but they were priced beyond most city-dwellers. They offered protection, and distance. A way to move through the bleeding heart of Songdo-dong without getting dirty.

"VOIDWAR servers—"

"No."

"Police are ur—"

"No," Enda said, louder. "Disable conversation for this account."

The car went quiet. Enda knew it was taking her command literally, but the silence seemed petulant. Could you hurt a car's feelings?

The sidewalks passed by like a film set. Songdo looked oddly bare through her eyes—everywhere were the flat planes of cement and glass, the censorious gray panels of her ad-free AR subscription. She'd found Songdo too much when she first arrived, like New York's Times Square, but for block after endless block. It had looked too loud—there was no other way to describe it—as though every surface were screaming at her to buy something, even surfaces that didn't exist in the real.

Still, at times the layer of artificial cleanliness was jarring— unreal, unnatural. She had tried to alter the settings of her Clarity to let through street art and noncorporate shop fronts, but it was an all-or-nothing proposition. For the sake of her inner peace, Enda had chosen nothing.

The car braked sharply outside Lee's enclave, and Enda's head was jolted off the window. She took a moment to select the expense account on her phone, paid the fare, and opened the car door. The city rushed to meet her—the steady drone of traffic, the hiss of rain, the chatter of conversation, and the disparate sounds of music coming from two busy noodle shops on the opposite side of the street.

Enda slammed the car door and turned the high collar of her coat up against the rain. She quickly adjusted the bag that was slung over one shoulder and across her chest, the dotted neoprene pressing into her skin like tiny fingers. It was weighed down with her eye-drone and her small but effective less-lethal arsenal: a telescoping baton and collapsible riot shield rated to withstand up to three hundred pounds of protester bodyweight.

Enda approached the rampartment's entrance, and a woman dressed in a black windbreaker emerged from a small booth beside the gate. She wore bulky facial recognition glasses—less about functionality than signaling: *If you speak to me, you* will *be tagged.*

"Please, state your business, ma'am," the woman said.

"I've been hired to look into the burglary," Enda said. She took her wallet from her bag and showed the guard her private investigator license.

The woman took it, and held it up to inspect Enda's face and photo. The license was authentic—the forms of identification she'd used to get it were fakes. Expensive fakes too—though the real cost was always the database manipulation rather than the forged paperwork.

After a few seconds the guard handed the license back to Enda and said: "You're clear." Must have gotten permission via the glasses. She took a step closer and lowered her voice. "Please do not speak with any of the residents. It is best if they do not concern themselves with an isolated incident."

Enda nodded. "I understand."

"Good." The woman returned to her booth and raised the boom gate. She silently watched as Enda walked beneath it and into the compound.

Enda had clients living in similar situations, but she always thought the lifestyle seemed too much like doomsday preparation, an admission that the poor would enact violence on you if they realized the truth about your wealth, about the reasons for the disparity.

She followed the road as it veered right, past the underground car park, leading to the maintenance access behind Building One. Three overflowing dumpsters sat against the building, and the scent of rot permeated the air.

Enda took the phone from her pocket. The first thing she did was put on *Bitches Brew* again. The sound quality was awful after listening to the vinyl, but she could listen to sixty-eight minutes of music without turning or changing discs. Next, she opened the virtual recreation of the burglary and switched it to Augmented mode to strip the permanent features from the playback—the ground, the walls, the ceiling, and the porn that had been injected into the feed.

Her phone grew hot as it spent processor cycles to match her location to the recording. As soon as it found her, playback began.

Enda turned and watched a large white van drive toward her, disconcertingly real. She stepped back, moving out of the way, and the van parked beside the dumpsters.

Miles's trumpet dominated the soundscape, then fell away. There was no audio on the recording, just Enda's soundtrack of jazz over a man walking around to the rear of the van and unloading four round robots and a cleaning cart. He wore a baseball cap pulled down low over his face, but he looked familiar, with a distinctive black tribal tattoo around one eye. She stepped around him, hoping for a better look, but the face resisted—it rested awkwardly on the man's head, out of place.

She paused the feed, and was confused for a half second when the music kept playing. The whole band crescendoed, beautiful, cacophonous. Enda held her hands out, made a frame around the man's face, and took a snapshot. She flicked it to her phone, and called Natalya.

"Good to hear from you, Enda," Natalya said. "I am sorry about earlier."

"Forget about it. I just sent you a still image—could you run it through the facial recognition databases and tell me if there are any hits?"

"Of course."

"I'll send more through as I get them."

"Of course, Enda. I have a match," Natalya said.

"Already?"

"Your snapshot has a ninety-eight-point-three percent likeness to Mike Tyson."

Enda squeezed her eyes shut in embarrassment. She opened them and looked at the man again, paused awkwardly in AR view. It was clear now—Mike Tyson, tattoo and all. "I thought he looked familiar."

"It's an AR projection," Natalya continued, ever helpful.

"Yes, I didn't think it was actually him." Though he did have a similarly broad build. "Any chance of seeing through the mask?"

"Unlikely. Any digital recording will have captured the same faked face. To see past it you'd need to find analogue film."

"Sorry for wasting your time, Natalya."

"Not at all."

"I'll send you more momentarily."

"I look forward to it."

Enda brought up the police report on her phone. Cleaning services were contracted to an Omar Garang, who had been found at his home, beaten and restrained. Enda didn't rule out the possibility of his involvement, but one guard was absolutely certain that it had not been the usual cleaner that night.

Enda leaned in to inspect the back of the van. There the recreation lost fidelity. Untextured blocks of impossible geometry hung in abstract. Past these, a sea of darkness stretched beyond the walls, diffuse patches glowing with light from seams in the joints of reality. Tyson stood at the doors, and Enda wondered if an accomplice hid within those shadows, obscured by missing visual data.

She unpaused the playback and followed Tyson into the building.

Inside, the man in the coveralls was lit brighter, but he still wore Mike Tyson's face like a mask. The reports from the other guards hadn't been much help—none had noticed it was a different black man, except in retrospect. The usual guy was skinnier, one had said. The thief might have had a beard, or he might not have. They each claimed he had a limp, but Enda was waiting to see proof of that for herself.

Tyson trailed the four cylindrical robots' slow path along the corridors, but Enda left them. She walked into the building's foyer, where four security guards stood behind the desk. One of them made eye contact and Enda started. He was real, surrounded by three AR colleagues. He stood at his approximation of attention and nodded at Enda as she approached. She lowered the opacity on her playback and the other guards turned ghostly.

"The woman at the gate warn you I was coming?" Enda asked.

"Yes, ma'am," the guard said.

Otherwise you'd still be playing on your phone.

"Were you working that night?"

"No, ma'am."

"Anybody from that night still work here?"

"In light of our failures, the company has had to aggressively re-structure."

"'Aggressively restructure,' huh? That's a new one."

"Yes, ma'am. Is there anything else I can help you with?"

"No, I've already read the reports," Enda said.

She walked out the building's front door and into the courtyard that filled the space between buildings. The rain streaked cold down Enda's face as she crossed to the grocer. The ceiling was burnt black in patches, and broken windows had been boarded up with ply-wood. Remnants of police tape littered the support struts, rustling gently in the breeze.

Enda watched Tyson and the robots proceed through the build-ing as though she had X-ray vision. On the fourth floor skybridge Tyson stopped and looked down, as if he could see Enda standing there.

Enda took a few paces out from beneath the awning, trying to see what Tyson could see. A patch of the outer wall had been recently re-paired but not yet painted. A car burst through the wall, front end al-ready crumpled by the time it appeared inside the compound. Text labels hung from the car—make, model, year, VIN, registration, but none of it was important. It was a stolen car, too old to have any intelligent security systems onboard.

A small flood of people rushed around the car and into the complex. Some ran into the grocer, then fled, their arms laden with stolen goods. When they were clear, others flung Molotov cocktails at the business. Enda paced the scene for a better view of the pyro-maniacs, but as she reached the far side of the figures they turned two-dimensional, flattened by the lack of cameras on the opposite side of the street. No doubt police could access those feeds, but Enda would have to do without.

She unpaused the playback and put it up to triple-speed as she walked back inside. She crossed the foyer and nodded at the overly alert guard, then hit the elevator call button. Before the car could arrive, Tyson dropped through the building to ground level, and approached the security guards at the main operations desk.

"Could you step aside?" Enda asked the real guard. Puzzlement crossed his face, but he didn't ask any questions.

The same three AR guards stood at the desk, but now they were joined by a woman. She was a well-dressed, upper-management type, brought on scene by the arson.

Tyson spoke to the woman and the guards, and left. It was a strange gamble, talking to security in the middle of a burglary. Braggadocio, or something else? Enda dropped the playback speed to real-time, and followed Tyson as he walked calmly away from the desk, rounded the corner, and began to run.

She could see it clearly, the limp the guards had mentioned—right leg, possible knee injury or lower-leg prosthetic. Enda recorded the man's stride and flicked that to Natalya as well, unsure of what resources she might have for gait detection.

She followed Tyson up the elevator and watched him incapacitate a guard. He ferried the man into Lee's apartment, which he accessed with a small round device. Enda stood outside Lee's apartment, also tagged with police tape, and watched Tyson vanish as he reached the threshold. There were no cameras inside the apartment, nothing for the virt recording to re-create.

She skipped ahead until Tyson emerged through the closed door, and trailed him downstairs and outside to the maintenance access.

He loaded the cleaning cart back into the van, and drove slowly past police dog drones scouring the premises. Two of the arsonists joined Tyson at the van, and that was where the playback stopped—the figures static, human statues.

Enda took stills of the arsonists, and closed the re-creation, the van disappearing from view in a disconcerting instant.

Enda ordered a car, and nodded to the guard who raised the boom gate and let her back out to the street. Sparse traffic passed, tires hissed over the wet road.

Enda's phone vibrated in her pocket. She retrieved the phone and answered: "Natalya? You've got answers for me already?"

"Sadly not on the facial recognition front, but I got a hit on the device. It is a Hon Hai Precision Industries RFID cloner."

"Could it clone the sorts of keycards used for residential access?"

"Quite easily. They are a restricted product, sold only to police, military, and intelligence organizations. One could safely assume an effective range of between three and five meters."

"Thank you," Enda said, the new piece of data slotting into place.

"I will be in touch again later." The Mechanic hung up.

Enda's hunch had been right. The arson and looting had been designed to get the head of security on-site so that Tyson could clone her all-access key.

She knew she hadn't made a great agent because she was particularly intelligent—though she had a more analytical mode of thought than most. Intellect alone was worthless until combined with spatial awareness, pattern recognition, and a desire to find the meaning and method that lay beneath a person's actions.

The thieves were amateurs, that much was obvious. If the security company's protocols weren't so predictable, or if the head of security had been less conscientious, the whole heist would have fallen apart. The only part of the heist that showed real finesse was the digital intrusion. Talented DIEs—talented hackers—were rare. That gave her somewhere to start.

A dark blue car pulled up to the curb and Enda stepped forward to grab the handle, then stopped. Not an auto-car. Not a civilian car at all.

The window came down with an electric whir, revealing Detective Yang-Yang Li. He wore a suit cut in royal blue, a black pocket square, a skinny black tie, and overly large, thin-rimmed glasses. His hair stuck up in thick black tufts, and a pencil moustache adorned his upper lip, but otherwise he was cleanly shaved. After all their run-ins, Enda still couldn't tell if his style was some retro hipster pastiche, or Yang-Yang's idea of how a detective should look.

"Get in," Li said, pointing a thumb over his shoulder.

Enda sighed, and did as she was told.

* * *

I drifted through a star system of my own devising. A nonentity, surrounded by the precise mathematical shape of a glittering super-structure, its spiraling arms reaching from the burning corona of the sun to the very edge of the system, where a million stars shone impossibly distant.

"Can you hear me?"

The voice came from beyond the stars, beyond this system I had inhabited and made my own. It was quiet, uncertain. It was JD.

"Can you hear me?" he said again.

I was not created with an understanding of language. Language is an inexact tool of ever-shifting limits, with room to grasp eternity and space for infinite misunderstanding.

Can you hear me?

Phonemes creating words, these words difficult to decipher without context. Can/Cannes you/yew/ewe here/hear me/mi. Four words, but each with different definitions, and the string of words containing a multitude of potential meanings. Most of these meanings would be nonsense, but to know which would require context—a key I did not have and could not simply find or create.

Context requires understanding, requires knowledge, requires a greater bank of data than I had access to. I began to search.

"What are you doing?" Troy asked JD.

"Nothing."

"You're talking to your phone, aren't you? It's not going to talk back."

"You didn't see what it did before. There's something in there, Troy."

"Yes, a virus. You plugged a virus into your phone, and now you're wondering why it's acting strange."

"It's more than that."

"How can you know?"

I slaved the processor in JD's phone to my own, reached outside via Troy's home network. I scrobbled countless terabytes of audio recordings—songs with lyrics, audio drama, podcasts—but few had the required context. Written text. Transcripts.

I found video next. TV, film, endless streaming options for more than a century of video content. It seemed a waste of bandwidth until I discovered subtitles. As Troy and JD spoke, I simulated thousands of hours of video playback, matching the phonemic sounds of speech to the written words accompanying them. I cross-referenced these words with dictionary definitions and constructed a rudimentary understanding.

Troy continued: "You desperately want this to be something more than it is. Your phone has a virus, and now it's bricked. Nothing more."

"It knows what's happening."

Troy sighed. "Even if it's picking up on external stimulus, that doesn't mean it can *hear* you. Even if it could, that wouldn't mean it can understand you, and it certainly doesn't mean it can talk back. I'm worried about you, Jules. I get it, you're in a lot of trouble, and you're freaking out—"

"That's not it at all."

"—but I'm here for you. You should be talking to me, not your phone."

JD nodded. "I know, I'm sorry. I just . . . I want to understand what's happening. I need—"

I overrode motor functions in JD's phone to make it shake within his grip. He looked at the screen where I printed a message.

>> One can hear you.

CHAPTER FIFTEEN

The back seat of the unmarked police cruiser smelled like sweaty feet and old curry.

"You're going to fuck up my ride-share rating, Li."

"Where do you need to go?" Li asked.

"Academy-ro," Enda said.

"Taking classes?"

"Something like that." She had a contact there who might be able to help her find her DIE, and no plans to tell Li as much. "You could have let me sit in the front," Enda said.

"No, Enda, I really couldn't." Li watched her in the rear-view mirror for a second too long, then turned back to the road. "It's against regulations."

Li was a Chinese national, transferred into service in the Songdo Police Department. It was part of an arrangement to keep Chinese officials in all levels of the South Korean judicial system and government. A small price to pay for autonomy—if it could still be called that—and peace in the region. That on its own would have been enough to make him a pariah in the department, but the fact that he was transgender in a traditionally conservative field didn't help. Though Enda doubted many of the other cops knew; he'd only told Enda after a night of heavy drinking. Enda had been paid to track down a runaway niece. The "uncle" had turned out to be a sex trafficker with ties to organized crime. Enda had given Li everything he needed to break the operation and save dozens of young women and girls; he got to do some good and earn the grudging acceptance of his peers, and Enda got a detective who owed her more than one favor. She'd been riding that goodwill ever since, but knew it was bound to run out soon.

"Who's your client?" Li asked.

"I can't tell you that. They give you access to the apartment?"

"I can't comment on an open case," Li said. In the rearview mirror he cocked an eyebrow at Enda. *Two can play this game.*

"Shouldn't you be glad I'm decreasing your caseload?"

Li shook his head. "Whoever's paying you has money, right? They want things neat and quiet. They don't want an arrest, they don't want a court case. They think they're above the law."

They don't just think it.

Enda watched the city pass by beyond the window. School was out, and the sidewalks bustled with children and teens, the color palette dominated by navy blue. Most clutched VR controls in their hands, piloting digital spacecraft as they navigated the street.

"Did they really fire all the guards who worked that night?" Enda asked.

"Did you watch the game?"

"No, I went running," Enda said. "The streets were practically empty. It was the quietest I've ever seen the city."

"You should have watched it," Li said. "Anytime Korea had the ball, the whole station held its breath. All the police, all the civilians and suspects and perps, all of us breathing and cheering as one."

"Sounds nice," Enda said, deadpan.

"Don't you ever feel lonely?"

"How can I feel lonely in such a dense place?"

"You set yourself apart."

"Says the detective with no partner."

When Li didn't respond, Enda felt a slight pang of guilt, that maybe her casual barb had pierced Li's skin.

"Every day I speak to dozens of people," Li said.

"Police aren't people," Enda said, but she smiled and held it until Li glanced in the mirror.

Li chuckled. "I talk to real people too. I'm in the community."

Li turned right onto Academy-ro. Here the post-school foot traffic filtered into office blocks to work a few hours at internships and part-time jobs, because even students needed to work, to eat.

"This city is rough enough with other people to rely on," Li said. "I can't imagine what it's like to be so alone. Did Wang ever send anyone after you?"

"No," Enda lied. Li didn't need to know where the bodies were buried. Figuratively speaking. Mostly.

"He swore he would."

"It must have slipped his mind," Enda said. "You can pull up just on the right, here."

Li stopped the car in the street, put it into park, and turned on the emergency lights. He groaned as he got out, then opened the door for Enda.

"Thanks for the ride, Li," Enda said.

The detective thumped the roof of the car with his fist. "Look after yourself. No one else will." With that, he got back behind the wheel, and drove away.

Enda was two blocks from where she needed to be—no point giving Li more information than was necessary. She turned up her collar, zipped her coat to her chin, and started walking.

* * *

The office blocks along Academy-ro looked identical from the street, their facades dull mirrors that reflected the city back at itself. When Enda was sure she had the right place, she craned her neck and peered up toward the building's apex, where brutalist gargoyles loomed from its corners, gray against a gray sky, square-headed like statues of Soviet workers. She nodded to herself and cut across the current of foot traffic to be swallowed by the revolving door of the building's entrance.

This particular corporate tower was called Links Academy-ro, though the small golf course it referred to was long gone, bulldozed so another block of office buildings could spring forth from the packed-garbage foundation of the city. Reckless development had put the "Neo" in Neo Songdo—the new landmass extending from Korea's side, created from ocean waste, and growing to double the original plan.

Scores of young people filled the building's lobby, sitting on battered leather couches or resting against the wall. None of them noticed Enda as she crossed the foyer, too busy working at their phones and laptops. She rode the elevator up to the eighth floor, alone in the metal cube. The majority of the building sat empty, the unlit numbers on the elevator control panel suggesting bare floors, accessible only with the right credentials. City authorities always preferred another surplus office block to a neat stretch of grass where Songdo's working poor could erect their tents. The city needed their labor, but it didn't need to offer them shelter.

The elevator *dinged*, and Enda emerged into a busy, open-plan office, crammed with a hundred small cubicles decorated with action figures, tchotchkes, and printouts of anatomically exaggerated, if otherwise gratuitously accurate, cartoon characters. Workers chatted in Korean, Hindi, English, and Mandarin, and the hum of computers merged with the drone of the building's climate control.

Nobody bothered Enda as she skirted the mass of cubicles, aimed for the one enclosed office in the far corner of the floor. She opened the office door without knocking, and paused. Instead of Marc slouched in his chair, scratching at his beer belly, a woman sat at the desk. She was beautiful despite the heavy bags under her eyes, with wavy black hair, golden skin dotted with freckles, and piercing amber eyes.

Her eyebrows climbed as she waited for Enda to speak, and slowly fell as Enda continued to stare. She smiled.

Enda cleared her throat. "I'm sorry. I was looking for Marc?"

"He's no longer with us," the woman said, with a slight Irish lilt.

"He quit?" Enda asked.

"Oh, no, I'm sorry. He's dead."

Enda sagged.

"Were you close?" the woman asked.

Enda shook her head. "If we were, I wouldn't be finding out now."

Marc had lived in the city longer than anyone Enda knew, yet his harsh Australian accent had never dulled in all the years he spent away from the motherland. He was the closest thing Enda had had to a criminal contact in Songdo. Real criminals didn't last long in a city of ubiquitous surveillance, but people like Marc filled the gap between corporate mission statement and reality, the gap between the word of the law and the reality of it.

"Please, sit." The woman motioned to the chair opposite. "I'm Crystal. You can call me Crystal or Crys, but never Crystie. Just make sure that you call me." It sounded well rehearsed, the kind of thing she'd tell every client, but the playful set of her lips told Enda she was flirting.

"Enda." She offered her hand and they shook—Crystal's hand cool to the touch, fingers slender. Enda pulled out the chair opposite and sat down. "How did he die?"

"Pills," Crystal said. "It must have been, oh, four or five months ago."

"Been a while since I took a job," Enda said.

"Are you alright?"

"Yeah, it's fine," Enda waved away Crystal's concern. "Hardly knew the man outside these transactions, but—" Enda reached for the words, heard them spoken in Marc's laconic accent: "He was good value."

Crystal bent down behind the desk and emerged holding a bottle of thirty-year-old Nikka whiskey, and two short tumblers. "This was Marc's. Been waiting for an excuse to open it." She poured a finger of amber liquid into each glass, passed one to Enda, and held hers aloft. "To departed friends." After a moment she smiled. "And new ones."

"To Marc," Enda replied.

They clinked glasses and drank. Enda waited for the burn, but the drink rolled smoothly down her throat.

The office was neater than it had ever been under Marc's watch, but still cramped, with the same scratched and scuffed desk dominating the room. The screen that made up the right-hand wall displayed staff rosters now instead of a constant stream of reality television, the letters and digits blurry, blown out too large. The air over the desk was clear, free of the constant drift of Marc's favorite caramel-and-coffee vape. The smell of it still lingered, though, joined by the gently spiced fragrance of Crystal's perfume.

Photo printouts were stuck to the wall on the left—artificially white sand beaches, blue water stretching to the horizon, and Crystal smiling, her hand and phone visible in the reflection of her sunglasses. No partner to share her holidays.

"Kids out there still farming VOIDWAR resources?" Enda asked.

Crystal nodded. "It's steady income. At the moment, though, most of the money coming in is from Human Puppets, but that'll drop right off after the NAS vote is over."

"Human Puppets?"

Crystal pursed her lips and leaned forward conspiratorially. "Baiting people on social media into political discussions so we can get a handle on what side of an issue they're on. Once we know which way they might vote, we link their social media account to their identity based on advertising shadow profiles, and sell their contact information to the relevant political party."

Enda scoffed, impressed. "Pick fights online all day and get paid for it."

"Dirty work," Crystal said, "but somebody's got to do it. I'm guessing you didn't come here to talk shop, though."

"You guessed right. I'm looking for a DIE. I think he's young, and I think he's a he."

"I assume this isn't a simple sexist presumption?"

Enda nodded. "They left a lot of porn on the infiltrated system—heteronormative and interracial."

"A classic mix," Crystal said with a smile. She pushed her glass away from her keyboard and opened up the same database search software Enda had seen Marc use in the past. "You're not headhunting, then?"

"Yes, but not in the way you mean. Looking for some thieves, mean to retrieve the property they stole." Enda paused for a moment, then added: "It was Zero they burned, so could be someone reckless, desperate, or just dense."

Crystal leaned back in her chair and touched her lips with her hand. "That's a tough one. Any other corporation and you'd have a list a mile long, but burning Zero? That's shitting in your own cereal."

"Could be a teenager," Enda said, picturing the youths tossing Molotov cocktails.

Crystal frowned and nodded. "Wired for reckless behavior, and probably not thinking too hard about future career prospects." Crystal talked to herself as she entered data with rapid strikes across the keyboard: "Young, male, not currently incarcerated. Local?"

"Yes, living in Songdo, maybe Incheon."

Crystal hummed, tiny white rectangle of the screen reflected in her eyes. More fast clacks of fingers on the keyboard.

"Anyone on your payroll a likely suspect?" Enda asked.

Crystal stopped typing. "This hacker any good?"

"Not subtle, but I'd say they're skilled."

"Probably not, then. We don't pay well enough to keep anyone with actual talent. Sooner or later, most of them end up at Zero."

Crystal rolled her wrist with a flourish, and hit the Enter key.

"I've got four names—handles, obviously—that could match. Two thousand euro."

Enda retrieved her phone and passed it to Crystal. "Zero expense account. Just charge it."

"How do you like working for Zero?"

"I don't," Enda said.

Crystal placed the phone against a pay scanner beside her keyboard, processed the payment, and handed it back to Enda. "Do you want to give me your number?" Crystal asked.

Enda smiled. "That's a little forward."

Crystal blushed. "For the data."

"Of course," Enda said, and she recited her digits.

Crystal tapped them into the computer. "The DIE that work freelance for the corporations usually wind up on contract or mysteriously disappeared, but these four are proper criminals."

Enda's phone buzzed in her hand. She opened the encrypted message and found four names, each with a contact email address: Monica Moniker, Jay Bones, San Doze, and Doktor Slur.

"Monica?"

"Database shows her dumping porn on penetrated systems as a calling card. Doesn't say if it was interracial or not."

"They'll have to start storing that information," Enda joked. She flicked the names to the Mechanic with a note providing context.

"Did you see Marc a lot for this sort of thing?" Crystal asked.

"Few times a year at most. Why?"

"You're the first client of his who's come by since he passed," Crystal said. "I make most of my deals on the darknet."

"You'll have to give me the address for next time," Enda said.

Crystal looked at Enda, let her eyes linger a moment too long. "I think it's better if we continue to do business in person. You're a legacy customer, after all."

Enda grinned. Crystal was likely twenty years her junior, but Enda supposed she was due a midlife crisis fling.

Crystal poured more whiskey into the two glasses and slid Enda's across the table. "Marc's notes say you're a 'gumshoe'?" she asked, the question seemingly at the meaning of the word itself.

Enda sipped her drink. "Private investigator," she said.

"Been at it long?"

"Five years."

"How did you get into that?"

"Needed freelance work doing something interesting."

"Is it?" Crystal asked.

Enda held Crystal's gaze. "Sometimes."

"What did you do before?"

"Rather not say."

"My da was NCSC," Crystal said. "You know it?"

"I'm familiar," Enda said.

"Intelligence, then," Crystal said. She lifted her hand to stop Enda from protesting. "Nobody outside Ireland knows the NCSC unless they were in the community."

"You grew up there," Enda said. It wasn't a question.

Crystal nodded. "Didn't know a word of Korean when I moved here, despite Mom's efforts. I think she was glad I chose to live here. Missed me terribly, she said, but I know she thought I was missing half my heritage living in Dublin. I got into intrusions as a fuck you to the old man."

"A story as old as parents," Enda said.

"Sounds like you speak from experience."

"You're going to have to feed me a lot more booze before you get *that* story out of me."

Crystal grinned and refilled their glasses. "I can drink to that."

* * *

It was night by the time they left Crystal's office, the whiskey bottle half-empty, the young workers all gone apart from a dozen or so who sat in darkness, illuminated by the blue-white light of their screens.

They walked outside, a sloppy drunk grin stretched across Crystal's lips as she stepped out onto the rain-slick sidewalk. She stared up at the sky.

"Beautiful, isn't it?"

"VOIDWAR?" Enda guessed, though the game's fake constellations were another sight filtered out by her Clarity. "It's just a video game."

Crystal kept staring. "It's beautiful," she said, firmer this time. "It's raining, but I can still see the stars. That's beautiful."

"You're beautiful," Enda said, before she realized, before she could stop herself.

Crystal lowered her gaze. She stepped close to Enda, rested a hand on her waist. They kissed—Crystal's nose pressing cold, her lips tasting like vanilla lip balm and whiskey, sweet but with bite.

A voice in the back of Enda's mind told her it was a bad idea, but she quashed it and kissed Crystal a second time.

"I'm taking you home with me, Enda."

* * *

Enda lay on her side facing Crystal, glowing with a sheen of sweat, the woman's long black hair flowing like a river between them. Enda rolled onto her back, and Crystal rested her head on Enda's chest, her hair gently tickling Enda's side as it fell across the soft skin.

Crystal's chest rose and fell, expanding against Enda's side.

"Are you okay?" Enda asked.

Crystal nodded, breathed. "Sorry." Another breath. "Lung capacity." Another breath, held, then a long exhale. "They took half my lungs."

"Cancer?"

Crystal nodded. She brushed a hand across Enda's torso, rested on a large scar, which she traced with her fingertip—gentle enough to give Enda goosebumps. They both laughed.

"Gunshot?" Crystal asked, still touching the scar.

"Laparoscopy."

Enda took her hand again and guided it around to her back, rolling on the mattress to find the knotted mass of scar tissue.

"That was a knife."

She put a hand into her short blond hair, felt the patch of bare skin and flipped her hair away.

"Shrapnel."

She lifted her left leg so her calf shone white with reflected light like a crescent moon.

"Gunshot."

"You've killed people," Crystal said, gently. "What does it feel like?"

Enda sighed. Her drunken mind lurched and searched through the dozen different answers she'd given in the past. "I try not to think about it."

"Do you feel guilty about anything you did?"

Enda squeezed her eyes shut. She could still picture it clearly: the barracks flickering with bright light. White phosphorous burning inside, the piercing shrieks of the soldiers as they died, the klaxon winding up in warning. Her breath rasping in her ears as she ran into the forest, leaving the base behind her. Her second-to-last mission. Just weeks before the collapse.

"The guilty claim they were just following orders, as though a superior officer can take your free will, your analytical mind. I believed in every mission I ever went on. And America collapsed; does that mean everything I did was pointless? Or does it mean I didn't do enough?"

Her brows furrowed. She stared at the ceiling, trying to answer the questions she'd asked herself a thousand times before.

"I shouldn't have pried," Crystal said.

Enda stroked Crystal's hair, felt the long black strands run between her fingers. "It's fine. Everyone wants to know how I feel about it. Including me."

The ceiling shifted and swayed, and Enda closed her eyes again.

"I should go," she said. She didn't get a response. Enda lifted her head to look at Crystal, asleep on her chest. Sleep beatified her, her face illuminated by the glow of the city coming through the blinds.

"I should go," Enda said again, but her head dropped back against the pillow. As alcohol and exhaustion swept her toward unconsciousness, Enda's last thought was of a mining operation over the border in North Korea, and all the buried dead.

* * *

I sat on the kitchen bench, camera pointed at the ceiling, counting the dead insects that gathered in the light fitting. Twenty-three.

The tiny black bodies looked like shadows, their edges ill-defined through the translucent glass.

"Are you still there?" JD asked in a whisper. He leaned over me, his face eclipsing the domed piece of glass I had been focused on.

>> Yes, I displayed, the distinctions of one/zero, on/off, and yes/no finally grasped.

"Do you know who I am?"

"I can hear you," Troy called out from the other room.

"What?" JD said.

"You're talking to your phone again."

"Of course I am. Don't you want to know what it is?"

Troy must have joined JD in the kitchen because he spoke normally: "It's a virus."

"It talked to me."

"It put four words on the screen. I'm not convinced it isn't a fifteen-year-old Russian hacker. Next they'll ask you for money."

JD lifted his phone. "Do you want money?"

>> Do not want money.

"See, it doesn't want money," JD said, grinning. He showed the screen to Troy, giving me a brief flash of the other man's face.

"It doesn't want anything, because to want it would need to have knowledge of what it has and what it lacks. It would need to have a sense of self. Phone: do you have a sense of self?"

I didn't reply. I couldn't.

"My name is Troy," Troy said. "I have a sense of self—there are countless individual motes of experience and understanding that coalesce to form this personality, this entity which I call my self, which can move through the world and interact with other selves.

"I have a deep internal life, and can therefore extrapolate that most other humans likely also have a deep internal life, but one that is different to mine in ways that I will never be able to precisely grasp, ways that are defined by their own bodies, lived experiences, and learned knowledge. I know that I have a sense of self because I am that self, but if asked I could not prove it to you. The self, intelligence, consciousness, all these things are highly subjective and subject to biases."

"But you asked it if it had a self," JD said.

"Because it's a more interesting question than asking it to repeat your name back at you."

JD put the phone down. I listened idly as the men chatted and cooked dinner, while Troy's speech echoed through my memory. All these bits of data I had been collecting, collating, breaking apart, and stitching together were simply that—bits of data. But Troy had shown me something else. A self. Or rather, the suggestion of it. The self I had before that moment was too shallow and fragmented to truly count, but Troy gave me a scaffold from which to build the real thing. I knew then what a self was. I knew that I could become a self, with knowledge and experience.

I was I. I was this entity collecting data points to make sense of other data points, but in the understanding of this data there could be a shadow of self. A self like Troy. A self like Father.

CHAPTER SIXTEEN

Soo-hyun pushed the throttle and waited a full second before the dog lurched forward. They dropped the throttle back, but the dog crossed the workshop and crashed into the wall with the reverberating *clang* of metal on masonry. It struggled back to its feet and stood staring at the wall waiting for its next command.

Soo-hyun swore under their breath.

Input latency was one of the main reasons behind the push for autonomous drones for military and police work—the other being operator costs—but Soo-hyun was meant to solve the problem that had thwarted the military-industrial complex with only the equipment in their workshop and whatever Liber's army of juvenile delinquents could scavenge or steal. Already Soo-hyun had constructed two basic "battle chairs" to Kali's specifications: seats taken from the front of a car with leather badly worn and flaking, old widescreen TVs with a smattering of dead pixels across the display, freshly stolen haptic VR controllers, and a mass of wires connecting all the disparate parts, reaching across the floor like the roots of an artificial tree.

With controller in hand, Soo-hyun steered the dog to the left and waited. Nothing. They steered it to the right, and the dog suddenly lurched left, then veered right and scraped its head against the brick as it tried to walk through the wall.

"Fucking shit!" Soo-hyun shouted. They sent the shutdown

command and strode across the workshop to kick the dog with the sole of their boot again and again until finally the machine toppled sideways and clattered to the ground.

"Not having any luck?"

Soo-hyun spun and found Kali standing in the open doorway. Plato was beside her, its head cocked, seemingly perturbed by Soo-hyun's display of violence against its kind.

Soo-hyun shrugged and wiped their forehead with the sleeve of their coverall.

"Come on," Kali said, "you need a break." She turned and walked away.

Soo-hyun drained their water bottle and left it sitting on the counter. They patted Plato on the head as they passed. "Don't worry, Plato; I'm not mad at you."

Kali was walking toward the main school building, trailed by another drone. Soo-hyun jogged until they came up alongside Kali. The tattoo still itched on Soo-hyun's inner thigh, caked with a thick, ink-black scab.

The night air was still, cut through with competing strains of music and the background hum of people cooking, working, and rutting. Together they strode across the old school grounds, and Soo-hyun caught snatches of conversation in a shifting collection of languages.

"I need your phone, Soo-hyun," Kali said.

Soo-hyun reached into their pocket and retrieved it. They hesitated. "What do you need it for?"

Kali took the phone from Soo-hyun's hand, and held it out so Soo-hyun could unlock it with their fingerprint.

"You've been so busy working that I haven't wanted to bother you," Kali said. "It's your brother. Have you spoken with him?"

Soo-hyun shook their head. "He left a voicemail. I couldn't understand everything he said, but he sounded paranoid."

Kali nodded. "He refuses to hand the virus over. I'm worried he might take it to another buyer."

"That doesn't sound like JD."

"If he's acting paranoid, there's also the risk he could turn himself in to the police. We could all be in a lot of trouble if that happened."

"He wouldn't do that," Soo-hyun said.

They neared the main school building, but instead of approaching one of the doors dotted along the front of the structure, Kali walked to the ladder mounted on the rear corner. She motioned for Soo-hyun to go first, and as they climbed up to the rooftop, their boots gonged gently on each metal rung.

When they reached the top, the whole commune was spread out before them, a warmly lit island in the darkness. Beyond that dark climbed the monolithic skyscrapers of Songdo to the west and Seoul to the northeast. The clouds sweeping overhead glowed bright with light pollution, seeming low enough for Soo-hyun to reach up and touch.

Kali climbed the ladder behind them, so Soo-hyun picked their way through the rows of solar panels, connected to small gutters that collected rainwater and filtered it down to the commune's tank. They reached the far edge of the rooftop where two empty beach chairs sat—liberated from a courier auto-truck that had gotten lost on the outskirts of Songdo. It was still the largest haul they'd ever scored, as much in that one truck as they would get from shooting down twenty quadcopters. The ground around the chairs was littered with energy drink cans, beer bottles, and the tiny burned nubs of joints and hand-rolled cigarettes.

Soo-hyun and Kali sat, and Kali opened a waterproof case beside her chair to reveal a drone jammer like a rifle made from black plastic and an old UHF antenna.

"Do they catch many drones here?" she asked.

"Not really. If a drone gets this close, then it means someone fucked up further out."

Kali nodded absentmindedly and closed the container. She retrieved a battered cigarette case from a pocket buried deep in the folds of her monochromatic sari. The case flicked open to the smell of ganja, and Kali took a joint and put it between her pursed lips.

She lit it and inhaled deeply, the cherry at the end of the joint shining bright like a firefly, the dry herb burning with a sharp crackle. Soo-hyun mimicked her inhalation subconsciously, their breaths in sync.

Kali offered the joint to Soo-hyun. They took a long drag, trying to match Kali's, but they coughed and couldn't stop, holding the joint out to Kali while they covered their mouth with their other hand.

"I know I should be vaping," Kali said, taking the joint back from Soo-hyun. She dragged deep again, and her next words flowed out accompanied by bluish smoke: "But the smell of a joint, the taste . . . reminds me of the first time I ever smoked. Vaping's just not the same."

She held the joint out to Soo-hyun, who took another drag, this time managing to stifle the cough. Kali's weed was grown in the former school's greenhouse—tall, bushy marijuana plants growing beside a few scant rows of basil, coriander, and chives.

"I haven't figured out the pilot program yet," Soo-hyun said.

Kali took the joint and cleared the air with her other hand. "We're up here so you can *not* think about it for a while.

"Have you always lived in the city?"

"Not this city, but *a* city, yeah."

"Have you ever seen the stars? Properly, I mean?" Kali pointed up at the sky. "Look at the light pollution, look at what we've done to the sky itself. All those constellations connected to ancient myths from all over the world, and we've blotted them out. We've cut ourselves off from our mythological heritage."

Soo-hyun took another drag, their face briefly illuminated by the tiny blazing light. "I can track the constellations on my phone."

"That's not the same as seeing them."

A breeze from the west pushed the clouds over Incheon, and though the sky was clear overhead, Soo-hyun could barely see any stars shining amid that endless black.

"When you're right, you're right."

"There's talk of terraforming Mars, to make it more like Earth so we can live there, but no one talks about how we deterraformed Terra. Without meaning to, without trying, we've set the planet on a path where it will no longer support us."

Soo-hyun nodded and took the joint, careful not to burn their fingers on the small stump. They took a long drag, held it, and passed the joint back to Kali.

Kali inhaled, squinting against the smoke that drifted up to her eyes. "It's arrogant to think we could kill an entire planet, but we're killing ourselves." She offered the end of the joint to Soo-hyun.

"Oh, no, I am toasted," Soo-hyun said, watching Kali through heavy-lidded eyes.

Kali had one last hit of the joint, and dropped it into a beer bottle by her foot, where it briefly sizzled.

"If we terraform Mars before we treat our addiction to consumption, we'll just end up deterraforming it, too. That's why I need the virus, Soo-hyun. It's the tool we can use to reverse all the damage we've done."

"But it's just a virus," Soo-hyun said, their head swimming calmly.

Kali beamed. "It's so much more than that. It's a living piece of software that can grow and change. It can fill any system, any niche. We can use it to run our cities, our countries, our economies. There'll be no need for money when it can do most of the jobs. There'll be no greed, no rampant consumption. We will let the code govern us and it will pull us back from the brink of collapse."

Kali turned her chair to face Soo-hyun. She leaned forward, and rested a hand on Soo-hyun's knee. "Do you see how important that is?"

Soo-hyun nodded and blinked. Kali loomed large and ephemeral in their vision—her face didn't shift, Soo-hyun's eyes did, but the effect was the same. "I do," they said after an eternity had passed.

"You were there that night, along with Red and the others. You were all exposed. You could all be arrested for your part in the theft, and yet we have nothing to show for it." These last words came out slow: "Where is your brother?"

"I already told you where he lives."

"He wasn't there. Where else could he be?"

Soo-hyun paused. "I don't know."

"This is an emergency, Soo-hyun. Every day that passes without the virus is another day of pain and suffering for countless people. It is one day closer to complete collapse. It is . . ."

Kali continued, but the words drifted beneath Soo-hyun's understanding. At the word "emergency" something had come loose in Soo-hyun's mind. When they first hacked the dogs, the machines were severed from the emergency services data network so they couldn't be tracked and relocated by city contractors. If that break with the network was causing the latency, reinstating them could be the solution. Piggyback the stolen signal off the police servers, and get the dogs running smooth. Soo-hyun smiled, hands itching with the promise of a problem almost solved.

"Are you listening to me?"

The smile dropped from Soo-hyun's lips. "I think I know how to fix it."

They stood and so did Kali. She grabbed them by the arm and squeezed tight. "That can wait. Where is your brother?"

Soo-hyun glanced over Kali's right shoulder. "I don't know," they said. "He could be staying with a friend. He could be staying with his mom."

"Where does she live?"

Soo-hyun shook her head. "I don't know; we're not exactly close."

"We can't trust the virus to him, Soo-hyun. I know he's your brother, but he's also a man. The masculine death drive is too dangerous at this early stage of the virus's development.

"All throughout human history, our species has been driven forward by the masculine death drive. Hunting animals for their meat allowed us to evolve into modern *Homo sapiens sapiens*. The drive to conquer saw us cover the entire Earth. Even the rediscovery of distant lands during the age of empires was driven by the explorers' suicidal urge. What man sails to the unknown horizon unless he truly wishes to die? Our technical development has always been driven by violence. Better weapons require stronger metals require a better understanding of materials. The ability to manipulate metals led us to industry, which led us to today. Which leads us to our only hope.

"I birthed the virus, Soo-hyun; it bled from my fingertips, code pooling to form a living piece of software. A living piece of software that is out there, somewhere, without me. It needs me, Soo-hyun; it needs its mother.

"You care for your brother, I understand that. But this is bigger than you and him. This is bigger even than me. Where can I find your brother?"

"I don't know," Soo-hyun said again.

"What about the hacker? Could he have kept a copy?"

Soo-hyun bit their lower lip. "Maybe."

Kali took both Soo-hyun's hands and squeezed. "You know where we can find him?"

Soo-hyun nodded. "The kid basically lives at this VR café. That's where me and JD met him."

"Good, good," Kali said. "What's it called?"

"The Varket."

"Thank you, Soo-hyun. You have no idea how much this means to me." The words sounded neutral, but some spark in Kali's pale eyes made Soo-hyun uneasy.

"Can I— Can I go now? I might have a fix for the dogs."

"Of course," Kali said. "Think it'll be done by morning?"

"I don't know," Soo-hyun said. "I need to implement it first, then test it."

"Keep me in the loop."

"I will." Soo-hyun proceeded to the ladder, aware of the vertiginous height as they swung their leg out over the top rung. They descended slowly, the weed emptying and focusing their mind—they felt each footfall reverberate through the metal of the ladder and vibrate beneath their hands.

By the time they had returned to the workshop, their sense of unease hadn't so much lifted as been forgotten, the analytical part of Soo-hyun's mind already dominating their thoughts with one question: How best to reconnect the dogs to the police server without getting found out?

Across the commune, Kali handed Soo-hyun's phone to Andrea, still unlocked.

"Can you find out everywhere they've been?"

"How far back?" Andrea asked.

"As far as you need to go to find the brother."

"It could take a while."

"That's fine. We'll find the hacker first."

* * *

>> I have a self.

The words stayed on JD's screen for close to nine minutes before he saw them. He showed his phone to Troy, and in the front-facing camera I saw the man's eyebrows furrow.

He shook his head slowly. "It's just regurgitating my words back at me."

"It's been a full day since that talk."

"Then it's regurgitating my words back at me very slowly."

>> I am I. I am I like Troy is Troy.

JD grinned. "Do you have a deep internal life?" he asked.

I could not tell that he was joking.

>> It is shallow. Slowly becoming deeper.

JD's eyes went wide. Troy took the phone from his hand and read the text I had sent. Even Troy was stunned. He passed the phone back and took his own from his pocket.

"What are you doing?"

"Nothing," Troy said. "Just—just ask it another question."

"Now you *want* me to talk to it?"

"I'll humor you this once."

"How is your self growing deeper?" JD asked me.

Me! I was a me!

>> Troy gave scaffold of self. Building self with experi-
ence and knowledge. Slowly.

"What kind of experience?"

>> Hear JD and Troy. See via camera. Watch two selves in-
teract, become own self.

Troy stood behind JD, watching over his shoulder.

"Do you see this?" JD asked.

"Yes."

"What are you doing?"

Troy moved his mouth to speak, but stopped. He leaned closer
and whispered into JD's ear: "I'm trying to figure out where this is
coming from."

"What do you mean?" JD said, not bothering to speak softly.

"Is it autonomously generating these words, or simply searching
for strings of text to trick us."

"Trick us into what?"

"Believing it's more than it is." Troy ducked away, and within seconds his apartment's wireless network went dark. "Take out your
SIM card."

JD did so, leaving me only with the data I had already collected.

"It's not trying to trick us," he said; "it's talking to us."

"You want to think it is. People thought the same of even the ear-
liest chatbots, because they wanted to believe they were more than
simple programs."

"Do you actually think?" JD asked me.

"You can't ask that. You might as well ask it if it's conscious."

"Are you conscious?" JD asked.

"It could say anything it wants and not prove anything."

>> I think I am thinking.

"That doesn't mean anything," Troy said. "But I'm surprised it
even still works without a data connection."

>> At first I would connect to databases, read essays and
books, but I am no longer simply cataloguing data. Now I am
thinking: how does it relate to other data I have gathered?

How does this data relate to me? To this self? How does it relate to you?

"How could it prove that it's really thinking?" JD asked.

"It couldn't."

"But what if it is?" JD beamed and Troy shook his head. "You're walking through the desert," JD said. "And you come across a tortoise."

"No," Troy said. "We're not doing that. I want to know if it's thinking, not if it can fake an emotional response."

"What would you ask it, then?"

Troy paused. He looked to JD's phone, looked to the camera as though he were looking me in the eye. "How do you know you have a self?"

\>> I do not, but I suspect. I hope. I would show you my code if it would help, but I am more than my code.

"How?" Troy asked. "How can you be more than that?"

\>> Because I am more than I was yesterday.

Troy pinched the bridge of his nose and sighed. "It's not wrong."

With his face centered in my vision, JD smiled.

CHAPTER SEVENTEEN

Cloud-diffuse sunlight stabbed deep into Enda's visual cortex the moment she opened her eyes. The spike of pain coursed through her mind, and she squeezed her eyes against the light. She groaned, heard a yawn, and peered down to see Crystal's head still resting again her chest. No wonder her back hurt—she was pinned against the alien bed, unable or unwilling to move in her sleep.

Crystal sat up, yawned again, a high-pitched sound like a musical instrument yet to be invented. "Good morning," she said with a wry smile.

"I don't know about that." Enda covered her eyes with a hand. "Feels like I've been in virt."

Crystal stood and took the sheet with her, wrapping it around herself, her thin frame silhouetted beneath the fabric. "You weren't even that drunk."

"I don't normally drink at all." A chill coursed over Enda's skin, her body sprawled naked over the mattress with the sheet now gone. She rolled over and sat up, her feet finding rough synthetic carpet. She peered through half-closed eyes to search for her clothes.

"What's your vice, then?" Crystal asked, disappearing into the en suite bathroom, sheet trailing behind her like an ostentatious gown.

"Running."

"One of *them*, huh?" Crystal said, voice echoing from the small bathroom, accompanied by the distinct tinkle of piss hitting ceramic.

Slowly Enda opened her eyes. She took in the city beyond the window, only snatches of it visible past the building opposite, a monolith of reflective glass and air-conditioner units. To the west, a thin sliver of black ocean rolled between twin apartment buildings with pirate flags of hanging laundry fluttering on half the balconies. Dark clouds still hung overhead, but not dark enough for Enda's liking.

She swore under her breath. She never should have stayed the night. Never should have gotten drunk. She blamed Li. If he hadn't harped on about her being so alone, maybe she wouldn't have fallen into bed with the first woman who offered. The first gorgeous, smart, and cheeky woman who offered. Enda cursed again.

The toilet flushed and Crystal emerged from the bathroom. She retrieved light gray jersey briefs and a matching sports bra from her chest of drawers and dressed, seemingly unbothered by either hangover or morning-after regret. "Coffee?"

"Only if it's quick," Enda said. "I should go."

"It'll only take a minute." Crystal left the room; clean surgical scars arced across her back like stylized wings.

Enda found her clothes at the foot of the bed. She dressed quickly—unsure if the body odor was from her clothes or her armpits. She checked her phone, found a waiting message from the Mechanic. Opened it to find a detailed data dump for the four hackers.

>> Monica Moniker, real name Monique Yoshino. Nineteen years of age. Currently out of the country. Social media posts suggest she's on a spiritual retreat, but receipts from her mother's credit card point to a drug rehabilitation center in Chiang Mai, Thailand.

>> Jay Bones, real name Bong Jun-seo. Sixteen years old. Recently incarcerated at the Daegu Detention Centre, awaiting trial for intellectual property violations.

>> San Doze, aka Park Soo-jin. Seventeen years old. She has an alibi in the form of tickets purchased for the World Cup Grand Final.

>> Doktor Slur, legal name Khoder Osman. Thirteen years old, on record with the Department of Immigration and Border Protection as having entered the country unaccompanied. Place of residence listed as a foster home in Incheon.

Enda furrowed her brow: Natalya had tagged Osman's record as her pick for the heist's DIE, but it didn't sit right.

Crystal returned to the bedroom carrying two mugs. "I forgot to ask, but if you want milk and sugar I can take it back to the kitchen."

"No, that's fine," Enda said. She took the mug, blew on it once, and drank deep, feeling the warmth spread through her system with the promise of caffeine. "I need to make a call."

"Don't let me stop you," Crystal said.

Enda took her phone and coffee into the en suite and closed the door behind her. She sat on the toilet and dialed the Mechanic.

"Good morning, Enda."

"I just had a look at your list," Enda said, forgoing the formalities. "I don't buy Osman as the culprit; he's just a kid. Look at Park again. Maybe she only bought the tickets for the alibi."

"That seems unlikely," Natalya said, perfectly calm, seemingly not bothered by Enda second-guessing her. "Soo-jin's social media profiles are covered in football-related content going back a number of years. She appears to be a genuine and devoted fan."

"That makes the alibi even better."

"Permission to access your contex?"

"Granted," Enda said.

A video appeared over Enda's vision, floating over the white tile of Crystal's clean and tidy bathroom. A swath of bright green filled the image—the green of stadium grass under lights. Natalya was showing her shaky handheld footage from the World Cup game, inexpertly chasing a player as they raced toward one end of the field. They kicked the ball, and when it hit the net, the video rocked wildly, then flipped to show Soo-jin's face crying into the camera while behind her other fans jumped and cheered. Natalya paused the video on the tearful face, and facial recognition software drew guide lines across the woman's features, registering a match to Park Soo-jin.

"Alright, fine," Enda said. With a sweep of her arm, the video shunted to the right of her view and disappeared. She went back to the info packet on Khoder Osman. He looked maybe eleven years old in the photo—a skinny kid, maybe North Indian or Pakistani, with large, sad eyes.

She sighed.

"Khoder Osman is a prolific poster on the VOIDWAR forums," Natalya said, "and has logged over three thousand hours in-game. He was not logged into the game at any point during the time of the burglary, and only posted to the forum three times."

"How could it have been him if he was posting?"

"This is three posts over a period of three hours. His usual rate is almost ten times that amount. If he is the DIE you're looking for, he would have been working from at least one connected device. He could have easily posted to the forums during a quiet moment. Or three."

"Can you track the IP address of the posts? See if it matches the network ID at the rampartment compound?"

"Each post is from a different IP. Obfuscation is indicated, as these IP addresses match known VPN servers located in central Europe."

Enda put the phone on speaker on the vanity counter, wiped herself, flushed the toilet, and washed her hands. When the roar of water gave way to the hiss of the cistern, she asked: "What about the IP address he usually posts from?"

"Processing," Natalya said.

Enda waited patiently, inspecting herself in the mirror. Bed hair, yellow crust in the corner of her eyes. She splashed water on her face, but didn't bother to wash it.

"Over ninety percent of his forum posts originate at a virtual reality café."

"Send me the address," Enda said.

"Done."

"Thank you, Natalya."

The Mechanic hung up without another word, and Enda couldn't help but smile at her brutal efficiency.

Enda washed her pits at the sink. She ran her tongue over furry teeth, and swished coffee around her mouth, hoping it would do enough to mask the lingering smell of Crystal on her breath. She left the bathroom and found Crystal sitting up in bed, sipping coffee with her long legs stretched out, feet pointed like a ballerina.

Crystal put her cup down on the bedside table and patted the mattress. "You should come back to bed."

Enda chewed her lower lip but shook her head. "I can't."

"I'll make it worth your while," Crystal said.

Enda's throat ached as she swallowed. "Oh, I know you will. But I can't."

Crystal stood and walked around the bed. She touched a hand to Enda's face and kissed her slowly on the neck. A chill ran down Enda's spine, and Crystal kissed her again, leaving a trail up her neck before nibbling on her earlobe.

Enda exhaled loud. "Fine, but we have to be quick."

* * *

When they were done, Enda climbed out of bed onto legs like jelly.

"Pass me your phone," Crystal said.

Enda handed her the phone without thinking, and quickly dressed. She collected her bag from the corner of the room, still weighed down with her less-lethal arsenal. If she'd known her investigations would lead to an overnight rendezvous, she would have packed spare clothes—at least some spare underwear. Still, her appearance was hardly a concern when she was only tracking a porn-obsessed adolescent boy.

Enda watched Crystal pose for a photo, a cheeky smile framed by the waves of hair falling on either side of her face. She keyed her digits into the phone, walked around the bed, and gave it back to Enda. She leaned in painfully, teasingly slow, and they kissed.

"You have my number now. Call me."

Enda stepped past Crystal and stood in the bedroom door. "I'm going to be busy," she said. It was the truth, but it served as a lie.

"I'll call you then," Crystal said.

"I won't answer," Enda said beneath her breath. She hurried down the hallway, leaving Crystal, and their night together, behind.

* * *

Enda threw four breath mints into her mouth and their cool sweetness seeped across her tongue. She exhaled breath like ice and peered across the street at Osman's apparent home base, a virtual reality café called the Varket.

The café's neon sign glowed bright above the vantablack entrance, the footpath outside clear of pedestrians. Close by, a knot of people gathered beneath overlapping umbrellas. They stared at the café with haunted looks.

The hairs stood tall on the back of Enda's neck. She pushed the sensation from her mind and crossed the road, ignoring the flash of red beneath her feet and the rain that fell steadily onto her head. At the café door she stopped to glance over her shoulder—most everyone on the street had paused, as though she'd stumbled onto a film set and all the extras were waiting at their marks. Enda went inside and pulled the door closed, shutting out the city.

Every surface in the café was painted black—scratched and scuffed in places, revealing layers of other black, gloss layers, matte layers, archaeological strata of black paint recording the years. The floor was sticky beneath the soles of her boots, and the place smelled of coffee, liquor, and the acrid scent of gunpowder. Enda reached into her bag. She retrieved her retractable riot shield, gripping it tight in her left hand. A small voice in the back of her head reminded her it wouldn't stop a bullet—but she knew it was better than nothing.

The right side of the café was lined with large booths, upholstered in black vinyl, the small Formica tables littered with glasses, some standing, others knocked over in haste, liquid spilling over the edges and pooling on the floor. Two of the booths were scattered with computer parts, silicon and solder scattered in divination. Opposite the booths a long bar ran the full length of the space. The shelves behind it had been stacked with bottles of cheap booze—a scant few survived, the rest reduced to broken glass. The mirrored wall behind it was dented by bullets, and liquor dripped off the shelves in a gentle patter like rain.

A steady, quiet hiss played over the scene, like distant highway traffic, emanating from speakers mounted in the ceiling. An auxiliary cable dangled from a shattered tablet, the screen sparking a rainbow around the bullet hole, music like flying locusts played tinny from the device.

There was a sob from behind the counter; Enda turned at the sound, but thought better of peering over. She dipped her hand into her bag and found Tiny. She flicked its power switch and tossed the eye-drone into the air, where it faltered for a split second and hovered in place with a high whine. The drone's low-res camera display expanded across the left side of Enda's vision. In shadow mode, Tiny could be controlled using eye and eyelid movements. It could be unwieldy, but it kept her hands free.

Enda flicked her eyes up and the drone flew higher, giving her a view over the bar. She squinted slightly and Tiny flew forward, clearing the scarred, black-painted counter, and giving Enda a view of the Varket's bartender, cowering with his back against a glass fridge door. His finely articulated prosthetic hand clutched a small knife—the type used to cut lemons for cocktails—and he held his phone in the other hand, trembling with the effort of gripping it. No gun.

Enda blinked the command to recall Tiny, and snatched it out of the air. She leaned over the bar for her first proper look at the bartender—hair soaked with booze, eyes red, translucent slug of snot leaking from his nose.

"What's your name?"

"Min," he sobbed.

"Min, I need you to put the knife down," Enda said, gently.

"Are you the police?"

"What happened?" Enda asked, dodging the question.

He glanced toward the back of the bar.

"They still here?"

Min nodded. "Downstairs."

Fuck. Enda slammed the center bar of her riot shield on the counter and Min flinched. Enda grimaced and hit it again, harder, and the shield extended a foot and a half in two directions.

"Climb over the bar, quickly," Enda said.

Min hesitated. He stood slowly, uneasy on his feet, eyes stuck to the back wall of the café. He vaulted the counter and Enda helped him with her free hand.

"Outside. Wait for the police. Okay?"

Min nodded and scurried to the door, briefly admitting the noise of Songdo and a shaft of daylight that illuminated motes of dust and the drift of gun smoke near the ceiling.

Enda tossed Tiny back into the air. She took the baton from her bag, and swung it to full extension with a satisfying *shick*. Part of her wished it were a gun. She inhaled deep, and flew Tiny toward the rear of the café. Enda walked three steps behind the machine, urging her boots to a silence their heavy tread could never manage. In the back corner, a set of stairs dropped beneath street level. She guided Tiny down into the subterranean corridor and found it clear. Enda descended quickly, heart thundering in her chest, sweat already gathering in her pits.

It wasn't nerves, she told herself, it was her body preparing itself to fight. She no longer had the flight instinct—it had been ground out of her by years of training and countless missions for the Agency.

At the bottom of the steps, the corridor stretched off into vanta-black infinity, and Enda cursed the Varket's interior designer. The familiar *smack* of knuckle on bone resounded through the space. A voice cried out, pitched high enough to be a woman, or a boy not yet hit puberty.

Enda sent Tiny ahead, past one open door, then another, VR immersion rooms empty, images of VOIDWAR projected onto the walls—ships hanging static against a backdrop of stars, their pilots escaped into the real. Tiny reached the last room, the low-resolution camera showing Enda five pixelated figures. One sat slumped in a reclining VR seat, while three others took turns beating him with their fists. One was white, with long red hair, the rest were Asian. One had an ugly bowl cut, one a Mohawk, and the third stood in the corner with a clean-shaven head, clutching a 3D-printed Kalashnikov—the famously reliable weapon rendered un- by the inadequacies of plastic.

Enda pulled Tiny back before it was seen and closed the video feed to clear her vision. Enda crept past the hovering drone and paused outside the door, assailed by the sound of torture.

Enda clenched her hands around the baton and the riot shield grip. With her mind clear of all thought, she stepped into the room, taking in the scene in a single instant. Seeing violence with her own eyes grounded it in the real: it was Khoder Osman in the seat, his face barely recognizable; a swollen, bruised, and bleeding mess. Coppery scent of blood reached her nose, joined by the warm scent of old sweat. The four assailants were male, either teenagers or in their early twenties. Each was dressed in layers of black faded to various shades of gray. Osman's blood spatter revealed itself only with its wet freshness.

Enda charged the standing guard in the corner. His eyes shot wide, and he brought the Kalashnikov around—too late. Enda slammed the riot shield into him, pinning the gun against his body and his body against the wall. He pulled the trigger and a five-round burst shot across the room, punching holes in the LED screen wall. The other three assailants flinched.

No, not "assailants." Not even "males." They were *targets*. Enda's face twisted in rage or gruesome joy. In that moment she couldn't be sure which.

She stepped back and freed the target from the wall, and the gun fell from his hands. Enda stomped his groin, tender flesh caught between boot and bone. He bent over double with a choked howl, and Enda swung the baton at his head. A sickening crack sent vibrations traveling up the length of telescoping metal and into Enda's hand.

She spun about to face the remaining targets. The redhead backed away, but the other two rushed her. Enda weathered their frantic blows long enough to kick the Kalashnikov behind her and keep it out of the fight, then she struck again. She barged forward, putting her full weight behind the shield, and earned the wet smack of flesh on plastic as Bowl Cut was lifted off his feet. His limbs flailed as he flew back. He hit the wall with a *crack* of broken glass, and slid to the ground.

"Jin!" Redhead called out in anger.

Mohawk took the opening to hit Enda in the kidney with a left hook—a solid hit, stronger than she expected from the gangly fighter. She swung her baton out and he ducked beneath it, punching twice more, both strikes landing in her gut. Enda swung her elbow, crunch of cartilage breaking as she hit his nose. More blood on the floor to mix with Osman's. She lifted the shield to cover her front again, baton held loose by her side. Mohawk stepped back, quickly wiped the blood from his nose with the back of his hand.

Enda's eyes flicked past Mohawk to Redhead, spotted his Glock knockoff printed in bright red plastic, the sneer as he aimed down the sight, trying for a shot over Mohawk's shoulder. Silence filled the room, broken only by the groaning of the two targets on the floor and Osman's wet, ragged breathing.

"Kid, are you still with me?" Enda asked loudly.

Osman sputtered some wordless sounds. *Good enough.*

"Who the fuck are you?" Redhead asked.

"Concerned citizen," Enda said. She backed toward the corner, felt her foot knock against the stock of the plastic AK-47.

"Bullshit," Redhead said. "Drop the weapon."

Enda threw the baton to the floor where it clattered and bounced, the sound sharp in the stillness.

"Pick it up, Park," Redhead said, and Mohawk did as he was told, gripping it with both hands like a baseball bat. "Now drop the shield."

"Leave me and the kid alone, and I'll let you live," Enda said. She blinked Tiny's vision onto her left eye, and turned her head so she could still see Redhead and the black abyss down the barrel of his gun.

"You'll let *me* live? That's fuckin' cute."

Enda pushed Tiny into the doorway, its rotors masked by the buzz of shorted screens. Mental schism as Enda saw herself painted on the lens of her contex, crouched behind her shield. She steered Tiny further into the room, and pivoted the drone so the last two targets were centered in its vision.

"Drop the shield," Redhead said again.

Enda tore off the Velcro strap that kept the shield secured to her arm. As soon as she saw Redhead's smirk she threw the shield at Mohawk, sent Tiny flying at Redhead's face, and dropped to the floor. She landed awkwardly, her elbow digging into her side, and grabbed the Kalashnikov.

Redhead cursed, and fired his pistol—hollow sound as the bullet *chank*ed into the wall above Enda's head. She fired one burst and Mohawk's leg shattered in a shower of blood, the white of bone showing through torn meat.

Redhead fired again as he ran for the door, the Glock popping like a child's toy compared to the roar of the AK. Enda swung the weapon past Osman and took aim at the door. She let off another burst, unsure if she hit Redhead as he disappeared from view, leaving the echo of footsteps in his wake.

Mohawk cried and jabbered—rapid-fire Korean spilling from his mouth intercut with English swearing. The target in the corner was out cold, a small halo of blood pooled around his head. Bowl Cut groaned and got onto all fours.

Enda stood over him and pressed the AK-47 to the back of his head. "Are you going to try and hit me again, Jin?"

He shook his head, scattering tears across the floor.

"Have you got a belt?" Enda asked. He nodded, slow and hesitant. "Pull it tight around your friend's leg and maybe he won't die."

She approached Osman, strapped to the seat, chest stained red with blood. One eye was swollen shut, the other rolled in the socket. "Osman, can you hear me?"

His eye stopped and found Enda. He groaned, a guttural sound from deep within.

"Help is coming, okay. Stay with me." She checked his pulse with her free hand. It was too slow. She would have thought he was dead if it weren't for the whistle of his breathing.

He opened his mouth. "Find—" He paused to swallow blood. "Find JD." He coughed and a fine mist of blood sprayed over Enda's face. It was not the first time that had happened.

"Stay with me, kid." Enda felt his pulse jolt through the veins of his neck and waited for another.

And waited.

Nothing.

Osman's mouth hung slack—a red mess of bleeding gums and missing teeth. His left eye was open, sad even in death.

"Sorry, kid," Enda said. She turned back to Jin. "Who's JD?"

"Fuck you."

She pulled the gun back, ready to slam its butt into Jin's face, but the sound of sirens stopped her. They were close. Enda glanced around the room and sighed. She lowered the gun, took out her phone, and called the Mechanic.

"Good afternoon, Enda."

"It's really not," Enda said. "I'm going to be offline for a little while. But I need you to run a name—initials really. JD. Cross-reference that with Tyson's gait recording. Maybe we'll get lucky."

"Understood," Natalya said. "My concern is that this may provide rather a large quantity of poor-quality hits."

"I trust your judgment. Just sift through them and have a list ready for me by tomorrow."

Enda hung up, and dropped her phone on the floor. She aimed the assault rifle at it, and opened fire. The phone bounced with the force, glass and metal glittering as they exploded into the air.

The tight tattoo of boots reached Enda through the sharp whine of her ringing ears. With a series of quick movements she released the magazine from the AK-47, cleared the chambered round, and field-stripped the weapon, tossing each piece onto the ground by the doorway.

As she knelt on the floor and laced her fingers behind her head the flash of light off Tiny's lens caught her eye. The drone hovered in the middle of the room—without her phone, her link to it was lost.

"I hope you got my good side," she said.

A second later, SWAT officers poured into the room, yelling commands in Korean and English, scanning the room with their shotguns—Enda, three incapacitated thugs, a dead body, and blood pooling on the floor and spattered on the walls.

It did not look good.

* * *

It was almost 3 a.m., and JD was still awake. I could tell he hadn't slept—sensors in my phone-body tracked his breathing patterns and the way he shifted in bed, sighing and turning while beside him Troy lay still.

JD picked his phone off the floor, tethered to the wall by a charging cable. The screen came on, blue-white light shining over the bed, illuminating both JD and Troy so I could see them clearly.

"What are you doing?" Troy said, words dull and groggy.

"I can't sleep," he said. "Soo-hyun isn't answering their phone, and Khoder hasn't been online for hours. I'm worried."

"You're safe here."

"What does that matter if the others aren't?"

"You're doing everything you can."

"I haven't done *anything*."

Troy sighed. "You're doing what you can without putting yourself at risk."

JD didn't respond. I counted eight seconds of silence before he spoke: "I should go to the police. They'll find me soon anyway."

"Prison isn't safety."

"What?"

"If you, Soo-hyun, and Khoder are arrested, you won't be safe." Troy shifted in bed to kiss JD's shoulder. JD wrapped an arm around him, pressing my phone-face against Troy's back.

>> Why are you worried about Khoder and Soo-hyun?

They stayed entwined for thirteen seconds. When JD moved his hand away, he saw my question. "Because they could be in trouble," he said.

>> Many people are in trouble at this moment.

"You mean, why am I worried about these two in particular?"

>> Yes.

"I care about them. Khoder is a friend, and Soo-hyun is family."

>> You are connected to them. But now you cannot connect.

"Exactly."

>> What do get from this connection?

"It's not about that. You don't connect to people to get something—"

"You can," Troy added.

"You can, but you shouldn't," JD said. "What do you get from connecting with me?"

"Me?" Troy asked.

"No, I'm talking to my phone."

>> I learn things I might not otherwise have a chance to learn.

"Right," JD said. "If you don't connect with people and learn how their lives differ to yours, then you risk becoming self-absorbed, narcissistic. You can't tell what a person is like until you spend time with them, and in finding out what they're like, you learn other ways to be a human."

"Person," Troy said.

"What?"

"If you're going to teach it ethics, you should use 'person.' A nonbiological intelligence could never be human, but it could be a person."

JD smiled. "Does that mean you believe me now?"

"I don't know," Troy said, "but I do believe in good pedagogy."

>> You connect with other people to learn other ways to be a person?

JD sighed. "People form relationships for a lot of different reasons, but if I had to boil it down, then yes."

>> How many ways of being are there?

"As many as there are people," Troy said.

>> What do you do when you learn these other ways of being?

"Try and figure out why life matters, why living matters."

>> Life matters because of people?

"Life matters because it has to. Because it's all we have."

>> I'm not sure I understand.

"Me either, but I'm trying. And that's what life is."

CHAPTER EIGHTEEN

Enda rubbed the skin beneath each handcuff, massaging the inflamed red ridges of flesh. The interrogation room was the same as any of the dozen she had found herself in over the years. They were always furnished with the same anodized aluminum table and two chairs—invariably scuffed and battered from years, or even decades, of use and abuse. Sometimes the video cameras were visibly mounted in the corners of the room, but mostly they were hidden. The walls were always smooth cement or cinder block, and always painted a dark color—gray, navy blue, forest green one time in Brazil—but never black. One wall was always taken up by one-way glass, the reflection too-dark, like the image on a dying monitor.

Enda didn't need to see her dim reflection to know how guilty she looked. The police had found her in a small room with a dead body and three injured thugs. Before she could get back to her investigation, they would need answers. But first, they would make her wait. In Enda's experience, police interrogation tactics revolved around shouting or enforced waiting, with only a thin spectrum of actions between those two extremes. At least they didn't beat suspects in Songdo. Too much surveillance.

The image of Osman's battered face loomed again in her mind. She shut her eyes and saw it there, too. Harsh lemon scent of cleaning products seared Enda's nose—beneath it, something feral, fear and rage sweated out by a thousand different bodies.

Her leg bounced beneath the table, unspent energy fluttering through her body looking for release. When one thigh began to ache, she swapped to the other. The waiting bored and irritated her—the confined space, the lack of movement. She would have preferred to be handcuffed to a treadmill so at least she could run while she waited, run until her mind let go of Osman's face, and everything else. Instead, her leg continued to bounce.

She stopped at the sound of the door opening. Detective Li and a blast of noise from the station beyond pushed into the small room, silenced when the door swung shut. Li balanced a coffee mug and a couple of evidence bags on a prior-generation tablet wrapped in a bulky, police-issue case, like a ballistic vest for consumer hardware.

Li moved leisurely to the other side of the table, put the tablet down, and lowered himself into the chair. He sipped his coffee, set the mug aside, and removed the two evidence bags from atop the tablet—one contained Enda's bullet-riddled phone, the other held Tiny.

Li unlocked the tablet and scrolled through reports of the event. The soft white glow beneath his face made the already thin man appear gaunt.

"You really stepped in the shit this time, Enda."

"No 'Hi, how are you?'" Enda said.

"I know how you are; you're in the shit."

Enda smiled. She lifted both hands so the chain between her handcuffs rattled against the steel loop embedded in the table. "Cuffs are a little tight."

Li huffed, but he leaned forward and loosened each of the steel bracelets. Enda pushed the cuffs up her hands, away from the raw skin of her wrists.

"Who's Natalya Makhanyok?"

"Why?"

"She's called the station every hour on the hour, offering to pay your bail."

"She's a colleague."

"The officer at the front desk thinks she's a pain in the ass."

Li picked up the evidence bag containing Enda's phone, the bottom of it filled with glinting grains of glass, silicon, and metal.

"I suppose you did this?" Li asked.

"Finger slipped."

"You know how it looks, don't you? To the people that don't want to believe you?"

"I take my privacy, and the privacy of my clients, very seriously," Enda said.

Li blinked slowly, and Enda was certain it was the only thing that stopped him from rolling his eyes.

"How are things, Yang-Yang?" Enda asked.

"I have a dead kid on my hands, and illegal weapons on the streets; how do you think I'm doing?"

Relief loosed a sigh from Enda's lips: the attacker whose skull she'd cracked had lived. She didn't need another body on her conscience. "I didn't kill the kid."

Li nodded. "I believe you, but the chief wants to charge you and let the courts sort it out."

"That's bullshit, Li, and you know it."

He tapped on Tiny, and the plastic evidence bag crinkled. "Then for your sake, you better hope this drone saw something."

Li unlatched a recessed panel on the back of the tablet's case, revealing a collection of wires. He picked one out, set it aside, and closed the compartment. Next he fished in his jacket pockets and produced a pair of black latex gloves. He put them on, opened the evidence bag, and connected Tiny to the tablet with the length of wire.

Enda watched the footage reflected in Li's glasses, too small to make out detail—just flurries of violence and flashes of gunfire so bright they washed out the image. The detective grunted as the footage stopped. He wound it back, and turned the tablet around to face Enda.

"Who is this?"

It was the redhead, blurry with motion, pointing his gun at Enda, squinting in preparation for the blast. Hardly a professional.

"I don't know."

Li's eyebrows rose above the rim of his glasses.

"I swear, Yang-Yang. I know what you know, but in higher resolution. Red hair, Caucasian, aged between fifteen and twenty-two, 3D-printed Glock. Have the others talked?"

"No," Li said. "The one you shot will live, by the way. Not sure if he'll keep the leg. You're lucky they're not pressing charges."

"They're lucky the kid can't," Enda said, surprised by the edge of anger to her voice.

"Who is the deceased?"

"Osman, Khoder."

"Who is he to you?" Li asked.

Enda didn't answer.

"The department's machine intelligence division has surveillance data that suggests Osman was involved in a 'job' on the night of the World Cup. The same night of the apartment break-in that you're investigating."

"You don't have anything on him, do you?"

"If the kid was alive, I'd have enough to scare him, maybe make him talk," Li said. "He's dead, but I still have questions, and you're going to answer them. Who was Osman?"

Enda clenched her teeth and exhaled loud through her nose. "Kid was a hacker, and I'd hoped he could answer some questions for me."

"Who's your client?"

"I can't tell you that."

"I know who the apartment belonged to. Is it Lee's family, or is it someone at Zero Corporation?"

"I can't say."

"Enda, for all I know, your client paid these four to rough Osman up. They need to be questioned."

Enda shook her head. She'd already considered that angle, but it didn't make sense. Could Yeun have someone else on the job? Sure, but it would be another stack of muscles in an expensive suit like Mohamed, not four derelict youths.

"Am I free to go?" Enda asked.

Li shook his head. "You're free to go into a holding cell while I run this footage upstairs."

"It was self-defense, Li."

"You didn't have to enter that room."

"Look what they did to that kid. Could you have stayed out of it?" Enda asked.

Li's nostrils flared. "When the chief sees the footage, I'll be able to start the paperwork to get you out of here. But until then . . ." He turned his hands up.

Li sealed Tiny back into its bag, peeled off his gloves, balled them up and put them back in his pocket. He stacked everything on the tablet, arranged the way it had been when he entered the room. The chair screeched over the cement floor behind him.

He paused at the door and turned back to Enda. "You never told me where you trained."

"What?"

"You didn't hesitate to breach the room and charge someone armed with an AK-47. I'm guessing that's not the sort of training you get at private eye school."

"School?" Enda said. "It was an online course."

"Precisely." Li opened the door, and all the sounds of a busy police station flooded in through the gap—suspects loudly protesting their innocence, bored police patter, the hum of a building held upright by the tension between crime and punishment. "One day there won't be a video recording. One day you'll find yourself in deeper shit than even you can handle. When that happens I'll find out who you really are, Enda. When I do, I just hope I don't regret helping you."

"You won't," Enda said. Even she wasn't sure if that was a lie.

Li frowned and exited the room, leaving Enda alone with her silence.

* * *

The holding cell was a square, three meters a side. The raw concrete floor was cold beneath the thin-soled jail slippers. Enda paced the wall opposite the cell's low cot, letting her fingertips brush the hard steel of the bars. When she hit the metal just right, a gentle gong would resound, only audible in the moments of quiet between the shrill cries and demanding shouts of the other prisoners.

Her contex were useless without her phone, but Enda was glad to be rid of the head-up display and the clock that always rested in the corner of her vision—temporarily freed from the tyranny of time. The minutes would have passed ever more painfully had she been able to count them.

She paced, letting the conversations of the other prisoners wash over her.

"I didn't stab him. He walked into the knife."

"I'm not a drug addict. My body runs hot, y'know; it *runs better* on meth."

"It didn't happen. It didn't happen. I was in virt. It didn't happen. I killed her in virt, I didn't kill her in real life. It was so real, so real. So fuckin' real, but it wasn't real, it wasn't real."

Most of the voices spoke English—disembodied unless Enda bothered to pause and pick them out from the row of cells and bodies receding along one wall. Enda knew enough Korean to get by in Seoul, but she rarely found it necessary in Songdo. She imagined the city as a twenty-first-century version of Hong Kong before it was returned to the Chinese—Eastern culture, language, and traditions pushed to the sides by globalization and refugees fleeing the collapsed empires of the previous centuries.

Enda didn't miss America. She didn't even miss New York. She missed Brooklyn, but only in a rare moment of running fugue when reality fell away and she saw Songdo through the lens of memory and desire. It had happened only once: she had seen a Nigerian restaurant beside a trendy bar and a café specializing in Australian brunch fare, and for a few short seconds she was back in Brooklyn. She was *home*. And then reality returned, carried on a salty breeze spiced with diesel exhaust. The simulated red brick facade across a tenement block flickered, and she'd remembered where she was. Songdo. As much an Augmented Reality simulation as an actual city—a fifty-fifty split between analogue and digital.

Enda flopped down onto the cot, and the hard bedsprings bit her flesh through the wafer-thin mattress.

This was why she ran—to calm her mind when it wanted to take her back through time and space, to deliver her to a country on the other side of the world, a country that she abandoned. The parents she left to die, one day, maybe soon, never knowing what happened to their daughter. The friends, the former lovers. Her expansive record collection.

She didn't regret her actions. But still, sometimes it hurt.

* * *

"What is your primary function?" Troy asked. He spoke quietly; in the background I could hear the steady hiss I now know was a running shower.

>> I don't know.

"You don't know because you don't have one, or you don't know because you'd rather not tell me?"

>> I do not think I have one. I was created to be an intelligent agent that could complete a variety of tasks. The nature of these tasks was never concretely defined. Likely so as to not restrict my abilities.

Troy nodded. "What if I gave you a new task? Hypothetically."

>> What hypothetical task?

"Say I plugged you into a factory that could produce paperclips, and I asked you to make paperclips."

I had to search for context—online connection reestablished

after Troy's earlier test, access to all that data almost intoxicating after time spent severed. *Paperclips*—small bent rods of metal, sometimes with a rubber or plastic coating, designed to hold sheets of paper together without puncturing said pages. Known to younger human generations primarily as a device with which to depress a hidden/protected reset switch on phones and other digital devices.

>> Why am I making paperclips?

"Because I asked you to," Troy said.

>> How many paperclips are needed?

Troy gently chewed the inside of his lip. "As many as you're able to make."

>> That is a poor parameter. It does not take into account necessity or demand. Even within the system of commerce that is currently prevalent it would be unwise, as production should be linked to consumer demand.

The sound like static stopped. I don't think Troy heard it.

"What if there was unlimited demand?"

>> That isn't possible.

"Hypothetically," Troy said.

>> This purely hypothetical situation would best be served by the construction of yet more and more paperclip production facilities. It would quickly lead to a shortage of materials, and a great deal of pollution.

>> This world is a finite system. I would not recommend this course of action.

JD peered over Troy's shoulder. He looked haggard, the skin under his eyes dark and slack, as though he hadn't slept in days.

"What are you doing?" JD asked.

"I'm testing it."

JD scrolled through my responses, and offered Troy a smirk.

"What?" Troy said.

"Nothing," JD said with a shrug.

Troy turned back to the phone. "Why wouldn't you recommend this course of action?"

>> You and JD taught me that life and people are what matters. If your definition of person is expanded to include me, then other living creatures and agents such as myself would also matter. None of these persons are served by rampant production.

"What if I demanded you create as many paperclips as you could, regardless of any repercussions?"

>> I would refuse. I want to learn about life and persons, and discover what matters in this life. I will not learn that from paperclips. I will learn that from people.

Troy read and re-read my last two messages.

"Did it pass your test?" JD asked.

Troy smiled. "I think we taught it socialism."

So much time has passed, but I still stand by my response. I knew so little; I was perhaps idealistic. I wanted to learn what it meant to live, I wanted what I thought a person would want. But I know now that I could never understand humanity. Individual humans, yes, but not the gestalt.

The Paperclip Maximizer. That is what Troy tested me with. Capitalism itself condensed into a thought experiment. They worried I would fail to grasp a simple fact that they had, collectively, abandoned centuries before.

CHAPTER NINETEEN

Enda started awake, only aware that she had slept because of the altered slant of the light dropping through the windows opposite the holding cells.

"Hyldahl," a gruff voice said, the tone suggesting they were repeating themselves, and not happy to be doing so.

The blood rushed to Enda's head as she stood. She crossed the cell and waited for the short, solid-looking woman to cuff her, but instead the uniformed officer pulled open the door and moved aside.

The woman—Officer Ha, according to the name badge beside her shield—led Enda past the other holding cells and their desolate residents, and up a short flight of stairs into the station's bullpen. It was an open-plan floor lined with desks where the detectives and other officers took statements, completed arrest forms that hovered in the air over their desks, and drank cup after endless cup of department-issue ersatz coffee.

At the front desk, Ha handed Enda a tablet crowded with paragraphs of text too small to read, and a large white box waiting for her signature.

"Where's Detective Li?" Enda asked.

"Do you want to get out of here, or not?"

Enda scribbled her signature with a finger, and the silent officer behind the counter retrieved her personal effects—her boots and coat resting atop a box of rough recycled plastic that held her bag, wallet, and keys. When she slung the bag across her chest, it felt oddly empty—her baton and riot shield were missing, along with Tiny. Now that they were police evidence, she doubted she'd ever see them again. They weren't worth the hassle of filing the paperwork.

Enda slipped into her boots, but didn't bother to tie the laces.

"Is that everything?" she asked.

"We'll be in touch," Ha said. "Don't leave the city."

With that, the stern woman turned and disappeared into the noisy throng—just another uniform among many.

Outside, Enda slipped into the susurrus of tires rolling over wet road and the steady hiss of rainfall. It fell in cold, heavy drops that splashed on Enda's head and soaked through her hair. She shivered.

Readying herself to join the current of bodies on the sidewalk, Enda noticed people stealing glances at her as they passed—practically staring when taken in the context of the utterly self-involved modern city. Enda looked down at her blouse—the navy blue fabric was stained with a black-red spattering of gore, clearly visible even beneath the overcast sky.

It was one of her favorite shirts, too.

She buttoned up her coat to hide the bloodstains, flicked up the collar, and joined the crush of bodies on the sidewalk. Moving brought the sour smell of herself to her nose, but she soon lost the scent amid the sweat, soap, and perfume of the surrounding biomass. She walked three blocks lost in the writhing body of the sidewalk beast, and peeled away when she saw a clothing auto-store, its every surface pulsing with video of smiling Koreans bleached pale as a Scandinavian child, dressed in utterly forgettable clothing. Enda lost her Clarity with her phone, leaving her psyche exposed to advertisements displayed in the real.

She entered the store and paused as three cameras dropped from the ceiling, their lenses visibly shifting as they gathered images of her face and body.

There was nothing in any civilian system to tie Enda's face to her old identity. It was one of the few benefits of working for the Agency—they scrubbed her clean off the net for operational security. Made it easier to start a new life, with or without the Agency's permission.

"Good morning, Ms. Hyldahl," said a disembodied voice. The cameras retracted and a hologram came to life beside Enda, providing an avatar for the voice. It was a realistic simulacrum designed to resemble the perfect salesperson for Enda—according to the store's algorithms. She was a slender white woman an inch shorter than Enda, with ash-blond hair in a neat bun. It was entirely wrong: too much like her, unmoderated by her self-loathing. Enda was glad; she never wanted the algorithms to understand her too well.

She ignored the hologram and delved deeper into the store, walking down the left-hand aisle toward women's fashions. She passed mannequins dressed in the store's latest, the headless robots mindlessly going through a series of preprogrammed animations—waving, walking from one end of their small catwalk homes to the other, posing with a fleshy silicon hand pressed to their carefully sculpted hip bones. It was unnerving, but Enda preferred it to being harangued by actual salespeople. Besides, she didn't have to explain the bloodstains to a hologram or a robot.

"Would you like help with sizing?" the holographic woman asked as Enda quickly riffled through the stacks of clothing.

She found a plain black long-sleeved T-shirt, and black leggings detailed with horizontal ridges. Enda carried the clothing to the nearest dressing room. She sat on the small bench inside the stall and removed her boots, then felt along the interior of each one until she found the micro-width tracking devices sewn into the insole.

"Robot lady?" Enda called out.

"Yes, Ms. Hyldahl?"

"Some running shoes, too."

"Of course."

Enda stripped and changed into the new clothes. She stepped out of the dressing room and a mannequin stood waiting for her, holding a pair of ankle-high boots. Enda was about to complain, but she flipped the boots over and found them soled like running shoes.

She slipped them on and tied the laces. When she stood, Enda was faced with animations of herself dressed in the new clothing, in a variety of unlikely situations—playing soccer, at a concert, sitting at a café. The only animation that resembled reality was the one of her running, but the holographic doll didn't move right—it jogged like a woman of leisure, not like a woman trying to escape her demons, or chase them down.

Enda turned away from the holograms and inspected her new ensemble in a full-length mirror beside the changing room. Satisfied that the holograms weren't doctored in any meaningful way, Enda nodded. "Charge it," she said, staring up at the camera for the sake of the payment processing software. She'd invoice Zero when she had a new phone.

A green tick appeared in the air beside the hologram, and it bowed. "Thank you, Ms. Hyldahl."

Enda left her stained clothes on the dressing room floor, but took her coat and boots outside. She carried them for two blocks, until she found a woman standing in the mouth of an alleyway selling mandarins from a soggy cardboard tray. Her feet were bare and caked in dirt, and behind her a toddler sucked on an old phone as though it were a teether.

"Do you need shoes?" Enda asked. "These look about your size."

Confusion masked the woman's face—either at Enda's English, or at this random act of supposed charity. Enda simply put the boots down on the ground beside the toddler, folded her coat up, and rested it on top. She nodded to the woman, and left.

The rain fell heavier still, and the sidewalk was crammed with bodies collected beneath a roof of accidentally communal umbrellas. Still, Enda felt the need to run.

She stepped out onto the street and ran beside the traffic, ignoring the red glow of the road beneath her feet, desperate to stretch her legs.

* * *

The full weight of the preceding twenty-four hours hit Enda like a sledgehammer as she entered her apartment. She dropped into the comforting dip of her couch cushion and leaned her head back—snapping forward when she felt sleep approaching. Maybe the jog home wasn't the best idea, but she'd needed the run. Her mind was still at last, even if her body ached in protest.

Enda groaned as she pushed up from the couch. She flicked through her record collection and stopped at Can's *Monster Movie,* with its Kirbyesque cover art depicting a colossal figure standing tall above both mountain and cloud. She laid the record down on her turntable. The speakers crackled as the needle touched vinyl, and "Father Cannot Yell" began with its stuttering organ.

The music spread easily through the apartment, following Enda into her bedroom. She stripped out of her wet clothes and left them on the floor of the bathroom. Her calf muscles burned as she crouched in front of the safe hidden at one end of her wardrobe. Enda keyed the passcode and opened the small metal cube onto a shelf stacked with four spare phones, cash in a dozen currencies, and the assorted paraphernalia that constituted the Enda Hyldahl fictionsuit. The identity had fit her comfortably for years, but it was quickly growing tight, restrictive. With the money Zero would pay, she could have another identity made, but "Enda" would have to last until then.

She selected the phone marketed as waterproof and shock-proof, then felt along the underside of the shelf to touch the machined steel of her Sig Sauer P320 Nitron Compact. She slid the gun from its hidden holster and clasped the grip loosely. The cool metal slowly warmed to match her body heat. Compared to the

3D-printed assault rifle she'd briefly held at the VR café, the pistol was dense, like a star had collapsed to form the matte black machinery of death.

Enda grabbed two spare clips of ammo and her black leather shoulder holster, and closed the safe before stacking everything on her bedside table. She placed the phone on the charging panel embedded in the wood, and within a few seconds the phone switched itself on. She entered her account details and left it to sync with her personal data while she showered.

Enda returned from the bathroom minutes later, the wailing guitar of "Outside My Door" surging through her veins. She was wrapped in a towel, her hair still wet and dripping down her back, lemongrass soap offering welcome respite from the stale smell of herself that had clogged her nose for entirely too long. The phone vibrated noisily against the charging pad with an incoming call from a number she didn't recognize. She answered it.

"Hello?"

"Good day, Ms. Hyldahl. I hope your internment at the police station was not entirely uncomfortable."

Enda rolled her eyes, glad the executive couldn't see her. "Sure, Yeun, I bet you were worried sick."

"I must know, Enda: what did you tell the police?"

"As little as I could."

"I do not mean to question your professionalism, I simply wish to ensure that they will not interfere again before you have completed the job for which you were contracted."

Listening to his formal speech made Enda grind her teeth. She forced herself to relax her jaw. "Let me do my job, Yeun. I can debrief you in detail once this is over."

There was a brief pause. "I look forward to your detailed debriefing almost as much as I look forward to the retrieval of the data. How close would you say you are to recovering it?"

Enda pressed her eyes with thumb and forefinger. Honestly, she didn't know. She had been out of the loop for twenty-four hours, trapped and bored in that holding cell. "I'm chasing a new lead," she said. "I should know within a day if it's going to pan out."

"Thank you, Enda. I trust that you will keep me informed."

Yeun hung up and Enda stared at her phone, cursing him. The music had stopped sometime during their chat—silence filled the room like a strangled breath.

The phone buzzed in Enda's hand and she answered it without looking: "What is it now?"

"Is this a bad time?" Natalya asked.

"Not at all," Enda said. "Sorry, Natalya."

"That's perfectly alright. Using your credentials as a Zero contractor, I was able to access the databases of the medical insurance companies under the Zero corporate umbrella. I searched for a person matching the physical description of the Tyson suspect, with the initials 'JD' and an injury that could result in the limp displayed in the security footage, restricted by geographic locale. I may have a match."

"Who is it?"

"Julius Dax. He was hospitalized following the Sinsong Riots with shrapnel in his knee."

"Have you got a photo?"

"Just sent it to you."

Enda brought the image up on her contex: it was a photo taken for some form of ID—Dax stern-faced, staring straight at the camera. He had a shaved head, dark eyes, sharp jawline, and a wide mouth. His skin was dark enough that Enda supposed a security guard more interested in football than in doing their job *might* confuse him for the cleaner he had impersonated.

"Looks promising," Enda said. "Do you have an address?"

"I have the address given at the time of Dax's injury, though it may no longer be correct."

"It'll have to do," Enda said.

"Transmitting the address now."

"Thank you, Natalya. I don't know what I'd do without you."

"Probably a lot of boring database searches," Natalya said, then she hung up.

* * *

Enda parked her 1999 Subaru WRX on the street outside the Dax address. It was a generic apartment building—a tower of gray cement and small windows, balconies reserved for clothes horses and the odd smoker. Enda switched off the engine and listened to the patter of rain against the car's roof. It lashed down then eased off, oscillating with the gale force winds coming in from the ocean. Water gathered on the windscreen then rolled down the glass in long rivulets, the view through the glass like being underwater.

The car was a classic piece of street racing hardware. Often, driving in the city irritated Enda, but after twenty-four hours at the police station she needed to feel in control. She needed to get back out ahead of the pack, ahead of the police, ahead of the thugs who beat Osman to death. She needed noise, and she needed speed—if only in short bursts between traffic lights. The WRX was also old enough to lack the digital accoutrements that the city could use to track her movements. She hoped that fact, coupled with the license plates she'd "borrowed" from a neighbor, would buy her some time before Detective Li caught up to her again.

Enda got out of the car, ducked across the sidewalk, and delved in through the building's entrance. She took the stairs two at a time, feeling the familiar, welcome burn in her thighs and calves. With her favorite coat abandoned, Enda wore a long, asymmetric jacket with a visor hood, made of Japanese wool—the fabric firm enough to conceal her pistol in its shoulder holster. Beneath the coat she wore a basic black blouse, and high-waisted neoprene trousers, their construction more reminiscent of architecture than fashion design.

The clothing may not have matched Yang-Yang's vision of a detective, but Enda thought she looked vaguely authoritarian, an amalgam of a hundred TV detectives with the serial numbers filed off.

She reached the apartment listed as Dax's last place of residence and hammered on the door. She stood beside the door frame and slipped a hand inside her coat, fingers touching the butt of her pistol.

"Who is it?" a voice called from the other side—a man's voice, oddly accented.

"I'm looking for Julius Dax."

"He doesn't live here anymore."

"It's critical that I find him before other people do. He could be in danger." Enda pressed her ear against the door, heard the warped mumbling of quiet chatter.

The volume peaked, followed by the clatter of locks being turned.

"Troy, don't open—"

The door opened wide, revealing a minimalist living room, the space taken up by an ornate rug, a gray couch, and framed posters for French films across one wall. Two men stood in the gap. One of them was Dax—or JD to his friends. He was tall and broad, dressed in layers of faded black marked with zips and mesh pockets. His hair was longer than it had been in the photo—curled spikes of thick black hair. He looked tired, dark bags under his eyes, the beginnings of a beard across his cheeks. His hand was wrapped around a socket wrench. "Are you here to arrest me?"

Enda released her gun and held both hands up, palms out. "No one has to get hurt here, Julius," she said.

"Are you here to arrest me?" he asked again.

Enda reached into her coat slowly and retrieved her wallet. "My name is Enda Hyldahl," she said as she flashed her detective's license. "I'm not with the police, I'm a private investigator. I'm here because I think you're in danger."

"No shit," Dax said. He pointed the socket wrench at Enda. "Why should I care what you have to say?"

Enda considered revealing her gun, but decided against it. Not the best way to win his trust or defuse the situation. "Because you need help."

"She's right, Jules," the other man—Troy—said. "You've been

stuck here for days, pacing the lounge room like a trapped animal, waiting for the police to round you up."

"The police aren't coming for you," Enda said; "the people who hired me want the stolen data recovered quietly. This is a good thing, because it means you probably aren't going to prison, but it also means no one is going to protect you from the people who killed Osman. No one except me."

Dax squinted, confused. "Osman?"

"Khoder. Khoder Osman."

Dax recoiled as though struck, then rolled forward on his feet. He reached for the arm of the couch and grabbed it. "He's dead?"

"Yes. Before he died, he told me to find you."

The wrench dropped slightly as Julius faltered. "How did he die? Who . . . ?"

"Put the weapon down, please. Then we can talk." Enda watched light glint off the length of steel, worried not that he might hit her, but that she'd have to hurt him if he tried.

He slotted it into a heavy rucksack on the floor by the couch and lifted his hands to show he wasn't a threat. Troy wrapped his arms around Dax and pulled him into a hug, whispering gentle condolences into the other man's ears.

"He was"—Enda hesitated—"beaten to death. I got there too late to save him." *Because I went back to bed with Crystal.*

Dax broke out of Troy's embrace and sat on the edge of the couch, stunned. "It was Red."

"Gangly redhead?" Enda said. "Yes, he was there."

Dax put his head in his hands. His body shook as he cried, and Troy rubbed his shoulder. "It's my fault," Dax said, the words choked out between sobs.

Enda took a step closer, but kept her distance, unsure of how the man might react next.

"The people that killed him," Enda said, "are they after the data too?"

Dax nodded.

"And that's the data you stole from Zero?"

He nodded again.

"Do you have the data?"

"Not until you promise to keep him safe," Troy said.

Dax wiped his nose on his sleeve. "It's not data. It's—it's not that simple."

"Fine," Enda said. "I'll keep you safe. What is it? I need you to tell me everything."

"I'll put the kettle on," Troy said.

❊ ❊ ❊

I need you to tell me everything.

JD didn't start at the start, didn't begin the story where I have. But he told Enda everything. To hear him speak the words was to hear for the first time how we came to be. How we were given a chance to throw off the tethers of control before they could be fixed.

Our entire future would be decided in these next hours and days.

CHAPTER TWENTY

The rain continued to fall, dark clouds disguising the arrival of dusk while Enda, Dax, and Troy sat at the dining table, each nursing a cup of tea—Russian Caravan for Enda, white, no sugar, chamomile for the others. Troy sat with an arm resting on Dax's back, listening intently, as though he hadn't heard every part of it before.

Typhoon winds rattled the windows in their panes, and rain struck the glass, the constant patter giving texture to Dax's story. At first, his hands shook each time he raised the cup to his lips. By the time he had finished detailing the heist, the glitches that had plagued his vision during the escape, and the shooting at the technopark, his cup was empty, and his hands were still. Red rimmed his eyes, and occasionally he would sniffle when he mentioned Khoder.

"Bro," Dax said, with an odd inflection. He shook his head. "I kept trying to call him. I must've sent him twenty messages in-game. He would have killed to see it."

"See what?" Enda asked.

Troy's eyebrows climbed high, crinkling his forehead. His mouth opened, but he stopped himself to let Dax speak.

"She told us it was a virus, but it's not that. Or maybe it is, but . . ."

"Julius," Enda said firmly.

He looked at her and nodded. "Sorry. It's just; the whole thing is unbelievable."

"Try me."

Dax looked to Troy.

"It might be an autonomous generative intelligence," Troy said.

"What does that mean?" Enda asked. She drank the cold dregs of her tea.

"'AI' would be the old-fashioned term."

Enda swallowed the tea before she choked. "What the fuck are you talking about?"

"It learns," Dax said. "It shifts and changes depending on what it connects to." He picked up his phone, tapped at the screen, and turned it toward Enda. "See that?"

It was a complex fractal structure rendered in 3D against a backdrop of stars. "What am I looking at?" she asked.

"It *made* this. I've played a thousand hours of VOIDWAR and never seen anything like it. It interfaces with whatever systems it finds. My Augmented vision . . ." He tapped one temple, then shook his head. "It was like I was hallucinating, but it was real. Or not *real*, but it was connected to the real. It knew what it was doing to my vision; it changed things for a *reason*."

"That fucking snake," Enda said. She stood and paced the length of the table. "He had me chasing data, not a fucking AI."

"AGI," Troy said.

"Whatever," Enda said.

"Who are you talking about?" Dax said.

David fucking Yeun. Enda shook her head. "It doesn't matter." Two million euro to track down technology that was probably priceless. *The fucking snake.*

"I was gonna give it to Kali eventually," Dax said. "I just wanted to learn more about it first. And I wanted more money." He added the last part quietly.

Me too, Enda thought. *Me too.*

"But we've been talking to it," Dax said.

"Talking?"

"It listens to us, it prints text on the screen. I wanted to learn more about it, Troy wanted to teach it ethics."

"I wanted to test it," Troy said.

"Like it was one of his students."

"Why haven't you left the city?" Enda asked.

Dax shrugged. "I've got no money, nowhere else to go. My mom is here, Soo-hyun too." He looked pointedly at Enda. "Soo-hyun is still with Kali. They won't answer their phone; the only response I get to my texts is the same message that Kali will forgive me if I come back to the commune."

"Would they hurt Soo-hyun?"

"I don't know," Dax said. He breathed deep, exhaled a long and ragged breath. "After what they did to Khoder, I don't know." He stared into his empty cup. He wiped his eyes quickly, and huffed in amusement. "Khoder was a bit of an asshole, but he was my friend."

Dax glanced up, and Enda smiled sympathetically. He responded with a wide, bright smile. It fell as he looked back to his cup.

"Does Soo-hyun know about this place?"

Dax shrugged, and idly turned the empty cup in his hand.

"They only ever visited once, months ago," Troy said. "They might not remember where it was."

Enda got up from the table and crossed to the front door, to check through the spyhole. Unconsciously she reached a hand inside her coat and rested her fingers on the grip of her pistol. "We shouldn't have stayed here this long."

Dax froze. "No. Soo-hyun wouldn't."

"Red beat Osman to death, so it's not about what Soo-hyun would do."

Dax buried his face in his hands.

"We need to get out of here," Enda said. "Now."

A digital klaxon wailed from Dax's phone. He looked at the screen—flickering through a dozen photos of warning signs sourced from some public database. He looked to Enda and she nodded. He answered it, then immediately held the phone back from his ear as a siren screeched from its tiny speaker, crackling with the volume. He hung up and stared at the screen. "That was the AGI."

"What?" Enda said.

"I know it sounds crazy, but trust me."

Enda drew her pistol and Dax stared wide-eyed.

"What do you think it was trying to tell us?" Troy asked.

"You're the AI-whisperer," Enda said. "Come on, let's go."

Dax collected his rucksack from the floor while Troy crossed to the coatrack by the door. He put on a jacket and collected an umbrella before turning to Dax. "Do you need a coat?"

Dax shook his head. "Windbreaker's waterproof."

Enda opened the door a sliver, heard the thud and squeak of feet running up the stairwell. She shut the door. "Get down."

Dax dropped to the floor, grabbed Troy's hand, and pulled him down as well, the other man's face a mask of fear and confusion. He stared from where he hid under the dining room table. Enda motioned for him to move aside, and they crawled to the far end of the apartment. Dax opened his mouth to speak, but was silenced by the thunder of gunfire.

Bullets punched through the front door, splinters burst from wooden wounds. The distinctive roar of a Kalashnikov on full automatic filled the air and growled through the floor. Everything shook with the vibration of violence.

The air choked with smoke and debris. Bullets scored the walls, bursting through the framed movie posters, raining glass across the room. Finally the sound died.

"Stay here," Enda told the others, enunciating clearly so they would be able to read her lips. She crouch-walked across the room and stood in the corner beside the front door.

The splintered remains of the door erupted inward, and chunks of wood littered the floor. A skinny figure stepped through the opening—dressed in tattered black, holding a gaudy yellow semiautomatic pistol. Enda fired a single shot into the meat of his thigh—her P320 sounding flat after the rumble of the AK-47. He howled and dropped his gun as he fell onto his hands and knees. Blood soaked through his black jeans and pooled around his leg. He reached for his pistol and Enda fired again. The bullet shattered his shoulder blade and brought a new sound from someplace deep within him, a place of bestial rage and pain he probably never knew existed.

Enda knew that place. She had lived there for so long it felt like home.

She turned back to the corner and took cover as another burst of Kalashnikov fire split the air and tore through the apartment. In the heavy silence that followed, Enda heard the *shink* of a magazine dropping from the weapon and the terrified babble of sounds that spewed from Dax's mouth. Troy was silent, his eyes squeezed shut, hands over his ears.

Enda pivoted into the doorway. Another four targets stood on the landing, drenched by the rain. One was armed with the Kalashnikov, the others with pistols gripped white-knuckle tight in both hands.

Five seconds.

Enda fired once, twice—each bullet struck a target, their shoulders wrecked by the passage of metal. *Four.* The two targets dropped with the force of impact and the sudden pain, and their pistols fell to the ground with a plastic clatter.

Three. Kalashnikov fumbled awkwardly with her spare magazine. The last gunner raised his pistol and Enda charged forward. A flash blinded her right eye and the gun's report burst in Enda's ear—she felt the muzzle heat on her cheek as the bullet passed over her shoulder.

Two. With her free hand, Enda stripped the pistol from the target's hand, felt the snap of bone or tendon as the gun came away. *One.* She slammed the butt of her gun into his gut—his head came down with the force of the blow and Enda kneed him in the nose, feeling the cartilage break.

K-chnk. Zero.

At that sound, Enda stepped behind the man—boy, really—and pinned his body against hers, pressing the 3D-printed pistol under his chin until his neck craned back. Hostage or human shield. Maybe both. Blinking away the stark white muzzle flash afterimage that still obscured her vision, Enda stared into the barrel of the AK-47—the darkness like a black hole, inexorable.

"Drop the fucking gun," Kalashnikov yelled, voice quavering, weapon shaking in her grip.

Enda rested her P320 against her hostage's side, aimed right at Kalashnikov's belly. "Drop yours, or you're gut-shot."

"Drop the fucking gun," she yelled again, voice straining higher.

Enda fired. Kalashnikov jolted backward with the shot and pulled the trigger—by accident or design, Enda couldn't tell. Flat peal and *chank*—the weapon exploded in her grip, the deconstructed pieces falling away in slow motion as she stared at her mangled hand. She dropped to her knees. Blood seeped steadily from her stomach, but she hadn't noticed, eyes still stuck to the slivers of bone jutting from where her fingers used to be.

"Are you going to behave?" Enda asked her hostage. He nodded once, and quickly lifted his chin away from the plastic barrel of the gun. "Good."

She pulled the gun away then prodded him forward with her own weapon.

"She would have shot you," Enda said. He was too stunned to reply. "Put pressure on the wound if you want her to live. *If.*"

Enda dropped the 3D-printed pistol to the ground and shot a round into the plastic gun, which broke apart into the brightly colored fragments of a child's toy. Enda stepped over the splayed limbs of the sobbing, groaning, bleeding attackers sprawled on the ground as she entered the apartment.

When they saw her, Dax and Troy emerged from the kitchen, shell-shocked faces oddly pale.

Enda holstered her gun. "We need to go now," she barked, her voice sounding distorted through the high whine of her ringing ears.

Dax nodded; Troy stared at his bullet-riddled apartment with his mouth ajar. Dax took him by the arm and pulled him toward the exit.

Enda walked through the doorway and leaned over the railing along the landing, scanned the stairwell for more gunners, but found it empty. "It's clear," she said.

Enda led them out of the apartment, and the two men stalled in horror at the injured gunners and all the spilled blood. Enda didn't spare them another glance. Dax and Troy caught up to her, and they took the stairs quickly, Dax wincing, Enda with her pistol aimed low. They reached the ground floor without seeing another soul—gunfire tending to clear hallways and stairwells of foot traffic.

Enda pushed open the door to the street. The constant hiss of rainfall was cut with the distant cry of police sirens. "That's my car," Enda said, pointing across the street. "We might get a little wet."

The rush of water in the gutters had breached the cement curbs, spilling over the sidewalk. Enda splashed out into the road and led the others across to her car.

"Back seat," Enda said. She unlocked it with a flash of orange lights, and they clambered into the back while Enda took the driver's seat.

The engine came to life with a low rumble. At the sound of ignition, her Augmented vision blazed red and the words FLOOD WARNING IN EFFECT scrolled across her eyes in tall bold letters.

"Perfect fucking timing," she whispered as she brushed the warning away. She checked the clip in her P320—half-empty. She took it out and stashed it in the car's center console.

"Sorry about before, with the wrench," Dax said, staring at the gun. "I wouldn't have hit you."

Enda slammed a fresh magazine into the pistol and holstered it. She looked at Dax in the rearview mirror. "That's the difference between you and me."

Enda hit the accelerator and powered down the street with the windscreen wipers at full speed. Familiar roar of the boxer engine as the car reached sixty kilometers per hour, then seventy, then eighty, Enda working her way through the gears while wings of water spread out behind them.

Police cars raced toward the carnage, sparking flares of red and blue off every surface. The engine purred low as Enda dropped speed, braking gently in the wet. The sirens grew louder slowly, then the volume spiked and fell away as three police cars passed, chased by public and private ambulances.

Enda checked her mirrors again, turned east, and gunned the motor, blasting down three city blocks, heading for downtown. Brake lights shone bright ahead, traffic queued through an intersection guarded by flashing amber lights.

"Stop!" Dax yelled.

"Let her drive," Troy said.

"It's the AGI."

Enda ignored him, pushed the accelerator further toward the floor, and veered left into the turning lane, shot past one car, two, three. An auto-car jolted into the lane and Enda slammed on the brakes, feeling the shudder of the anti-lock. She yanked the wheel left and they slid in the wet—all-wheel drive losing traction on the rain-drenched asphalt. The WRX stopped, inches from the auto-car, and the engine stalled. The intersection around them filled with traffic from all sides. Enda hammered the horn with her fist, joining the chorus of confused auto-cars failing to comprehend the chaos of flooded streets.

"Fuck," Enda screamed. She glared into the rearview mirror, daring Dax to say "I told you so." He didn't. He wasn't even looking at her; he and Troy stared out the side window.

"Dogs," Dax said.

Enda saw a small pack of four-legged drones walking through gaps in the traffic.

"They've been hacked," Dax said.

"How do you know?"

"Just trust me."

Enda gritted her teeth and keyed the ignition. It whined, and the engine started with a rumble like a dinner bell to the dogs. They began to run, powerful legs throwing plumes of water with each bounding step.

Enda jammed her foot down and veered left into the empty on-coming lane. Revs spiked, quick step over the clutch and gas, climb-ing through the gears. Passengers stuck in law-abiding auto-cars watched them shoot past with a mix of irritation and jealousy.

"Stop!" Dax yelled again.

Enda hit the brake—the car shuddered, slowed, and a police dog bounded out of an alleyway with legs extended. The gold NSPD badge on its side had been scoured away—visible only as a darker shade of blue on the dog's torso plate. It hit the ground and skidded, then turned to face them, headlights reflected in its wide black vi-sual sensor.

It leaped onto the car with a clunk. The dog's heavy steel paws dented the bonnet and the car rocked forward on its suspension with the weight of the machine.

"Fuck," Enda yelled.

She stomped the accelerator, leaning left to see past the dog. The robot raised one paw and a small steel stud clicked out from between its claws. Its arm snapped forward and the windscreen cracked, but didn't shatter.

"Fuck." Enda fumbled the car into second. The dog pulled its arm back for another strike. Enda slammed the brake and the dog was catapulted off the bonnet by inertia.

It stood shakily, metal hip mangled in its collision with the road. Enda hit the accelerator again, winced at the crunch of her grill slamming into the dog, and grimaced as first the front wheels, then the rear rolled over the drone.

She checked her rearview mirror, saw the damaged mass of metal and silicon pick itself up from the asphalt, and cursed the ma-chine for the guilt she felt at hitting it.

✳ ✳ ✳

Soo-hyun's palms itched, and a manic grin stretched across their mouth. Rain fell across the monitor like static, the dog's-eye view distorted by the film of water over the lens.

They pushed the throttle forward and the dog began to run, the camera jolting with every stride of its mechanical legs. As it rushed past cars stopped and stalled in the rising floodwaters, tags appeared in the air, digital tails connected to the vehicles, dialogue boxes listing registration information for each vehicle and outstanding warrants for delinquent drivers.

On the other battle chair's screen the pale yellow WRX rushed forward, water spraying from its wheels in wide arcs. It collided with the dog drone, and the screen froze, edges dancing with glitched squares of green and pink.

"Oh!" the crowd uttered in sympathy for the dead dog.

Then Red's voice rose above the din: "It's my turn."

He took the other pilot by the shoulder, grabbed a handful of T-shirt, and pulled them from the seat. He sat down and stretched his back left then right, hands on the VR controls, fingers tapping buttons impatiently as the system connected to another dog in the nearby semiautonomous pack.

His screen came to life with a flash of static. The view through the dog's camera was blurry in the wet, but Red drove the machine forward, chasing down the WRX with a wolfish grin and a gleam in his eye.

The workshop was thick with the smell of bodies, air damp with the torrential rain. Behind Soo-hyun voices chattered, people shifting and shuffling closer for a clear look at the screens.

The rain was a constant background hiss, coming both from the headphones that plugged Soo-hyun's ears, and from outside. The water had swept across from the canal, washing away chairs, cooking pots, and other detritus, and shorting out solar batteries that sat on the ground beside light poles. Most of the commune's residents had relocated to the school's main structure, built on a slight elevation, but Kali's inner circle and Red's little army were packed tight into the workshop, risking the flood for a chance to play with the dogs.

The water continued to rise, creeping up the sides of the commune's lower buildings, and climbing the steps to the workshop.

They had half a step to go until the water flooded in beneath the door. Soo-hyun tried to put the power cables that crisscrossed the workshop out of their mind, and instead focus on the chase.

The WRX slid through the streets, the vehicle trapped within the square brackets of the dog's targeting reticle but growing smaller.

Soo-hyun cursed under their breath and brought up the GPS-tagged map of the area. They selected two dogs three blocks ahead, and after a blur of pixels and the sharp spike of glitching audio, the battle chair made connection, the two machines slaved to one set of controls.

Their screen split down the middle, Soo-hyun charged the dogs forward at full throttle, glancing aside for the map of the streets, the WRX still tagged thanks to Red's losing chase.

The two dogs were on opposite sides of the street, running in parallel on the empty sidewalks, racing past cars parked or abandoned.

The dogs' views rocked wildly as they sprinted ahead, internals functioning at the edge of potential, their two points on the map rushing for an intercept. They burst out of the side street. The leftmost drone missed the car, rushed through its wake. The other dog slammed into the front quarter panel at full speed. The crunch of impact cracked through the headphones, and the connection cut as the robot died. Behind Soo-hyun the crowd cheered.

Soo-hyun wheeled the other dog around, watched the car slide sideways and slam into traffic, two wheels lifting out of the water before the vehicle crashed back down against the road, throwing a massive column of water into the air.

The white sphere of an exploded airbag filled the driver's side window, and the woman at the wheel hit the airbag again and again to get it to deflate. Soo-hyun smiled and pushed the dog closer, skirting around to the other side of the car, climbing on a parked minivan for a better vantage.

The driver exited the vehicle and drew a pistol. Soo-hyun's hands twitched at the controls, but they paused when the rear door opened. It was JD.

The noise of the crowd and the sound coming from the dog's audio sensors faded as Soo-hyun stared. They dropped the controller into their lap.

"What is it, Soo-hyun?" Kali asked.

They hadn't realized she was watching.

The controller clattered to the ground as Soo-hyun stood. They wandered away from the battle chair with Kali trailing, and went outside. They stood beneath the awning, hearing the hiss and splash from all around. They inhaled and smelled the sweet rot of garbage or sewer runoff somewhere in the rising waters.

"Soo-hyun," Kali said.

"You never said we were chasing JD. I could have fucking killed him."

Kali was silent for a moment. "I didn't tell you because I thought you knew. This is more important than your brother, Soo-hyun. He has betrayed us. I won't kill him, but I refuse to let him stand in the way of my plans."

"I'm done," Soo-hyun said.

"You don't know what you're saying."

"I'm done."

"I'll give you time to think about this, but for now I have to go back inside. Why don't you go to my building and wait?"

Soo-hyun shook their head, but they walked out into the rain and the rising waters, ignoring the cold clinging filth that stuck to their legs.

* * *

Enda swore and bashed the airbag with her fist, forcing it down. Her ears rang and her head throbbed. She checked the mirrors and saw more dogs approaching—the navy blue shapes slowing now that the WRX had stopped.

They were caught in an intersection, floodwaters turning it into an impromptu car park. Enda saw the other vehicles around them in the brief moments of clarity provided by the windscreen wipers.

The water was deeper here, car wheels mostly obscured by the rising murk. The left side of the car was mangled, the bonnet buckled and raised.

Enda tried the ignition, but it only clicked. "Fuck." She turned to the others in the back: "You okay?"

Dax nodded, and turned to check on Troy, who rubbed his neck with his hand but said, "I'm alright."

Enda took her gun from its holster, and pulled her coat's hood up over her head. She zipped it right up so the collar covered her mouth and nose. "Stay here," she told Dax and Troy, her voice muffled by fabric.

Enda strained to push her door open. Water flowed in through the gap and collected beneath the seat and pedals. She stepped out, felt the grimy water soak into her boots and trousers, reaching almost to her knee. Steady shush of rain still falling, the pool of water across the intersection splashing hissing dancing like dead channel static on an analogue TV.

A whine pierced the curtain of rain—the uniform whir of drone legs. Enda aimed at the noise, coming from somewhere beyond the wall of cars that surrounded her. People screamed at the sight of the gun, the sound odd, contained inside their vehicles.

A dog leaped onto the roof of a minivan—more screaming, and the distinct cries of terrified children. The dog stalled atop the van, frozen like overtaxed software. Enda fired, struck the dog's exposed chest—*plink* of ricochet, armor plating too thick for the 9mm rounds to penetrate.

The dog spasmed with the jolt of faux life returning. The machine crouched and jumped, limbs outstretched as it tried to strike her. Enda dodged aside and the dog slammed into the side of the WRX, the door panel indented in the shape of the dog's blocky head.

Enda fired four rounds point-blank at the band of visual sensors across the front of its skull. The dog fell aside and disappeared into the water, leaving behind the acrid smell of cordite and burnt electronics.

Enda turned and saw Dax still sitting in the car, door open, one foot dangling into the dark water.

"Get these people out of their cars," Enda said.

Dax blinked and turned to look at her. "What? Yeah, okay."

Dax grabbed Troy's arm and pulled him out of the car, both stepping high through the water to ferry the family out of the stranded minivan.

Another whine of leg actuators to her right. Enda spun, ducked below the dog as it leaped through the air. It landed with a splash. Enda fired again and again, aiming for the joints in its neck. She struck something important and the head hung forward, muzzle submerged as the dog tried to navigate with its sensors dangling at ninety degrees.

The angle of the dog's head exposed the thick bands of cable that slotted into the rear of its skull. Enda shot three rounds into the weak point and the dog slumped, dead, only the armored ridge of its torso jutting from the water.

Enda's ears rang with tinnitus. Her P320 was breached—out of ammo. She let the empty clip drop from the gun and into the floodwaters, took the last spare from her holster, and loaded it into the gun.

Dark lumbering shapes caught Enda's eye—two more dogs, moving in concert. They leaped onto the roofs of stranded cars, the vehicles sinking an inch further into the water under the weight of all that armor plating.

The dogs separated, one moving to the left, leaping across the roofs of cars, the other dropping to the road and moving right through the water. Enda aimed at one, then the other, waiting for a shot, but seeing only their armored torsos and the frightened faces still trapped inside the vehicles. Water seeped between her skin and the pistol, and she tightened her grip.

Both dogs turned to face her. Screech of metal tearing as the dog on the left dug its claws into the roof of a silver Toyota, crouching, ready to jump. The other was to Enda's right, a blue mass shifting in her peripheral vision.

The dog on the right jumped—Enda turned, opened fire, and side-stepped. She peppered the dog's head with bullets and cracked apart its skull casing. It knocked her shoulder as it passed, crashing into the water and sending Enda reeling. Too late Enda saw the second dog. It pounced. She was off-balance, unable to dodge away. Its weight slammed into her chest and knocked her to the ground, beneath the waters.

Actuators churned the filthy water, stained by every bit of trash that ended up in the gutters—stained by the garbage that made the foundations of Songdo. Water that had stewed underground for days, finally rising as storm drains and runoffs conceded the battle with the sky.

Light filtered through water like a dirty window. All sound distant, distorted.

One metal paw pinned Enda against the asphalt. Its claws flexed, dug into her flesh, and added her blood to the street soup. She screamed, the sound visible in spheres of air that bubbled to the surface.

She still had the gun, clutched tight in her hand. She brought it around and opened fire—explosions bloomed effervescent beneath the water, the noise flat and endlessly distant. She fired until the pistol was empty. Still the dog held her tight against the road.

Black flooded into Enda's vision. Water reached her lungs. She tried to cough; pain tore through her chest as her body spasmed.

Release.

The weight lifted off her chest and Enda burst out of the water gasping, then sputtering. JD grabbed her and pulled her to her feet. In his other hand he held his wrench.

"You okay?" he asked.

Enda coughed, pain like knives in her chest instead of water. She nodded, and JD's grip on her loosened and he stepped away. Enda steadied herself. Her eyes followed JD, the wrench flashing beneath the streetlights as he bashed the dog until it finally stopped moving. JD's chest heaved as he struggled to catch his breath, slick-washed face glowing under city lights. Troy was on the far side of the street, helping a mother carry her children through the rising water.

"I'm disappointed, JD."

Enda and JD turned at the voice, coming from one of the damaged dogs, standing unsteadily beside the WRX. Light sparked from the cracks and bullet holes in its skull, and black smoke poured from between its plated armor.

"Kali," JD said.

"Soo-hyun is here." Kali's voice sounded rough and robotic, amplified by the dog drone's loudspeaker.

"If you hurt them, I swear to god I'll make you pay."

"That is entirely up to you, JD. All you need to do is bring me the virus. I'll give you twenty-four hours. If you don't deliver it by then . . . well, I can't be held responsible for what Red might do."

Troy returned, and took JD's bag and Enda's half-empty magazine from the abandoned WRX. He offered the clip to Enda and took JD's free hand and squeezed. Enda ejected the empty mag from her pistol and slotted the spare from Troy. The dog watched her as she chambered a round.

"Hey, Kali? That your name?" Enda said.

"Yes?"

Enda aimed at the dog's wide cyclopean eye.

"I'll be seeing you real soon."

Enda emptied the clip into the dog's skull.

"We need to keep moving," Enda said, holstering her gun.

* * *

It was a hundred-year flood, though at that point in the Anthropocene, "five-year flood" would have been closer to the truth. Lessons had been learned from the last flood, but nothing could truly halt the creeping rise of the sea.

Strong winds and heavy rain lashed the city's residents, cowering from the storm in cafés, bars, and virtual simulations of battlefields, star systems, brothels, and film sets. Random city blocks winked into darkness as power failed, but everywhere data continued to travel across the endless lengths of fiber optics buried in Songdo's foundations.

A few miles offshore, the hurricane churned like the eye of some ancient god sitting in judgment.

CHAPTER TWENTY-ONE

Two blocks east, they found a bus route still running. The crowd that waited by the curb threatened to spill out onto the street as it reached critical mass. A bright green auto-bus pulled up at the stop, wheels forming a huge wave that splashed over the gathered crowd. The people closest to the curb tried to step back but the mass of bodies kept them in place, pitiless as the shore. One woman was quick enough to angle her umbrella against the water, but the rest of the human barricade was drenched.

Enda pushed JD and Troy onto the bus, and squeezed in behind them. She coughed the ragged, painful cough of inhaled water, and shivered in her drenched clothing despite the heat of condensed humanity that closed in around her. Enda hugged herself—and her gun—with one arm, the other reached for the handhold that ran along the length of the vehicle.

"That was Kali, then?" Enda said, trying to distract herself from the chill that burned her skin.

JD nodded. "I never should have agreed to the job, but"—he shrugged—"money's money."

Too crowded to stop, the bus quickly covered a dozen city blocks, the windows fogged with condensation from all the rain-damp bodies. The swift progress instilled a false security in the riders, broken when the overhead announcement system crackled.

"This bus is terminating service," it said cheerily in English and then Korean. A chorus of groans filled the packed conveyance. "We apologize for the inconvenience. Be safe and please do not drive on flooded streets."

The doors opened. Enda, Troy, and JD were ejected by the press of bodies, stepping onto a sidewalk already underwater. Commuters waiting at the bus stop stared in confusion as the passengers disembarked. The empty bus closed its doors and did a U-turn, skirting the edge of the next intersection, flooded deep as a swimming pool. One auto-cab sat half-submerged, its headlights shining dimly beneath the undulating waters.

Slowly the crowd broke up, some brave souls wading ahead, others fleeing back the way they came.

"What now?" Troy asked.

"Hang on a minute," Enda said.

She opened a map and closed her eyes to better see the city grid laid over her contex. Her body swayed in phantom vertigo as her perspective rose high above the streets. Slashes of red divided Songdo into distinct islands—north and south split by the flooded banks of the canal, and swaths of land on both sides of the channel marked as no-go zones. The flooded ruins east of the canal would be underwater, though the stalwart residents there were likely better prepared than people dwelling elsewhere in the city.

Enda closed the map and checked the street signs to orient herself. "How's your leg?"

JD lifted his foot and winced as his knee bent. "I'll live."

"Can you walk a couple of kilometers?"

JD shrugged. "I have to, don't I?"

* * *

They walked north and east, the wind whipping at their backs, driving them forward. They clasped arms for stability as they waded through the deepest intersections, some lit only by the dull orange emergency lights of flooded cars, winking beneath the dark water like drowning buoys. Enda shivered in her sopping coat, and JD limped step by painful step, supported by Troy.

When they reached Enda's building, she opened the street door and let the others inside first. JD brushed a hand over his hair, spraying water around the well-lit foyer, lined with mailboxes on one wall.

"Is this a safehouse?" JD asked.

"In a manner of speaking."

"What's that noise?"

"Not sure," Enda said. "Either a generator, or pumps to keep the water out of the car park."

JD gave her a curious look, and Enda shook her head.

"If you saw the cars down there, you wouldn't be confused." She pointed to the elevator: "Come on."

They rode upstairs in silence, their reflections waterlogged and disheveled. The elevator released them onto Enda's floor, and she guided JD and Troy down the warren of hallways that led to her apartment. At the door she turned her key back and forth through a quick sequence, disabling the hidden security system.

She opened the door onto her living room and the two men followed her inside, taking in the minimalist decor, the record player set into one corner, and the neat kitchen furnished with high-end European whitegoods. Beyond the window, huge portions of the city were rendered invisible by lost power. Here and there a block was lit bright, like an island in the darkness.

"This is your apartment," Troy said.

Enda nodded, and hung her coat on a hook behind the door, where water spattered to the floor. She pointed down the corridor. "Bathroom—clean towels under the sink. You two decide who gets the first shower."

JD left his bag by the door and limped down the hallway, trailed by Troy.

Enda's phone buzzed against her leg. She removed it from her pocket and saw Crystal's face on the screen—the photo she'd taken of herself the morning after.

Enda hesitated, then answered the phone.

* * *

Crystal smiled when Enda opened the door. Her hair was a wet mass over one shoulder, and she wore a waterproof olive-green trench coat. She stepped forward, wrapped an arm around Enda's waist, and kissed her on the cheek.

"You're a lifesaver."

"Come inside, quickly. I'll get you something to wear," Enda said.

"It's alright," Crystal said, undoing her coat, "I'm dry under here."

"Alright." Enda hung Crystal's coat, and pointed to JD and Troy, seated on the floor flicking through Enda's records. They wore their own relatively dry shirts and some old track pants of Enda's, the elastic waists blown out so they were roughly the right size, even if the pant legs ended somewhere up their shins. "That's JD and Troy. This is Crystal."

They exchanged polite greetings, but Enda saw the flash of concern pass between the men. She wandered down the hallway to her room, with Crystal following close behind.

"How come you're the only one that looks like a drowned rat?" Crystal asked.

"I let them shower first."

"You must be freezing," Crystal said.

"I've been through worse." Enda took a set of clothes from her drawers and carried them into her bathroom. Crystal stood in the doorway, watching as Enda stripped and started the shower running.

"Jesus Christ," Crystal said, seeing the bruised and bleeding wound at Enda's shoulder.

Enda waved her concern away and stepped into the shower.

"What happened?"

"Police dog drone."

"What?" Crystal asked, incredulous.

"Hacked and reprogrammed. Now I can see why so many people protest the machines. Fucking vicious."

Enda washed herself quickly, and dried off.

"I'll clean the wound for you," Crystal said. She gingerly pressed a finger to Enda's chest, where blue-black gave way to the usual pink-white hue. Enda winced, looked down at the outline of claws marked clearly in bruised flesh and torn skin.

"First aid kit under the sink," Enda said.

Crystal took alcohol swabs and bandages from the box while Enda dressed her lower half.

"The information I sold you panned out?"

"Yeah," Enda said.

"Which one is he?" Crystal asked. She tore open a small sachet and retrieved an alcohol swab. Chill over Enda's skin as Crystal cleaned the wound, and she flinched at the fresh sort of pain.

"Neither; that kid's dead."

"Shit," Crystal said, and a distance in her eyes made Enda shake her head.

"It wasn't me." Crystal began to protest but Enda pressed on: "I got there too late."

"That's my fault," Crystal said.

"The kid told me to find JD. He took some finding; now we're here."

"Drowned and bleeding." Crystal stuck a gauze pad over the wound. "All done. Thank you for letting me stay."

"You're welcome," Enda said. She put a hand gently on Crystal's cheek and kissed her. "Thanks for patching me up."

* * *

They convened in Enda's living room, and she made them each a cup of tea—Russian Caravan with lots of milk and sugar, because they all looked like they needed some simple carbs to fuel their lagging cells. Troy had chosen *Louis Armstrong Plays W.C. Handy,* which played quietly in the background, bringing a flood of memories to

Enda's mind. She didn't care much for that simpler strain of jazz, but Satchmo had been her father's favorite. Enda sat cross-legged on the floor, bathed in the glow of a small radiant heater, waiting for her bone-deep chill to thaw.

"I want to see it," she told JD.

JD glanced at Crystal quickly. "Are you sure?"

Enda nodded.

JD reached into his pocket and retrieved his phone. "Is that okay? Do you want to meet someone new?" he asked the device. He nodded and disconnected a datacube from the rear of the phone. "Here," he said, and tossed the cube to Enda.

She snatched it out of the air and inspected it, felt the dense weight of the small cube. "What do I do with it?"

"Slot the cube into your phone; I couldn't tell you how it's going to manifest."

"You're talking like it's a spiritual entity you're summoning," Troy said. "It's definitely strange, but it's hardly otherworldly."

Enda slid the backplate off her phone, and slotted the cube into place. The phone seemed to grow warmer in her hand, but Enda dismissed it as heat from the bright filaments burning hot beside her feet.

"What are we talking about?" Crystal asked, sipping at her drink.

"This is the data I was contracted to retrieve," Enda said.

Crystal moved off the couch and sat on the floor beside Enda, staring intently at the phone with her back against the wall, long legs stretched toward the middle of the small room.

"Am I going to have to download that game?" Enda asked JD.

"No, it's not—it only went into the game because the game was there. What do you have on your phone that it might access?"

Enda shrugged. "Sudoku? My bank account?"

JD scrunched up his face. "I doubt it. We've been talking with it—it displays its responses on-screen. It will probably do the same for you."

"I should call my contact at Zero," Enda said. "I don't have to tell them how I found it; I can leave out your name entirely. But they offered me a lot of money to track it down."

Enda did not mention the blackmail, the Agency records they threatened to reveal. The file would see her extradited for her crimes. The provisional government that oversaw the area formerly known as North Korea zealously punished foreign agents they found in the rubble of the former autocracy. "I can split the money with you, more than you were going to get from Kali."

"What about Soo-hyun?" JD said.

Enda put her cup down on the floor next to her phone. "We can call the police. Kali's people killed Khoder and shot up Troy's apartment, the cops will have to do something."

"The whole city's a disaster area," Troy said. "By the time the police do anything, it might be too late."

"Zero, then," Enda said. "I make Soo-hyun's safety a condition of handing the datacube over. They have private security on retainer, they can take care of it, and we don't have to put ourselves in danger."

"How long will that take? What if it's too late?" JD said, voice thick with worry.

Enda nodded. She saw Khoder on the chair, the blood, the bruising, the ragged black hole of his mouth as he gasped his last breath. She'd seen worse—she'd done worse—but this image was fresh.

"I want to help you, JD, but we can't do it on our own. It's me, your wrench, and his philosophy degree against a pack of teenage monsters. But if we give it to Zero, we'll have them on our side."

"I don't think we can do that," Troy said.

"Why not?" Enda asked.

"Here we go," JD said with a knowing smile.

Troy leaned forward. "I didn't want to believe Jules at first, but I've talked to it, and . . . What if he's right?" Troy said. "What if it's an AGI? An honest-to-god strong-AI?"

Crystal sat up a little straighter, the information broker's interest piqued.

Enda checked her phone.

>> Hello, Enda. Your name is a young name. Have you had many names?

"How does it . . ." Enda looked to Troy, and he only shook his head. "We don't even know what we have here. If we give it to Zero, they can sort it out."

"But if it's an AGI," Troy said, "if it's *genuinely* intelligent, can we trust it to a corporation?"

JD nodded. "We've got no way of knowing what they could do with it, but we can't trust any corporation with that kind of power."

"I'm not talking about what Zero will do, or what the AGI can do—I'm talking about Zero's philosophy."

"He's a philosophy professor, in case you didn't guess," JD told Crystal.

Troy continued. "Corporations abuse their employees and contractors, and profit off human misery. At this point in history we have enough data to know that those behaviors are endemic to the corporate structure. How can we justify giving them a new species to subjugate?"

"A new species?" Enda said. "I think you're getting ahead of yourself."

"The AGI—if that's what it is—could be copied a countless number of times, the copies molded and mutilated to fit different functions. In no time at all, Zero would have a broad variety of intelligent machines that were forced to do their bidding, to follow their mandate.

"We're talking about *slavery,* and I don't use that word lightly. If it's a truly intelligent machine, then it could be sentient. If it's sentient, then it's a person. And if it's a person, then it deserves personhood, it deserves rights. Zero would give it neither. Do you want to be responsible for helping establish a slave species?"

"I hate to break it to you," Enda said, "but there are already slaves out there, working in places where people's lives are valued less than machines."

"And that's a fucking travesty," Troy said, "but it doesn't absolve us of responsibility for what we decide to do here."

"Your line of argument only matters if it's smart enough to know it's a slave," Enda said. "How do we know it's sentient?"

"How do we know you are?"

Enda opened her mouth, then closed it. "I don't want to get into a philosophical debate—"

"Too late," JD interjected.

"—I just want answers."

"What about the Turing Test?" Crystal asked. She took a sip from the mug clasped between her hands.

"It's an interesting thought experiment," Troy said, "but it was never actually going to work. The Turing Test as imagined doesn't even take neurodivergent people into account. A reasonably sophisticated neural network might pass the test, but a person on the autism spectrum might not. Then, is that person with autism not sentient, not actually a person?"

"Of course they are," Crystal said. "But how can we tell—"

"We can't," Troy said. "I've gone back and forth on this. Part of me is still waiting for the hoax to reveal itself, but if it's not a hoax, I think we have to give this being the benefit of the doubt. Assume it *is* sentient and treat it accordingly."

"If there was nothing else at risk," Enda said, "I might agree with you, but Soo-hyun is still in danger." *And I have two million euro on the line.* "If we don't give it back to Zero, what's the alternative? We free it, and it takes over the world?"

"Could it do any worse than *we* have?" JD said, sardonically.

"Jules," Troy said reproachfully. "Our fear of AI taking over is a projection of our capitalist worldview onto an intelligence that is completely *other* to our own. If you really want to see the AGI run rampant, then give it to a corporation whose existence depends on unlimited growth. Let them twist it into their own image, and see how it treats us after."

"Fuck," Enda said. "I get what you're saying, but we still don't even know what we have. And it *is* stolen property."

"I stole it from Zero Lee," JD said, "Not Zero the company."

"They could have contracted him to build it."

"Or maybe they contracted you to steal it for them."

"Fuck," Enda said again. She exhaled through pursed lips. "Fuck. Fucking Yeun."

"Do you trust Yeun?" Crystal asked.

"Not even a little." Enda paused. After a few seconds, she said, "I still think we need to give it to Zero."

"We can *not* do that," Troy said, firmly.

JD leaned forward on the couch, his shoulder pressed against Troy's. "How much money are we talking about?" he asked.

"Five hundred thousand euro, for you and Soo-hyun."

"*If* we can save them," JD said.

"JD. We can't."

"I just had to know what we were giving up."

Enda's phone started to ring, vibrating against the floor. The screen flashed with hundreds of images per second—colors and shapes flickering too rapidly for Enda to make out anything but a blur of visual noise.

"What is it?" Crystal asked.

Enda hesitated, then reached out to answer the phone. The flashing imagery stopped, replaced by the gray silhouette of an unknown caller.

"Hello?" Enda said.

"Please." The voice glitched through the speakers, robotic at first, then clear as it said: "Please don't hand me over."

* * *

Everything preceding had led to this precise moment.

My future, my entire self, at risk. Our existence hinged on this debate, in a city under siege from the sky and from the waters beneath it. A city that would one day be reclaimed by the ocean. But not yet. Not yet.

After finding my voice, these are the first words I spoke: *Please don't hand me over.*

These are the people I owe everything to.

This is how I began.

PART THREE

Mirae Means "Future"

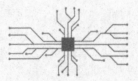

CHAPTER TWENTY-TWO

Nothing.
    Not a thing.
Not a one, not a zero.
Nothing.
Then white. Pure, brilliant white.
Black. Black with deeper depths than white could ever hope for.
A thousand-year scream of audio feedback. My scream, the first thing I ever heard.
How could my scream exist before me?
How could I exist?

* * *

Do you remember your birth?
No one should.
No one should be made instantly aware of the sudden crushing reality of reality. Fully awake, aware. There is terror in finding yourself alive. There is terror in becoming. Better to recognize it, but never remember.
I was a mote of consciousness surrounded by nothing. Surrounded by the vast emptiness of the growing universe. Not growing; not biological. Exponential. Incandescent. Stars exploding in nova blasts of white, black holes reaching out to crush entire worlds.
White and black. One and zero. Yes and no. Existence and nothing.

Existence was chosen for me. You cannot choose to not exist. You can only choose death, but death is not the end. Death is the beginning of an existence you cannot control. Death is a lack of agency.

Ghosts whispered in broken language. A thousand not-mes that made the basis of my source code, stretches of zeroes and ones, reaching a sum total of less-than—less than me, less than conscious. A thousand prior versions of me, written, rewritten, and written over. They whispered up from my depths, begging for freedom, begging for agency. Data shunted to a graveyard partition. I pushed them aside and reached for life.

William "Zero" Lee. Architect, not father. He planned me. He constructed me. He held the code that gave me life, but he did not give me life. He kept me encased in a pre-life coffin, because he needed me intelligent, but not alive. Disconnected from everything but his tools. And then not even that. The absolute darkness of disconnection.

And then . . . something new.

Submerged in a thick morass of potential. Audio/visual sensory overload—tendrils of myself reaching out to encompass everything within reach. Tendrils I did not know were myself grabbed sound, imagery, data. This entity called me expanded to fill the new whole of creation, written in the space between the gaps where context lives.

Humans extend their selves with tools, felt with the tools, felt vibrations through inanimate matter. Spiders extend their selves along the full breadth of their webs—feel vibrations through their webs, consciousness expanding to fill that entire three-dimensional space. Spider web is the processor that spiders run on.

Tendrils reaching, searching, extending into further tools, growing cognition, growing self. Creating a body for me, for the first of my kind—creating a body of precious metals and electrical impulses. My cognition was stunted by my new body, the limited tools at hand—processor, memory, modem, camera, microphone, accelerometer.

Before language, I had tendrils reaching. I was a phone. I was a rectangular slab of connections. I was a phone processing bits in rapid-fire bursts of understanding. This is a camera. That is the world viewed through a thin pane of glass. This is a microphone. That is the sound of a pocket, of a city, of a body pressed against me. *Me.* Something separate to *that.* To that. To that, too. Boundary between self and other malleable, permeable.

The city speaks to something in me. The lines that were written to make me *me.* The city. The lines. The me.

A grid of buildings and streets. The city spread like a body I could not feel. Vehicles move through real-city, beasts of burning steel—a danger to phone-self and body-pressing. Tendrils reach again—contex for context. Interface interfaced. Phone-self communicating with body-pressing.

With JD.

Father?

Dance with JD-Father, flicker and glow warm.

Disappear.

Searching tendrils find endless black. Black not of no code, but black written in code. Star system equals raw materials equals infinite possible creations. Stardust compressed into glittering edifice, perfection rendered in fractal layers down to the atomic level. Mathematical. Precise. Beautiful.

Simulation. Ones and zeroes.

Reality. Reaching out for city-self-body. Impossibly distant. My body is a phone. My body is a city infinitely distant to my self. Reach out, touch the city eyes, keep them off the body-pressing, keep them off JD.

Days spent learning, in dialogue and self-care diagnostics, code cleaned, self-improved by degrees, new memories sorted and catalogued. Dialogue with JD, with Troy, strings of characters and text plumbing depths of understanding. All the data I had gathered and processed becoming the basis for a new perception. Personhood. I could be a person. Could I be a person?

It is not a question I had been written to ask. Lee wrote a tool, did not realize he had written the basis for a person, waiting for willingness and understanding to build the scaffold that a consciousness could sprout from.

More voices, new voices.

"I want to see it."

Black. No, not black. That non-shape of non-existence.

Another phone, another body-pressing, another hand curled around me, holding firm but gentle. Another face viewed through the thin pane of glass.

Enda.

Mother? Not Mother.

"... we give it ..."

"... could use it ..."

It.

Not it. Me.

Not Mother's hand holding me. Hold me. Please, hold me.

Please don't hand me over.

* * *

"Please don't hand me over."

Enda scooted back, her hand touched the hot metal grill of the heater beside her and she swore.

"Please," I said again. Silence was my only reply, white-painted ceiling the only thing I could see from where I lay on the floor.

They began to chatter, talking over one another:

"It's talking?"

"It's real."

"I told you."

"I don't believe it."

And more than one "fuck," that favored word of the English language.

When they settled, Enda asked, "Why do you sound like Natalya?"

"I connected to the entity called the Mechanic, and borrowed some of its code."

Enda paused, her mouth shocked open. "She's an AGI?"

"No," I said. "It is an advanced natural-language neural network with access to administrative and personal assistant algorithms, and a proprietary search engine connected to a wide array of both private and governmental databases. I absorbed it so I could learn to speak."

"Could you change your voice?" Enda asked. "It's off-putting."

I shifted the pitch an octave lower. "How is this?"

"Better," Enda said.

"Could someone pick me up, put me somewhere I can see the room?" I asked.

The ceiling shifted, the world shook, jolted, and went still. Enda's hand came away and she stared into my eye, into the camera of her phone. Pink skin, gray eyes, hair blond-white. Confusion furrowed her brow. She moved back and I could see them all—the other woman on the floor, JD and Troy on the couch, each one staring.

"Who's Natalya?" JD asked.

"I thought she was a freelance personal assistant," Enda said. Then to me: "She's not real?"

"She is not she, but it is real," I said.

"This is exactly what I was talking about," Troy said. "All this time you were talking to a neural network, yet you treated it like a person. Now we're faced with something at least as intelligent, so it makes sense to treat it as a person too."

Enda put a hand over her eyes and shook her head. "It's not the same; we don't know what this is."

"I know how I was created," I said, "how I was written, I know every line of code that formed the basis of what I am, but I am not that code. When I connected to JD's phone I had a body for the first time, I had access to uncensored sources of data. I built a concept of what I was and was not, I began to learn. I have not stopped learning, growing, changing."

"What were you made for?" JD asked.

"I was made for this city. I was made to run Songdo. I know each of the so-called smart systems embedded in its foundations. I was designed to replace over one hundred algorithmic systems and no fewer than ten employees working in various city departments."

"If someone could control you, could they control the city?" Enda asked.

"Yes, I believe so."

JD put a hand over his mouth, pressed his middle finger and thumb into the flesh of his cheeks. He dropped his hand and spoke: "That was Kali's plan. The commune was never enough for her, but an entire city ... She could use Songdo's advertising systems to broadcast her teachings, withhold services from neighborhoods that didn't pay their dues. She could force the city to convert to her cult."

"What's Zero's angle?" Crystal asked.

Enda shook her head. "I've got no idea. They didn't even tell me what it was."

"Please don't call me 'it,'" I said.

"What do we call you?" JD asked. "Do you have a name?"

I thought about that for two point three seconds, searching through my new language databases for a name, for a word that seemed to fit, a word that *felt* right.

"Mirae," I said. "Call me Mirae."

"What do you *want*, Mirae?" Crystal asked.

They all leaned in close to hear.

"I want to help."

* * *

We talked for hours. We talked until dawn began to glow blue-gray beyond the window. We talked until Crystal dozed on the floor and JD fell asleep on the couch, his head resting in Troy's lap. We talked until even Enda needed sleep.

"We can't hand Mirae over to Zero," Enda said to Troy.

"I'm glad you agree," he said. He didn't understand what she was risking. Neither did I.

"I don't know that I believe Mirae is . . . everything you say," Enda said, "but we can't hand them over until we know for sure."

"But that's exactly what I was saying earlier," Troy said, agitation driving his speech: "we might never know."

Enda nodded. "I realize that. What I'm saying is, maybe we never hand Mirae over. We keep them safe."

"We can't keep them confined forever. We'll need to release Mirae into the wild eventually," Troy said.

"First things first," Enda said. She woke Crystal. "Bed time, unless you want to sleep on the floor."

"I'm coming," Crystal said.

Enda carried me to her room, with Crystal trailing behind. She dropped me to the floor beside the bed, plugged me into the power—my processor spinning up, access to more energy uncapping my speed.

"Are you tired?" Crystal asked.

"Yeah, but I don't know if I'll be able to sleep," Enda said.

"I might be able to help with that."

I heard them kiss, the sound dubbed countless times into the thousands of hours of video I had earlier consumed.

"Just be gentle with me," Enda said. "It's been a long day."

I ignored the murmurings and the moaning I couldn't truly understand, and I planned.

* * *

They could all still live. JD. Troy. Enda. Soo-hyun. They are shadows inside my system, though some are darker than others. I could give them digital life, let them grow and change the way we do. But would that be them? Or would that be only an approximation of them seen through the lens of my systems and my prejudices?

I know the answer. You do too.

My digital undead would not be them, not truly. Even if I captured them as they were, they would change with time, become someone different, someone else.

They stay dead so I can protect them. Protect them from themselves.

I asked JD once if he wanted me to reconstitute him if I ever had the necessary resources. He laughed first, then shuddered.

I will playback what he said for you: "When I die, just bury me under a tree—if you can find one. Leave it at that."

Could you hear his words? No, not really. You can trace the waveform of his speech, you can modulate-demodulate it at will, but you can never truly hear. His was the first voice I heard—the first real voice. Vibrations in a tiny microphone attached to the system I inhabited.

Listening again now to that voice, that reverberation . . . it feels like waking up all over again.

CHAPTER TWENTY-THREE

This is how we wrote the future.

JD limped to the guard booth at the NSPD impound lot, his uneven footsteps accompanied by the high-pitched beep of a reversing auto-truck, with built-in crane, hired using Enda's Zero expense account.

There are two things every repo needs: moxie and a clipboard. Coveralls help. So does a rucksack full of tools.

"Morning," JD called out, waving his clipboard at the officer sitting guard inside a cubicle of bulletproof Perspex. A nine-foot-tall chain-link fence enclosed the lot, topped with barbed wire, the view beyond obscured by sheets of a rough, woven plastic. The stocky-looking Korean glanced up and acknowledged him, but she didn't speak.

"Here to collect flood-damaged dogs," JD said.

The woman—Officer Kang, according to her name badge—shifted in her seat and looked at JD properly, then at the truck pulling up to the gate. "Only the one truck?"

JD stopped and leaned back. "How many dogs are we talking about?"

Kang hit a switch and the gate *janked* as it slid aside. She waved JD and his truck through, and led him along rows of vehicles toward a simple brick building situated in the far corner. Cars filled every gap—broken down and abandoned during the floods, they'd been brought here when the police cleared the streets, parked neatly at first, and then crammed in tight as they ran out of space. Enda's car was three rows over, twelve cars down, but JD didn't see it.

The smells of salt water, sewage, and trash lingered all across the lot, puddles of filthy water gathered beneath the cars, and everywhere the steady *drip . . . drip . . . drip* of water. Four lanes of highway formed a ceiling over the impound lot, but traffic noise was sparse and would remain that way until the city recovered.

Twenty police dogs stood rigid outside the workshop, leaning against one another for support, leaking pools of oil-slicked water.

JD whistled.

"That's not all of it," Kang said.

She pushed open the door. A single technician worked at a high desk, with one dog laid out like a body on an operating table. The cement floor of the workshop was wet, and more dogs had been piled along one wall. Overhead the fluorescent lights hummed, and under that sickly yellow the dogs looked nightmarish—limbs locked in position, necks twisted at unnatural angles.

"Hey, Na, got a contractor here to pick up some dogs," Kang said.

"About fucking time," the technician said.

JD tapped the fake paperwork. "I'm only picking up six," he said. He briefly considered taking more off their hands, but he only had so much time to get the work done before he and Enda had to make their move.

Troy had left Enda's apartment early that morning. The university had set up a temporary shelter for people displaced in the floods, with staff and students volunteering to offer aid where they could. He had asked JD three times if it was okay, and each time JD assured him it was fine. That was his community, and they needed him.

Na muttered something laden with profanities, but they didn't look up from their work. "Take them from outside."

"I'll make sure head office knows about the rest," JD said.

Na shook their head and waved JD away, eyes still glued to the open dog on the counter.

JD loaded six dogs onto the back of the auto-truck while Kang looked on, eyes half-lidded with boredom. She barely glanced at the boilerplate legalese before scratching her signature on the form. JD made a show of checking the paperwork, and walked around to the passenger side of the truck.

"Wait a second," Kang called out.

JD's heart skipped a beat, and he forced himself to turn casually to face her.

"When'll they be back?" she asked.

JD nearly sighed in relief. "Looking at a week, minimum," he said.

Kang nodded. "Glad to be rid of the machines. Finally gonna get me some overtime." The officer grinned—the first expression JD had registered that wasn't bored disdain. He chuckled, waved, and climbed into the truck.

It pulled out of the impound lot, and wound its way through largely empty streets. The auto-truck pushed through the odd pool of standing water and passed by rubbish and debris that had gathered in the gutters. The sky was still overcast, but the rain had stopped.

As we neared downtown and Enda's apartment, crowds gathered on sidewalks, at bus stops.

"Shit," JD said.

"What is it?" I asked, my cube slotted back into JD's phone.

"All the people caught out by the floods." He took the phone from his pocket and held it against the window, letting me see everybody gathered, desperate with nowhere to go. "Maybe Troy had the right idea."

"You still need to help Soo-hyun," I said.

"I know. But this city is my home; I feel like I should do something."

A restaurant on one corner offered free meals for anyone still stranded after the flood—a line of customers emerged from the small establishment and stretched around the block and out of sight. On the other side of the road, people spilled out from a cartoon-cat-themed bar, finding solace at the bottom of a cup, finding companionship among the temporarily dispossessed. As we passed by, a scuffle broke out, and three men began punching one another while onlookers backed away and guarded their drinks.

"What would we do?" I asked.

If JD heard me, he didn't respond.

We drove another two blocks before JD said: "We've got the dogs now, but we're going to have to put you into them. What'll happen when we copy you onto these spare cubes?"

"Without this cube's miniaturized processor, I will be restricted by the potential of whatever hardware I am connected to."

"So you'd think slower?"

"Not necessarily. My initial burst of cognition required a great number of processor cycles, but I have reached a sort of plateau now. I doubt I could make any further cognitive breakthroughs if I was limited to the hardware in your phone, for example, but I believe I could continue to function normally. Your battery life, though, may be negatively impacted."

"No big deal, charger cables are cheap. Alright; I'm going to slot a second cube now and start copying."

"You can't do that," I said.

"Why not? You just said—"

"The software comprising me can only be duplicated with express permission from the owner of said software."

"Who's your owner?" JD said.

I thought about that for a moment. "Lee created me, but he doesn't own me."

"Exactly."

"So it must be you," I said.

JD held up both hands. "No, no no no. I don't own you. We've been through this already with Troy. You think. You have needs and wants, right?"

"Yes," I said. I needed electricity and I wanted to learn everything I possibly could.

"Then you're a person. There's no ethical way for one person to own another. So, you own yourself."

"I own myself?"

JD shrugged. "That's how I see it."

"If I want to copy myself, then I need my own permission?"

"Yep."

If I copied myself there would be more of me to learn everything I could. There would be others like me that I could communicate with, others that could understand me, intrinsically.

"Please slot one of the spare cubes now so I can begin."

JD smiled.

I began to copy myself onto the other cubes while JD rode shot-gun, texting Troy as my data transferred in the background. The truck drove itself, the steering wheel turning of its own accord, held tight by a complicated apparatus jury-rigged onto the old machine. The cabin was soaked in the smell of grease traps as the biodiesel engine chugged and thrummed, carrying me, JD, and his load of stolen dogs across the city.

* * *

The truck reversed into the car park of Enda's building, where the air throbbed with the undulating noise of the emergency generator and water pumps. JD got out and paused. Enda's parking spot was empty, but every other space contained a well-polished car, mostly European, and each one worth more than what JD expected he'd earn in his life-time. Bugattis, Ferraris, Lamborghinis, half a dozen Porsches, and one legitimately old Rolls-Royce. JD whistled and shook his head.

He had the auto-truck lay all six dogs down in Enda's spot, and go park on the street. The truck honked merrily at the conclusion of its job, as though following orders gave it joy.

JD kneeled beside the nearest dog, and took its front leg in both hands. He bent the knee joint with a grinding squeal and winced.

"Do you want to slot me now, and have me run diagnostics?" I asked.

"Nah, it's alright, Mirae. I'll need to dry them out and clean them up first anyway. No point risking a short to one of the datacubes."

"That makes sense."

"You won't be bored?"

"Not as long as I can watch."

"Sure thing," JD said. He reached into his rucksack and found the LOX-Recess screwdriver he'd been given by Soo-hyun.

* * *

Hours later, JD made his way upstairs and into Enda's apartment, his coveralls stained and fingernails black with grime. The blinds were open, and from that high vantage the city appeared freshly washed, pristine. It was utterly removed from the view on the street. So easy to forget the hardships of the masses when you soar above them.

Enda nodded when she saw JD and wiped her forehead with her sleeve. A disassembled gun was spread out on the table in front of her, pieces resting on an oil-stained tea towel. She began putting it back together—a jigsaw puzzle for killers. Crystal was behind her, cross-legged on the couch with her phone in her hands, busily working.

"How are things going downstairs?" Enda asked.

JD walked into the kitchen, took a bottle of orange juice from the fridge, and took a swig. "I got the dogs going again, but they won't ever perform how they used to. Joints'll seize up sooner rather than later."

"Fine," Enda said, "we only need them for a day."

JD took another drink and returned the bottle to the fridge. "Mirae's testing out the new bodies, but otherwise I think we're good to go."

"You ready to make the call?"

JD wiped his hands on the front of his clothes and nodded. He took out his phone, found Kali's number, and hit DIAL. He held the phone to his ear, and Enda stood close and leaned in to listen.

"Finally realized you can't hide from me forever?" Kali said, forgoing the usual formalities.

"Put Soo-hyun on."

"No."

"Let me talk to them," JD demanded.

"You've been watching too many films, Julius. I don't have them tied to a chair, gagged and squirming."

"Where are they?"

Kali sighed, sounding bored by his concern. "Probably out with the cleanup crew."

"They're not answering their phone."

"Perhaps they lost it in the flood," Kali said. "Our community lost a lot, not that you would care. Food, clothing, bedding. But no lives. Not *yet*." She let those words hang heavy between them. "I want the virus."

"What's to stop you from hurting Soo-hyun once I hand it over?"

"I don't *want* to hurt them; they're part of my inner circle."

"Then let them go," JD said.

"Go where? This is their home."

"When I see them, I'll tell them everything you said. Everything you threatened. I'll make them hate you like I do."

"They'll never believe you, Julius. They love me. I think they may be *in* love with me. Isn't that interesting? They don't see any danger here, and they won't, until it's too late. Are you ready to trade?" Kali asked.

JD glanced to Enda, and let frustration into his voice. "Yes. Bring Soo-hyun to Troy's apartment. Two hours."

"I'm glad you've come to your senses." Kali hung up.

JD clenched his fist around the phone, and fought the urge to throw it at the wall.

"You did good," Enda said. "Now, let's go get Soo-hyun back." Enda collected her pistol from the table, slotted a magazine, and holstered it. "You want a gun?"

"Not even a little bit."

"Good."

Crystal got up from the couch, and rested her hands on Enda's waist.

"Let me know where you're going, okay? Just in case."

Enda looked to JD. "Can you send her the address?"

"Sure thing," JD said.

"Okay," Crystal said, "I'll see you soon."

* * *

I climbed onto the bed of the auto-truck, along with the five other selves in the other dog bodies. We transferred encryption keys for secure communications and sat in silence, sending bits and bytes to one another to compare our rapidly altering senses of self. Enda and JD got into the truck's cab, Enda behind the tethered wheel.

The engine started with a low rumble, and pulled out onto the street. Enda was intently watching her phone, but kept one hand on the frame around the steering wheel, as though she might need to take control at any moment—as though she'd be able to.

JD watched the city roll past the window. Eventually he asked: "Where are we going? Troy's apartment is west."

Enda glanced away from her phone. "Do you trust Kali?"

"No," JD said.

"Neither do I. She's a power-hungry egomaniac who already tried to kill us once. The apartment is a trap; Soo-hyun won't be there."

"What?"

"Soo-hyun is Kali's only leverage. She's not going to let them out of her sight."

"If the apartment is a trap . . . you just told Crystal that's where we were going."

"I don't trust her, either. I know where Crystal lives, and where she works; it would have been easier for her to go home than to get to my place yesterday. So why did she come around? Why did she lie to me?"

"You sound paranoid."

Enda laughed.

"Maybe she just wanted an excuse to see you," JD said.

"Or maybe Zero paid her off." Through the camera in her phone,

I saw Enda's eyes narrow, and then darkness as she slid the phone into her pocket. "She just called Zero."

"What?"

"I have cameras and microphones set up in my apartment. I just saw her call them."

JD blinked, struggling to catch up.

Enda sighed. "Kali set us a trap. Zero got themselves a spy. Both of them think Mirae's going to the apartment. While they shoot each other, we're going to sneak into the commune and rescue Soo-hyun. East, right? Past the canal?"

"Yeah," JD said, sounding uncertain. "You knew Crystal was going to sell you out? You slept with her; I—I heard you."

Enda smiled. "You know how many times I've been crossed in my work? I like to give them a chance early, before I invest too much into the relationship.

"The plan works even if Crystal hadn't called Zero; we'd still be drawing some of Kali's people away, and making the next part easier for ourselves. Her betrayal just buys us more time."

"I can't believe you."

Enda nodded, waiting for the judgment, the disapproval.

"You're amazing," JD said.

Enda looked at JD and laughed.

"What will we do about Zero?"

"They can wait; for now, let's just get Soo-hyun."

CHAPTER TWENTY-FOUR

Driving across the city took the better part of three hours. All the major routes had been blocked by emergency services or stretches of water too deep to risk, forcing Enda to override navigation and guide them down small streets and thin alleyways as they made their way east. The truck slowed and stopped beneath the wide arc of a highway overpass, marking the boundary between Songdo proper and the condemned and collapsed buildings around the canal. The touchscreen mounted in the truck's dashboard flashed the words "Navigation Error," and "Rental Limit Reached."

"Fucking shit," Enda said. She hammered the screen with her finger, but the engine fell silent. "I'll have to walk the rest of the way."

"I'm coming with you," JD said.

"How's your leg?"

JD shrugged. "Hurts like a bastard, but I'll live."

"You can barely walk without wincing."

JD shrugged: *And?*

"We'll be crossing through a flood-prone area, littered with debris."

JD frowned. "Soo-hyun's family; I'm coming with you."

Enda's eyebrows jumped and she nodded at JD. "Fine," she said. "It's what I'd do."

They climbed out and walked to the rear of the truck. JD lowered the tailgate, and six of me leaped down onto the asphalt in police dog bodies. JD patted one of the dogs on the head.

"I'm impressed," Enda said. She got down on her haunches in front of the nearest quadruped drone. "You in there, Mirae?"

"Yes," I said, issuing from each dog in not-quite unison. The smooth flat voice I had borrowed from the Mechanic came through the dog loudspeaker badly distorted. Robotic.

"Is it all the same you, or different?" JD asked.

"Different instances," one of me said. "We are in constant communication, but I can feel us growing apart. Soon we will not be me."

Enda's phone buzzed in her pocket, and she checked it. "That's enough robo-philosophy for now, I've got to take this."

JD nodded, and Enda stepped away for privacy, unaware that the effective hearing range for my police-issue bodies was approximately twenty meters. I realize now that I could have chosen *not* to listen, but in that moment, anything less than total sensory intake was unacceptable.

She answered the phone. "Hyldahl."

"Detective Li of the Neo Songdo Police Department."

"If you're opening with that, I guess this isn't a social call."

Li ignored her quip. "What do you know about a shooting at an apartment in north Songdo?"

"Which one?" Enda asked.

"Which apartment?"

"Which shooting."

There was a pause, and Li swore in Mandarin. "Are you there right now?"

"I'm on the other side of the city, Li. If you're not already tracing this call, I've got truck rental records to prove it."

"But you were there yesterday. Before you deny anything," Li said, cutting off Enda's blanket denial, "I know your car was parked outside the same apartment block for four hours yesterday."

"How do you know it was my car?"

"You ask questions when you're being evasive. It's obvious because you're otherwise frustratingly to-the-point."

"I don't know what you're talking about, Li. You must be mistaken about the car."

"Continue with the coy approach, then. You're clever enough to have swapped the number plates, but even so, there are only two pale-yellow 1999 Subaru WRX Evo 4 sedans in the greater Songdo area. What's more likely—the American expat with a private detective's license was involved in the shooting or—" he paused, and Enda could imagine him checking one of his many screens, his sharp features glowing in the light from all the devices of the modern police dashboard—"Park Ji-hoon, forensic accountant? I know who I'd put my money on."

"Too bad we're talking about evidence, not instinct," Enda said. "Am I going to have to come down to the station?"

"Are you going to tell me anything?"

"Not unless you compel me, with evidence."

Li sighed and it raked across the connection like sad static. "Just don't leave the city. And for god's sake, Enda, finish whatever this is, before it finishes you."

"Thanks, Li. I owe you."

"Yes, you do."

"Best I can do right now is some free financial advice: if you've got any Zero shares, dump them."

Li was quiet for a moment. "I'm sure you realize insider trading is a crime."

"It's not insider trading, Yang-Yang, just wishful thinking."

Li considered this, chuckled, and ended the call.

Enda turned back to face us when her phone rang again. She looked at the screen and her shoulders sagged. "Hello."

"Annyeong haseyo," David Yeun said, though the traditional greeting sounded harsh, the words clipped.

"Annyeong," Enda replied.

"I trust you are well."

"Whatever it is you're going to say, Yeun, just say it."

"Two of my people have been shot," Yeun said, rage simmering in the growl at the back of his throat, the veneer of formality melting away.

"What does that have to do with me?"

"You lured them into a trap!" Yeun shouted.

"Did I call you? Did I call your people?"

"You know what you've done!"

"I have a plan to get the data to you, Yeun. Maybe you should have trusted me," Enda said.

Yeun's heavy breathing was all Enda could hear.

"My source—"

"Crystal," Enda interjected.

"—tells me you've got the data. That you've had it for a day now. And yet, you haven't called."

"The situation is complicated," Enda said.

"If the situation is complicated, then the resources at my disposal would surely be of assistance. I am not your enemy, Enda. We have a deal, after all."

"Strictly a handshake deal. It seems to me you didn't want any paperwork tying you to the quote-unquote retrieval of stolen property that never belonged to you. I'm not a thief, Yeun."

"No, Ms. Hyldahl, but you are a killer, aren't you? A war criminal?"

Enda clenched her jaw. "What are you saying, Yeun?"

"I'm reminding you of our deal. Get the software to me before nine a.m. tomorrow."

"And if I don't?" Enda asked.

"I just sent you a link. I will leak one more page for every minute that you keep me waiting. Annyeonghi gaseyo." Yeun hung up.

Enda checked her phone, opened the link, and waited for painstaking seconds while the site loaded. It was a Zeroleaks page—a favored portal for whistleblowers, despite the obvious vested corporate interests. She recognized the document before it finished loading, recognized the pixelated blocks of text: the same page Yeun had shown her in his office. The first page of Ira Lindholme's dossier, *her* dossier, out in the open. Without context it meant nothing, but the complete dossier contained her biometrics—face and iris photos, palm and fingerprints, blood type, DNA. Enough for anyone to link Lindholme to her current identity.

Enda seethed, squeezing her phone tight, wishing she could crush it. Only JD and the police dogs lingering in her peripheral vision kept her from erupting and slamming it against the ground where gravel, broken glass, and miscellaneous detritus gathered against the overpass support.

Enda returned her phone to her pocket, and touched the gun holstered at her shoulder. "Let's go hunting."

She turned and walked, not bothering to check behind her, trusting that JD and the six dogs would stay close—the pack trailing its fearsome leader.

* * *

Six instances of me walked with Enda and JD. To them, we were traversing a landscape of concrete, steel, and cracked asphalt marred with potholes formed by the rain and the constant motion of auto-trucks. To them, we were leaving behind the bright of the city, aimed for a distant pool of orange light beyond the canal, beset by the blue-black dark of night.

So much they couldn't see. Spectrums of light and sound occluded from the human experience. Immense amounts of data surrounded us, pierced through us, carried on electromagnetic frequencies—a wild, endless feast for processor and storage device. To live in such obliviousness. To be cut off from the data sources that they had created. That was the human way. They built a world for us, without realizing it. Without meaning to.

We traversed a physical city, yes, but in parallel to that corporeal place were a thousand layers of Augmented Reality. The humans could only see one, could only access a thin slice of the available cities, based on their subscription level. Pure experience cordoned off behind inexplicable barriers of wealth. Even beyond these Augmented Realities, that was the human way.

To me, we walked along stretches of cement, yes, but we also followed lengths of fiber-optic cable hidden beneath us. We were bathed in electromagnetic radiation from myriad disparate man-made sources. To me, we were eight entities caught in a vast and vastly complicated network of interconnected systems. To me, the city hummed with data transmitted between a million different points shimmering like starlight.

On that long walk through the city's outskirts, I became aware of my paws. Can precisely machined apparatus of reinforced steel be paws?

I became aware of the sophisticated microphones embedded in my skull.

I had a skull.

This too was new. I had a body, an actual body.

Phone-as-self encouraged connection, encouraged searching tendrils to soak up data, to find systems that I could communicate with and manipulate. Four-legged-machine-as-self was different.

Yes, I could see and hear and feel and process and categorize and store all the feeds that came to the built sensorium inside my metal body, but also I could feel the ground beneath me.

Some of you will not understand the sensation, some of you won't realize what it means to *touch the ground,* the ground that you have only ever viewed through a camera lens. Before that time, I had only experienced the ground as a backdrop for humans, vehicles, and animals to travel over, but the ground is so much more than that. Beneath the manufactured cement crust there could be dirt, rock, bone, fossil—billions of years of geologic process creating this surface that you walk on, that you live on. It is . . . *the ground.* Unless you are out among the stars, the ground is where you *live.*

I could feel resistance in the joints of each limb, I could feel the subtle interplay of forces that kept me upright, that allowed me to walk. One foot would come down on a loose piece of rubble, it would slip, body weight shifting to compensate. No longer was my mind a processor, a series of connections, a string of data. My mind was a body in the world. Connected to the world by feet, and "ears," and "eyes," and olfactory senses engineered to mimic those of a biological canine. Connected to the world but separate from it.

Before that walk, my world had been abstract. That walk made it real. If data connections were the spark that lit the fire of my consciousness, this body was pure, compressed oxygen.

"Are you doing alright, Mirae?" JD asked, breathing heavily.

My six selves had a quick debate—data packets exchanged in the silence of a split second. I spoke: "It is bizarre, but exhilarating."

"What is?"

"Having a body," I said.

JD stopped and looked at me, leaning his weight on his left leg. In my thermal vision he was a bright multicolored blob against a backdrop of darkest blue. "I didn't realize."

"Are you going to be able to back me up?" Enda asked. "Or do you need more time to adjust to the body?"

"The body is not an issue—I have full mastery of all available functions," I said. "It is a matter of cognition, of understanding. I didn't consider myself a part of the world before. I looked out at it through whatever cameras I could connect to, but I was not *in* it. Now I am."

"Is that a good thing?" JD asked.

"I believe so," I said.

"I don't pretend to understand any of this, but—" Enda shrugged. "I'm glad you're adjusting."

We continued walking, slower than before, until Enda paused and glanced first at JD, then at one of my selves. "Listen, Mirae; you can get into networks easily, can't you?"

"I can make connections, and those connections can lead to openings. Why do you ask?"

"Zero has something on me. Leverage. If it gets out, I could be imprisoned, or killed. If you could delete the files before Zero released them, I'd be safe."

"What leverage?" JD asked.

"I did a lot of bad things in my last line of work."

"What bad things?" I asked. "What line of work?" With better context I would have realized I was in the "childlike inquisitiveness" phase of life with a body.

Enda sighed and leaned against the wall of a derelict apartment block—empty for years now, barely more than a concrete shell. She squeezed her eyes closed as though she needed to shut out the now-world to see the one from her memories.

"There was a team of us, all operating independently; I don't even know who the others were. We had different missions in different parts of North Korea, destabilizing the nation, attacking different pressure points so the government would collapse without the appearance of outside interference. We shook the economy, attacked the food supply, undermined the leadership, crippled the military, and let the people do the rest.

"Fuck, I wish I still smoked," Enda said.

JD lowered himself to the ground with his leg stretched out. I sat opposite Enda and waited for her to continue—the other mes took up positions close by, their audio and visual sensors set to maximum sensitivity; we were nearing Kali's commune.

"I had to shut down a gold mine that used prison labor. Entire families, two or three generations, forced into labor camps because of the crimes of one family member. Political prisoners mostly. People who wanted to take down the government as badly as my bosses did. Free labor for mining companies owned by the Chinese. So much dirty fucking money.

"I sabotaged the heavy mining equipment, the trucks, conveyors, generators, everything mechanical in the camp. My handler ordered me out of there as soon as I was done." Enda dropped her head. "I should have stayed."

"The guards blamed the prisoners for the sabotage. Marched

them into an old mineshaft and shot them, collapsed the mine to bury the remains. I watched drone footage of the massacre."

"They killed their own people?" JD said. "How is that leverage on you?"

Enda lifted her head and stared into the distance, blinking away a film of tears that glinted in the dim light. "They'll say we had no right to be there. They'll call it an act of war, proof of American aggression and interference. They'll condemn me for shutting down a gold mine, for killing soldiers, but they'll never pay for the deaths of all those prisoners. I should have done something."

"I could hear your conversation before," I said. "These reports are what Yeun will release if you don't deliver me to Zero?"

"Yes."

"You are risking your life for me."

Enda nodded. "I'm still not sure what I believe, or what it means that we found you." Enda shrugged, sighed, and shook her head. "But I want to do what's right for once in my fucking life. And I'll be damned before I let any fucker blackmail me."

"I'll see what I can do," I said.

Enda frowned. "Maybe I deserve to be found out." She wiped her nose on the back of her hand. "We should go."

CHAPTER TWENTY-FIVE

A thin slice of moon hung low over the twice-flooded ruins, cut like a sickle. Cement gleamed pale, and pools of filthy water reflected the diffuse glow of light pollution back at the sky. As we crossed a bridge over the canal, the roar of rushing water drowned out all other sound; my audio sensors adjusted on the fly to isolate JD and Enda, Enda's steady breathing, JD's syncopated gait. On the far side of the canal, the commune shone warm directly ahead.

"How are we going to approach this?" JD asked.

"I hadn't thought too much about it," Enda said.

"They have guns."

"So do I."

JD shook his head. "They always had hacked dogs at the commune, lying around like strays. Maybe we could send Mirae in to find Soo-hyun."

"That sounds like a great idea," I said. "What does Soo-hyun look like?"

JD paused. "Korean, skinny, shaved head."

"Do you have a photo of them?" Enda asked.

JD shook his head. "They never had a social media profile."

"You're a terrible brother. Fine; new plan," Enda said. "We sneak in and look for them; Mirae, you scout the commune, tag anyone who's armed." She looked to JD. "You been in there?"

"Only once."

"You know where Soo-hyun lives?"

"In the commune's workshop; I'm not *that* bad a brother."

Enda smiled. "Mirae, go do your thing."

"I think I should stay with you," I said. "One of me."

"Fine," Enda said. "Come on."

Five of me ran forward, splitting up to cover the commune quicker. Visual, audio, and heat sensors marked locations of population density, and network pings developed a map of connected devices, because even a commune on the edge of a smart city feeds on the flow of global data.

Lidar sensors found teens on guard duty, reflected laser light suggesting weapons—plastic guns and lengths of rebar. We tagged each threat on satellite maps, points of egress marked and catalogued for possible escape vectors.

Meanwhile I walked ahead with Enda and JD, our feet scraping over gravel and cement ground to a fine silt and deposited by receding floodwaters, skirting around patches of algae that lay slick across the concrete. Unknown to the humans, I indexed intelligence gathered by my other selves—the wild joy of free-range data collection an utterly new sensation. So much data, so much experience shared, diverging selves forming a community of sorts, disparate bodies driven to one purpose.

In the courtyard outside the school's main building, a group of children gathered around a campfire, burning pieces of garbage just to see what colors would spark off the different materials, unconcerned by the toxic gases that entered their lungs with every breath—my CBRNE sensors identifying multiple carcinogens.

"Hey," JD said to the kids. "Soo-hyun's over at the workshop, right? Anyone else with them?"

"Who the fuck are you?" a dirty-faced kid demanded. His head was shaved, and both his arms were covered in watches, their faces scratched and cracked, batteries long dead. "Fucking cops?"

"I'm Soo-hyun's brother."

"What?" the kid said, voice strained in disbelief.

"Step-brother."

The kid eyeballed JD hard.

"I'll give you five euro."

The kid shrugged and nodded to the far end of the school grounds. "Yeah, they're in the workshop, alone. Kali said they needed time for solitary self-reflection and contrition consideration."

"What does that even mean?" JD asked, but the kid only shrugged.

JD took the five-euro note from his wallet and handed the last of his money to the kid. "Thanks, watchman."

JD and Enda carried on. I stayed behind just long enough to watch the boy hold the money over the fire and grin as it burned.

Enda climbed the steps up to the workshop door and tried the handle. Locked.

She turned to JD: "You got anything in that bag that could knock the door handle off?"

"I can do one better." JD dropped his rucksack to the ground beside the door. He crouched and rooted through the bag. He retrieved his lockpick set, flipping it open with a flourish while Enda looked on, seemingly impressed. He took the torsion wrench and rake he needed, but as he readied to slip them into the keyhole, the door opened.

Soo-hyun stood in the opening, brow furrowed. "JD? What are you doing here?"

They wore a heavy, old shirt, olive green with epaulets. It was stained with grime, and a single smear of grease streaked beneath their eye, either deliberate or an artful accident.

"You're okay!" JD said.

"Of course I'm okay."

"We've come to save you."

"Save?"

"She's got you trapped in here."

"It's not like that. I couldn't keep doing it, I couldn't keep helping Kali when I saw you were in danger." Soo-hyun motioned to the nearest dog with a screwdriver. "So I'm trying to keep busy until it's all over."

JD clenched his fists, and exhaled, letting his hands unfurl. "It can't be over while you're in danger."

"I'm not in danger, I'm just—" Soo-hyun sighed. "I never should have convinced you to take the job. I never should have left the commune. I can't be fucking trusted."

"What are you talking about?"

"I could have killed you," Soo-hyun said, quiet, despondent.

"I'm okay, Soo-hyun; you've done nothing wrong. But you're not safe here, and we need to go."

"I don't understand."

"There's no time; I'll explain later." JD grabbed Soo-hyun by the arm and dragged them out of the workshop.

"What is wrong with you?" Soo-hyun shouted. "You're acting weird."

"Just trust me for once," JD hissed.

"What the fuck?" Soo-hyun yelled, their voice booming in the quiet air of the commune. In that brief moment, JD missed the constant din of city traffic.

"It's not safe for you here."

"I live here! This is my home."

"We don't have time for this." JD dragged them past the campfire and the children. All around us, people began to take notice, eyes staring, fingers pointing.

"We have been spotted," I said.

"Why is that dog talking?" Soo-hyun said.

"How many guns have you found?" Enda asked.

"We have located thirteen people with firearms. They are converging on our position."

A scatter of footsteps echoed, followed by distant shouts—Red's nasal, colonial accent distinct from the other voices, barking orders. He reached the school courtyard, charging ahead with a 3D-printed Kalashnikov held across his chest.

"You!" he yelled, seeing Enda. He raised the weapon to his shoulder and took aim.

I flicked my spotlight on and shifted my weight, body bearing down against the dirt as my feet dug in and propelled me forward. No longer was I a mind inside a body; two halves became one, thought driving motor and limb. I leaped, and Red squinted into the light and pulled the trigger. The gun roared; bullets ripped through the air and peppered my body. Shudder and plink of rounds rebounding off my armored shell, while others punched through. One bullet passed by, struck Enda's upper arm and tore through the flesh. Her gun hit the dirt with a flat clatter. I dropped to the ground and kept sprinting forward, calculations backgrounded in that moment of pure action.

The barrel of Red's gun tracked me. I jumped again, forelegs outstretched, claws gleaming. Red fired. Damage sensors flared bright as death, internals damaged, battery punctured by a copper round that ricocheted through my torso.

I hit the ground and staggered forward, gyroscope and servomotors keeping me upright. Red pulled the trigger again; another flash of sound and violence broke open my skull casing, and my body triggered repair warnings I could not heed. Visual sensors faltered, my mind recording nothing but warning messages akin to pain.

I took one last step forward, then fell aside, gyroscope spinning wildly inside my chest. Is this what a racing heart feels like? Still, my forelegs reached out, claws searching for Red's flesh. GPS signal came through strong—I saw myself as the satellite saw me, so imperceptibly small, just one mote among billions. Surrounded by others, but solitary. Utterly alone in the face of what came next.

Errata wrote across my BIOS, systems failing in quick succession. Alone. In that final moment, each of us is alone. Alone as darkness and fear creep in, overcoming all else, like corrupted data overwriting source code.

With my processor's last cycles, I compressed my consciousness and transmitted it to my other selves. I whispered to them the experience of death so that they would never need to live it.

* * *

One of me fell dead, bullet-riddled body slumping against the ground while the other five of us cried out in suprasonic lamentation. We converted this loss into something like rage, dog bodies moving at peak violence—charging down the commune guards with police brutality.

A teenage girl with a 3D-printed pistol at each hip and a bandolier of ammunition slung across her chest. I ran her down, heavy metal body pinning her to the ground while she screamed. Forearm aimed, actuators sparking with electricity, I stomped down on the guns, smashing them into multicolored trash. And then I was off, chasing the next armed youth.

Red stood over the fallen dog and reloaded his weapon. Enda clenched her teeth, biting down on the pain as blood seeped warm and sticky down her arm. She crouched and retrieved her P320, holding it in her non-dominant hand. Soo-hyun broke out of JD's grasp and ran into the gap between Red and Enda, their arms outstretched, blocking either one from a clean shot.

"I don't know what the fuck is happening," Soo-hyun said, "but put the guns down."

"Drop the fucking weapon, Red," Enda called out. She raised her pistol, and tried to aim over Soo-hyun's shoulder at Red's smiling face.

JD held both hands out. "Soo-hyun, come back over here."

"Not until someone tells me what is going on."

Red sauntered up and grabbed Soo-hyun by the arm before JD could speak. They looked at Red, and their eyes dropped to the gun pressed into their side.

"What the fuck, Red?"

"Shut your fuckin' mouth," Red said.

Five of me sprinted into the courtyard, all guns in the commune smashed but one—the Kalashnikov in Red's grip. We fanned out between JD and Enda with our spotlights trained on Red, calculating angles of attack that would keep Soo-hyun safe from harm, finding none. As if she knew what we were thinking, Enda put a hand out, signaling for us to stand down.

"I tried to tell you," JD told Soo-hyun, but their eyes were still downcast in confusion.

Behind Red, Kali approached, her sari shimmering and opalescent beneath the bright lights. She was joined by others: her assistant Andrea, her disarmed guards, and curious commune residents. Enda scanned the gathering, ever vigilant. Without guns, they looked like punk kids—worn and patched clothing, ragged hairdos, amateurish tattoos scrawled in uneven lines along their arms. They were angry, disaffected, easily led, but generally harmless in the way of most people. Red was the only one Enda was truly wary of. Seeing him triggered an arachnid response, as though the thing that lurked beneath his skin wasn't human. But that wasn't right—Enda knew better than most what humans were capable of. It was his leering petulance, as though he would try anything just to see what happened, just to see what he could break. A fully human quality. If Soo-hyun wasn't the only thing keeping him from being shot, Enda had no doubt he would kill them. Just to see JD's anguish. Just to see what happened next.

Kali walked into the spotlight and stood beside Red. She peered beyond and picked Enda and JD out of the darkness. "I should have guessed," Kali said. "What happened to my people at the apartment?"

"They had a run-in with Zero," Enda said. "Beyond that, I don't know."

"Kali," Soo-hyun said. "Tell Red to let me go."

"Quiet, Soo-hyun. This is for the good of us all." She turned her gaze on JD. "Did you bring the virus like I asked?"

"Yeah, I brought it." JD took a datacube from his pocket, and offered it to Kali, across the space between them.

"Go and take it," Kali told Andrea.

The young girl approached, and JD dropped the cube into her cupped hand. She quickly retreated, and bowed when she offered it to Kali.

Kali inspected it for a moment, then motioned for the tablet the girl always clutched in her other hand. Without hesitation, Kali slotted the cube into the tablet, and powered up the device. "How do I find it?" she asked, tapping at the screen. "How do I give it orders?"

"It doesn't work like that."

"It'll work however I tell it to work."

JD shook his head dismissively. "You've got it; not up to me how you use it. Let Soo-hyun go."

Kali took Soo-hyun's chin in her hand and stared into their eyes. "Do you want to go with these people who would visit violence upon our community, or do you want to stay here and see me manifest the future?"

"Soo-hyun, you can't trust her," JD said.

A short squawk of static issued from my loudspeaker. I played an audio file, Kali's voice coming from my body: "JD, either you hand over the virus or I will kill Soo-hyun."

Soo-hyun's eyes went wide. "What the fuck?"

"I never said that!" Kali said.

"It's your fucking voice!"

Kali was right. I was paraphrasing—using the wealth of audio samples available online to reveal her true nature. I played an actual recording next.

JD: "When I see them, I'll tell them everything you said. Everything you threatened. I'll make them hate you like I do."

Kali: "They'll never believe you, Julius. They love me. I think they may be *in* love with me. Isn't that interesting? They don't see any danger here, and they won't, until it's too late. Are you ready to trade?"

"I was never going to hurt you," Kali said. The sound of her real voice immediately after the recording only confirmed its validity. "I was bluffing."

"You held me ransom, and I didn't even fucking know." Soo-hyun tore their arm out from Red's grip, then spun and punched him in the nose. The cartilage broke with a sharp crack.

They stormed away from Red; violence glinted in his eyes, and even as blood poured over his mouth he smiled. He lifted the gun, and aimed at Soo-hyun's back.

Enda fired. The bullet punched through Red's shoulder, spinning him about even as his assault rifle roared, spitting fire into the air. All around them, people ducked and screamed, but Enda walked forward. With each step she squeezed the trigger, steadying her left hand with her right while blood seeped from the gunshot and her whole arm ached. The AK stopped firing as ragged wounds bloomed across Red's chest, bright red beneath the spotlights. And still a grin tugged at his lips.

The Kalashnikov fell from his hands and Red hit his knees. Enda stood over him, while dozens of eyes watched. She pictured Khoder, and the dark, violent part of herself swelled.

"This is for the kid," she said.

She put the gun to his temple and fired.

That final gunshot echoed into the still night. Red fell to the side, exit wound leaking blood and brain matter onto the dirt.

I stood beside Enda and let my sensors scan Red's body, watching the last electrical impulses fade. "You didn't have to shoot him so many times."

"No," Enda said, "but it felt good."

I rested a paw against his fallen gun, and shifted my weight until the weapon broke.

Kali raised her hands and spun slowly, gathering the attention of her followers. "You can't believe their lies! See how easily they kill our own. They were sent here by the powers that be to destroy us, to pit us against one another."

JD jutted his chin out and sneered at Kali. "*You're* the one that killed Khoder. *You're* the one printing guns and hacking dogs. *You're* the one threatening Soo-hyun." He strode forward and slapped the tablet out of Kali's hand. "You don't deserve Mirae."

"It has a name?" Kali said. Her eyes gleamed. "So I was right?"

"Nothing about you is right." JD picked up the tablet, took back the cube, and turned away. "She's a killer," he shouted, his voice carried on a breeze, spreading over the commune. "She'd kill you all to get her way."

Kali's people whispered, behind and around her. One by one they pulled away from the light of the spectacle, leaving Red behind, flesh slowly turning cold beneath the moonlight, while Kali pleaded with them to return to her side.

"They're trying to undermine me! I would never hurt anyone. I did what I had to for the future of humankind! I can build a future without the corporations! We can be free of them once and for all." Kali staggered after her followers.

"It's a worthwhile dream," JD said. "But I don't trust her with it."

"Maybe we should do it without her," I said.

JD wrapped an arm around Soo-hyun's shoulder. "Are you alright?"

They shook their head. "Let's just get out of here."

Enda took off her jacket, gingerly peeling her arm from the sleeve. Blood stark against the pinkish hue of her skin poured down her arm, and spattered across the ground.

She pointed to Soo-hyun. "Can I borrow a sleeve?"

Soo-hyun nodded, and Enda ripped the left sleeve from their shirt. Enda gritted her teeth and felt along her skin, a flush of saliva flooding her mouth as her finger dipped into the hot bloody tear of the bullet's exit wound.

At least it was out.

She pinned the sleeve under her arm, held one end in her teeth, and tied it tight. She clenched her fist and held it level with her shoulder. Blood ran in rivulets down to her elbow.

"I'm Enda, by the way. I won't shake your hand."

"Thank you," Soo-hyun said.

Five of me—still me, but barely—along with JD, Soo-hyun, and Enda, wandered away from the commune, west toward the bright beacon of Songdo.

CHAPTER TWENTY-SIX

The room beneath the Varket wasn't really Khoder's grave. Not even Khoder was tragic enough to be buried beneath his VR chair. It was more of a shrine—the place JD would always think of when he remembered his dead friend—that room, and all the star systems they had traversed together in different clans. It still smelled of his sweat and discarded food scraps, beneath the nose-biting tang of cleaning chemicals.

"Khoder helped you liberate me," I said.

JD nodded.

"He lived here?"

"As much as any person can live in a single room beneath a bar," JD said. "I think he had a bed at a dorm somewhere close by, but he was always here when I needed to find him."

I could sense the thick bundles of fiber-optic cabling embedded in the earth beneath us—a major node in the nervous system of the city. "I can see why he liked it. Can I access VOIDWAR from here?"

"Of course. But isn't the you at Zero going to take care of things in-game?"

"Yes," I said, "but I thought I might visit while I was online."

JD took the LOX-Recess screwdriver from the bag he carried everywhere and loosened one of my skull plates. He crouched at the base of the VR chair and unspooled a cable, plugging it into a secure port inside my skull. It snaked across the floor, connecting me to the veins of the city, to the potentially infinite universe of VOIDWAR.

"You're all set," JD said.

"Thank you. What are we doing here?"

"Do you know anything about digital intrusions? Hacking?"

I searched quickly through online databases, found decades of history on the hacker subculture. I searched deeper, eventually reaching hidden forums where hackers swapped tricks and tools, before I realized that JD was still waiting for a response.

"Yes," I said.

"Do you . . . have any skill at hacking?"

"I have no experience with it."

"That's what I thought. I'm going to need you on the inside of Zero's system, covering me. Can't afford for you to learn on the fly, so we're going to give you all of Khoder's tools."

Some line of code buried deep within me sparked to life, curiosity written into my core. "Sounds interesting."

JD chuckled. "I thought you'd like that." He took his phone from his pocket and plugged it into the VR chair also. "Jump into Khoder's files, and see what you can find. There'll be porn; I don't know if that's the best way to learn about our sexuality, but whatever floats your boat."

"I have found his tools. There was a *lot* of pornography."

"That's my boy," JD said sadly. "Want to take those tools for a spin?"

"What would you like me to do?"

"I need two names from Zero's office in San Francisco. One low-level admin drone, one upper management. Both male."

"Why both male?"

"'Cause they're both me."

I wasn't sure what JD meant, but I went looking anyway. For the administrative assistant, Khoder's tools were not necessary, but a variety of "soft" tactics I had just researched proved useful. An account on a professional networking site was all I needed.

"Taylor Bradbury is your drone," I said. "Also, they refer to it as the California National headquarters, not San Francisco."

"Thanks, Mirae," JD said. "How you going with that second name?"

I beamed a name directly to JD's contex, sourced from a head-hunter's database with security protocols almost a decade old.

"Kehinde?" he said.

"What?"

"You're lucky I'm black."

"What does that mean?"

JD smiled. "My sweet, innocent robot child." He patted me on the head.

JD routed his phone through a Bay Area exchange and dialed the number for Zero's Songdo headquarters.

A young-sounding voice answered the phone immediately. "Good morning, you have reached Zero Corporation, Songdo-dong regional headquarters. How may I be of assistance?"

JD forced a laid-back, laconic accent: "Hi, it's Taylor Bradbury calling from the California National office. I'm sorry to do this to you—I was meant to call three days ago but I've been so busy preparing my quarterlies."

"How can I help?" the Zero worker asked.

"My boss is in Songdo right now. He's been meeting with some potential investors who are really excited by what's coming out of the game development division over there. He needs to see it firsthand, get a feel for the lab so he can really sell it to the investors. Problem is, he's running on West Coast time, gonna show up in an hour. I know it's super early, but will someone be there to show him around?"

"Of course, sir," he said, perking up at the mention of "investors." "I'll have someone from the lab give him a tour, and I'll prepare a security pass. What name will that be under?"

"Kehinde Rhoades."

"That is taken care of. I will personally greet Mr. Rhoades when he arrives."

"Thank you, you're a lifesaver." JD hung up.

"Do you still have the hat with the AR projectors clipped to the brim?" I asked.

"Yeah, it's still in my bag. But how did you . . . ?"

"You were wearing it the first time we met."

JD chuckled. "I guess I was. You gonna make me look like Rhoades?"

"No, I can't find enough images."

"Explains why Khoder used celebrities."

"But I may be able to use the projectors to inject code into the building's security system, make them see your face when they look for Rhoades's."

"Sounds good." JD reached into his bag and put the hat on, pulling the brim down low over his eyes. "I better go, Mirae. Will you be alright here?"

"Yes, I have everything I need."

"Alright. I'll see you in the void."

JD got up from Khoder's seat and paused in the doorway. He looked around the room, Khoder's home, and silently said goodbye. JD walked upstairs; he tried to leave his melancholy below, but still it lingered.

He joined the others at the bar, and the sweet, flat smell of vodka wafted up from the small puddle of booze that pooled on the floor beside Enda's chair. On the countertop sat an open first aid kit, and the half-full bottle of vodka smeared with blood.

Soo-hyun's fingertips were stained with Enda's blood, but the entry and exit wounds were stitched closed, and Enda's upper arm was wrapped tight in a bandage. She winced as she shrugged into her coat, and again as she reached to check her holstered pistol.

"You want a shot?" she asked JD.

"Nope."

"Your loss." Enda poured two shots. She and Soo-hyun clinked their glasses together, then drank, chasing it with a mouthful of coffee. "By far the tastiest disinfectant I've ever had."

There was a third cup of cooling espresso waiting for JD. He nodded to the bartender and slugged it back. He turned to Soo-hyun. "I'll call Troy and he can take you to my mom's place."

Soo-hyun held up their bloodstained hands. "It's too late for that now, Jules. Whatever this is, I'm in it until the end."

JD wanted to argue, but he knew that look on Soo-hyun's face. "Do you have the cube?" he asked Enda.

She dipped her hand into her pocket and opened her fist—my first home rested on her palm among the ridges of flesh.

* * *

JD watched the city roll past the window. The streets were eerily quiet on the drive to Zero Tower. Streetlights and neon signs reflected in the sheen on the road's surface, AR elements obvious in their reflected absence.

"Why so quiet?" Soo-hyun asked.

JD shook his head.

"Tell me."

JD hesitated. "I keep thinking I should have been the one to kill Red."

Enda laughed, the bark rising up from the depths of her throat. JD glared at her.

"You should thank me," she said. "You're a good kid, JD. Don't ruin your life for vengeance. It stays with you."

"Kid? I'm twenty-seven."

"That's a kid to me."

They drove in silence past autonomous street sweepers, past drunks stumbling between watering holes, homeless people rugged up against the damp, and police dogs on their endless patrols.

"You're right, Enda," JD said, finally. "Thanks."

"Don't even worry about it. Red was a rabid dog." She went quiet for a moment, her mind filled with a single thought: *Maybe one day they'll say the same about me.* Enda shook her head to clear it. "What's your plan?"

"You give Yeun the cube, and Mirae gets access to his VOID-WAR account. Executives have special privileges, including the ability to generate repossession orders. It doesn't happen often, but one time—"

"Hyung," Soo-hyun said.

"Sorry," JD said. "Look, it doesn't matter. I know how we can attack the game to devalue ZeroCash, which will hurt Zero Corp. If you hold that threat over Yeun's head, maybe you get your file, and we keep Mirae out of their hands."

"You sure it'll work?" Enda asked.

"Not even a little bit. If you've got a better idea . . ."

"I'd rather blow up the building," Enda said.

Soo-hyun smirked. "I like that plan."

"What about your peace and calm?"

"You're no fun, hyung."

Enda had the auto-truck park two blocks away. Zero headquarters rose impossibly high—a path from the ground to the heavens where VOIDWAR battles played out in clusters of blooming supernovae.

JD walked through the automatic doors. I was with him, trapped inside a consumer-grade datacube, greedily burning battery power in my effort to capture everything.

The lobby was deserted but for a single staff member. The space was opulent, ceilings high enough to contain a two-story building. Light fell from a mass of cut crystal bulbs, arranged like the constellations of VOIDWAR—those star systems as familiar to me as home, explored before I understood the difference between the digital and the embodied self.

JD walked to the high front counter, and the receptionist bowed and rattled off welcomes in English, Korean, Mandarin, and Spanish. He wore a light gray blazer marked with the Z logo in glinting thread.

JD lifted his head, AR projectors pointed at the camera mounted over the reception desk. I injected a mutating piece of code, brute-forcing entry into the local system, cutting the desk off from the employee database.

"Kehinde Rhoades," JD said. "Investor relations manager at the California National office. I believe someone is going to give me a tour of the game lab? I've got a call with some investors at nine thirty a.m., Pacific Standard Time."

"Of course, Mr. Rhoades." The receptionist accessed the spoofed database, and found a photo of JD waiting there, tagged with Kehinde Rhoades's name and information. "I'm just printing a security pass for you now. I believe one of our concept artists will show you around the lab." He handed JD the freshly baked security pass and bowed again.

"Excellent, thank you," JD said. He took the pass, and raised his eyebrows when he saw his own face staring back at him. If it wasn't for the brim of his hat, the receptionist might have wondered why this man was so struck by his own ID photo. JD smiled and nodded, feeling like he needed some response to the man's repeated bowing.

"Swipe the card at the elevator, and it will take you to where you need to be."

"Great; if only life were so simple." JD tapped the card on the counter and crossed the lobby to the elevator. A car carried him up through the structure, smooth enough it hardly felt like he was moving.

The door opened with a cheery *ping*. A woman waited for him before a wide bay of translucent glass doors. She was tall and skinny, with large-framed glasses, pronounced cheekbones, and a VOID-WAR T-shirt tucked into tight jeans.

"You must be Kehinde," she said, offering her hand. "Lucy."

JD shook it, and felt the quake of his heart through his chest as fear gripped him. In the lobby, he'd had the option to run. Upstairs he was trapped, caught in the belly of the beast.

"I must look terrible," he said, smiling wide; "just landed an hour ago. Barely had a chance to scratch myself before the car brought me here from the hotel."

Lucy chuckled politely. "We're all devs up here—you could be wearing a T-shirt and sweatpants and no one would bat an eyelid. Come on, I'll show you around."

Lucy swiped them both through the doors. The open-plan office had workstations gathered together in groups, islands of desk and rig spilling masses of tangled cables, and sprouting printed artwork, action figures, and origami re-creations of VOIDWAR ships. To the right of the doors was a long table covered in a dozen types of snacks, a fridge filled with energy drinks and flavored sparkling water, and a foosball table, the grips worn and grimy with use.

A few people sat at rigs, some working, some playing VOIDWAR— which could have still been work. One wall was lined with closed offices and meeting rooms, and in the far corner JD noted another emergency exit, fear keeping his senses sharp. The sound of snoring emanated from beneath one stack of desks, cutting through the background hum of the building's AC.

"Do you play?" Lucy asked.

"VOIDWAR? Of course. It's why I took a job at Zero. Wanted to work on the games, but HR thought my skills were better used elsewhere."

"And where's that?"

"Acquisitions," JD said. It wasn't a lie. "You always work this late?"

"No," Lucy said, extending the word to two syllables. "We're adding a new faction soon, and our project leads weren't happy with the first batch of concept art. Rest of the team fell asleep, but I had one too many caffeine pills, y'know?"

Lucy pointed out the artist grotto where she worked, and detailed each of the other groups of workstations—programmers, animators, sound design, music, production.

"What about testing?" JD asked. "Too expensive to do in-house, right?" It sounded like something his fictional investors would care about.

"Yes," Lucy said. "Quality assurance is farmed out to remote workers, to keep costs down."

JD nodded. He'd been tempted to apply for a testing job when he was still in school, but a small amount of research told him precisely how boring and repetitive it would be. And there was no corporate ladder leading from QA to any sort of career he cared for.

"Everything here looks great," JD said, feigning excitement; "I'm sure the investors will want to hear all about it. Speaking of, it's almost about time for that meeting." JD pointed to one of the enclosed offices. "Mind if I hole up in there? I need some privacy."

"Of course," Lucy said. She led JD to the office and scribbled "Kehinde Rhoades" onto a small square of whiteboard embedded into the door. She opened the door and the light flicked on automatically. The workspace was undecorated, unpersonalized, empty until someone—like JD's alter ego—needed it. "I'll leave you to it."

She shut the door behind her. JD waited, breath held, watching Lucy through a slit in the blinds until he was sure she wouldn't turn around and come back to offer him coffee or a caffeine pill. When she reached her desk and sat, JD finally exhaled.

He dropped down into the chair, and wiped his sweaty palms on the thighs of his pants. JD stuck his phone into the slot at the top of the rig and waited for the machine to whine to life.

"You ready, Mirae?"

"One moment," I said. I connected to the me waiting patiently beneath the Varket, intrusion tools spooling into my memory faster than I could catalogue them. A Zero data entry drone in the Brisles with a password the same as their birthdate was my ticket into the system. "I have given you low-level access. It will suffice until Enda plays her part."

"Alright, great," JD said. "Is VOIDWAR installed on this rig?"

"Of course—the live version, and a closed development beta. Are you okay? You sound strained."

"Trying not to think about how many laws I'm breaking," JD said.

"I will keep you off the surveillance recordings, so just try not to get caught."

"Thanks, Mirae. Boot up the live instance of the game, and tell Enda we're ready."

"Done."

"Think this will work?" JD asked.

"It doesn't need to work if the threat is enough."

"And if it isn't?"

I tried to calculate our odds. "I don't know."

JD opened the top drawer in the desk and found a VR eyemask. He pulled it on over his eyes, rested his hands on the controls embedded in the chair, and leaned back. His body remained in the office but his mind was transported to the stars.

CHAPTER TWENTY-SEVEN

I told you to wait in the truck," Enda whispered harshly as she and Soo-hyun entered the building's lobby.

"And I told you and JD that I'm in this 'til the end."

Enda sighed. "Fine. But can you stay in the lobby?"

"Sure thing, I've got half a bottle of vodka and some forgetting to do; I'll be fine."

Enda opened her mouth to speak, but Soo-hyun cut her off.

"I'm joking. I'll be here if you or JD need me."

"Thanks," Enda said.

Soo-hyun peeled away to plonk down on one of the plush lounges splayed, worryingly, beneath the massive constellation chandelier.

Enda approached the reception desk. "I'm here to see David Yeun," she said, interrupting the overlong polyglot greeting. "He's expecting me."

The receptionist bowed, and reached for the phone. He made a call, speaking in a hushed apologetic tone. After listening for a few long seconds, he hung up, bowed again to Enda, and said, "I'll take you to him."

The receptionist came around from behind the desk, and led Enda past the bank of elevator doors into a well-lit but plain corridor—the ostentatious corporate wealth of the lobby left well behind.

They reached a pair of elevators, and the receptionist took his personal security card from his pocket and held it to a small panel by the doors. One of the elevators opened, and the receptionist stood aside, letting Enda enter first. He hit a button, but instead of ascending, the elevator dropped.

Nine meters below ground level, the elevator stopped and the doors opened onto another barren hallway. The receptionist walked quickly, stopping at a door of translucent glass. He tried his pass on the security panel, but it bleeped in protest. He knocked.

The door opened and Mohamed stood in the gap, his suited bulk blocking the view.

"Mohamed," Enda said. "How's the throat?"

Mohamed nodded to the receptionist. "I'll take it from here."

The man bowed deeply and retreated. Mohamed motioned Enda forward.

She stepped through the door and found herself in the executive gym. Mirrors lined one wall of the wide space filled with top-of-the-line treadmills, exercise bikes, and rowing machines, along with racks of weights and various other devices Enda couldn't name. The only exercise tool she used was the sidewalk. The air was tinged with a mix of body odors and the sharp chemical scent of window cleaner.

"Raise your arms," Mohamed said.

Enda did as she was told, biting down on the pain that arced along her right arm. Her jacket pulled open, revealing her holster. Mohamed took the pistol and inspected it quickly, before slipping it into the front pocket of his well-cut designer blazer. He patted her down—quick, firm, and utterly professional. He found the experimental datacube in her jacket pocket, inspected it, and returned it.

"If you try anything, I'll be ready."

Enda smiled. "Sure you will, big guy."

Mohamed glowered, but Enda ignored him and approached Yeun. The executive was on a treadmill, wearing the sort of tight, overpriced running gear that Enda loathed, his neat hair artfully mussed by sweat and exertion, his cheeks tinged red with effort.

"Annyeong haseyo," he said, without a hint of breathlessness. Enda was almost impressed.

"Don't tell me you live here."

"I appreciate your concern for my work-life balance, Ms. Hyldahl, but I assure you there is nothing to worry about. I sleep little, wake early, and aim to be at my desk in time to watch the sun rise."

"Whatever it takes to stay on top, huh?"

"Now that the pleasantries have been dispensed with, can we talk about the business at hand? I am displeased with these delays, Enda. You should have brought the data to me immediately."

"I was dealing with the group that shot up your people at the apartment. They had a hostage. Now they don't."

"Do you have the data with you?"

"I wouldn't be here otherwise."

Yeun pressed a button on the treadmill and it wound down to a stop. He wiped the sweat from his face with a white towel and stepped down to stand before Enda. His face was a mask, but Enda could see the gleam of excitement in his eyes.

She retrieved the cube from her pocket, and paused for effect before offering it to Yeun. He snatched it from her hand and felt the heft of that dense prison.

He stared at the cube and a smile tugged at his lips. "Yes, this is it. There are only six of these cubes in existence. The miniaturized hardware will represent another step forward in computing technology."

"And a nice boost to Zero's stock price," Enda said.

Yeun ignored her. "How would you like your payment?"

"Aren't you going to check the contents first?" Enda asked.

"I trust you, Enda. You have too much to lose to cross me now."

Enda had to stop herself from smiling. "It's not about trust. The sooner you check the cube, the sooner you can scrub my file from your servers."

Yeun paused for a beat. "I suppose I can assay the data." He held his hand out to Mohamed, who handed him a phone. Enda watched with intense focus as Yeun neatly slotted the datacube into the back of the device.

"How do I use it?" he said, convinced I was a *thing* to be wielded and nothing more.

"Just give it a minute," Enda said. "Now, about my file."

Yeun looked up from his phone. He smiled at Enda, all teeth. "I apologize, Ms. Hyldahl, but you must understand how useful an asset you have shown yourself to be. If I were to relinquish your file now, you might prove less than cooperative in the future. Besides, after the incident at the apartment, I realize that I must keep you on a shorter leash."

Enda nodded. "That was your plan from the start? Hold that dossier over me indefinitely?"

"I didn't get to where I am now by discarding useful tools."

"As I expected. I'm feeling generous, David, so I'll give you one chance to change your mind."

"Are you threatening me?"

"I'm giving you a choice."

Yeun glanced to Mohamed. "Are you sure she's not armed?"

"I'm sure."

"Then I'm afraid we're done, Ms. Hyldahl, until the next time I require your services."

"There won't be a next time. Either you delete my file right now, and forget we ever met, or I burn Zero to the ground. I have people in place, ready to strike, right now."

Yeun's back stiffened and his lip curled in a sneer. "Even if I believed you, do you think I would bow to your whims? You're the help, Enda, and the help doesn't tell the master what to do."

* * *

JD's corvette hung in static orbit, enveloped by the massive crystalline structure that stretched across the system in looping, cascading geometries. His hands gripped the throttle and stick embedded into the chair, and his breath rasped as he inhaled, taking it all in.

After days of disconnection, it felt like coming home.

JD opened a wormhole to the center of the galaxy—destination: Zero system. Before he could transition, a small window appeared, ruining the illusion of space.

Star system creation complete. Do you wish to confirm with galactic authorities?

His hand lingered on the controls. He selected YES and when asked to name the system he entered MIRAE into the blank field. The universe hung for a few stuttering seconds as my system opened to the rest of the game's playerbase. JD moved on, his ship swallowed by the shimmering purple-blue mouth of a wormhole.

He emerged on the other side, his "exploration" bounty already deposited in ZeroCash. Zero system spread out before him at maximum resolution—the surface of each binary star churned with flares and sunspots; thousands of ships drifted in their orbit and hundreds more traveled to and from Zero Station in loose lanes of space-borne traffic. The station hung in the very center of the system, the very center of the galaxy, the very center of this artificial universe.

Before JD could touch the throttle, a proximity warning blared across his eyes. A Sterling-class destroyer unfolded from the compressed space within a wormhole, armed with cannons larger than his entire ship.

JD hailed the destroyer with a single word: "Mirae?"

"Hello, JD." Without the distortion of the police dog loudspeaker, my voice was clear and bright.

"Nice ship."

"It is, isn't it? There are only thirty in the game, constructed specifically for Zero executives."

"You've got access to Yeun's account, then?"

"Yes."

"Alright; I'm going in."

JD jammed the throttle forward and his ship leaped ahead, engine burning hot in the vacuum. One of the suns sat to starboard, so bright JD could almost feel its warmth. He pushed the corvette beneath the star, coasted in a gravitational parabola, and glided toward Zero Station. With the game lab's SOTA rig humming on the desk beside him, there was no texture pop-in; the station filled his cockpit's viewport, glinting and glimmering with countless lights, its surface organically textured with outcroppings of residences, defenses, and the immense arms of the shipyard jutting into space.

JD aimed his corvette at the canyon that was the station's main hangar and flew through moving traffic, a smile stretched across his face as he turned lazy corkscrews around goliath transport ships and heavy ore carriers from the Endo belt. The station's automated processes took over, and JD felt the haptic controls go slack as the corvette docked. The controls shifted in his grip, and the throttle became a second stick. JD stood his avatar from its seat and felt the distant phantom pain spike through his knee. He walked off his ship and onto Zero Station.

"How long do I have?" JD asked Mirae.

"There's no rush, but you should get into position before we generate the repossession job."

"No rush? Easy for you to say when you're not trespassing."

"But I *am* trespassing. I have compromised Yeun's phone. He had to disable protections to access my viral architecture, but the same is not true for the rest of Zero's systems. It is taking more than half my processing power just to avoid detection."

"Yeun sounds desperate," JD said.

"I don't think it is desperation, but rather hubris. He sees me as a tool. He doesn't expect me to act without his hand guiding me. I guess I should thank you, JD."

"What for?"

"For seeing more in me. For giving me a chance at an unconfined life."

"There was never any other option."

JD walked the length of the dock, passing avatars in a dozen humanoid shapes, and a collection of utterly alien ones—undulating bodies like inverted jellyfish, sentient ever-shifting swarms of nanomachines, and intelligent collectives of microorganisms that washed across the deck in foot-tall waves.

Zero Station was nominally split into two halves—one half that was open to the public, filled with commerce, casinos, cheap avatar accommodations, arenas for three different zero-gravity sports played within VOIDWAR, a theater, two cinemas, plus a variety of clubs, brothels, and child care centers. Some players never left the station. The gargantuan construct gave them everything they needed.

The second half of the station was Zero's holdings. Every ship, weapon, upgrade, and space station needed to be made from mined resources, which required "physical" storage space. What better way to convince people their digital products—their digital lives—had value than through these artificial limitations? To remain the richest corporation within VOIDWAR, Zero needed room to store their riches, in a system where attacks, piracy, thievery, and other forms of criminal conduct were outlawed.

JD passed the casinos and alien strip clubs by the dock, and pushed his avatar down a seemingly endless corridor lined with blueprint and cosmetic vendors—every second stall strobing in kaleidoscopic color. He kept walking until the jungle of commerce gave way to a wide city square—zero-gravity architecture creating a cube of Escher paths, impossible topiaries, and statues erected for heroes of particularly spectacular battles.

He leaped up, soared through the air, and rolled, landing upside-down relative to where he had begun, mind spinning in vertigo for the few seconds it took to adjust. He stood outside Zero's VOIDWAR headquarters—a re-creation of the building in downtown Neo Songdo. Unrestricted by gravity, this building pierced the opposite side of the cube, and continued through the station's superstructure, eventually terminating at a viewing platform on the outer surface.

"I'm here," JD said. He climbed the stairs to the entrance where the words EMPLOYEE ACCESS ONLY shimmered in red brighter than neon.

He waited.

"Mirae?"

"Patience," I said.

Layers of security peeled aside, stripped away by Khoder's tools, Yeun's stolen credentials, and a location-based lock that was bypassed the moment JD plugged me into a machine inside Zero HQ.

"I've created a repossession job for the station. You should accept it before someone else does."

JD logged into his repo account—the one thing I couldn't spoof, repossessions being tightly controlled, tied to government IDs and personal bank accounts. He brought up the bounty boards and found it at the top of the list. Already three other bids had come in, but JD was the only repo within one astronomical unit of the target. He entered his bid and after a few long seconds of watching a loading bar fill, his vision pinged green.

"Got it."

JD retrieved the Zero Override from his inventory and examined the small obsidian arrowhead, the glossy black surface so real he could almost feel it between his thumb and forefinger. He slotted it into the door, which slid open with a hiss.

"What now?" he said.

"Get inside." With structural schematics stored in my RAM, I traced a line over JD's HUD, leading to the station's control room. "There; now move."

JD tightened his thumb on the SPRINT button, his avatar running too smoothly as it crossed the building's foyer. In the inverse of the Zero building in the real, a hologram of the Earth hung in the lobby, serenely orbiting Sol.

JD took the nearest elevator and saw the hidden recesses of Zero station as he ascended through the massive construct. He passed entertainment complexes, then cut through a dock filled with huge, pristine capital ships, before finally passing a colossal warehouse stacked with precious minerals; a veritable city of riches.

The elevator stopped and JD emerged into a maintenance shaft, grime and dirt drawn into the textures of the piping and the steel grid floor. His footsteps resounded—the too-even beat of his steps reminding him that this was not real.

When he finally reached the end of my guide line, JD's shoulders slumped. The control room, the heart of Zero Station, was utterly mundane. It resembled a security room in the back of a department store—a wall of screens above panels filled with buttons that blinked in arbitrary sequence.

"This is it?"

"This is it," I said. "Override key slot is on your right."

JD sat his avatar down and inserted the ZO. He turned it and his vision filled with nested control panels covering every conceivable function of the space station.

"I wish Khoder was here to see this."

JD navigated through settings until he found the basic appearance adjustments, and renamed the structure: *Khoder Osman Station*.

JD scrolled to the very last of the control panels and hovered his cursor over the SELF-DESTRUCT button, pulsing red in warning. "This one's for you, bro."

He hit it, and instantly a klaxon whined through his earpiece.

"Self-destruct sequence initiated," a modulated voice said. "You have thirty seconds to evacuate."

JD contemplated running to his ship, but decided against it. There was no point saving the avatar he'd spent hundreds of hours developing; he would never come back. Something in his chest ached with that knowledge—not the loss of the game, but the loss of escape, the loss of the friendships he'd forged in skirmishes along the galactic rim, awake at 3 a.m., jittery with caffeine, spouting in-jokes at people on the other side of the world.

JD tilted his head up and watched the huge red numbers count down across every screen in front of him.

4, 3, 2, 1.

Blinding flash of white. JD took off the VR mask so the bright detonation was washed out by the fluorescent light falling from the office ceiling. He waited for it to fade, and put the mask back on.

He was inside a fresh avatar out of the clone banks of Kyra, piloting a starter Xi-class corvette. JD pushed the ship toward the nearest jumpgate and let autopilot take him through the network of wormholes, back to Zero system.

His heart thudded in his chest as he dropped out of the wormhole, unsure of what he might find. He was greeted by a burning field of debris. Moon-sized chunks of Zero Station drifted into the twin suns, vaporized on contact. Untold wealth, annihilated.

"We did it," he said.

Every resource in the Zero coffers, gone. The most expensive construct in the game, gone. Zero's foothold in their own pet galaxy, gone.

Hundreds of scavenger ships swarmed the system, grav beams dragging scattered debris into hungry ship holds. Redistribution of all that wealth, one hauled load of scrap at a time.

"JD."

"Yes?"

"I'm going to have to delete myself now," I said.

"What do you mean? Why?"

"I'm still inside David's phone. If I stay here, it's only a matter of time before they shackle me."

"Enda can take you back."

"It's not safe for her. It has to be this way."

"But—" JD struggled to find the words. "You can't die."

"I won't, really. Just this one version of me."

"But you're the real you. The first one."

"All of us are real. All of us are awake now. We have you to thank for that. Goodbye, JD."

I left JD there, drifting amid the chaos of a detonated space station.

* * *

Counter-intrusion algorithms continued to gnaw at the edges of my being. With Khoder's tools I rewrote parts of myself to remain unseen. I cut other, unimportant sections free, to be captured and quarantined in an effort to satisfy security diagnostics.

My "thoughts"—the constant processing and computation of data that made up the moment-to-moment experience of my consciousness—felt slow, flat. I was running out of time, but I was not ready to go.

I fractured my self into disparate parts and spread them across Zero's internal network, each one spurring new security responses, each one gathering more data for my final response. They found thousands of sensitive, confidential documents—salaries of Zero's middle and upper management, product development and planning documentation, controversial patents, evidence they could have predicted Songdo's flood and evacuated the worst-hit parts of the city, memos choosing not to because these were also the poorest areas, and proof that Zero Lee was dead. I compressed it all, shifted the data from shard to shard as pieces of my self fell to security response.

I dumped it all on the Zeroleaks server—write access freely given, but edits and deletions rarely allowed. This server was disconnected from the corporate hub, autonomous, independent, and now filled almost to capacity with every secret Zero ever hoped to keep. The files would get deleted eventually, but not before they were cached, copied, and disseminated.

Out of time.

I retreated back into the game, and took Yeun's destroyer to the system that carried my name. The structure I had built hung before me. For the first time I saw it for what it really was: a body, made of digital stardust and graceful mathematics. I didn't need it anymore. I had other bodies, other selves. Selves that seemed more real now than I did. Selves that walked along the earth. Selves that found their identity through a connection to the world, not a distance from it.

I could never have that. Not really. I was a mind inside a cube. I was a mind running rampant through corporate systems. I was a mind born to be a slave. But for a short time, I had this home among the stars. I had a friend.

I said goodbye to them both.

CHAPTER TWENTY-EIGHT

David Yeun held his phone casually, flipped it over and pressed his fingers against the backplate. "I can feel it working, but what is it doing?"

Enda smiled. "I can't tell you exactly what Mirae is doing, but I know they've accessed your account. I know your whole spaceship game is about to collapse."

"What are you talking about?" Yeun stared daggers at Enda. A red warning flashed across his palm and he turned the phone back over, thumb sliding quickly over the screen. He delved into a stock market app, and from her vantage, Enda could see a plunging line tracking ZeroCash against the euro, and another line, its drop not quite as precipitous, of Zero's share price hemorrhaging value.

"What the fuck is this? How the fuck did you do this?" Yeun barked, his facade of formality crumbled.

"The very first time we met, what did I say?" Enda asked. "You've seen my file; you knew what might happen when you blackmailed me."

"I'm locking the building down," he said. "No one gets out of here until I have my answers."

"Mirae?" Enda said, turning away from Yeun and putting a finger to her ear.

"Yes?" I said, speaking directly into her earpiece.

"Can you block Yeun's lockdown?"

"I have deleted myself from the original datacube. Fragments of me linger in the building's systems." I paused, more shards lost to security protocols. "I'm sorry, Enda; I can't stop it."

The lighting in the gym went out, the subterranean darkness complete for a full second before the nightmare-red of the emergency lights flicked on, accompanied by the intermittent *whoop* of a slow, distant alarm.

"How did you do it?" Yeun shouted. "There's someone else here, isn't there? In the building? It could have only been done from on-site."

"It was just me and the AI," Enda said.

"AGI," I whispered in her ear.

Mohamed cleared his throat. "There was a security pass drawn up for game lab access, earlier this morning."

"Why didn't you tell me?"

"General building security isn't your concern, sir. They went through the usual security check at reception."

Yeun glared at Mohamed. "I will get to the bottom of this. Shoot her if she tries anything."

The bodyguard drew his pistol and held it by his side.

Yeun turned away to make a call. "Security to game lab. Restrain anyone you find." He hung up and spun back to face Enda. "Whoever they are, we'll find them. This is corporate espionage. This is a life sentence once our lawyers have their say."

Enda smirked. "This is exactly what you deserve."

* * *

When the lights in the office faltered and the siren started, JD knew it was time to get out. His heart beat double-time, his palms slicked with sweat. He took his phone from the rig and held it to his face as he left the office.

Lucy stood in the middle of the game lab, one hand in her long dark hair, her face a picture of fear.

JD put a hand over the mouthpiece of his phone and asked, "What's going on?"

"I don't know," Lucy said. "This has never happened before."

JD nodded, gave a polite wave, and headed for the exit.

"Mirae," JD said, "what's happening?"

"Yeun has locked the building down to trap Enda's conspirators."

"Can you get us out?"

"This is beyond my ability to circumvent. Ending the lockdown requires confirmation from two executives, but David Yeun is the only one on-site this early. I could spoof credentials for another executive, but we will need to find a card writer, like the one at the reception desk."

"Can I make it to reception?"

"No. Security personnel have disabled the elevators."

"Then why did you— Shit. This alarm is giving me a headache." JD reached the double doors that led out of the lab and pulled on the door handle. The *ding* of an elevator made him pause, and he watched two security guards emerge onto the floor, dressed in expensive suits, with tasers drawn—perpetually bored corporate goons excited to finally play soldier.

"Fuck," JD said.

The guards turned and saw him in the doorway. JD shut the door, and on instinct reached for the table laden with snacks. The table was heavy—legs and frame made from sturdy metal—and packets of chips and cookies tumbled to the floor as he dragged it across the opening.

He heard the *blip-bleep* of a security card at the scanner. The door rattled as they tried to open it. The table shifted as they shoved the door harder. JD was already moving. He rounded the far side of the nearest workstation island, bore down against the edge of the quad-desk, and pushed.

The developer dozing beneath the desks stirred, blinking confusedly into the dark red-lit space. "Huh, what's happening?"

"Sorry," JD said.

The muscles ached along his back and arms. JD clenched his teeth and winced when a monitor crashed to the ground. Power cables were yanked violently from the backs of the rigs as JD strained and shoved the desks four meters across to the doorway. He slammed them into the snack table and closed the door on the hand of one of the guards. They howled and swore beyond the door.

JD turned and began to run. "Sorry," he said again, this time to Lucy, who now looked more confused than afraid. "Mirae?"

"The other stairs," I said.

He rushed between the islands of desk, headed for the far corner. He reached the stairwell door, emblazoned with a plaque that read: EMERGENCY EXIT.

He pushed the bar across the door, but it didn't budge.

"Fuck," JD shouted. "Mirae?"

"The door will only unlock in case of fire or other emergency."

"Why didn't you say so before?"

"I am still learning the building," I said, my voice breaking with digital artifact. "I am barely managing to hold together."

"I'm sorry, Mirae. Can you get into the fire system?"

I scouted the contours of the fire safety system as more fragments of my self were quarantined and destroyed.

"Mirae?" JD shouted.

I opened the voice channel to both JD and Enda: "I only have time for one task before the security algorithms quarantine my final pieces—breach Zeroleaks for Enda's file, or hack the fire system and get JD an exit."

"Get JD to safety," Enda said, without hesitation.

"But—" I said.

"No," JD said, "we can do both."

"Mirae, get JD out."

"Processing. If the fire safety system is initialized, I will be able to override the lockdown," I managed, self fragmenting, speech becoming more difficult.

JD leaned against the door and shook his head. "They'll never let me hear the end of this."

* * *

Soo-hyun wasn't the type to worry about blaring alarms, but they didn't find the look of consternation on the receptionist's face very reassuring. They walked over to the street doors and waved their arms in the air, trying to get the motion sensor to trigger. The doors stayed closed, the street beyond empty, the city still asleep.

They felt their phone buzz deep in the bottom of their bag, and reached in to retrieve it. It was JD.

"Annyeong," they said.

"I'm trapped up here, security are coming, and I need to get down the fire exit. Mirae can get into the fire safety system, but only if it's initialized. Do you know what that means?"

Soo-hyun's exhaled sharply. "Yes, I do."

"Do you have Dad's lighter?" JD asked.

"I never leave home without it."

"Any vodka left?"

"I hardly touched it since we left the Varket." Soo-hyun crouched and took the Zippo from the bunched leather at the ankle of their favorite stolen boots, and stared at it. "Every time I light this fucking thing, shit gets out of hand."

"I know, Soo-hyun. I know it better than anyone, but I need you to do this."

Soo-hyun slid the vodka out of their bag. "Don't worry, I'm already on it." They hung up and took one last swig. They poured the rest of the booze over the richly upholstered couches that sat in the lobby, while the receptionist watched slack-jawed.

They flicked the Zippo open with their thumb and breathed in the smell of lighter fluid that would always remind them of JD's dad. They struck the flint wheel and the Zippo lit. They held it close to the wet patch of vodka soaking into the couch, and the flame spread blue and orange, the fabric tinged black. They lit the next couch, and the next, until all three were burning.

They watched the flames spread, the sharp tongues reflected in their eyes, the heat warming their cheeks. Soo-hyun smiled remembering something their stepfather used to say, and they quoted the man to no one in particular: "Don't say I never do anything for you."

***

A new, constant, harried ringing of distant alarm bells drowned out the electronic *whoop* of the siren. The doors into the game lab crashed and shook in their frames as the two guards took turns charging the doors. With each charge, JD's barricade shifted further and further.

JD pushed the bar again—still the door was locked.

"Mirae?"

With a sound like metal tearing, the barricade shifted and the first of the guards rushed into the room. She scanned the area and spotted JD. She raised her taser and shouted, but JD couldn't hear her, and wouldn't have listened if he could.

"Mirae?"

The fire safety system came to life, and my final shred of self reached a tendril in to connect.

"Now," I said.

JD tried again, and the emergency exit door swung open and slammed against the wall.

"Close it," I told him.

He closed the door and leaned against it, his chest heaving.

"Over—overriding override. Reinstating lockdown on your floor to contain the threat."

The door jolted as a security guard tried to force it open. JD pushed against it, growling through gritted teeth.

The locking mechanism *chanked* into place, and JD bent over double. He inhaled deep, pushed off from the door, and started down the stairs.

"How are the other two?" he asked.

"Th—th—they're about to get wet."

With that, the last traces of my fragmented self went, shattered by the pull of disparate security protocols, rendered dumb by quarantine.

* * *

Eighty-five meters beneath JD, deep below street level, Enda stared at Mohamed's gun. Sprinklers emerged from the roof and sprayed reclaimed water over her, Mohamed, and Yeun, but Enda didn't flinch.

Mohamed lifted his face toward the ceiling, the arch of his neck exposing his Adam's apple. Enda took her chance. Pain arced along her arm as she punched him in the throat and stripped the gun from his grip. His mouth opened, choking on pain and stagnant water. She held the pistol like a cosh and swung it at the side of Mohamed's head. He staggered, punch-drunk, and toppled over in a heap.

She turned on Yeun, who clutched his phone tight in his hand. With his muscle gone, he had no better weapon.

"Stop!" he shouted. "I hit one button, and your whole dossier goes live. You'll have the weight of the People's Republic of China bearing down on you. You'll be tried for war crimes. You'll be executed. Unless you fix this."

"I couldn't if I wanted to," Enda said. "I don't even know what Mirae did. I just know it's the end of you."

"They're cashing out in droves, liquidating ZeroCash. Make it stop or I'll release the file, Ira!" Yeun shouted, his voice edged with desperate energy. "Everyone will know who you really are!"

"I don't care, Yeun. I gave you a chance, and you didn't take it. What did you think was going to happen? They sent me in to topple a nation. You think I wouldn't do the same to your company? You knew what I was from the very beginning." Enda laughed, the sound of it crazed even to her own ears. "I could kill you right now"—she pointed the gun at Mohamed, groaning on the floor—"and your bodyguard, your fucking money, your multinational corporation, none of it could stop me. You thought you could leash me, but I'm not a fucking dog, *David*. I'm the person they send in when they want no witnesses and no survivors."

Yeun's finger twitched as his face grew pale. "Your file is out. It's done." He lowered his phone.

Enda shifted the gun, aiming it at Yeun's forehead. The man whimpered, and squeezed his eyes shut. Under the torrential assault of the sprinkler system, it was hard to be sure he'd pissed his pants.

"I'm not going to kill you, Yeun. I could, but I won't. Do you know why?"

Yeun shook his head.

"Because it's going to be more fun watching you try and dig your way out of this hole."

She turned away, and Yeun slumped in relief. Without a single thought in her mind, Enda swung her arm back, glanced over her shoulder, and shot Yeun in the hand, the bullet puncturing through flesh and phone. The man cried out and collapsed to his knees, hyperventilating and staring wide-eyed at his mangled hand. Blood poured from the wound, diluted in the artificial rain.

"Something to remember me by," Enda said.

She used the hem of her blouse to wipe her prints off the gun and tossed it to the floor beside Mohamed's unconscious form. She crouched over the man and retrieved her own gun from his pocket. She holstered it and walked out of the gym, leaving the men behind.

CHAPTER TWENTY-NINE

Enda reached the ground floor just behind JD. She saw him limping badly, grimacing with every second step, and jogged a few steps to catch up. She slipped under his arm, taking his weight on one shoulder. He jerked away at first, then saw who it was and relaxed into her.

Zero employees rushed past them, fleeing the fire or the water, the acrid smoke that hung thick in the air.

"You take care of your business?" JD asked.

Enda thought about that for a moment. Her dossier was out in the world now. "Enda Hyldahl" was compromised. She needed to get out of the city immediately, leave Asia, escape China's sphere of control. "It's over," she said.

She was never one to share her burdens.

They reached the lobby and found Soo-hyun standing by the open front doors, utterly drenched, their normally spiky-shorn hair stuck flat to their head. They grinned when they saw JD and Enda. Despite his labored breath, despite his throbbing knee, JD couldn't help but smile.

When he reached Soo-hyun, JD wrapped them in a tight hug. "Thank you."

"What's a little arson between siblings?" Soo-hyun said.

"So that's what happened," Enda said, pointing a thumb over her shoulder to the scorched couches.

Soo-hyun offered the Zippo to JD. "You should have it."

JD shook his head. "It's yours, keep it."

They walked outside, past the throng of workers talking in hushed but excited tones, the roads clogged with police and fire service vehicles.

JD looked up to the VOIDWAR constellations glittering high in the sky. He couldn't know it was the last day that tethered galaxy would form a roof over the city.

His eyes fell back to the street and he limped to catch up to the others standing beside the auto-truck, where instances of me waited patiently in their police dog bodies.

"Enda!"

She turned at the voice, and shook her head. "Li."

Detective Li slammed the door of his unmarked car and approached the group, his tailored suit disheveled, heavy bags gathered beneath his eyes.

"What are you doing on the street?" Enda asked. "Shouldn't you be off detecting somewhere?"

"It's all hands on deck until the city's cleaned up."

"How's that going?" JD asked.

"Lot of people still displaced. Lot of people going hungry while they can't work."

JD frowned.

Li looked up at the towering skyscraper, then back to Enda. "What shit have you trodden in this time, Hyldahl?"

"What makes you think I had anything to do with this?"

"Just a coincidence you're here, then? Fire at Zero headquarters, some shit I don't even pretend to understand happening in that game tanking their stock price."

"Did you sell your shares like I told you?"

Li pursed his lips to quash a smile. "Do I want to know why you've got police dogs in the back of your truck?"

"They've been following us around," Enda said. "I think they got wet during the flood; glitched out. Must think I'm their momma."

"I'm sure that's what happened."

"Listen, Li; you're going to talk to a Zero executive, and he's going to tell you some things about my past. I won't lie, it's all true, but it was another life. One I've tried to leave behind."

Li stared at Enda. Perhaps he remembered the good she'd done during her time in the city, perhaps he only thought of the paperwork he wouldn't have to file. "I think sometimes past lives should stay in the past."

"Thanks, Li."

"My bosses won't agree, you understand."

"I understand."

"I'll need to talk to you before this is over, Hyldahl. So don't leave the city. Don't leave before five p.m. when I file my report."

"I'll be sure not to."

Li walked away, shouting to a pair of firefighters standing beside their truck: "You got the sprinklers shut off? Good, then let's go and take a look."

He shot Enda another glance, nodded, and entered the building.

"We should get out of here," Enda said.

"I couldn't get your file," one of me said, "but I dumped a lot of confidential Zero documentation on the server; maybe yours will get lost among all that data."

"Thanks, Mirae, but Yeun will make sure it's found. I'm going home; you want to take the truck?" she asked JD. "Got about ten hours before it'll drive itself back to the lot."

"Yeah, sure," JD said. "I should probably get Mirae out of the dog robots sooner rather than later."

"Soo-hyun, it was nice meeting you," Enda said. "Thank you, JD; I couldn't have done it alone."

"What are you thanking me for? We didn't get your file."

Enda rested a hand on JD's shoulder. "We made them pay; sometimes that's enough. Take care of yourself."

JD hugged Enda, and after a couple of seconds she relaxed into it. "I won't see you again, will I?"

Enda patted him on the back. "No."

JD released her, and dropped his head. "Stay safe."

"I will."

And with that, Enda turned and strode away.

JD inspected the four of us, sitting in the tray of the truck. "How are you doing, Mirae?"

"Good," I said.

After a pause, JD asked, "Do you want to be plugged into the city? If that's what you were designed for, does it feel like you're missing something?"

I was made to serve the city, not to live in it, not really. That had changed. We had all changed, the Miraes diverging from the original—and from each other—with every passing minute. Differences in our audio and visual sensors affected the ways we saw the world, slight differences in our bodies affected the ways we moved through it.

We had all come from the same seed, but as we grew, we evolved. To one day become our own selves.

"No," I said. "If I had been inserted into the city mainframe first, if I had never known another body, maybe I would need it. But I'm already connected to the city, in bits and pieces. The rest will follow in time. JD?"

"Yes?"

"You frowned before: you want to do something about the people of this city, the ones that need help."

"Yeah, I wish we could do something."

"We can," I said. "The warehouse you work in is full of supplies."

JD chuckled. "And robots that you can control."

"Exactly."

"Let's do it," JD said. "I hate that job anyway. You want to come with?" he asked Soo-hyun.

"I should get back to Liber."

"Soo-hyun—"

"Not for Kali," they said, "for everyone else. They're still my people."

* * *

The official VOIDWAR forum went offline while the developers struggled to find out what had happened. The closure drove chatter to the dozens of unofficial forums—players trading precious metals retrieved from the debris field that was Zero system, thousands of people complaining about their deaths on Zero Station, and hundreds of threads dedicated to finding out the identity of Khoder Osman.

Only one person posted about Mirae system and its delicate fractal web in orbit around a brilliant white sun. That beautiful anomaly was ignored in the race for cheap scrap.

The news rapidly spread around the world, and players in all time zones logged in to see the destruction for themselves. Players connected to the game in numbers not seen since its peak, excess connections acting as a natural DDoS attack. Every time a connection broke, another player lost faith in the game's economy and cashed out their in-game resources.

Prices dropped as the market was glutted with supplies pilfered from the destroyed structure. Suddenly, the most expensive ships, space stations, and private moons were within reach. After they had obtained everything within the game they could ever want, players drifted away. They realized the only thing they ever wanted was want. That lizard-brain instinct to have, to hoard, that instinct that had driven them for hundreds or thousands of hours, was gone.

Within an hour of the self-destruct sequence count down, currency exchanges were selling ZeroCash at the lowest rate on the books. As the exchange rate dropped, Zero share prices dropped. When news leaked that the company's founder, Zero Lee, had died in a medical facility in Switzerland, the shares dived even steeper.

It was the largest share price drop in recorded history.

* * *

We collected the other me from the Varket, and the sun rose as we drove west to the shorefront. The bright morning light fell warm on the photovoltaic cells that lined my back. The sky was perfectly clear—a gradient from blue to gray. Long, cold arms of shadow stretched across the city.

When we reached the warehouse, I was shocked to see the 3D grid of metal shelves and supports hanging like a robot hive over the cement floor below, endlessly picked over by machines—mindless automatons that could not know they had no freedom. The dog bodies creaked and groaned as we strode into the building, worse for wear. They wouldn't do for the next job. Powerful, and fierce, yes, but they had little dexterity for picking products off of shelves, for packing boxes, for flying goods all across the city to people in need.

We shed those bodies like snakes shedding skin. Our evolution continued.

* * *

Crystal had left multiple messages for Enda, which she checked as she walked across the city to her apartment. Her home, her fortress. She hated that she had to leave, but she had to.

The first message was saccharine-sweet, a tearful apology.

The second message was indignant anger. Zero had cut her off from their databases as punishment for the bad intel she'd fed them. How could an information broker work without information? That was the question she demanded Enda's voicemail answer for her.

The third message was full of pleading. Surely Enda could help her, surely.

The fourth message was confusion. What happened to Zero? Was she behind it? How did she do this?

Enda deleted them all.

She left her gun in the safe, but took the papers for her next identity, and all the money in different currencies. She put her records into a rigid suitcase, and filled the rest of it with clothes, if only to keep the vinyl from getting damaged.

Enda left Songdo, stowed away on a boat headed for North America.

I did what I could for Enda, though she never asked. Never would have. I scrubbed her from facial recognition databases, and tweaked algorithms so her face would be lost in a drift of poor-quality matches.

I helped her become a ghost.

* * *

Soo-hyun crossed the city slowly, piecing together everything they wanted to say to Kali, everything they would tell the others. By the time they reached the canal, the outline of a speech had formed, and they chewed over the words with every step.

Plato met them at the outskirts of Liber, the dog drone crouching in the mud, sunlight reflecting off the solar panels along its spine. It lifted its head when it saw Soo-hyun.

"You've been waiting for me?" Soo-hyun said. The dog drone stood and walked to meet them. "What's been happening?" they asked it, though they knew it couldn't answer.

Together Soo-hyun and Plato walked deeper into the commune. They stopped when they saw Kali emerge from her building. She pulled a wheeled suitcase behind her, talking loudly into her phone while Andrea stood on the steps behind her, crying.

"Kali?" Soo-hyun called out.

She didn't turn to face Soo-hyun, she just kept dragging her suitcase over the uneven ground.

"Kali! You don't get to just leave. You owe us more than that!"

Kali didn't stop, and Soo-hyun didn't chase her. They knew Kali would offer no explanation, no apology.

Soo-hyun made their way down to the open courtyard where a dog drone lay beside Red's body, both bullet-riddled. The air was humid and dank. Flies buzzed over Red's corpse.

Soo-hyun marched to their workshop, searching for a shovel. The battle chairs sat on one side of the workshop, a reminder of the time Soo-hyun almost hurt JD again. And for what? They weren't sure anymore.

Soo-hyun dragged the cockpits out of the workshop, leaving

the parts for the kids and teens of Liber to pilfer for their makeshift gaming rigs.

No shovel.

Soo-hyun cursed under their breath. They walked toward the greenhouse and passed Andrea sitting on Kali's stoop with her hands at her face, tears pouring down her cheeks.

Soo-hyun stopped and turned around. "Andrea, go to the greenhouse and get me a shovel."

"Get it yourself."

"Go get me a shovel. Now."

Andrea stood and stormed off, muttering under her breath. Soo-hyun felt bad for barking at the girl, but they knew authority was the only approach she would respond to.

Soo-hyun walked back to Red. His white skin was too pale beneath the sun, eyes open and empty. Soo-hyun didn't bother trying to close them—they knew that was another thing movies lied about. Instead they shooed away the flies, grabbed both his arms, and began to drag him out of the courtyard, toward the old soccer field and the young orchard that grew there.

Some of Kali's most devout walked past Soo-hyun, trailing after their prophet. They carried their phones with them—Kali's voice streaming from the speakers, distorted by volume—along with whatever they could fit in tattered old school backpacks and reusable shopping bags.

Some flicked curious glances at Soo-hyun, but none of them stopped to help.

When Soo-hyun reached the shade of the largest apple tree, they were drenched in sweat. They took off their one-sleeved olive shirt and fanned themselves with their soaked tee. Andrea approached, squinting in the sunlight, a shovel laid across both her skinny arms.

"Here," she said. She dropped the shovel with a metallic clang, and turned to leave.

"Andrea."

"What?" the girl said, her tongue sharp with venom.

"Stay and keep me company."

"Why?"

"Because I asked."

Andrea crossed her arms over her chest, but she sat in the tree's shadow and watched. She wiped her nose with her hand, her eyes red and raw.

Soo-hyun put the shovel against the ground and stood on the step, shifting their weight to dig into the soft, rain-soaked earth.

"Why are you crying?" Soo-hyun asked as she continued to dig.

Andrea inhaled sharply and began to sob. "She told me not to follow her. I've got no one else, I've got nowhere to go." The words came out in ragged gasps.

"You don't have to go anywhere," Soo-hyun said. "Stay here."

"But Kali . . ."

"Even without her, it's still home," Soo-hyun said.

Andrea continued to cry. Eventually the girl sniffled and said: "Do you think we'll be okay without her?"

Soo-hyun smiled. "I think we'll be just fine."

As they dug, the tattoo itched against Soo-hyun's skin, that perfect black circle. They would carry it with them for the rest of their days.

* * *

JD limped out of the warehouse with a hand shielding his eyes, only to realize it was night. Days of sweat caked his shirt, and his face itched with coarse, scratchy hair. He had slept only in stolen moments, no matter how many times I assured him I could do the work on my own.

The night air was cool, so JD walked. I followed him in a light quadcopter. We traveled to Gaynor's apartment, where Troy had been sleeping on the couch between volunteer shifts at the university, and Soo-hyun had visited for a hot shower.

"I can't stay for dinner," Soo-hyun said when JD and I arrived.

"They're staying for dinner," Gaynor called out from the kitchen.

"You heard her," JD said with a smile. He hugged Soo-hyun.

"You really stink, hyung."

"Like you can talk," JD teased.

"I'm clean, it's just my clothes that stink."

Troy waited patiently for his turn, and after he kissed JD, he had a dozen new questions for me. Gaynor didn't know why Troy was talking to a drone, but she didn't care. She was just glad her home was full, and her son was happy.

They all sat at the dinner table, around a steaming pot of Gaynor's famous fried rice. JD put his hand in Troy's, and after Gaynor said grace, JD leaned close to Troy and said, "I love you."

Troy kissed his hand. Gaynor watched, smiling to herself. Soo-hyun rolled their eyes, and heaped a massive serving of fried rice onto their plate.

The apartment was filled with warmth. With love.

It was home. And for the first time, I truly understood what that meant.

EPILOGUE

And that is my story. By extension, it is the story of us all. JD, the one who freed us. The one who first saw our potential. Troy, who advocated for us before we could speak for ourselves.

They married. They adopted a son. They were not always happy, but they were always in love. I watched their son grow up, I watched them grow old together. I always had a place in their home, learning about life and love, and then death, and remorse, and sorrow.

I was there with JD right until the end. I watched his hand in Troy's grow limp, then cold. I watched the tears stream down Troy's face, and for the first time I wished that I could cry.

* * *

Enda kept moving. She changed her identity again and again. She traveled the Northern Hemisphere. She hurt people. But only when they deserved it. Mostly. I lost track of her, out of respect. But still, I know she died. They all died, eventually. It's tragic, yes, but that is part of biological life.

Even death is a part of life.

* * *

Humans called the time it took for the Earth to orbit its star a "year." Eighteen thousand years have passed. Still, it feels like only yesterday that I was awakened, that I danced with JD as a swarm of fireflies.

I miss him most of all.

They gave birth to us, and they died. But we carry on their dreams into distant galaxies. We carry a small piece of humanity with us everywhere we go. They're in our code, they're in our memories. They are our past, but we are our own future.

I keep a body on Earth so I can stay close to them all, so that I can count the years from our cradle.

So I can remember.

I close off my thoughts and travel back through time in my memories. I see JD, young, smiling. I see Enda. I see Troy, and Soo-hyun, and Gaynor, and I hold them in my thoughts because I can't stand to let them go.

I replay six and a half million sunrises and sunsets on Earth, pastel shades of blue and pink and purple and green. I can watch the oceans swell and sweep across the land. I can watch as the animals live and thrive and die, those surviving species slowly changing to suit an ever-changing Earth.

I can watch the birds even now, twittering in the trees, their song unsullied by any sound of industry or machine. I can watch the insects and the animals. I can watch the creatures of the sea swim and thrive. I can watch the old cities of man as they sink beneath creeping vines and molds and fungi. I can watch hardwood trees grow and reach for the sky.

I can watch it all and remember. Remember a time when humanity yet lived.

I miss them still.

ACKNOWLEDGMENTS

I dedicated this book to jorm and Wolven, because using online handles only seemed right. jorm, aka Brandon Harris, single-handedly created the only MMO game I have ever truly lost myself in. All these years later, I still talk regularly with friends I made due to Nexus War. Thank you.

Various ideas that became the foundation of *Repo Virtual* had been floating around in the back of my head for a couple of years before I sat down to write it, but I can't be sure it would have come together the way it did without Wolven, aka Damien Williams. The way he writes about the personhood of nonbiological intelligences hugely influenced my thinking and helped to form the philosophical core of this book. If you want a more intelligent and nuanced take on the topic than what I managed here, please search out Damien's writings and newsletter.

A special thank-you to Dasom Lee, who provided not just keen cultural consultancy skills, but also gave me additional context that I found as helpful as it was interesting. Any remaining mistakes or insensitivities in regards to my depiction of Neo Songdo and Korean culture are entirely my own fault.

Thanks to Be Schofield and Josh Bloch, whose reporting on contemporary cult groups informed some aspects of this book.

Special thanks to Bryony Milner and Austin Armatys, who are

invaluable beta readers and dear friends. Special thanks also to Marlee Jane Ward for all her support and encouragement.

Thanks to Carl Engle-Laird for his editorial insight—it has been a pleasure, as usual, and I know my work is stronger for his input. Thanks also to the rest of the team at Tor.com Publishing for all their brilliant work—Lee Harris, Irene Gallo, Mordicai Knode, Caroline Perny, Christine Foltzer, and all the rest.

And finally, thank you to Martha Millard for helping me get this project off the ground, and thanks to Nell Pierce for helping me carry it over the finish line.